To Tread on Kings

Book III of the Epic of Hotspur
Liz Sevchuk Armstrong

Print ISBNs
Amazon print 9780228638032
Ingram Spark 9780228638049
Barnes & Noble 9780228638056
BWL Print 9780228638063

Copyright 2025 by Elizabeth Schevtchuk Armstrong
Editor Victoria Chatham
Cover artist Michelle Lee

"And if we live, we live to tread on kings..."

Shakespeare

Table of Contents

Chapter I

Late July 1402: Tower House,
Northumberland, England

Ciarry DeCorbett Fitzwyatt was tending a kettle of soap when the summons came to provide counsel at Berwick Castle to the noble Sir Harry Percy.

The fact that the courier bearing the message was none other than the noble sir himself made acceptance all the sweeter. Dropping the kettle ladle, Ciarry crossed the yard at a run. "Harry!"

He embraced her with an ardor she returned and bestowed kisses as she rested in his arms. "Dearest..."

Tall and lean, with slightly wavy dark hair, deep-blue eyes, and seemingly endless energy, Harry served as warden—military commander and governor—of England's East March, or borderland across from Scotland, and in a similar capacity as lieutenant of North Wales. Years earlier, the Scots had nicknamed him "Hotspur," as if his spurs never cooled, for his uncanny ability to thwart them when they tried to raid. Now, at age 42, he still ranked as England's leading knight, a champion in tournaments as well as battle. Inherently optimistic, despite the increasing dangers and frustrations of duty to a troubled nation, he was known for his audacity and courage, and treatment of all as equals. Despite a sometimes fiery temper, he had a rough-hewn charm that prompted older women to want to mother him and younger men to train alongside him.

Romance, though, had long eluded him, and after the breakdown of an arranged marriage, he had forsaken all notion of love—until, in 1400, riding alone on a back road in Northumberland, he had encountered Lady Ciarry.

With copper-bronze hair, eyes of an unusual sable-plum color, and short, thin body, Ciarry was the daughter of a low-level knight. She had survived marriage to a loutish lord; founded a reform-oriented abbey that thrived, until lack of support from the church hierarchy forced its closure; and proved adept at both scholarship and farming. As Harry had learned the day they met, she also could shoot like an archer, ride like a *chevalier* and leave many a man in the dust when it came to walking.

He had been smitten immediately. Ciarry had lost her heart, too, and after they'd rambled together for two days, he had made her co-owner of Tower House, a vacant estate along the Coquet River in the remote Cheviot mountains. She had restored it as an active farm, complete with sheep, chickens, and cows; grain and vegetable crops; and a stone peel tower, resembling a small castle keep, as her home—and his. For no matter how long he was gone, he always came back to it. As he had now.

They kissed again before she pulled away, protesting that the soap-making left her steamy enough even *without* him. So he let her return to her cauldron but soon followed to ease the ladle from her grip. "Leave your bonny witches brew for a bit."

"You're summoning me to a conference?" she wondered.

"Aye, set for a fortnight from now. I'm concerned about relations with Scotland and various other matters. As you know, as warden of the East March, I outrank even my venerable father, Henry Percy, even though he's earl of Northumberland and warden of the West March. So I'm ultimately responsible for much of the north. I want to convene not just my captains and the area lords but churchmen and others, to plan, before a crisis occurs. You're intelligent and experienced; you can help by giving us your own ideas and acting as a scribe, too.

"Moreover, not only did I bring the summons myself," Harry continued with a mischievous look in his eyes. "I brought the means of answering it more expeditiously."

Hand encasing hers, he led her toward the gate.

On the other side of it, his favorite saddlehorse, the black-coated, white-stockinged Redesraven waited patiently. But so did a smaller one, whose slate-grey coat darkened to jet on ankles, mane and tail.

"A worthy gelding, aye?"

"He's beautiful!" Ciarry sprang forward.

The horse looked at her with soft, intelligent eyes, ears flicking amiably. She let him sniff her palm and rubbed his neck, as he nuzzled her fingers.

"Where's he from?"

"Most recently, from Cottingham, that estate King Henry foisted on me in lieu of pay a couple of years ago. But he was foaled, in 1399 or so, on a property my late stepmother, Maude, bequeathed me in Cumberland."

"And you want me to stable him for you?"

"Aye. However, he's yours, Ciarry."

Her puzzlement turned to delight. "But... I never asked for a horse. Why ... how?" Tears brushing her eyelashes, she embraced him and bestowed another kiss, before wrapping her arms around the grey's neck and kissing him, too.

Harry smiled. "I've been meaning to give you another horse e'er since you lost the chestnut mare last year. You've managed all right, borrowing one if needed, but 'tis better for you to have your own again. I considered leaving Redesraven here, but as you know, from having tried him, he's a bit tall and large for you."

"Yea!" She rubbed her legs. "It stretches my muscles merely to mount him. So I didn't mind that you kept him. Besides, he prefers you. Not that I blame him." She grinned impishly. "*I'd* far rather be ridden by you than anyone else!"

"Bawdy wench!" He pulled her close. "So who do you want to try out first today? Me or the grey?"

"You, of course. Neither, though, until I finish up with this soap!"

* * *

Two days later, on a sunny late afternoon in the fruit garden, Harry and Ciarry planted a few more violets on the graves of their twins, taken by death before birth the previous year. Remembering his frantic ride to Ciarry's side, after months away, only to find one baby already dead and see the second emerge equally lifeless, Harry felt his eyes misting. Then, glancing down at Ciarry, he smiled softly. At least she had survived, and their life together continued to unfold in joy, notwithstanding all the separations and difficulties they endured. His dirt-stained fingers found hers, and they ambled down to the pond, where they washed their hands and fed the ducks remnants of their lunchtime bread.

With the sky turning from blue toward lavender and dusk, they headed back to the house, pace quickening when Dogmael's barking shattered the tranquility. Named for an early Welsh saint, Dogmael, had been a neighbor's gift to Ciarry upon her arrival at Tower House. He'd grown into a rambunctious off-white mongrel who resembled a small wolf and combined a fierceness against potential intruders with the disposition of an affectionate kitten.

"Dogmael: What?" The shout came from Enochie, the partly lame youth who lived on the adjacent property and assisted Ciarry with chores. Approaching the front gate, Harry and Ciarry saw Enochie coming toward them, escorting a man whose riding boots were typical of a knight but who

10

otherwise wore the clothing of a commoner, black leggings topped by a brown tunic whose hood hung low around his head. But the newcomer carried no sword or knife and, apparently regarding him as acceptable, Dogmael trotted alongside, tail wagging.

"Lord Harry," Enochie began. "This fellow rode up, saw me out front, and asked to be taken to you. Says he's an old friend, from Scotland."

The stranger removed his hood, and Harry almost jumped. "John Montgomery! Oh my God..." Striding forward, he hugged his visitor. "I'm both surprised and honored."

"Och, 'tis good to see you too, lad," Montgomery responded. "And I've a bit of tale to tell, if you can put me up for a night or so."

"Definitely," Harry affirmed, still surprised, for he hadn't seen Montgomery in two years. "First, though, let me introduce Lady Ciarry."

She offered her hand, which Montgomery gallantly kissed before stepping slightly aside.

"I've heard much about how you and Harry fought on opposite sides at Otterburn, where he charged into battle—despite having been wounded earlier when the Scots besieged Newcastle," Ciarry said. "You bested him in swordplay, captured him, had his wounds tended, and saved him from a violent mob."

Neither man contradicted her, so Ciarry continued. "After that, you took him to Ayrshire, to your castle, at Eaglesham. There, for over a year you treated him more like a brother than a captive, until the English Crown finally allowed his ransom. And, since then, you've been friends, trying to maintain peace between Scotland and England." She smiled warmly. "Welcome to Tower House, Lord John. I'm very pleased to meet you."

"'Tis all true, what you said," Montgomery confirmed. "And 'tis the matter of peace between Scotland and England, that brought me here."

Harry rested a hand on his old friend's shoulder.

"That sounds serious. But let's talk at supper. For now, let Enochie and me help you stable your horse and supply you with whatever you might need, after such a long ride."

"A bath," Montgomery replied. "And then, the night is ours..."

With the men temporarily occupied, Ciarry entered the tower through the kitchen door to inform Agnes of the sudden guest. Lean and strongly built, the grey-haired Agnes had been rescued by Harry from destitution and death in 1399, when her family was murdered and its mill destroyed by brigands, as King Richard II and Henry Bolingbroke clashed and law enforcement broke down.

Richard had robbed and exiled Bolingbroke, Duke of Lancaster, but after months in Europe, the duke had surreptitiously returned. Exuding tolerance, he had launched a campaign to improve royal governance while letting Richard to continue to rule, reined in by Parliament.

Having also been exiled by Richard for voicing dissent, Harry had joined thousands of others in welcoming Bolingbroke and endorsing his reforms. But simultaneously, Bolingbroke had secretly schemed to seize the throne for himself. Within months, he succeeded, after executing perceived opponents following sham trials, imprisoning Richard, and inciting an armed mob to surround Parliament when it debated whether to let Richard remain king or to instead install Bolingbroke. Intimidated, Parliament had chosen Bolingbroke, who became King Henry IV. Objecting to Henry's deceit and violence, Harry had refused to attend his coronation. The two had subsequently reconciled, but friction continued.

Meanwhile, recognizing her talents as a cook and baker, Harry had made the whip-sharp but unschooled Agnes supervisor of the kitchen at Berwick Castle. Later, upon meeting Ciarry and bringing her to Tower House, he had invited Agnes to move there, too. Agnes had promptly agreed, ready to trade the demands of feeding a garrison for farm and household tasks alongside Ciarry. Thinking that she might also sell baked goods nearby, she had increased her pastry-making and flourished at local markets, especially after Ciarry had taught her to read and write. At Tower House, she also had found an ad hoc family. Kind and nurturing by nature, she had long since been a foster mother to Harry and his military companions and soon wrapped Ciarry and the motherless Enochie in her embrace as well.

Now Agnes and Ciarry responded with their usual aplomb to Montgomery's arrival. Together, they arranged chairs and added an extra plank to the oak table in the parlor, the main room on the tower's first level. A cozy chamber, it had whitewashed stone walls, rugs on the flagstone floor, a fireplace with a heavy mantel along one wall, and bench chests available for extra seating and storage. Ciarry retrieved plates, cups, and cutlery, while Agnes scurried down the winding stairs to the kitchen and cellar to begin preparing the meal: smoked ham, fresh kale and carrots from the garden, creamed barley, local cheeses, and summer fruit and butter cookies for dessert. When all was ready, the women carried it upstairs as Harry stoked the fire in the hearth and set out beverage options of water, ale, and wine.

"Damn!" Montgomery reproached himself as he stepped into the room. "I should've brought some whisky."

"Next time," Harry answered. "For now, you can open one of those bottles of Bordeaux."

"Gladly!" Bathed and changed into different leggings, shorter boots, a white linen shirt, and a thigh-length leather vest, Montgomery looked much the same as ever—well built, of almost the same height as Harry, and beardless, though he had a mustache of medium brown, the same shade as his eyes and his ear-length hair. Of uncertain age, he appeared to be 15 to 18 years older than Harry, whom he tended to call "lad."

Agnes usually ate supper with Ciarry, but on this occasion, at Ciarry's invitation Enochie also joined the two women, alongside Harry and Lord John. Everyone chatted pleasantly about non-serious subjects, until the final course of cookies and fruit.

"As you're all probably wondering why I barged in on you like this, I'd better tell you," Montgomery began. "I come from a privy session with King Robert and the high lords of Scotland. They were pondering what to do next regarding England, since the truce talks last autumn resolved nothing, and the incursion King Robert ordered afterward had cost us money and blood but hadn't accomplished anything, either. You and your captains are too good at kicking us back to Scotland, Harry.

"For that matter," he went on, "apparently 'tis not just you and your troops that are good at defense. According to talk across Scotland, last November, when our army stalled in Cumberland, some malcontents took off without permission to pillage Northumberland on their own. But they came to a sorry end, right here at Tower House, when they encountered two women and a farm lad."

Montgomery's eyes twinkled as he continued. "These women were right smart, too. They were up on the roof, behind the crenellation, and one, an archer, shot two of the reivers dead while the second woman poured scalding water down. The women also had lit the signal fire on the roof, and folks around here saw it and rushed to their aid."

Enochie nodded sadly. "One of the first was my brother. The reivers killed him."

"I'm sorry," Montgomery said, pausing momentarily. "However, it seems that the farm lad, equally brave—*you*—had the wits to unpen a couple of frightened bulls and drive them into the rest of the mob. Then more neighbors, bearing weapons, joined in and the raiders high-tailed it away. They only got a short distance up the road, though, before your squad captured them, Harry. Scotland is well rid of them. So I toast you all, in particular you three." Montgomery tilted his wine cup toward Agnes, Ciarry and Enochie. The boy blushed shyly, dropping his curly dark head but smiling at the praise.

Harry nodded. "They well deserve recognition. I only wish I'd been able to get here sooner. We were on the mountain when we saw the beacon fire. We raced here, but by then 'twas all over."

Montgomery added a splash more wine to their cups and raised his own. "To courage—in English, Scots, or whatever person it manifests itself." Five cups clinked.

"I'm just hoping that we don't have more fighting this autumn," Montgomery added. "Scotland's troops aren't ready for it. More importantly, on both sides of the border, we've got crops to harvest, cattle and swine to slaughter and lay away, fish to salt or smoke, hay and straw to stack in our barns, vegetables to stow in cold cellars, and fruit to dry, all afore winter. War would be a calamity for us all."

"Aye," Harry said. "May your barons and king concur."

Montgomery groaned. "That's the problem. At the privy session with King Robert, there was endless bragging and crowing about our might and about taking action, to convince your King Henry to forget all notions of obtaining Scotland's fealty, which he keeps demanding. I advised against an invasion, but my views were hardly shared by all."

Ciarry and Agnes exchanged worried glances. Enochie looked glum.

"Hell!" Harry swore. "So you think Scotland will attack?"

"I honestly don't know," Montgomery replied.

"And I'd best not say anything more. I just thought that you ought to know. I don't want more fighting. But it won't be my decision. And if Robert does go to war, Earl Douglas will probably be the commander, and, as his vassal, I'll have to be there, too."

"Aye." Harry understood. "If war comes, you'll have to do your duty to Scotland, as I must do mine, to England. But, whatever happens, we'll still be friends."

"Always," Montgomery agreed. "Hence my arrival here. Initially, I considered sending a message with a courier. But I didn't want to risk having him discovered and getting myself accused of treason against Scotland. Then I remembered that Edinburgh isn't all *that* far from here, 70 miles, maybe."

"But how did you know Harry was here?" Ciarry asked.

"Oh, we've got scouts watching comings and goings from Berwick. During that privy session, one reported to us that Harry had ridden to Berwick from London or somewhere, spent several days, then gone west toward Rothbury. As you know, families in Northumberland and our Scottish Lowlands have kith and kin hither and yon across the border. They visit often. Farmers, bards, livestock sellers and many others go back and forth, too. As long as they behave, no one cares. Anyway, that scout I referred to proceeded to Rothbury, where he noticed two prime sheep for sale, bought them for his own holding outside Edinburgh, and at a tavern heard someone mention that Harry frequently bides nearby, at Tower House. The scout, with his new sheep, then went back to Edinburgh to pass along what he'd learned."

Montgomery turned to Harry. "I decided I might as well try reaching you myself. I borrowed simple garb from my squire, sent him back to Eaglesham, and rode cow tracks and backroads through the Cheviots until I got here."

"I'm damned glad you did," Harry said. "Stay as

long as you like. Then I'll ride with you to the border. After that—well, let's hope we don't once again face each other in battle."

Montgomery nodded vigorously. "Amen!"

* * *

Early August 1402: Berwick Castle

When Harry convened his advisory panel, Scotland topped the agenda. "Several of you have notified me of rumors that the Scots plan a major raid," Harry told the attendees, mostly knights and men-at-arms, plus two mayors, a reeve, and two aldermen, as they gathered in the castle hall. "I'm grateful to you for keeping me apprised. In a sense, there's nothing new. We've got sentinels keeping watch on the Scots, just as the Scots keep an eye on us, and we haven't seen any increases in army activity there. But the Scots like to attack in late summer and autumn, and folk here worry about the coming weeks. So I thought it prudent to confer. Moreover, a Scottish knight whom I greatly respect recently informed me that various of his hot-headed peers want to attack soon. What he told me 'twas nothing more than what many of us already suspected. Nonetheless, 'tis sobering. So let's review our preparedness."

They went around the table, reporting on the staffing of castles and peel towers and how many levies might be called into duty, given the reality of harvest-time and the fact many men who were not fulltime soldiers would be busy in fields; the adequacy (or not) of weapons, equipment, and fortifications; and the availability of everything from food for soldiers, civilians, and animals alike to water supplies and medicine.

To allow John Hardyng, Harry's principal secretary and squire, to freely contribute to the discussion, note-taking responsibilities fell to Ciarry, one of the two females present. The other was her good friend and neighbor, Sister Etheldreda, the physician at Holystone Priory, which housed Augustinian canonesses, nuns who split their time between private religious devotions and service to others.

When military matters had been addressed, Harry explained the women's presence. "I asked them to come," he said, "because along with our defenses, we should remember the effects of warfare on the whole region: farms, villages, churches, shops, and everyone and everything else. Enochie, a partly lame youth who's my apprentice farm steward, Lady Ciarry and Agnes Bymiller showed how crucial non-military folk can be. Several of you undoubtedly know Agnes, who ran the kitchen here for a while."

"And is sorely missed, along with her pastries!" Thomas Knayton put in. A spare, lithe but strongly muscled man-at-arms, with the pale blond hair and blue eyes of his Norse ancestors, he was Harry's top lieutenant in the north and often commanded troops in Harry's absence.

"Aye," Harry laughed. "Now you'll just have to visit her more often. Anyway, as most of you know, Agnes, Ciarry and Enochie successfully defended Tower House last autumn until reinforcements arrived. That should make all of us think: What should we be doing to better protect ourselves in ways we've probably forgotten since centuries back, Anglo-Saxons and Vikings—including women—fought over this land? What buildings on farms or in villages have roofs that could hold archers, or could be updated to accommodate them? Are folks here sufficiently trained in archery to help in a crisis, or would it endanger them too much? Enochie used bulls against the reivers at Tower House. Would that work elsewhere?"

"Only," the reeve, a former bowman, interjected, "if the attackers don't include any archers or spearmen able to bring down a bull."

"Fine observation," Harry nodded. "Here's more to think about, too: In an invasion or other crisis, can places like Holystone and our rural churches be better equipped to act as shelters and hospitals, if needed? I know they traditionally have been employed that way, but can we take things further?"

Etheldreda—short and slightly plump, middle-aged, and trained in both medicine and learning, responded. "I've been educating more of the sisters at Holystone in nursing and the use of herbs and other plants for healing," she said. "Perhaps we could likewise instruct women—and men—from villages and farms. It'll take money and other resources, though."

Ciarry nodded. "As for archery, I can certainly provide basic lessons to anyone who wants to hone his or her skills. It'd be good for me, too. I can always use more practice. But we'll need more arrows and longbows, plus other gear."

Bishop Walter Skirlaw of Durham spoke next. "I've a little extra money in my episcopal chests. I'll gladly give some of it for the purposes you describe. Also, at Durham we have our large cathedral and all the other ecclesiastical buildings and rooms. Certainly, we could use those for teaching laity and clergy alike." A lean man of middle years, prematurely silver-haired but as quick and agile as a young squire, Skirlaw drew respect both inside the cloister and in the world beyond. His support for Etheldreda's suggestion prompted others to ponder what their own castles or towns might do.

Sir Gerard Salvayn, a veteran captain in the north, thought aloud. "What about diverting becks and other streams, or flooding some fields, to stop an invading force? I'm not sure if it'd work, but farmers and millers, river fishermen and others familiar with the waterways might help us figure that out. They aren't as expert in arms as we are, but they know the lay of this land extremely well."

Heads nodded approval.

"We can also fell trees across paths and roads, to hinder advances. And we can construct abatis, so your soldiers don't have to," an alderman added. "Our elders and youngsters can help: cutting saplings, whittling the tips to make them like spears, then setting the blunt ends in the ground, with the sharp points at the other end sticking up."

"And we might do what you did in that battle you won in Wales, Lord Harry," the other alderman put in. "You dug pits and covered them with sticks and then sod, so they looked like normal ground. But they were traps for your opponents to fall into when charging on foot or horseback."

Harry nodded. "Aye, and I borrowed that tactic from the Scots, who used it against an English army in Scotland a century ago."

More ideas began tumbling out around the table. An hour later, they recessed briefly.

To relieve Ciarry, when they resumed Hardyng took on the scribal chores. Raised in Harry's household from childhood, Hardyng, now age 24, was slightly above average in height, slim but strong like his lord, whom he emulated in his clean-shaven chin and the short cut to his light-brown hair. Harry had always regarded him more as a younger brother than a servant, ensuring that Hardyng received a good education in history, law, arithmetic, English composition and grammar, plus French, Latin, and music, along with all the training squires needed in weaponry, riding, and military activity. Some 15 months earlier, in Wales, Harry had given Hardyng his first command of troops, and the squire had handled it well. But he was also fond of books, kept a private journal, and hoped one day to write a history of

England.

Before he started taking notes, Hardyng proposed that since his lord had posed questions to the others earlier, they might now question him.

Harry agreed, and Knayton began.

"You recently rode all the way to London, Harry, trying to get our pay—yours, too—and the money we need to sustain ourselves, both in arms and otherwise," Knayton recalled. "Some of us here know what happened at the Exchequer. Others do not. Did anything occur?"

Harry smiled grimly. "Only the usual. I presented my tallies—those wooden slats, marked with notches indicating the amount due—that directed the king's financial officials to provide payment. Once again, the Exchequer could not, or would not, exchange them. Hence, I came back with tallies—and no gold or silver, no coinage at all. Nor did they provide any alternatives, such as jewels to sell and get compensation that way."

Sir Robert Umfraville, a prominent northern baron, sighed. "We've just spent a couple of hours talking about a possible Scots' invasion. How're we supposed to deal with them without sufficient money for supplies and weapons and all the other needs we've mentioned?"

"Fine question," said Aelred Talbot, one of the younger Northumbrian lords.

"I'll have to dig into my own coffers again, and my father's, and also provide what we can from our own stores," Harry answered. "Luckily, crops have done well this summer and there's a bit of a surplus, which should continue as we harvest more. I might be able to sell some, and any of the unneeded livestock and get money that way. If every other lord and knight in these parts does the same, as far as he can, I'm hoping we'll get by."

"You've got my pledge," Umfraville responded, and, around the table, others echoed him.

Skirlaw, too, promised to do all that he could, along with what he had already offered. But he looked troubled. "Do you think, Sir Harry, that this difficulty with the Exchequer arose because King Henry dislikes you for rejecting his order last spring to duplicitously kill Glyn Dwr, the Welsh chieftain—even though, as lieutenant of North Wales, you'd used the very authority the Crown gave you to successfully negotiate with Glyn Dwr to end the Welsh revolt—"

"—A revolt," Salvayn groused, interrupting, "that the king himself instigated by enacting laws that make the Welsh inferior to English, treating them like lowly creatures to be spurned."

"And a revolt that largely began after Henry had wrecked Welsh monasteries and villages, while you were on duty here in the North, Harry," added Sir Rauf de Eure, lieutenant of Roxburgh Castle, an English possession although located on the Scottish side of the border.

"Yea," Bishop Skirlaw resumed, "anyway, as we heard in church circles and beyond, you and Glyn Dwr reached this pact to end the war. Glyn Dwr even rendered fealty to you, as the Crown's lieutenant there, and volunteered to render it to Hal, the Prince of Wales, as well. But King Henry wanted you to return to Wales and, under the guise of further conversations, to seize Glyn Dwr and execute him. You refused."

"As would any knight who accepts the rule of law and declines to commit murder," Harry emphasized.

"Yet Henry probably resents you for contradicting him," Skirlaw added. "He might be retaliating by withholding money."

Harry rested his chin on his hand. "I don't know... Henry declined to pay me long before we argued about Glyn Dwr. He was in arrears even before he rejected the settlement I reached—again under authority granted me—with those insurrectionists at Conway Castle in 1401. I think the problem is his greediness and the corruption, or ineptness, of many around him, who never counter him. Henry should have more than ample income accruing from his own vast Duchy of Lancaster. English kings are supposed to 'live off their own'—their personal family estates, like Henry's duchy. They're not supposed to squander the government of England's money—the taxes and tariffs and fees and everything else we pay, whether high lord or lowly laborer. Yet Henry drains the Exchequer and gets away with it. But I'm not giving up..."

"What can others do?" Umfraville asked.

"Implore God for a miracle, a miracle in which Henry changes his ways," Sister Etheldreda suggested.

Skirlaw smiled, almost mischievously. "Yea, my brothers and sisters. Pray—*like hell*—to heaven!"

With that, they adjourned.

* * *

In the days that followed, summer hastened toward its end with wistful beauty. Mountainsides blazed with shades of gold, red, and dusky green, interspersed with swathes of lavender-blue heather and purple thistle. Along footpaths, mushrooms displayed red caps splotched with white dots and wildflowers in brilliant colors lined the roads. In mowed fields, rolls of straw awaited retrieval; elsewhere, sheep and cows grazed lazily. Apples hung heavily on orchard branches; in nearby thickets, blackberry patches brimmed with lush, dark fruit.

And Northumberland kept a wary watch...

Chapter II

September 1402: Northumberland

The Scots crossed the border like a horde of angry wasps.

Nearly 10,000 strong, they forded the River Tweed near Norham, spilling into meadows and clogging the roads, as if every knight, man-at-arms and lancer from south of the Firth of Forth (and many from beyond) chose to go a'reiving at once.

As impressive as their numbers was their leadership: not only lairds attached to their leader, Earl Archambeau Douglas, but the very cream of the Scottish nobility—even Murdoch Stewart, Earl of Fife, the king's nephew, young but already known for his arrogance. Two other Stewarts participated, as well: Sir Robert of Durisdeer and Sir William of Teviotdale, a turncoat once-English knight. Except for their surname, though, Robert and William had little in common, for the former regarded the latter as an untrustworthy opportunist. Another noble, Patrick Dunbar, likewise knew the taint of family disgrace, for Patrick's brother George Dunbar , who had once held Douglas' job as Scottish commander, had quarreled with King Robert, fled Scotland, and cozied up to England's King Henry instead.

The august company also included both Lord John Swinton and his arch-rival Andrew Gordon; three more earls—of Angus, Moray, and the Orkneys— whose domains lay far from the Anglo-Scottish border, and a delegation of French knights.

Lord John Montgomery was there as well, partly at his overlord Douglas' bidding and partly because he thought he might offer a seasoned voice of prudence, lest too much aristocratic glitter blind common sense and invite disaster.

After a few hours' rest and a meal of cattle butchered in nearby fields, they entered Norham, avoiding its small castle but scattering frightened residents in the village and sacking houses, stables, shops, and sheds, setting most ablaze as they left.

Outside of town, they paused, bickering over approaches. A large faction of lords and knights pointed to the obvious. They had entered England unchecked, although massive Berwick Castle was only six miles from Norham. Already, they were collecting easy spoils without any interference from Berwick's commander, the famed Hotspur. Nor did other English troops threaten them. Thus, they maintained, their army could take a leisurely approach, conserving energy, enabling them to raid over a wider area, perhaps down to Durham and even farther, to York. Some further urged that lords and men wanting to pillage on their own, while the bulk of the army moved more slowly, should be able to do so, as long as they later reunited.

Montgomery disagreed. "I thought this was supposed to be a raid, not a Sunday stroll," he argued. "We can't allow any troops to hie off on their own, either. That could fracture us, dissolve our strength. We need to move fast, as a united force: Hit, run, and be back in Scotland before the English realize what's afoot."

Silently agreeing with Montgomery but not wanting to rile the others, Douglas deliberated. Now about 40 years old—he wasn't certain of the exact year of his birth—he had become chieftain of Clan Douglas and military commander in the Scottish Lowlands at the death of his father, Earl Archibald "the Grim" Douglas, in February 1401. Taller than his late father as well as slimmer and more fit, he had short reddish-brown hair, a neatly trimmed mustache, his maternal grandmother's lightly freckled pale complexion, and alert grey eyes. Although named Archibald after his sire, he had, while still a boy, become known as "Archambeau" instead.

Surveying the knights and lords, he settled on a compromise: They would camp for a day or two to replenish energy depleted on their trek through lower Scotland. Then, as Montgomery suggested, they would strike hard as a single force—but within a limited range. "We can target the eastern coast of Northumberland and move southward," he said. "When we've taken as much as possible from there, we can go home by the same route. The English won't expect us to retrace our steps. Yet as soon as we cross into Scotland and unload our spoils, we can hit England again, but farther west, raiding upper Coquetdale and Redesdale and Cumberland."

A round of "Ayes" followed.

Montgomery, though, unfurled a map on the ground, studied it for a few seconds, and then placed it in front of Douglas and the rest. "You mean we use a two-pronged approach, like an arc?" He traced it on the map. "Down and back; over and back."

"Exactly."

Montgomery thought further. Douglas' scheme meshed well with his own desire to keep their force organized and focused, and thus less likely to suffer a bloody setback. Also, by the time they'd burnt and plundered eastern Northumberland and lugged all their booty back to Scotland, they might have lost any desire to attack western Northumberland and Cumberland at all.

"All right," he said, although he was still dubious.

Douglas slipped an arm around him. "You'll see, John. Our run through eastern Northumberland will be like a Midsummer dance. We seem unlikely to face opposition. King Henry has marched off to bring fire and sword to the Welsh again. Sir Harry is lieutenant of North Wales. His father, Earl of Northumberland, is not only warden of their West March here but England's high constable. Harry and Earl Henry will both have to be with their king in Wales. I know Harry was sojourning near Rothbury, but that was weeks ago. By now, they've got to be miles from here."

"Do they?" Montgomery replied. "Never underestimate Harry's ability to do what you'd least expect." His misgivings lingered, though he kept them to himself.

After Douglas' promised two-day respite, the Scots began raiding northeastern Northumberland, hitting the monastic island of Lindisfarne before moving inland to rob and burn villages, manors, farms, and churches. Skipping around, they stole several hardy white cattle from the park at Chillingham but withdrew before they provoked a fight with its castle. They also avoided other castles and peel towers but rampaged through the town of Morpeth. Venturing as far west as Brinkburn Priory, they looted and set it aflame but stopped short of nearby Rothbury.

From Tower House, Ciarry and her neighbors saw the fiery haze and prayed for Brinkburn's monks. Yet even before the smoke lifted, the Scots oddly withdrew from the area. Startled, but relieved, Coquetdale residents resumed their normal pursuits.

Pressing south toward Newcastle and Durham, the Scots continued to prey on farms and hamlets, setting fields ablaze, nabbing cows, sheep, and horses, harassing residents, and stealing household goods even if they left homes intact.

No army challenged them.

The English had resolved to hold back until they could act decisively, stopping the Scots' raids, if not forever, at least for many years. Let the Scots lull themselves into complacency, Harry reasoned. To confront so large an enemy without like strength was foolhardy. Still, as reports of devastation multiplied, he began second-guessing himself.

"Perhaps we've delayed too long and should've struck a week ago." His fingers drummed on the table in frustration as he conferred with his father and captains at Warkworth Castle. "But we weren't ready a week ago. If only I'd been here all summer, preparing, instead of in Wales and riding hither and yon over half of England..."

"We're still short on men," said Sir William Clifford, who, like Gerard Salvayn, had long served with the Percies. "Thank God more arrive daily. We'll need everyone. Without them, we don't stand a chance against 500-score Scots."

"My troops weren't anywhere near ready till two days ago," de Eure observed.

"Nor mine," Umfraville echoed.

Salvayn looked at Harry and Earl Henry. "As wardens, you've called up not only the men of Northumberland and Cumberland but the levies from Lincoln, Yorkshire, and Westmorland, even those from diocesan and abbey lands." He dipped his head respectfully toward Bishop Skirlaw. "It takes time to muster troops from so far afield."

"Aye," Harry admitted. "We've also got to maneuver without drawing the Scots' attention. But being unobtrusive slows us down, too."

"Especially since you've done a lot of it in darkness," Skirlaw remarked.

"True." Harry smiled wryly. "I've been out many a night myself. Alas, I've a few more ahead of me. We're nearing the hour, though..."

Four days after the discussion at Warkworth, he was satisfied. He, too, had a force of about 10,000: pikemen, infantry, archers, men-at-arms, and knights. As the Scots continued their southeasterly course, he quietly moved his troops forward, concealing them in castles, towers, hidden riverbeds, and mountain passes to the west. Thanks to good reconnaissance, he also knew exactly when Douglas abruptly changed direction and began heading back toward Scotland.

And he knew that the Scots' pace had slowed.

Indeed, as the invaders proceeded north, they found roads—open several days earlier—blocked with large boulders or tree trunks, forcing them to detour into swampy fields that only grew soggier and more flooded, compelling them to veer even more off course. As they slogged along and took shortcuts through fields, they belatedly discovered another hindrance, camouflaged pits into which troops and wagons plunged. Several horses and oxen died, men suffered broken bones, and John Montgomery lost his armor, crushed when the wagon carrying it tumbled and smashed.

"Hell! Now what am I going to do?" he grumped. But the armor of an injured knight had been packed into a smaller cart that avoided ruin. He shared Montgomery's height and build, and, his leg shattered, loaned Montgomery the undamaged armor.

The Scots continued more carefully, encumbered by the heavily laden wagons and stolen livestock, but highly pleased, nonetheless. The 13th of September, a Wednesday, found them in a celebratory mood, congratulating themselves: They'd spooked the English. In a fortnight, they had encountered no English force at all. Moreover, once they deposited their booty on the Scottish side of the border they would raid again, into Coquetdale and beyond. Brimming with drink and hubris, they tramped merrily along, less like warriors than children on an afternoon romp.

The sun had already set when they reached Wooler, at the eastern edge of the Cheviots, nine miles from Scotland as the crow flies and a dozen by the road. A prosperous town, Wooler lured them, a final place to plunder as well as a pleasant place to stay until morn. Welcoming an opportunity for a decent night's sleep under a real roof, Douglas ordered that no building be burnt unless he demanded it. After a feast and rounds of song wetted by wine and whisky, they fell into slumber well after midnight.

By midday, Douglas told Montgomery as they retired, they'd be home.

* * *

Harry had sent messengers to all his outposts, telling his men to array outside Milfield-on-Till, five miles from Wooler, on the Feast of the Exaltation of the Holy Cross: Thursday, 14 September. They were instructed to arrive at least four hours before dawn but no earlier than nightfall the preceding evening, using darkness for cover. Aware that any Scottish sentinels atop the Cheviots might spot torches, he had some of his men march without light. Others carried two or three torches each; still others backtracked briefly, covering the same ground twice, to seem more numerous than they were.

The night of 13 September was clear and sharp, stars pricking the blackness like silver spear points as the moon rose full, glowing like a round, orange-white shield.

Most of Harry's forces reached Milfield about an hour after nightfall. He placed them under his father's immediate authority and, as lieutenants, tapped Umfraville, de Eure, and Lord George Dunbar, the erstwhile Scots commander who had turned against Scotland, fled with most of his notable wealth, and became one of Henry IV's favorite's in London.

Harry gritted his teeth in assigning Dunbar, whom he had first encountered over a dozen years earlier and who seemed to have hardly changed, either in appearance or morals. Old enough to be Harry's father, Dunbar still looked younger than a man on the cusp of old age. Of medium height, with clean-shaven cheeks, hard green eyes, a mostly bald pate, and just

30

enough wrinkles to make him look distinguished but not doddering, he might have stepped from the niche of a Roman villa, a marble emperor come to life. Like many an emperor, too, he sought to dominate the world around him, using whatever means possible, legal and ethical or not.

In 1388, when Dunbar had been a Scottish aristocrat, he and Harry had fought on opposite sides at the Battle of Otterburn, where an already wounded Harry had lost a sword fight with Montgomery, been captured, and become a hostage held for ransom. The next day, when fanatical Scots had sought to kill him to avenge their own dead, Dunbar had supported them, happy to dispose of an English adversary who otherwise would return to duty after being ransomed. Harry had been moments from death when an irate Montgomery, returning from a scouting mission with other knights, had intervened. Protecting Harry, he and his companions had accused Dunbar of trying to commit murder and violating the laws of both chivalry and Scotland. Cursing, Dunbar had backed down.

Years later, after Dunbar had landed at the English court, King Henry had dispatched him to join Harry on a campaign in Scotland, where Harry had caught him blatantly violating orders.

Now, King Henry had dumped Dunbar on him once again. "Hell!" Harry muttered, watching Dunbar, de Eure and Umfraville go off to confer with Earl Henry.

While retaining overall command, Harry had assigned himself to the advance force—500 knights and men-at-arms on horseback and a like number of mounted archers. He now led them off on a circuitous route to avoid discovery, crossing the River Glen near Coupland, following the narrow road to old Yeavering, and proceeding eastward across the base of the mountain known as Yeavering Bell to Tallon's Crag. There they turned hard north again, toward Gleadscleugh and a ford, to halt at the foot of

Harehope Hill, west of Wooler.

Separating them from the town lay Harehope's rounded hulk, some 800 feet high, and, immediately to its east, the larger Homildon, or Humbleton, Hill (or mountain, as some called it). Early inhabitants' earthwork defenses ringed Homildon's slopes and ancient cairns crowned its top, nearly 1,000 feet up.

Secure on the west side of Harehope, Harry let his men rest until early on 14 September, when a distant cock crowed, echoed by its fowl brethren. Light split the lingering greyness, turning the heavens to pearl and periwinkle above heathered slopes. Dispatching mounted foragers, he told them to find game and wild fruit and pay for whatever they took from the local folk, for Homildon Hill supported two hamlets—tiny Low Homildon and larger Homildon Village—and a few farms lay farther up the road. Then he went to fetch his warhorse, the dapple-grey Valdus, and tell Hardyng and Knayton to mount up, as well.

They rode up Homildon, dismounting on the summit—one of the most spectacular overlooks on the borders. Even in these sobering circumstances, the view brought the usual flash of delight to his face. Beyond the fields below on the north, the meager huts of Low Homildon grouped at the edge of the road, giving way to the plains that lay below Milfield. On a curved shelf partly up the east slope, Homildon Village's more substantial homes, barns, church, mill, sheds and paddocks ringed a green. The millpond reflected bright yellow, interspersed with purple and amber as wild irises began to exchange summer flowers for the pods and seeds of autumn. Farther away, Wooler's buildings appeared, grey and pink stone, neat and friendly, washed by the Wooler Water, which meandered like a country lane. Harry noticed that Wooler's manor sported Douglas' banner, while atop the church the Cross of St. Andrew fluttered alongside the royal Scottish lion.

We'll see how long they remain, he mused,

silently.

Beyond Wooler, the land flattened, undulating toward the sea 17 miles away. At the edge of the horizon the ocean sparkled.

Behind Harry, the south face of Homildon fell in a sharp precipice. Directly west, more mountains rose. A scree-strewn cleft, Monday Cleugh, split the west side of Homildon Hill from the east side of Harehope and disgorged to the north in a downhill swath of meadow. It bore the name Red Riggs from the color of the soil, though now it was as green and gold as neighboring fields. The main road west cut past Red Riggs and twisted along the bottom of the mountains to link Wooler to a few more English settlements before crossing into Kirk Yetholm, on the Scottish side.

Harry filled his lungs with the clear air. Beyond the scenery, he was pleased to see how efficiently his father and the others had moved the bulk of the army into place, filling in below Milfield and curving around to almost overlap Harry's own troops on Harehope. The army waited easily, men and horses alike.

Knayton pointed. "They look good."

"Aye," Harry replied, surveying the landscape.

To the north and west, the English barred the way to the border. To the south lay the intricate corrugations of the Cheviots, fine for hiding individuals or small bands, but daunting to an army fleeing with wagons of booty. The Scots could try to force their way down the road to Kirk Yetholm but would have to dislodge the men from Harehope and withstand a flank attack by the other English. The east offered another route, perhaps, but only if the Scots risked being chased all the way to the sea, or into it.

"Douglas is trapped," Harry said. "How long it'll take him to realize it?" The question still hung on the breeze when three men on horseback, in Douglas' livery, appeared in miniature on a back lane from Wooler, at a carefree pace.

Harry ducked behind a cairn. "They're doubtless coming up to have a look around, just like we did," he said, as Hardyng and Knayton slipped in beside him. Edging their way back to their horses, they remounted and rode back the way they had come.

* * *

With no great haste, the Scottish scouts began climbing Homildon from the eastern town side. As they twined upward and looked out, their light conversation gave way to cries, audible on Harehope across the way.

To the north, they saw the Earl of Northumberland's banners and a large English army, its right flank disappearing somewhere toward Harehope. Besides the earl's flags, the Scotsmen counted those of Umfraville; Eure; the towns of Newcastle, York, and Carlisle; Bishop Skirlaw's levies; the northern Talbots and more—even the traitorous rat Dunbar's banner. They stopped counting, plunged downhill, and sped toward Wooler.

In another quarter hour, their news brought a look of aggrieved disbelief to Douglas' face and one of glum acknowledgment to Montgomery's. "I knew it!" the latter said. "'Twas ridiculous to think Harry would let us go home without trying to stop us."

"Is Hotspur there too?" Douglas asked the senior scout. "Or just Earl Henry?"

"The earl, definitely, and the others we mentioned," the scout replied. "I didn't see Hotspur or his personal banner. But I saw the flag from the garrison at Berwick and flags from Alnwick and Bamburgh and those from his towers at Barmoor and Ford and God knows where else."

"He's out there. I can feel it in my bones," Montgomery warned. "He's hiding 'til he's ready for us

34

to see him. If we even get a *chance* to see him."

"You know him rather well," Douglas said. "You can probably guess what he'll do."

"Whatever 'tis, he's doubtless already done it," Montgomery replied "And we'd better be putting our damned fool heads together and figuring out what *we'll* do!"

* * *

Harry finished deploying his men on the slopes and top of Harehope, as Sean Irby waited with Valdus. "Why didn't you use Homildon instead?" asked Irby, a 20-year-old who had trained with Harry in 1399 and gone on to become one of his squires.

"We could be seen from Wooler," Harry explained. "Besides, our archers can get a better line of fire from here, up onto to Homildon should the Scots go up there, while also covering the road below."

"Ahhh..." Irby nodded.

Intermittently, the foraging parties began straggling back, delivering their goods and reclaiming their positions. Taking tally, Harry noted that only one group had yet to return.

Meanwhile, the Scots pulled their banners from Wooler and coalesced in what Montgomery considered remarkable efficiency, given the relaxation (if not inebriation) with which they had greeted the day. Trudging along the same path from Wooler used by their scouts, they drew up on the lower edge of Homildon Hill.

"I say we go up there," Douglas gestured toward the top.

"Then what?" Montgomery wondered.

"We bide our time. There look to be old walls and such up there, shelter if we need it. We can make the whole hill as secure as any castle and wait them out.

Or..." Douglas thought aloud, "or, from up there, we can charge. Coming downhill, we'll have that much more momentum. We can split their ranks and keep going all the way to Scotland."

Montgomery frowned. "We can try to outwait them for a while. But we can't stay on that damned hill forever, no matter how well we dig in. We'll run out of food and probably out of water. But if we charge, we'll get ourselves in a devil of a fight. The last time we met the English in open battle was at Otterburn. Look what happened there."

Douglas laughed. "We won the day, no less. And hauled Hotspur's English arse back to Edinburgh!"

"And lost too many men, including your cousin and clan chieftain, Jamie Douglas. We also so severely depleted ourselves we couldn't muster another decent army until now, well over a dozen years later." Montgomery spat. "Some victory!"

"So what would you have us do?" Douglas asked irritably.

Montgomery shrugged. "Our choices aren't good. But probably our best option is to retreat to Wooler and try to beat a path northeasterly, through Tillmouth and hard by Berwick. If Harry is here, with his Berwick garrison, there can't be more than a token force in Berwick itself. 'Tis risky, for sure, and 'twill take longer. But it may save our hides—and all these spoils we've collected."

"It's time to turn back," Swinton agreed. "We might even hold Wooler for a time."

"And let the English outflank us and surround us on four sides, instead of two or three?" Douglas retorted.

"Then do as Montgomery says and march east!" Swinton urged.

Adam Gordon edged his horse close and glowered under Swinton's nose. "Ye caitiff cunt, Swinton! I say we hit the English like the men we are, not run like scared squirrels." Although half a generation younger,

Gordon had been Swinton's bitter rival for years, continuing a feud begun by his father.

Swinton's hand went for his knife. "Who are you calling a coward, Gordon?"

Douglas jammed his horse between them. "Peace, friends. Spare your fury for the English. And I still say we'd best go northwest as we planned and be prepared to fight."

Murdoch Stewart, the royal nephew, side-stepped his mount over to them and addressed Douglas. "I think you're correct, My Lord. I'm certainly not afeard of this Hotspur or any damned Northumbrian. Let's regroup up there and charge them. They're no match for us. We'll be in Scotland apace."

Most of those around Douglas agreed. With trepidation but no further suggestions, Montgomery remained silent.

They began their ascent, barons and knights in the lead behind Douglas, followed by men-at-arms, archers and spearmen, all on horseback, with the wagons lumbering at the rear. Oxen and plough horses strained, sweat-streaked sides heaving, hooves struggling, as wagon wheels tipped and slid over the grassy, rock-strewn incline. Creaking and groaning, the army passed Homildon Village and plodded ever upward.

The wagons made it only two-thirds of the way. But there was hardly room at the summit anyway for 10,000 men, let alone booty and draft animals. Thus, Douglas and the other leaders, with some knights and men-at-arms, dismounted and proceeded to the top, while the rest spread out along the upper slopes. Winded and already weary, the men fumbled with their water bottles, but their horses had to suffer without water or retreat to the pond at Homildon Village and then climb partway up again.

Traipsing through the village, the Scots found it empty.

Yet, though the villagers had fled, the Scots soon

learned they had unwelcome neighbors to the west. An English force materialized on Harehope, training longbows and spears on them, while Hotspur's banner waved from a rock.

"Why doesn't he come after us?" Douglas asked Montgomery peevishly.

"Too smart," Montgomery responded. "He's like a cat at the mouse hole, waiting for us to make the first move, after we're sick of being up here."

"Hell!'" Douglas kicked the ground.

Gazing at the English armies, Montgomery did not answer.

Confidence eroding, the Scots sought a modicum of security in the shadow of their horses. Some fingered their weapons, others broke into their supplies for a cold meal, and still others, anticipating the worst, wrote final letters home or arranged with comrades for disposition of their spoils should their booty but not their bodies survive.

Montgomery removed pen, ink and a couple of pieces of battered parchment from his saddlebag and addressed the upper sheet: *"To Sir Harry Percy, to be opened in the event of our defeat and my death."* On the other, he scribbled a quick note:

Harry,

My compliments on your victory. Please accept my remains and provide for my burial ... on the Scottish side of the border, if you will! Use the English coins in my purse to defray the costs. If any remain, give them to the poor, or use them to repair the damage we left in Northumberland, or do whatever you think proper. We'll meet again, in paradise. Until then, Godspeed to you on all your paths.

He wrapped the message inside the outer sheet, tied the little bundle, and strung it around his neck, inside his borrowed armor. He finished as Douglas started aligning archers. The Scottish bows, in the traditional, shorter Gaelic style, were smaller and required less pressure to draw, but also had a shorter range than those of their English rivals. Scots bowmen thus had to be positioned judiciously, and Douglas chose their emplacement with care.

* * *

The last English foraging parties appeared in the distance at noon, trying to skirt Homildon and approach Harehope by the path running along the southern edge of both hills. At first, they assumed that the archers on Homildon were their own and waved merrily.

Reality hit just before the first arrows.

The English riders spurred faster along the path, and the Scots shafts fell short. Frustrated, some of the Scots dislodged a couple of boulders, which crashed down on the path in front of the lead Englishman. Skittering, his horse stumbled on a smaller stone and went down, throwing the rider. His companions checked their speed to avoid collisions, and the emboldened Scots crowded the west side of Homildon, shooting repeatedly not only at the men below but toward the west.

A volley raked Harehope.

"We're under attack!" An English soldier sounded the alarm and whirled, seeking his sergeant. To his surprise, he slammed into Valdus and a man's armored leg. "Sir Harry, we're—"

"Aye!" Raised high, Harry's sword abruptly fell.

"Loose arrows!"

Almost by accident, battle began.

Harry sent orders to his father and the others to close ranks and push forward toward Red Riggs. Then he concentrated on the immediate fight, one largely borne on the shafts of the archers.

Lacking the power of the English longbow, whose reach extended 350 yards, the Scots pulled back from the edge of Homildon. Those partly up the hill struggled to reach the top, which was already dense with Douglas' lords and their knights and men-at-arms. Confusion grew with the ever-tighter crowds. Pressed onto the eastern and northern fringe of the summit, men and horses alike lost their footing and tumbled downhill. Pushed backward, others fell to their deaths off the steeper precipice to the south. Caught amidst the chaos, his own horse rearing, Douglas commanded everyone to halt and stand in place. That stopped the rush, but not the dying.

Although the English on Harehope were on a slightly lower elevation than the Scots, the arc of their arrows more than compensated. They aimed, fired, notched another arrow to the string, drew, aimed, and fired again ... and again... a dozen arrows a minute per man, sometimes more.

The Scots fell in clumps—knights and men-at-arms, barons alongside infantry. Attempting to form their usual "hedgehogs" or schiltrons, the pikemen were encumbered, unable to wield the spears they normally discharged with lethal results.

Panicking, the Scots farther down the slopes again began pushing onto the hilltop, with crushing intensity. Pinned backwards against the stone cairns, two knights died when their spines broke against the rocks. Many suffocated, and more were crushed underfoot. Choosing to flee to the south, still others underestimated the perils, losing their tenuous footholds and plummeting below.

With the Scots largely driven back from

Homildon's west side, Harry guided Knayton and his bowmen down the northeast side of Harehope to the cambered mid-level fields, which in turn fell in gentle curves to Red Riggs and the road beyond. All but Harry dismounted, sending their horses back with squires. Then they formed archery lines. Led by Harry on Valdus, they advanced again—running, shooting, pausing, and dashing forward once more—onto the northwest front of Homildon.

When the Scots responded with tepid fire that mostly fell short, the English bowmen claimed Homildon's lower slopes. Inching on, they reached a relatively level expanse.

Their next volleys reached the summit.

Harry left them to Knayton's command and galloped away to join his father and the main part of the army on the plains below.

The archers under his father's command had already begun moving forward to join their comrades from Harehope. Increasingly, the Scots were assaulted on two sides, the west and north. Under Umfraville and Gerard Salvayn, another English battalion pressed ahead from the east as well, opening a new front.

And the Scots disintegrated further.

* * *

Murdoch Stewart clawed his way over the bodies of several men and a fallen horse to reach Douglas. "They're closing in on three sides. We've got to do something!"

"I know!" Douglas yelled above the din. "We're going to break out. Like I said afore, we'll knock them down and go home!"

"How?" Stewart eyed the sheer drop on the south, the deep crevice of Monday Cleugh dividing Homildon and Harehope, and the threats posed by Umfraville's men infiltrating the village to the east.

Douglas swept his hand in a slow curve northwest, showing they would have to avoid the pits of Monday Cleugh and ending with a thumb cocked toward the lower slopes held by Knayton's archers.

"You're daft!" Stewart exclaimed.

"Daring, rather!" Methodically reorganizing his tattered ranks, Douglas sought volunteers for an exploratory foray. Ten knights and 40 men-at-arms from Galloway, all remounted, took up the challenge. He nodded and raised his battle axe. Bringing it down, he sent the Galloway party off.

They began somewhat tentatively but picked up speed and courage as they rode along, swords, hammers and axes raised high, lances primed, shields affixed. Tightening their formation into a *V,* they bore down the curving hillside and over the wider levels toward the English archers.

The English bowmen held their fire and stood firmly as the wedge approached, the earth already reverberating under the hooves. Nearer and nearer the Galloway force came, until it seemed all but certain that Knayton and his bowmen would be overrun.

Sudden arrows swarmed darkly through the sky.

The foremost Scots fell, to a man, some with several shafts jutting from their shields and armor. To detour around the stumbling horses of the slain and injured, the next ranks slowed their pace. They too soon collapsed.

By the time each archer had shot his first two rounds and fallen back slightly to begin anew, not one man from Galloway was left unharmed. Many of the horses were severely wounded as well, thrashing on the grass alongside their masters and neighing in agony. A few men on uninjured mounts tried to flee back up the hill and were shot. The rest slumped to the grass or crawled along, wounded. One man got up, weakly lifting his arms into the air to show that he yielded, took several steps toward the English lines, and fell, blood pouring from his mouth.

As if their own bodies had been transfixed by the arrows destroying their companions, Douglas and his lords froze in place, disbelieving even as they watched.

Finally, with a curse, Swinton stepped forward. "I say let's get them again. I don't know of an archer yet who won't run out of arrows. When that happens, he might as well be a piece of dirt against a mounted knight." Visor lifted, he surveyed his comrades. "As you know, I would've taken a different way out of here, to the east. But now that we're here, I'll fight like hell to get where I have to go! Have we been turned to straw by some wizard? Why stand here, pissing on ourselves in fear? We can take them, if we try. So... are we knights and men—or not?" He drew his sword. "Who's with me?"

To everyone's amazement, Gordon shoved forward and knelt at his feet. "I am, Sir, if you'll but forgive me the enmity I've borne you and yours for too long. And," Gordon swallowed hard, "if, in forgiving me, you'll also knight me, I should like to go forth with you as a knight. S'truth, there's no one more fitting to dub me than you."

At first, Swinton gaped. Then he threw his arms around Gordon, to applause from the others. Pushing the younger man to his knees, Swinton hefted his sword, quickly tapped Gordon's shoulders with the tip, and laid his hand on his head. "Rise, Sir Adam, and be recognized as my brother and knight." They hugged again, to cheering, and then mounted. A small battalion quickly gathered around them.

Douglas, too, prepared to join in.

Swinton objected. "No, My Lord, better for you to wait and lead the victorious charge to follow in our path."

Douglas nodded and Swinton's force thundered off.

Once again the English archers waited until the

last possible moment and then let their arrows fly. Again, the Scots dissolved like chaff in the wind. Swinton and Gordon keeled from their mounts, alongside all the others in the first ranks. The second wave came on nearly as fiercely, to meet the same fate.

Knayton's archers moved with a precise rhythm: Holding their ground, aiming, drawing, firing, seeing their targets crumble; pulling back to form a fresh line, enticing the next wave of Scots and standing firm as the horsemen approached. Then aiming, drawing, firing anew.

The Scots kept coming, drawn on by the ever-retreating yet ever-shooting English archers. With each downhill step, the Scots gained more ground but lost more men, until the last of them had fallen. Gordon and Swinton lay side by side, Gordon's arm reaching out to embrace his erstwhile enemy, a final tribute to a friendship found too late.

Atop the hill, Montgomery made the sign of the cross.

Douglas turned away and raised his visor, face pasty, as if he were about to vomit. He sank to his knees, gulping air. Rising again, he shut his visor with a growl, turned back toward the field, and stared. For another several seconds, he said nothing. Then he cursed and slammed his battle-axe into the ground. "They will be avenged!"

* * *

Like seas merging in an ocean of blood, Scots and English had been closing the distance between them.

Now a vast emptiness seemed to separate them again, not so much a silence as an absence, heavy with grief and dread on one side, lack of triumphant outcry on the other, and a subdued astonishment on both. A lone Lothian piper began a dirge, but Douglas cut him off in keening mid-note, and only the moans and cries of the wounded or dying remained.

Forcing himself to move beyond shock, Douglas gathered his remaining barons. Despite the many casualties, he still had the larger share of his army, stunned and fearful, perhaps, but intact. Surely, the combined weight of several thousand men, mostly mounted, rushing downhill en masse, could cut the English lines and push on to Scotland. They'd risk being outflanked if the extreme left and right wings of the English army tried to enclose them. But most of his men were still in good shape, while the English had been up all night, marching and eating on the run, while the Scots had enjoyed both comfortable sleep and ample food in Wooler.

"What of the English archers?" the Earl of Angus questioned.

"Archers can only last so long," Douglas replied. "Swinton was right about that. This lot must be near the bottom of their strength and their quivers. If we charge them as one, I think we can get through. Besides, once we've scattered the archers, the rest will be confused. Hotspur's probably getting lazy, thinking his arrows can do all the work. He and his fine friends down there won't be expecting another charge so soon. By the time they've figured out what's hit 'em, we'll be in Scotland."

"Hotspur? Lazy?" Montgomery scoffed. "Don't even dream of it."

"Hah!" Douglas rejoined. "What's he done so far? Pointed his bowmen in the right direction and then hot-spurred back to his father's lines!"

The others rubbed their whiskers, whispering.

"Cutting through 'em might just work," Stewart of Durisdeer reasoned. "I guess 'tis either that or end our days on this hill, starved out."

"We might sue for peace," one of the Frenchmen spoke up hesitantly. "I understand that this 'Hotspur' is never vindictive. He might give us honorable terms."

"He would," Montgomery predicted. "I say we seek them."

"Never!" Douglas insisted. "Asking for terms means surrendering, and I don't fancy spending even one day as a hostage." He looked at Montgomery. "Hotspur might let you off with very little ransom, John, since he regards you kindly. I only know him slightly from our truce talks in the past. He seemed reasonable then. But after a battle like this?" His voice rose in incredulity. "The rest of us might not find much kindness."

"He'd hold us knights as hostages, Scots and French alike," Montgomery replied. "But he'd let our men-at-arms and squires and the rest go home. And they—and we, once ransomed—would live to fight another day."

Douglas's face froze in stubbornness.

Aware he was getting nowhere, Montgomery gave up. "Yet you clearly think otherwise, and you'll do as you willst."

"You'll be with us?"

"To be sure! Am I not Scottish?"

* * *

Through their constant shooting and retreating, the Harehope bowmen had pulled back far enough that the larger English army, moving forward, had overlapped them. Combined, the English troops formed a long, rough shape, like an *L* turned sidewise, with the non-bowmen units of Harry's vanguard, most still on Harehope, as the *L's* shorter piece.

Harry stayed below the hill with the longer line, the original bulk of the army.

Uneven shouts, backed by bagpipes, blared from atop Homildon, accompanied by a blur of activity.

Then the English heard a sustained roar, *"A Douglas! A Douglas! A Douglas!"* amplified by the pipes and the rhythmic beating of hands and weapons on shields.

Douglas appeared on horseback at the rim of the hill, armor gleaming, lance at the fore, shield covering his left side, close to his body. His right hand gripped his battle axe. It had been his late cousin Jamie's, and like Jamie, he preferred it to the sword, though he was proficient with both. He trotted downhill a short distance, and his cavalry began following, the flag-bearers with his pennant and the banners of Scotland in front.

Momentarily cutting back, Douglas cantered in a wide circle around the group and then took the fore again. *"A Douglas! A Douglas! Scotland and St. Andrew!"*

He charged.

The English archers let him approach until well within range. Fingers at bowstrings, arrows taut, they awaited Harry's signal.

"Loose arrows!"

Hundreds of shafts thickened the sky.

Four hit Douglas' uplifted axe, peppering it with dents. Another rocketed into his shield, tip emerging on the other side, to stab through his metal vambrace armguard. Jerking, he dropped his lance and his shield spun out across the ground. Three more arrows embedded in his armor, one in his chest and two at his waist. A fourth pierced the front of his helmet. Blood spurted from his eye slits, and the shaft still twitched when a fifth arrow penetrated his cuisse, the piece of armor protecting his upper leg. He sprawled from his horse. Nicked but otherwise uninjured, his frantic mount dashed into the English lines, where a bowman caught its bridle and brought it to a halt.

Blood seeped in an expanding pool through Douglas' chainmail, soaking his silk surcoat. The riders behind swept aside and raced on, forcing the English archers to fall back. But the bowmen continued their run-pause-shoot, run-pause-shoot even as they retreated.

As more Scots streamed downhill, the English archers shifted their formation, firing from two sides as well as the front. Three of the Scots' knights went down within a few seconds of each other. The fourth lost first his shield, after several arrows peppered it, and then his life, when another arrow tore into his lung. Struggling to retain formation, their companions got almost as far as Red Riggs before fracturing and splintering across the landscape. Hundreds collapsed with wounds or in death throes, and others staggered to their feet in a daze when their horses were shot out from under them.

The more daring sought to regroup, among them Montgomery and the Earl of the Orkneys, who had both been in the middle of Douglas' cavalry. Shields again in place, they started to gather men-at-arms, nudged the horses into an uneven wedge and refused to move. Initially, their fellows continued to course frantically around them, but then a handful paused alongside. So did some from the fresh waves pouring from Homildon—knights, pikemen, and the mounted infantry called hobilers.

From the English lines, the volleys started to taper off. The archers were tiring, beginning to deplete their supply of arrows, and becoming less dangerous. Harry raised his horn. 'Twas time to broaden the battle, before the Scots got away or re-assembled enough to be an army again.

His first three notes blasted forth clearly. The fourth sputtered out when Dunbar smashed his roan alongside Valdus and knocked the horn from Harry's mouth.

"What the hell you doing?" Harry yelled.

"What're *you* doing?"

"'Tis obvious!"

"Calling off the archers. And ordering a charge by the rest of us?"

"Aye!"

"Idiocy!" Dunbar's lips twisted. "Let the archers finish this, use up the rest of their arrows, every last fucking shaft!"

"To then get cut down, like sitting ducks, by whatever Scots are still out there?" Harry asked angrily. "I won't let archers go to slaughter like that."

Dunbar raised a contemptuous shoulder. "They might finish off the Scots before using up their arrows or slay them fighting man-to-man with their knives. There'll be no need for the rest of us."

"No!" Harry replied. "I won't let one part of my army bear the brunt while the rest sits on its haunches and does naught."

Dunbar sneered. "You and your chivalrous principles, Percy. You'll get us all killed!"

Others had drawn close, but Harry went on, unfazed. "I'm also the commander here. But if rank means naught to you, what of common sense? Once the archers exhaust their shots, even if they're not run through by the Scots, they'll hardly be able to fight hand-to-hand effectively. They lack the weapons and armor for that. That's the role of knights and men-at-arms. At the same time, when I'm leading horsemen into battle, I want us covered by archers. Archers can't do that if they lack arrows. But perhaps you're too stupid to see that."

"Oh, no," Dunbar smiled smugly. "I understand. I just disagree. Nor do I believe in lifting my sword when there's no need."

Harry turned his horse away, raising his horn again.

But the Earl of Northumberland wreathed his wrist with a sturdy old hand. "Wait, son. Mayhap Lord Dunbar has a point. What think the rest of you?"

Talbot demurred. "They both sound right..."

Eure sighed. "I guess I agree with Lord Dunbar."

Umfraville rubbed his cheek thoughtfully. "Neither seems *entirely* correct—with all due respect, My

Lords," he glanced apologetically at both Harry and Dunbar.

Salvayn shook his head at Umfraville and weighed in bluntly. "I'm with Harry."

Clifford nodded, and so did Knayton.

Earl Henry turned to Elyot MacKerny, long the master bowman for the English wardens of the March. "And your thoughts?"

"There be merit in what Lord Dunbar and Lord Harry both say," MacKerny replied. "Lord Dunbar is correct, in a way. The archers might finish off the Scots by themselves, with no need for our knights and men-at-arms. At the same time, my men *are* starting to run low on arrows. If even a small number of the Scots get back together—mounted, in armor—they could slay a multitude of archers. So Lord Harry speaks the more wisely," MacKerny concluded. "The archers need the support of the knights and men-at-arms; they can't finish this alone. But the knights need the support of the archers, too. My bowmen should cover them. That means keeping enough arrows to do so, just as Lord Harry says. Listen to him."

"Aye!" Umfraville changed his mind. "I'm with Harry, then."

"I, too," Eure added.

The rest concurred, except Dunbar.

Harry clapped MacKerny on the back. "Go. I'm going to call off your men. But have them ready to resume fire and follow at my command." Nodding, MacKerny left.

Undeterred, Dunbar surveyed the group. "Well, perhaps this little delay has been enough to let the archers continue softening up our enemies." He wagged a finger at Harry. "And don't forget who saved you from acting like a rash fool!" He cantered off.

"Insufferable prig..." Umfraville spat, but Harry scarcely noticed.

Raising his horn, he sounded his orders. Then his voice boomed out over the lines. *"Esperance! Onward for England!" Raising his sword, he galloped ahead.*

* * *

The Earl of the Orkneys had disappeared again, like the other earls. But Montgomery and Robert Stewart, assuming *de facto* command, succeeded in prodding the remaining knights and men-at-arms into a compact battalion, those on horses to the fore and sides and those on foot to the rear. Gamely, they started forward, less encouraged by the diminished arrow-fire than by the thought of Scotland, not 10 miles beyond. *"Scotland and St. Andrew!"*

"Esperance!" Harry's battle cry answered unexpectedly.

The Scots broke from a tenuous walk into a trot and then a low gallop.

The two sides closed with steel, shouts, and thuds.

Harry plunged Valdus into a tight knot of Scots horsemen. An axe confronted him, but he dodged it, and Hardyng knocked it from its owner. Two swords flashed in their faces a moment later, but Harry disposed of the first in a quick slash to the right and the other with a backhand cut to the left. Driving forward, he knocked another Scotsman from his mount, forcing those behind the man to back up until they toppled against others behind them. Valdus neatly crab-stepped over the thrashing limbs and shot forward again.

The Scots line gave way as Harry advanced, trading assaults on either side. Somewhere, he thought he caught a glimpse of Montgomery's tabard, but lost it in the melee.

Abandoning further attempts at unity, the Scots spilled beyond their tattered corps. Some tried to flee, but as the right and left wings of the English outflanked them, they threw up weapons and hands in surrender. Yet their thinning ranks allowed others to push past, avoiding both their remaining comrades and the English, to flee toward the border.

Switching his sword to his left hand, Harry pulled his horn out with his right and sounded another order to the archers to resume their fire. The resurgent arrows helped to confine the fleeing Scots to a narrow funnel of land stretching northwest from Red Riggs.

To create better cover, confuse the English, and carve out a wider escape route, a couple of dismounted Scots crouched behind shields and struck flint and tinder into dried heather and tufted hay. The grass and bushes were too lush to burn hard, but the spent heather blooms and hay scraps blazed. Smoke arose, mixing with a thicker, acrid film where the danker vegetation smouldered. In the murkiness, friend could hardly be distinguished from foe, and more Scots surrendered.

Even then, the fight was not over.

Horse hamstrung by an English axe, John Montgomery defended himself on foot. Knocking an English knight down, he raised his sword again when another mounted Englishman clobbered his shield with a nailed ball-and-chain. The shield cracked, the Englishman hit it again, and it split. Letting its fractured halves fall to the ground, Montgomery dove for cover. The horseman hurtled on past, and Montgomery strove to regain his bearings.

Eyes smarting from smoke, he lurched forward and tripped over a fallen Scotsman. Getting up, he realized it was Douglas. He bent down, lifted his lord's hand, and tore away the glove. Douglas' hand was chill, but a pulse beat beneath the whitened skin and blood continued to ooze from his multiple wounds. Ripping off his tabard, Montgomery wadded it against the biggest gash on Douglas's chest. The bleeding seemed to ease, and he thought he heard Douglas say something. But as he leaned closer, a tremendous force struck him from behind.

Flying headfirst over Douglas, Montgomery landed on a dead horse several feet away. Momentarily stunned, he lay quiet for a couple of minutes. Then, gingerly trying his aching muscles, he knew he would live. He pulled himself up and blundered ahead. An arm's reach away, a dazed Englishman slipped off a horse, and Montgomery groggily climbed into the saddle. At a touch of his spurs the horse galloped ahead.

Like Montgomery, Murdoch Stewart stumbled on foot, with his squires and several vassals. Coughing in the smoke, he stared, as a mounted Englishman, in the earl of Northumberland's colors, bore down on him at lance point. Falling to his knees just in time, he raised his visor, lowered his sword, and surrendered, vaguely relieved to discover that he was yielding to a fitting peer, Earl Henry himself.

On the field beyond, Harry's cavalry continued to encircle the remaining Scots. Heralded by Earl Henry's squires, the news that Murdoch Stewart and his entourage had surrendered convinced most of the Scots to give up, squads and sagging lines tossing aside their weapons as one.

Harry accepted numerous surrenders, including that of the Earl of Moray, whom he transferred to his father's custody to accompany Murdoch Stewart. The rest of his prisoners he left under the guard of Eure.

Squinting through the haze, he signaled to Hardyng, Salvayn, and a score of other horsemen, and addressed Umfraville. "You stay here, Rob. The rest of you: Come with me. I'm going after the Scots trying to flee."

Umfraville nodded, and Harry sped off, summoning MacKerny and a company of archers as he went. Remounted, the bowmen fell in behind. Then he waved to a regiment from Newcastle—merchants turned men-at-arms seeking to repay the Scots for their depredations—and they, too, joined the chase. After eluding their pursuers for a short distance, the exhausted Scots began straying across the countryside. Methodically, Harry dispatched squads in turn to round them up.

He rode with the remainder of his force initially but left it to Salvayn and Knayton when he spied a handful of Scottish knights hieing off along the River Glen. With Irby and Hardyng, Harry followed them.

Peering over their shoulders, the five Scots fled into a clump of oak and alder.

Harry and his aides galloped on, to find their quarry behind a massive fallen tree trunk. Gathering his muscles, Valdus cleared it in a fluid jump and landed amidst the Scots on the other side, knocking two from their mounts.

From their coats-of-arms, Harry identified one as a Beall and the other as an Elliot. Both promptly gave up. His squires, meanwhile, had edged around the trunk on foot to cross swords with two more men, one in a Stewart coat-of-arms.

Dismounting to join the fight, Harry nicked the Stewart in the neck.

Blood dribbling down his metal collar, the knight sank to his knees. "I yield to you, My Lord ... I am Sir Robert Stewart of Durisdeer..." His voice croaked, and thickening clots of blood stained his lips. Nodding, Harry turned toward his aides, but they had already forced the fourth man to the ground.

"Sir David Fleming." He offered Harry his sword and gauntlets.

Harry gave Irby the gloves and Hardyng the sword. "Stay here," he directed. "Tend to Sir Robert's wounds. I'm going ahead."

"What if you need us?" Hardyng questioned.

"I'll sound my horn." Remounted, Harry urged Valdus on.

Beyond a blackberry thicket, he found a horse limping in tall grass, saddle empty and bridle stamped with the crest of one of the Earl of Northumberland's manors. Broken branches betrayed the Scotsman's path.

Dismounting, Harry pushed into the bushes toward the River Glen, rounding a patch of dense thorns.

At the riverbank, a Scots knight turned, broadsword lifted, visor lowered.

Harry leaped forward.

Their swords met with a flash of sparks, then pressed tightly together. After several tense, long seconds, the Scotsman gave ground, edging backwards. Harry's blade smashed at his vambrace, though without drawing blood. The Scotsman almost fell. Regaining balance, he raised his own sword again and deflected Harry's next moves, though he had no shield.

As they went back and forth in thrust and parry, Harry realized he was dueling with someone whose skill he had encountered before and who had dearly tested him. Yet the man's black-brown armor was unfamiliar, and he had no coat-of-arms surcoat or tabard—the thigh-length, T-shaped tunic, bearing a knight's insignia, typically worn in battle. Swearing inside his helmet, Harry forced himself to conserve strength for what might be a long fight. Unexpectedly, though, the Scotsman retreated several paces, splashed backwards into the river, and, with a sigh, drove his sword into the muddy bank.

Harry stepped forward and simultaneously lowered his own sword.

"You've got me, Lad. I yield." Raising his visor, John Montgomery regarded Harry with a blend of chagrin, respect, and fraternal affection. "I could hold you off a bit longer, I reckon, but you'd best me in the end. So what's the point of carrying on one moment more?"

"None!" Harry raised his visor and sheathed his sword, as happy as he was amazed.

Montgomery waded out, boots squishing with each step and rivulets coursing down the greaves protecting his lower legs. Balefully, he beheld the dripping armor. "Oh hell, at least 'tis not blood."

Harry embraced him. "Damnation! I should have guessed 'twas you, John. I could tell I was crossing swords with someone I knew, someone cursedly good, too, but..."

Montgomery pounded his back. "'Tis 14 years since we dueled, erst time, Harry. And, praise God, this'll be the last time. Even so," he released Harry and pulled his sword from the mud, "however glad I am to see you and glad 'tis you that's taken me, I'm still beaten. So you may as well have my sword." He handed it over.

Harry returned it. "Keep it. I trust you'll not try to lop off my head the instant I turn around." He surveyed his friend. "You've lost your shield and coat-of-arms, though. You must've been in the heat of it, back there."

Montgomery nodded. "One of your men broke my shield, and I used my coat-of-arms to try to keep Douglas from bleeding to death. He's doubtless gone by now, though."

"He was alive?" Harry shook his head, astounded. "I saw him go down. How he kept from being trampled to death I can't imagine. He must've been hit with arrows thrice over, at least."

"Aye... I tried to do what I could for him," Montgomery explained. "Damned near killed myself falling over him, in fact. Otherwise, I never would have seen him. But he was about the worst I've found any man not yet dead."

Harry deliberated. "I was going to ride as far as the Tweed. But I'd best tend to things here. You can come with me." He chuckled. "That horse from my father's stables, too."

A hint of glee brightened Montgomery's weary eyes. "I only acquired him of necessity, when the man who'd been riding him had no use for him, temporarily."

"Doubtless. But I still want to fetch him back, and bring you along, too."

Montgomery smiled quizzically. "As hostage, prisoner, or friend?"

Harry laughed. "All the aforementioned!"

* * *

Below Homildon, Harry felt as if he wandered in a melancholy, red-tinted dream: Red in the crimson orb of the sun, suspended between streaks of brittle gold and dusty blue; red in the embers smoldering in hillocks; red in the shadows cast by the natural pink of the rocks; red in the pools of blood that stained green grass like so many hellish rubies...

He proceeded slowly, accompanied by Hardyng, who had unslung pen and writing tablet to note the names of the dead and wounded, and Montgomery, whose eyes filled with tears as he identified his fallen countrymen.

"The poor, stupid bastards..." Harry trod carefully among the carnage. "Why didn't they sue for peace after that first failed charge? I'd have given fair terms, taken some hostage, to be sure, but sent the rest high-tailing it back to Scotland, without their booty but with their lives. Why go on like this ... to slaughter, rank after rank?"

Montgomery answered hesitantly, for he didn't really understand, either. "Douglas ... we all, I suppose ... thought we could break through, that ... that you'd have to stop shooting. But we gave too little thought to how strong you were with the rest of your army, all your knights and men-at-arms beyond the archers. We'd deceived ourselves, I guess, riding as far as we did into England without hindrance. We began to think you powerless and ourselves invincible."

Harry shook his head again. "But you knew me, especially you, John. You must've known I wouldn't let you go unchallenged."

"Aye, but when I reminded them, they didn't believe me or didn't want to hear it. Now here we be." Montgomery's arm swept over the field. "Here's the flower of Scotland... Here's the glory of Caledonia..."

Walking on, Harry suddenly stopped, squatting beside two corpses. He looked up, astounded. "Adam Gordon, holding fast to John Swinton! Everyone knows they hated each other's guts. How?"

Montgomery explained.

Harry sighed. "They died together, as brothers. Why couldn't they live together as neighbors? Why can't any of us—English and Scots alike—live together as neighbors?"

They went another few paces, pausing over a dead baron, mutely shaking their heads when a pair of monks approached with a litter. The monks stopped, frowned, and hurried on to the next fallen man and, finding him alive, gently rolled him onto their stretcher. It was a sight repeated constantly across the field, for in a desperate bid to remove as many injured as possible before dusk or death overcame them, Harry's chaplain, Ian Kynge and a minor army of stretcher-bearers labored feverishly. Kynge had recruited priests and monks from churches and abbeys in every locale that had contributed military levies to the army. Villagers from Wooler and the Homildon communities lent assistance as well, a welcome contrast to the ghouls who often spread like maggots over a battlefield, to steal from the fallen, killing any still alive enough to protest. Priests from Douglas' army toiled with their English counterparts, nursing the wounded, dispensing drinks, administering the last sacrament, or offering whatever comfort they could.

Injured or dying horses were consigned to quicker fates. Harry ordered that those that could be saved be brought to town or fed and watered on the field, to mend as best they might overnight. Those irrevocably injured or deeply suffering—the majority—he ordered killed. He assigned that job to young squires not involved in caring for the human wounded, to reinforce their awareness of the horror and waste of war, lest they revel too much in the glory of victory. Three times, though, he drew his own knife, in one case dispatching a horse raised in his own pastures.

Nonetheless, most dead and wounded, human and equine alike, were Scottish.

Momentarily leaving his stretcher-bearing, Kynge came over. A big-boned man with strong arms and shoulders and no fat, he compared his tally of casualties with Hardyng's. They spoke in low tones, with an escalating hint of amazement. Then Kynge brushed his thick, short hair back from his forehead and tapped Harry's shoulder.

"Harry, 'tis a miracle, almost: We've only five Englishmen slain, among all these thousands."

Harry's sober expression changed to incredulity. "Five men?"

Kynge and Hardyng both nodded.

"You mean five lords? Or five knights?"

"No," Kynge informed him, "five men total, out of about 10,000 lords, knights, men-at-arms, archers, squires, *et al.*"

"How many wounded?"

"Less than 100, seriously hurt, including two from the foraging party at the beginning. Another couple hundred with minor cuts, sprains or bruises."

"Thanks be to God...'*Twas* nigh unto a mira—"

The arrival of an excited Irby interrupted him.

"Lord Harry: We've found Douglas."

"His body?"

"No. He's alive. Yonder." Irby pointed. "We only found him after we pulled four corpses from atop him. One of our men-at-arms thought he noticed movement 'neath the last body. Then we saw 'twas Lord Douglas."

"Huh? He was not under anyone when I left him," Montgomery said.

"Yea. We think it must have happened in their last charge. Mayhap it kept him from being further injured," Irby replied. "But when I identified myself and asked if he yielded, he cursed me. So I gave up. He hasn't yielded yet." The squire gestured again. "He looks very bad, and I don't think he can see. But he won't surrender and doesn't want any of us to come near, not even to help him."

"Let me try. The rest of you stay back." Harry hurried ahead a dozen yards.

It was hard to tell whether the broken hulk of a man on the ground was even a lord, much less the Scottish commander. Face up, he lay in a stagnating pool of his own blood and urine, dozens of flies crawling over his wounds. His chest was a sodden redness, obliterating his ragged coat-of-arms, and one leg was similarly covered in gore. Somehow, he'd wrenched off his helmet, and his face was swollen, bruised, and ugly purple and crusted where a scab had begun to form over a gash under one eye. Both eyelids were cemented shut with blood, dried on top and dusted with dirt, but still sticky and oozing slightly beneath. He'd lost his second gauntlet after Montgomery had removed the first, and his large, once-powerful hands lay lax beside him. Moaning, he banged a foot against the ground in agony.

Harry knelt, disrupting the flies and waving a hand over Douglas's eyes. No response followed. The man *was* blinded, if not permanently by his injuries, then temporarily by the mess on his face. Doughlas whimpered and threw his head back in a scream, biting his lip so hard it almost split. Writhing, he yelled a second time, a horrible, drawn-out wail.

Stomach tightening, Harry trailed his hand along his belt. For several seconds, he fingered his knife, pondering: It would be easy to slit Douglas's throat, to end the misery, as he had with the mortally wounded horses. *'Tis done... I know 'tis done, or has been, by Christian knights like me...*

Douglas screamed once more.

For another awful moment, the temptation to kill him retained its horrible appeal. Hand lingering on his knife, Harry winced. *But I can't ... I never have afore. Perhaps he'd want me to. But I can't.*

Douglas' cry descended into a low groan, and he lay still, breathing hard.

Harry's fingers continued along his belt to find his whisky flask.

As he untied it, Douglas moved again. His lips trembled, though no words emerged. Lifting his head slightly, he tried to marshal a remnant of strength before opening his mouth again. This time, hoarse defiance emerged. "I yield not ... to any damned ... Sassenach or squire!"

Harry brought his flask close to Douglas's face.

The Scotsman turned away with a murmured epithet. Harry grinned and signaled to his aides to rejoin him. "His spirit remains alive, as ornery as ever!"

"But Lord Harry," Irby raised a cautioning hand. "If he's not yielded, should you try to help him? What if he still has a knife somewhere?"

Harry brushed away both Irby's hand and admonition. "You mean well, Sean, but there's nary a chance in hell he could harm anyone." He held the flask to Douglas's lips again, using his left arm to prop up his head. Liquid dribbled down Douglas's chin, but then he sucked slowly and swallowed a little, paused, and took a longer gulp, followed by a second. He murmured something that sounded vaguely like "thank you."

Montgomery stood over them, in silent hope.

"Lord Douglas." Taking Douglas's right hand in his own, Harry squeezed it. "'Tis Harry Percy."

Douglas replied with a faint return pressure. "Percy... you've ruined me. And my army... I fear."

"Aye. We've beaten you roundly."

Harry gave him another sip, and Douglas spoke again, more strongly.

"Many of mine ... slain?"

"Aye."

"Dozens? Hun—hundreds?"

"Perhaps thousands."

Douglas moaned, emotional pain compounding the physical. "*Jesu...*" For several seconds, he made no effort to say anything. Then his strained voice came again. "Did... Did any of my lords ... knights ... survive? Yield?"

"Oh, aye. Murdoch Stewart—my father captured him, along with the French leaders. Then there were Stewart of Durisdeer, and a couple of Flemings, and a Beall, and Montgomery—among the many who yielded to me personally. The Earls of Angus and the Orkneys were taken by men from Raby, my cousin Neville's lieges, though Neville himself wasn't here. We also captured a half dozen Musgraves and two Crosiers and Humes, plus scores of others: knights, men-at-arms, hobilers, squires. Not all perished."

"You said Murdoch Stewart ... and ... those others... sur... surrendered?"

"Aye—and gratefully, most of them."

"Then..." Douglas began. "Then... I, too, yield ... to you ... on two conditions."

"Aye?"

"That you ... care for my wounded."

"'Tis already being done. My chaplains and yours are searching them out, binding their wounds and bearing them to shelter. We've got some of your men helping, too."

Douglas tried to nod again.

"Your other condition?"

"That... that should I live... you cede me to no one else—not to your Lord Father ... not King Henry, if he's here..."

"He's not," Harry replied.

"And..." Douglas struggled to go on, "don't cede me to that conniving traitor Dunbar."

Harry squeezed Douglas' hand. "Never."

"Nor cede any of my knights ... those you took yourself."

"Nor any of your knights."

"Swear it!"

"'Tis already well-understood practice, but...." Harry put Douglas's hand down and drew his sword, reversing it so that the cross-shaped hilt was on top. He gently placed the Scotsman's hand on it. "That's my sword, the hilt, in the shape of a cross. Can you feel it?"

Douglas nodded, fingers closing around it.

Harry wrapped his own hand around Douglas'.

"I swear," Harry began, "that I take you as hostage, that no harm shall befall you and that I shall safeguard you, care for your wants, and treat you as I would an honored knight and brother, so long as you abide by your bond..."

Douglas nodded again, clinging to the hilt.

"I swear further," Harry went on, "that, upholding good and true custom, I shall deliver you to no other man. And the same for any of yours that I've taken myself. I swear this by my own honor and integrity, and ... and so help me God."

His clasp tightened "Thus you have my vow, made on the cross of my sword. Fitting, 'tis the Feast of the Holy Cross, today." He smiled, though Douglas couldn't see it.

"Aye... H-h... Holy Rood... Day..." Douglas' voice ebbed, as if beneath the blood and dirt his eyes had closed.

At first, Harry thought he had died. But as he felt the wan pulse beneath his own, he realized that Douglas had succumbed to sleep or unconsciousness, not death. For a time, he remained kneeling, their hands still joined, not wanting to disturb Douglas by moving. Finally, he loosened his grip and stood, sheathing his sword.

He rested his arm on Montgomery's shoulder. "Douglas is a remarkably strong man, in all senses of the word. I think he might make it."

"Aye." Montgomery's relief was obvious.

Harry turned back to Irby. "Find a stretcher. I'll help bear him down to Wooler myself. And of he and I, 'tis I who'll leave this field with the far lighter burden."

* * *

Midnight loomed before Harry saw a chance to leave Wooler: After he'd helped carry Douglas down the hill; after he'd made arrangements for his other hostages and begun dispersing them to towers and castles in the region; after issuing orders for the burials of men and horses; after he'd set a guard on the battlefield to prevent looting; after he'd ensured the feeding of his army as well as the Scots and their animals; and after he'd taken reports from his lieutenants returning from the Tweed, where at least 200 more Scots had perished, either in fighting or in attempting to cross at a spot with no ford. Caught in rapids and undertow, weighted by armor and weapons, many had drowned.

"'Twas hideous," Knayton said. "We managed to save some, but a lot of them we couldn't reach. The Tweed runs with blood. The shallows and banks thicken with the dead."

Harry rubbed a tired hand over his chin. "They'll have to be removed, afore they rot and foul the water all the way to Berwick. It will have to wait till the morrow, but you'd best oversee it yourself. Take some bowmen to help."

"We'll start at first light. Anything else?"

"Just this, then get some sleep: Have someone saddle a horse for me; not Valdus, though, he needs to sleep, too. I'm bound for Tower House. I'll meet you here Sunday evening. Summon me if there's any cause meanwhile, especially with Douglas. Kynge thinks he'll be partly comatose for days, though."

"We'll send word posthaste," Knayton promised. "Give my regards to your lady."

Removing his sword belt, Harry shed his bloodstained tabard. But he left his chainmail cowl and hauberk in place, along with his ambraces, cuisses and greaves. Pulling on a thigh-length, tunic, he rebuckled his belt over it, slung his water bottle and a pouch over his chest, added a cloak, and left Wooler's manor. A squire led a horse into the paddock, and Harry dropped into the saddle. His squires had readied a sleek 3-year-old buckskin with dark stockings and crooked white blaze, stolen by the Scots from his meadow at Warenford. "So you're back with your rightful owner," he said softly, with a pat. Under another sky of brilliant stars, they set off for Coquetdale.

* * *

Night lingered as he rode into the yard, piercing the silence with his telltale whistle to announce himself. Dogmael barked from the barn and, as Harry dismounted, a sleepy Enochie pushed the barn door open, holding a lantern with one hand and restraining the dog with the other.

"Lord Harry!"

"Hullo, Lad. Sorry to bother you."

"'Tis nothing." The youth noted the chainmail. "Have you come from the north? Is there to be a battle?"

"There was." Harry stooped to pat a tail-wagging Dogmael. "Today, or perhaps yesterday, since it's now close to cock's crow. We defeated the Scots with great slaughter."

Enochie's face lit up. "The Lord be praised."

Harry replied with a bittersweet smile. "Aye." Then his brow knit. "Why are you sleeping in the barn? Has there been trouble?"

"No." The boy blushed. "It's just that if there *was* trouble, I wanted to protect the animals, with good weapons to hand, after what happened last time."

"You're to be commended, Lad." Harry slapped the boy's back and then rubbed the buckskin's neck. "You'll see to my friend here?"

"To be sure."

"Good. Afterward, hie back to bed. I'll help you with chores in the morning."

"Aye. Thank you, Sir." With Dogmael trotting alongside, Enochie led the horse to a stall, and Harry strode toward the house.

Aware that the back door would be securely barred, he continued around to the front and up the stairs. Despite his eagerness, in the darkness it took him a few moments to untangle the key chain at his belt. More seconds elapsed when the key he had selected would not work on the little hatch door, an inset in the main door. Swearing, he examined the jumbled keys, all long, heavy and scratched, glinting palely in the dimness. After running a finger over the teeth of several, he selected a second and tried it. The hatch unlocked and he reached in and removed the bar on the inside. It crashed to the stone floor within. Stifling another curse, he unlocked the big door, entered, and relocked it.

Banked low, the hearth offered a cozy welcome, and his annoyance vanished.

Whistling an old Borders ballad, he lit a lantern, hung his cloak on a peg, and slipped his cowl down around his neck. Filling his arms at the wood box, he stoked the fire to sustain it well into morning. Then he took the lantern and, still whistling, approached the staircase in the corner...

Upstairs, Ciarry tossed in bed, thinking—no, dreaming—that she'd heard a horse out in the yard.

Then a booming thud resounded.

Heart pounding, she sat up in bed, straining to listen. Footsteps echoed in the hall below—and the haunting melody of "Jock o' Hazeldean" drifted above the solitude. It was one of Harry's favorite songs.

Covers tossed aside, she slipped her feet to the floor, hand closing around the bedside candleholder. Ascending boots scraped the stone steps as she crossed the room, clad in a sleeveless linen shift. Then light gleamed under the door, brightening as a lantern came to rest on the hook on the other side. Rays seeping over the floor, the lantern light merged at her feet with the glow from her candle.

The bedroom door swung open.

"Harry!" She set her candle down with one quick movement; with another, she fell into his arms. "Thank God ... Oh, my love."

As she lifted her face to his, they kissed. From the rough new stubble of his whiskers she knew that he must have been up for a full day, at least.

He kissed her again, joyfully if inelegantly, in his weariness. "Ciarry, dearest."

His hold tightened, and she could feel the hard metal of the chainmail under his surcoat, the pressure of his sword belt and the prickling of the small buckles on the leather straps across his chest. Yet, even as he enfolded her, his body coursed with a fusion of coiled energy and frenetic exhaustion.

"We gave battle..."

"I knew you must have. And you've won, I think. *Laudate Dominum!*"

"Aye," he released her slightly, to look down into her dear, lovely face.

The half-lit room could not hide the dark rings under his eyes, or the shadowed sadness in them.

"Oh Ciarry, 'twas awful..." In the rush of duties after the battle, he had quashed his feelings; it wasn't fitting for a commander to give in to sentiment. But in pent-up rawness his emotions had ridden with him through the night. Now they spilled out, catching in his voice and coloring the expression on his face.

"'Twas less warfare than annihilation." His eyes closed in remembrance. "Never before have I been in a battle where I personally fought so little. And never have I seen one that took so many lives..."

She stiffened. "You lost a lot of men?"

"Not us, God be praised. The Scots: thousands of them, gone. Thousands..."

He told her everything, from his pre-dawn preparations to the charnel on the Tweed. "I stopped short of the border, though, and captured John Montgomery. He's with my men at Wooler. Douglas too, although I fear for Douglas' life. I still can't believe he charged as he did. They just kept coming on, and on. Doomed, foolhardy devils..."

She kissed him, resting her head on his chest as he continued, talking to himself as much as to her, struggling in his own mind to make sense of what he had seen, if it were even possible to make sense of it.

"I'd heard and read, many times, of what happened to the French at Crecy and Poitiers," he continued. "But I ne'er expected to see such a thing myself. I use archers all the time, always have. Even when I won that battle in Wales at Cadair Idris, 'twas nothing like this. I've seen death and terrible bloodshed. But naught like this, never like this."

Ciarry kissed him again. "Of our men, how many slain?"

"Five."

She nearly jumped in his arms. "*Five*?"

"Aye." Softly, he shook his head and stroked hers. "Hard to believe, but true."

"Then, Harry..." Ciarry hugged him fiercely. "You've just won one of the greatest victories ever, certainly one of the greatest for England. 'Tis every bit as significant as Crecy or Poitiers—mayhap more, since you lost so few men."

"Perhaps," he looked down at her, not having thought of the victory that way, and smiled ruefully. "Even so, it was a strange fete. I hardly drew my sword."

"Nonsense. You just told me you and your horsemen fought hotly at the end and chased the Scots back toward the border, capturing Montgomery and the others."

"Aye. Anyway..."

Hold tightening, he rubbed his hand over her back and across the delicate beauty of her shoulders. Again, he kissed her, more expertly this time. Tenderly, his hand eased its way down her spine to her rump, feeling its smooth roundness beneath the gauzy cloth of her gown, tracing the goosebumps of delight that his fingers and nearness evoked.

Lifting her arms around his neck, she rose on her toes, as if to extend her short frame to equal his. With a little help from his hand, her shift shimmied over her head and dropped to the floor, like a forgotten inhibition.

"Oh Ciarry, my love..." He embraced her, rejoicing in the wonder and beauty and sheer goodness of her, all the more precious after the horrors he had witnessed.

Without the scant layer of the shift to cover her, though, the metal of the straps across his chest bit into her skin. Backing up, she began unbuckling them.

"Here." Staying her hand, he slipped his water bottle and pouch over his head. A moment later, his sword belt clattered to the floor; then he shed his tabard.

Before he could remove his armor, she threw herself back into his arms, wanting only to have him close again. The metal waffling of his chainmail imprinted on her skin, but she ignored it, losing herself in moments that seemed stolen from heaven itself.

He drew his arms around her, almost afraid he would crush her but unable to pull himself away, exulting in her love and nearness, craving nothing—not even sex—except to hold her. Finally, he carried her to the bed and stretched out alongside her, still in his muddy boots, arm and leg plate, chainmail, and sweaty clothing underneath. For the first time in weeks, he truly relaxed, his head half on her shoulder and half on the pillow, whispering her name, he continued to caress her at first, then simply lay there as she wrapped him in her arms.

Before long, he was out.

For a few minutes, she watched him sleep, stroking his dark hair and rejoicing. Then, with a kiss to his upturned cheek, she pulled the covers over them both.

Chapter III

Wednesday, 20 September 1402: Berwick Castle

Bounding up the stairs, Harry met Kynge descending.

"Just in time," the priest said. "I could use help with Lord Douglas. I was about to fetch a squire, but you'll do—if you will."

"Of course."

They entered the tower room.

"He's asleep again, but it looks like he spilled the bedpan. The bedding is wet, and he's fallen half off the mattress trying to avoid it." Kynge sighed wearily. "It must've happened when I dozed off. I need you to help lift him while I clean it up. We'll have to remake the bed, too. And his bandage needs changing, also."

Collecting a blanket from a wooden chest, he spread it on the carpet. They picked up the wounded man and gently laid him down on it. Kynge whisked away the bedpan and soggy sheets and disappeared.

In his absence, Harry eyed the bed and then rooted in the linen chest. He wasn't used to playing chambermaid, though he knew how, from his uncle's household. Page boys, after all, had to tend to the lord's cot on campaigns in the absence of castle servants. Besides, he chafed at waiting for someone else to do things he might as well do himself. So he proceeded to remake the bed. Its corner location and the heavy curtains all around made the job more difficult than expected, however. No sooner had he finished than he realized that on the side facing the room, the blankets sagged to the floor while they barely reached the edge of the mattress on the other.

"Damnation!" He bent to the task again, loosening, tugging and tightening, glancing periodically at Douglas. But the Scotsman slumbered peacefully on the floor. From the garderobe, the clatter of Kynge's scouring sounded, followed by retreating footsteps as the priest hurried after fresh bandages from his quarters.

Since the bed was ready, Harry decided, it might as well reclaim its occupant. Squatting, he slipped his arms under the injured man's shoulders and knees. Strong and only a couple of inches shorter than the 6-foot, 2-inch Harry, Douglas was no featherweight. He'd never been fat, though, and pounds had melted from him after he was wounded. With years of practice in lugging armor-clad men from the field, Harry hefted him into bed.

Kynge reappeared and removed the old bandages from Douglas' chest and leg. "No suppuration. The moldy bread we applied worked. I can use the unguents now, though we must still be careful." After swabbing the still-vivid gashes with a mixture of whisky and water, he daubed them with a blend of herbs and beeswax, covering everything with clean cloths.

Douglas smiled faintly, without appearing to wake. A thick, red-brown scab glued his right eye shut. Below it, a second scab, almost as large, covered a deep cut on his cheek. His left eye, lightly bruised but apparently less severely injured, remained shut. Kynge gently wiped Douglas' face; bathed the scabs with whisky-water and patted them dry and smeared on salve, otherwise leaving them to the open air. Rising, he yawned.

"You're spent. You were with him half the night," Harry observed.

"No more than you."

"Aye, but I took the first shift and have had time to rest. You haven't. Get some sleep. I'll stay with him."

"All right. But come for me if he waxes hot with fever or any other problem arises." The door shut behind the chaplain.

Harry stretched his hand across Douglas' brow, to find it no warmer than his own. Tucking the duvet more securely around his captive, he picked up the book he had left the evening before, Sir John Froissart's *Chronicles of England, France, Spain, and the Adjoining Countries*, part of a series that covered the preceding 80 years. Purchased by Thomas Percy in London, this volume included an account of the Battle of Otterburn.

Settling into a chair by the window, Harry read: *"...Cries of `Percy' and `Douglas' resounded on each side. The battle now raged."*

The bedcovers rustled, but a questioning look revealed only that Douglas had shifted slightly. Harry went back to his exploits. *"Sir Harry Percy, during this last attack, had the misfortune to fall into the hands of Lord Montgomery, a very gallant knight of Scotland. They long fought hand-to-hand, with much valor..."*

The bedcovers scrunched again, harder. A sort of sigh followed.

Harry's head jerked up.

"I should hate you, you know." Surprisingly clear, Douglas' voice came from across the room.

Froissart slammed shut.

"You killed my brother, my cousin, and my father." Douglas followed the movement with his now-open left eye as Harry approached the bed.

"You cease dreaming at last." Since Homildon, Harry had only seen Douglas unconscious or sleeping. He laid a restraining hand on the blanketed chest. "Best not tax yourself with speech, lest you weaken and I still be accused of killing you."

Douglas went on. "You slew my bastard brother, Angus, when he tried to raid Northumberland. My cousin Jamie you cut down at Otterburn. Even if others had already stabbed him, 'twas you who struck him mortally."

"Aye. But only after I bade him to surrender. He wouldn't. And your brother Angus died because he wouldn't yield either and charged straight at me."

With the wave of a pale hand, Douglas dismissed the reply. "And my father sickened and died from chasing you that night in Lothian, 18 months ago. So you killed him, too, I think. Now you hold me, after your army shot me to pieces." A groan followed, half moan and half curse.

"Are you in much pain?"

"No." Douglas looked puzzled, as if just realizing this. "I was, but not now. 'Tis other things that discomfit me."

"Yet you're improving by the day. You won't die if I can help it."

Douglas blinked. "Perhaps that's all the more reason to hate you: You *didn't* kill me."

Brow furrowing, Harry dragged his chair over to the bed. "You want to die?"

Douglas didn't answer. Biting his lip, he began to pull himself up, failed, tried again, and failed anew. Reaching out with his right arm, Harry slipped his other behind Douglas' back. At first, the Scotsman tried to avoid assistance, leaning forward, trembling and struggling. Then he gave in. Falling back against Harry's left arm, he placed his hand on Harry's right wrist and allowed himself to be eased to a sitting position.

"Thanks," he acknowledged hoarsely.

Harry handed him a goblet, and Douglas sipped the wine-flavoured water.

"Again, thank you." After consuming half the cup, he gave it back.

"So, you want to die?" Harry repeated.

"In truth, no! But ... I know not what to think ... except that I feel I should hate you. Yet..." His voice disappeared in doubt, and he turned his face toward the bed curtains and wall.

"You want to hate me because I know you as you are now," Harry guessed. "You resent me for seeing you there, naked and injured, weak as a mewling kitten. You want to hate me, or even to die, because 'tis easier to do that than admit you're helpless and must rely on an enemy—or someone you *think* should be an enemy—and have that enemy see you so vulnerable."

Douglas turned back toward him, tears forming in his good eye despite attempts to blink them back. "Yea. You don't know what it's like, to lie here, dependent on ... on *Englishmen* to change your bandages, and turn you over, and wipe the puke from your chin, and help you drink when you finally can." His voice grew stronger as his emotions, confined within his maimed body too long, finally broke loose. "I can't even piss without you knowing how much and how often and how yellow it is. And I have to suffer you to carry me back to bed, like a babe in arms."

"I thought you were asleep. Did I wake you?"

"No." Douglas thought a moment. "What day is it?"

"'Wednesday, the 20th of September, feast of St. Eustace, a soldier and martyr."

"Eustace? I seem to remember him from my schooling. A Roman general, wasn't he? Won a great battle for his emperor, Trajan or Titus or something. But the emperor executed him because he wouldn't worship some inane false god, in homage for victory."

"Aye," Harry affirmed. "Most likely, Trajan wanted Eustace to worship Trajan, literally or figuratively. Probably Trajan envied him, too. But like any man with common sense, and as a good captain who loved his country, Eustace said 'no.' And died for it." A wry smile crossed Harry's face. "As a commander who's seen something of the way kings act, I can understand Eustace's plight."

"May *your* liege treat you better in victory," Douglas proposed, then took tally. "So 'tis the 20th, six days since you found me on the field. Clearly, I'm not *there* anymore. Where am I?"

"Berwick, in my quarters at the castle."

"'S'truth! Long did I wish to occupy the lord's chambers at Berwick Castle. 'Tis hardly the way I'd dreamed of, though." Douglas frowned. "Have I been here since the battle?"

"No. We carried you to Wooler first; put you to bed in the same one you'd slept in the night before."

"How long was I there?"

"Three days. We brought you here on Monday by wagon, very slowly." Harry smiled. "Mostly you've been unconscious or sleeping, barely noticing when we poured a little broth down your gullet."

"Yea. I *did* sense I'd been moved. And once, too, I heard you discussing whether I'd live."

Harry reddened. "Your heard that?"

"Yea, but fret not. You didn't say anything unkind. And I know everyone's been tending me with great care, even you, keeping watch and talking to me: `*Don't die, you brave fool! Live! Live!'*" He imitated Harry, who indeed had said that and more, willing him to live, goading him on. "Do you care for all wounded enemies so diligently?"

"No, regretfully. But most either die soon or aren't as severely hurt. Besides, I can't ransom a dead man."

Douglas's healthy eye narrowed. "Have you sent ransom terms to my king?"

"No." Harry found the question vaguely irritating, without knowing why. "Nor can I say when I might. I *did* send a messenger asking King Robert to alert whomever should be notified. I wasn't sure. And Robert is your father-in-law, is he not?"

Douglas nodded.

"I also wrote to the constable of Edinburgh Castle, asking him to send your personal belongings, whatever you might want that wasn't with your baggage at Homildon."

"I'm grateful..." Douglas thought again. "My squires?"

Harry's smile faded. "All slain, found near you on the field. Howe'er, if there's anyone else you want here ... your wife, maybe?"

"No... she and I ... live not as husband and wife. She's a princess, a fine lady beloved for her charity, but..." Douglas shrugged. "She never wanted marriage, to me or any man. She sought the convent, but her royal father forced her to make a match. He wanted her wed, and my father wanted me to have heirs—*legitimate* heirs, since my family..." he laughed lightly "...has oft produced the other kind. Thus, my wife and I came together in wedlock and begat two sons. She then retired to dwell separately, pursuing her good works and managing her properties. You know how such things go."

"Aye," Harry said somberly. A moment later, he brightened. "Maybe there's another woman who's close to you, heart and soul, who might be brought here?"

Douglas shook his head. "No such lass loves me, alas." Toying with the sheet, he looked down and then regarded Harry with deep frankness, as if nearly dying had robbed him of reticence. "In this world, I'm mostly alone … despite my armies and land. Now I'm left with naught but enemies to succor me."

"They're happy to do so."

"But I loathe having to be nursed." Douglas punched his fist into the bedcovers. "Loathe it!"

"Good!" Harry laughed. "Loathing it, you'll get better that much faster. Then, once you're well, you can loathe and hate *me*, if you wish."

Douglas shook his head again, almost sadly. "No… That's just it. I can't hate you. You've slain many near to me, but…" he sighed. How *could* he hate someone who had cajoled him into surrendering and bullied him into surviving, someone who had borne his torn body from the battlefield, helped wash him of blood and pus, lifted him back into bed, all, paradoxically, with no attempt yet at ransom? "Damn it!" Douglas cursed, exasperated. "It's hard to even think of you as an enemy."

Harry laughed again. "If not your enemy, then your slave—at least *ad interim*. Who else would be at your beck and call?"

"All right, slave. And overlord, for the time being, anyhow." Douglas laughed, too. He reached for his goblet, and Harry helped him drink. Then he sank back into his pillows.

Harry got up. "I should let you sleep."

"No." Douglas grabbed his hand.

So Harry sat down again, and Douglas closed his good eye, as if deliberating.

"I keep thinking of Swinton and Gordon," he confessed. "I've had a lot of time to think, lying here… They were mortal foes, Swinton and Gordon. Or so they thought. Once they stopped to consider it, though, they realized that didn't have to be. They could be friends instead, and maybe more than friends, be like brothers. Why did it have to take them so long?" Douglas seemed almost indignant. "Why did they have to wait until the moment they died?"

"Who knows? At least they died knowing friendship, at last."

"Yea. But I'd rather be wiser. Almost dying makes a man feel that way, I suppose. I don't wish to wait so long to begin mending fences, even across the border. I guess that's the real reason I can't hate you... Because after so much misery, after my rashness killed so many, after I knew for the first time what pain really is ... how pointless it all seems."

Harry nodded. "Borderer against Borderer, Scot against Englishman, St. Andrew against St. George."

"Yea. If Swinton and Gordon could reconcile, why not Douglas and Percy, why not you and I? In truth..." Douglas offered a lopsided smile. "In truth, these last few days, when you were hovering o'er me, I thought 'twas—"

"—a vulture!"

"Never! A mother hen or father goose, mayhap. No, I thought 'twas a friend or brother, not an enemy at all." Douglas' eye closed momentarily. "That ... that's the other reason I can't hate you. You almost seem like a brother..." His voice pitched in surprise. "*You,* who killed my real brother."

"A brother..." Harry repeated quietly. "I had brothers once. I miss them."

"I'm sorry. All gone now, aren't they?"

"Aye." So Harry told him about Tom and Rafe, who had died as young knights, and Alain, succumbing to disease as a child; and his little sister Margot, also taken away too soon.

In time, Douglas sank under the covers.

"Now I *have* tired you," Harry said. "You'd best rest."

"Yea. But first..." Douglas' hand poked from the blanket.

Smiling gruffly, they shook hands.

* * *

The next afternoon, Harry moved his chessboard alongside Douglas' bed, allowing them to continue matches from visit to visit. "Of course," he observed as they resumed playing Friday evening, "you've the advantage. You can plot strategy when I'm not here."

"Hardly does me any good."

"Aye!" Merrily, Harry seized Douglas' king, to join pawns and knight already captured.

"Hell! You're obliterating my men as easily as you did on that damned mountainside," Douglas sighed.

"If so, in much more pleasant fashion."

Douglas contemplated his chessmen again, only to look beyond the table. "Did you consider ordering your archers to stop shooting, at Homildon, afore so many of us died? Afore I charged?"

"Aye. Didn't consider it very long, though. Afterward," Harry dropped his eyes, "afterward, I asked myself whether I should've done as I did." His eyes met Douglas' good one. "I concluded that I hadn't a choice. Had I called off the archers, your horsemen would've overrun them. Many would've died, in sparing you. And you were the enemy. 'Twould be treason to let my own men die, to spare an enemy. Beyond that," he reached for his goblet, "you'd invaded Northumberland, pillaged and burnt, and were escaping with our livestock and goods. I couldn't allow that."

"True," Douglas acknowledged. "I would've done the same."

"As soon as most of you were down the hill in that last charge, and my archers had retreated safely, I *did* order them to hold their fire," Harry continued. "Then I led a counter-charge against the rest of your army."

"I can't remember that, though. I can't remember anything beyond riding downhill, and being hit, and waking to find you there, bidding me to surrender."

79

Harry squared his shoulders, stretched his long legs, and settled back in his chair. "What I've wondered is why you didn't sue for peace. You must've known what happened at Crecy and elsewhere, when the French attacked right into the ranks of English bowmen."

"I guess we didn't think it could happen to us."

"But after not only the men of Galloway but Swinton and Gordon and their ilk fell—you must've seen then. Why not surrender?"

"Seems foolish now. Probably seemed foolish to you at the time. Still, we thought we could break your lines. And," Douglas admitted, "a Douglas never surrenders, not while he's still standing, anyway."

"Oh, aye. I seem to recall encountering that attitude afore," Harry said.

"Consequently, here I am," Douglas said. "And here I'll remain awhile, for sure."

"Afraid so, My Lord."

"Please," Douglas objected. "There's hardly a need for titles here... I generally go by *Beau*."

"Better than 'Bald' from Archibald!" Harry joked. "And I'm guessing you didn't like 'Archie' much either."

Douglas shook his head.

"So," Harry went on, "where, in the first place, did *Archambeau* come from?"

"I picked it to distinguish me from my father," Douglas said, "and because my mother was fond of France. She ensured that my tutors were mostly French, though they all spoke perfect English, too, more polished than mine. They 'cured' me of Borders dialect before I was even 7 years old."

"That's why you talk more like a stylish English gentleman than I do," Harry assumed.

"Aye. Anyway, *Archambeau* sounded French, so I chose it—or coined it, perhaps. Whether it's really a French name, I don't know. And that led to *Beau,* which is what my sisters called me."

"So, Beau, it is. It suits you: a beau Scotsman, beau chevalier, beau friend."

"And should I call you *Harry*? I probably already have, since I think of you that way: 'Harry Hotspur'. How could you be anything else?"

Harry laughed. "In your stupor, you called me `Lord Percy' once or twice. More oft you called me a 'damned Sassenach!' Between those two, *Harry* is fine!"

They toasted each other.

* * *

A few days later, Harry breezed into the room with his usual gale-force exuberance. "I heard that the wild Scotsman is gone, replaced by a shaven and shorn lord."

Leaning on a chair by the window, Douglas turned, face freshly razored and hair trimmed. But his light-brown lashes brushed a listless cheek, a few freckles stark against his pallor, and as he gripped the back of the chair, his knuckles stood out white, in taut hands.

"What's wrong?" Harry rushed forward. "Cold? Overtired? Let me help you back to bed."

"No. I'm warm and stronger than I was. It's a relief to stand on my feet again."

"The scab has peeled from your eye. It looks good."

"It's not! I can't see on that side." Douglas stared, but only one eye focused or registered the light. "My right eye is blind."

"You certain?"

"Don't be an ass! How could I not be certain?" Tears welled in both eyes.

"I'm sorry. 'Twas a stupid thing to say." Unhooking a sheepskin cloak from a peg, Harry slipped it around Douglas' shoulders. "Let's walk."

Douglas fastened the cloak at his neck, and Harry ushered him onto a covered parapet, its thick walls cut by arrow apertures. Sunlight streamed through, dappling the floor with elongated crosses as they set off.

"Tell me about your eye."

"The barber helped me shave and cut my hair, as I wanted," Douglas began. "He filled the basin and put it on the stand near the fire, for me to use later. My skin did feel itchy around that eye. So after a couple of hours, I rinsed it and put more crème on it. The scab fell off. My eye opened. But I can't see with it."

They reached a tower with closed windows, with the River Tweed below, on one side, and the town on the other. Harry flung the shutters open, and a soft breeze stirred a cobweb in the corner.

Fields stretched beyond the town, but to the east, a wedge of ocean sparkled like lapis. Closer below, the roofs of Berwick jumbled together, tile, slate and thatch. The buildings were mixed, too, stone church next to wattled house, half-timbered shop adjacent to wooden barn. Down the castle wall from where they stood, a treacherous-looking stone stairway descended to riverside fortifications.

Harry leaned out. "I always enjoy the view of the river from up here. Of course," he gestured expansively, "yonder lies Scotland, from which too oft trouble has come."

"Can you blame us?" Douglas asked. "The Tweed is supposed to mark the border, but Berwick lies on the *north* bank. As long as you've been warden, though, there's been little chance to even get near."

"Good!"

"But once, as lads—you would've been a boy, too, then—my cousin Jamie and I rowed a boat right to the back steps there." Douglas pointed. "We'd snuck away—miles—from a hunting party in the woods. We had some silly notion of getting into the castle. What in

82

hell we thought we were going to do then, I don't know."

"*Did* you get in? I guess not, since I never heard of it."

"The sentries at the lower tower shooed us away. We'd dressed like urchins and they didn't know us, luckily." Douglas studied the narrow staircase. "Those steps scared us, too. One look at them ended any thoughts of racing to the top and fighting whatever guards we found there." He laughed. "Father was furious when he learned what we'd done. Said we'd damned near gotten ourselves captured."

"Did you count the stairs that day?"

"No. 'Twas enou' to know there were too many."

"There *are* a lot. Let's see. One, two, three..." Counting softly, Harry deliberately skipped one step as he neared 50. "forty-seven, forty-nine..."

"You're off," Douglas corrected. "You forgot number 48—that angular one, with the broken section and puddle of water."

Harry concealed a smile. "So I did. You can see why the Premonstratensians at Alnwick Abbey despaired of my arithmetic."

He moved to the town side. "And here's a pleasing sight! As lord of this humble burg, I'm happy to report that all the good folk seem hard at their labors. Down yonder," he waved toward a crowded street, "that fine fellow Albertus, the baker, has again stalled traffic so he can take his own sweet time unloading his wagonload of flour from the mill. Afore much longer, if Albertus doesn't clear the lane, young Hank-with-the-Shank, the butcher, is going to be raising a holy ruckus.

"And there," Harry gestured a lane over, "Mistress Fenton, the silversmith's wife, sets out more tankards in her windows. Probably she's already done a good day's trade. She's an excellent artisan, by the way, better than her husband, who usually takes the credit. So if you ever need cups or trenchers for Edinburgh Castle ..."

Douglas gazed at a street beyond. "Who's the farmer with the cart? Looks like he's got some terrific fruit."

"Aye." Harry turned slightly. "Samson Nixon, the green-grocer. His shop is down Marygate, but he brings a cart here most afternoons, gets more business from my garrison that way." His eyes darted again. "And there's Martha Wainwright. She parades up the lane about this time every day with her flock, picking up loose grain and scraps. Since they help keep the streets clean, no one minds, even if she gets in the way sometimes."

Douglas chuckled, watching the bent old figure bustle up Castle Foregate Street with chickens, ducks, and geese in her wake. Then his attention shifted to a rooftop two rows away. "I think one of her birds has gone astray. Up on that house with the wide chimney, there's a fat speckled hen. It's the spitting image of the one leading her little march."

Harry's hand shielded his eyes against the haze. Sure enough, on the house in question, a plump hen pecked along the gutter. "You're right. That's the sister bird to Mistress Wainwright's hen. Actually, it belongs to *her* sister."

Suddenly serious, he gripped Douglas' shoulder. "You worry about your eye, Beau. Perhaps 'twill get better in time. But I can tell you right now that even with one eye you can see as well as I can—and I've always had remarkably good vision—and better than many men with both eyes."

Releasing Douglas, he smiled. "Enou' of the sights of Berwick, though. I fancy some wine and another chance to beat you at chess."

But Douglas lingered, peering over the town. Then he confronted Harry. "You brought me here on purpose, didn't you? You knew I could still see quite well. You wanted me to know it, too."

Feigning innocence, Harry said nothing.

"You're probably well aware how many steps are in that staircase over there, and that the 48th is broken," Douglas added. "But you wanted me to see it, to prove I *could* see it, to keep me from pitying myself."

Harry grinned mischievously. "My, my. How you Scots always attribute ulterior motives to me!"

Douglas laughed. "You, my friend, would make a terrible liar. But that's probably good. Now, about that wine and chess…"

Two days later, Harry coaxed Douglas into forsaking the nightshirts (or nakedness) in which he'd lain for something approximating real clothing. Getting dressed was no easy task for a man as sore as Douglas, as vulnerable to the risk of reopened wounds, or as stiff as he had become. With Harry's help, though, he managed to don a thin, sleeveless men's shift, pull a monk's gown over it, belt that, and put socks and boots on his feet.

"But I've got no underdrawers," Douglas protested.

"So?" Harry cocked a quizzical eyebrow. "Guess the squires forgot those, but what of it? *I'm* not going to be looking under your skirts. And no one else is going to know."

He handed Douglas a long, open vest.

The Scotsman slipped it over everything else.

"Now you look like a right proper Doctor of Philosophy."

"I'd lief be in my armor."

"Aye, but you don't need armor to stroll through my garden. And if you don't start strolling more often, you'll be too fat and slack to ever don your armor anyway."

Turret steps posed another challenge. But by putting him in a sling and enlisting Hardyng's aid, Harry got Douglas down all three flights. Below, he sent Hardyng to fetch Thor, his pet hawk, and led Douglas into the constable's garden, enclosed in stone walls above the river.

"Michaelmas daisies," Harry paused on a gravel walkway. "Over there: wild roses, poppies, irises." He went on, proudly showing off nasturtiums, lilies, herbs, and a thicket of still-purple heather.

"You know how to garden?" Douglas marveled. Gardening was something monks and women enjoyed, and to which knights claimed to aspire for far-distant old age.

"Me?" Harry laughed. "No! I just know enou' to listen to the gardener and recognize a few bits of greenery. And those I know because they're really weeds at heart."

Hardyng brought Thor, all flapping wings and roving eyes, with a falconry glove and a bag of kitchen scraps. They transferred the bird, and Hardyng returned to the keep.

Harry tossed a piece of meat; Thor shot after it. The prize, a hunk of freshly killed rabbit, dangled from his beak as he landed on Harry's gloved wrist. A moment later, the meat disappeared in an avian gulp.

Douglas' good eye surveyed the bird. "His feet are maimed. Was he always like that?"

"Aye. Last year, some boys found him out in the woods, scrabbling on the ground, a mostly featherless baby, missing half his toes," Harry explained. "He must've been hatched that way. Or he was the last to break out of his egg and his bigger siblings greeted him by chewing on his feet. If so, they likely threw him out of the nest, too."

"And the boys brought him to you?"

"No. They took him to Berthold, keeper of the Berwick mews, who figured he should probably just wring the wee birdy's neck but couldn't bring himself to do it. So Berthold nursed him and then I chanced upon them and adopted him. He's grown up to be a fine hunter and an excellent companion—though he does get impatient at times."

As if he understood, Thor poked Harry with his beak, seeking another morsel of meat. Smiling, Harry threw one, before turning back to Douglas. "'Tis only right that I tell you," he began, his tone serious. "You know I captured William Stewart at Homildon."

"Yea."

"I've jailed him in Newcastle, pending trial for high treason. If convicted, which seems all but certain, he'll hang."

Douglas looked startled, then nodded.

"Do you object?"

"No. I suppose I should, since I'm his laird. But..." Douglas shrugged. "In truth, I've never liked him. Neither did Montgomery nor many of our other lords, including his kinsman, Robert of Durisdeer."

He glanced at a bench under an apple tree, and Harry guided him to it. With a twitch of unused muscles, Douglas seated himself and Harry joined him. So did Thor, who swooped down to perch on the back of the bench, alongside Harry.

"Stewart was my father's man," Douglas said. "To me, his head always devised more trouble than his hide was worth. If anything, I guess I wish he could've died at Homildon and saved himself the pain of hanging and a judge and jury the pain of trying him."

'It won't pain me at all to see him on trial and hanged," Harry said, with an uncharacteristic savageness. "He's long deserved it."

"Couldn't you pardon him, though?" Douglas wondered. "I'm not saying that you should, but..."

Harry shook his head. "I could arrest him. But I can't pardon him, or anyone else, for treason, nor can I reduce a treason sentence from execution to jail or exile or something else. Only the king of England can do that."

Douglas nodded. "Aah... He's forever been prickly, you know, insisting he's always been a Scot, regardless of where he was birthed. And he's related to the Scots king."

"So are many Stewarts, including some living peacefully in England," Harry replied. "He was an

English subject; swore fealty to Edward III and my grandfather. Then, with fire and sword, he helped your father subjugate Teviotdale, back when it was part of England. That's treason. Moreover, he took aid from France against us, sacked Roxburgh and did lots more. He wanted to kill me, too, after Otterburn, but that's beside the point."

"Is it?"

The question stopped Harry short but before he could reply Douglas answered it himself.

"Yea, even if you wanted revenge, what would it matter? Stewart's done plenty otherwise to bring on doom. 'Tis your prerogative as warden to put him on trial. Scotland would do the same, were the situation reversed." With a quick twist, Douglas snapped an apple off the tree. "You can imagine what I'd do with Dunbar if I captured him."

"Nor would you hear any protests from me."

Douglas bit into his apple. "What about Stewart's son?"

"I paroled him. He owes me a castle or two, in compensation, but..." Harry sighed. "What else could I do? Stewart junior can't help what his father is. And he's been Scottish his whole life, not a turncoat like his sire. I've no quarrel with him."

"I'm grateful, on his behalf," Douglas told him. "As for Stewart senior, well..." He shrugged. "He was never the friend to me that you've been already."

"Thank you." Harry too, plucked an apple and polished it on his sleeve. Drawing his knife, he sliced into it; the juice spurted out, glistening sweet. He passed a piece to Thor before bringing the rest to his neat white teeth.

"Stewarts aside, what happened to everyone else captured at Homildon?" Douglas asked. "Actually, how many are there?"

"About 1,000 hostages, French as well as Scots. My father's tending to those he took. It's the same with the other lords. Most I captured personally are paroled, to attend to their families and estates before reporting to me. Some have already turned over castles or towers with the appurtenant lands, in lieu of money. In truth, I haven't demanded money yet. Many Scots, especially the border lords, don't have much, anyway. Nor do I," after all these years of strife."

Nodding, Douglas cast his apple core away. "We're all land rich and money poor. Someday, maybe we'll see things change. For now, though, I'd just like to see the Tweed and dangle my toes in it, if you'll help me get that far."

Harry agreed. "But we'd best wait for tomorrow, so you don't exhaust yourself. We'll go down a back path, too. It's easier than dealing with all those stairs!"

Chapter IV

Thursday, 28 September 1402: Berwick Castle

Shown into the warden's parlor, Montgomery found Harry alone, finishing a lunch of cheese, bread, and fruit.

"John!" Harry eagerly got up. "Grab a chair and join me." He gestured with his knife and whacked off a fresh slice of bread.

"Don't mind if I do." Montgomery crossed the tiled floor. "But first…" With a flourish, he unhitched a bulging saddlebag from his shoulder and pulled out three suede sacks, each the size and shape of a fat grouse. He slammed them on the table, shaking the dishes.

"My ransom! Or part. 'Tis a tad weighty, so the rest is in a wagon outside."

"What?" Harry stared at the sacks. "I've asked for nary a pence from you, not yet anyhow. I just gave you leave to return home and arrange your affairs, as is usual, before coming back here."

"To be sure. Nevertheless, I thought I'd simplify matters. So I brought you something: to be precise, £4,600." He grinned. "Just what we got for you—eventually—after Otterburn. And like your ransom, this is in English coins, or mostly."

"Where did you get £4,600 in English coins? On second thought," Harry laughed, "I'm not sure I want to know."

"From King Robert. He happily changed my Scots groats and jewels into English coins from his treasury. Where *he* got them—well, you'd have to ask him. But, between you and me, I think some came from a couple of ships, bound for Eire and taken off our coast."

"Piracy!"

"Shipwreck would be more like it, but call it what you will," Montgomery winked. "And I expect another share came from sales of good old Scots whisky at the English court to your King Henry."

"What?"

"Aye. 'Tis one of the better things Robert's done, found new markets for our fantastic Scots creations, like whisky. And damned if one of his better customers isn't your very own king. Far be it from Robert to be denying the nice things of life to any man, even his enemies."

"Hell!"

"Aye, but cheer up and listen to this." Shaking a sack, Montgomery elicited a dull metallic sound. "King Robert suggested you use some for repairs and rebuilding at those kirks we sacked. He's real skittish about affronts to God, though he doesn't give a damn about affronting Englishmen."

He pushed the sack over to Harry. "Anyhow, I figured I'd give you the loot now, ere you asked, and make it easier on us both." He smiled shrewdly. "Besides, if you take it, all is resolved. And you don't get a chance to demand a larger sum after you've had time to think about it."

"Rogue!" Harry teased. "I accept, for holy kirk and a lot more. We can certainly use the money." Loosening the thong, he upended the sack. Golden English nobles and silver groats spilled out, with a sprinkling of French crowns. "My God!" Incredulous, he caught a coin about to roll off the table. "There's just one thing."

"What?"

"You vastly overpaid."

"Huh?"

"Aye! You said 'twas £4,600. What makes you think an old coot like you could be worth as much as *I* was?"

* * *

The next day, they were in Douglas' chamber when Hardyng brought dispatches from the Earl of Northumberland. "The courier emphasized that your lord father was anxious for you to have these."

The first consisted of a single line from the earl: *Harry, we must discuss these forthwith, and I await you at Warkworth.*

The other documents, addressed to Percy father and son, in care of the former, were orders from the king:

> ***Daventry, 20 September 1402:*** *The King sends his Council the news of the victory at Homildon on the 14th over the Scots and their French allies, just received from the Earl of Northumberland by special messenger, and the names of the chief nobles made prisoners and slain, with the loss of only five Englishmen; and orders the Chancellor to issue writs forbidding any one to be put to ransom without his pleasure being taken.*
>
> ***Westminster, 22 September 1402:*** *The King forbids the Earl of Northumberland and Harry Percy, his son, wardens of the West and East Marches; George Dunbar, Earl of March; Ralph, baron of Greystoke; Sir Henry Fitzhugh, Sir Rauf de Eure, the lieutenant of Roxburgh, and the constable of Dunstanburgh, to release*

Harry's cheerfulness evaporated. "Damnation! He can't do this!"

"Do what?" Douglas asked.

"This!" Harry waved the writs.

Montgomery touched his hand. "May I?"

Harry nodded.

Reading quickly, Montgomery summarized. "King Henry announces the victory at Homildon. Then he forbids Harry or anyone else to either ransom or free the men captured there."

Douglas's jaw dropped. "'Tis well established under the Law of the Marches as well as custom throughout England and Scotland, verily, all of Christendom: Knights can take hostages, reach ransom settlements with them, or free them. 'Tis a sacred right, and their agreements, captive and captor alike, are a sacred bond. A king can't violate that."

"I wouldn't think so," Montgomery said. "But Henry of England has never worried about the law." He smiled gleefully. "He's too late, for me, though. I've already paid Harry a ransom."

"But I haven't! Nor have I deeded lands or anything yet."

"Nor have I asked," Harry reminded Douglas. "Fret not."

"What will happen now?" Hardyng asked.

"Don't know." Harry sounded both defiant and discouraged. "All I know is that I can't jeopardize the lives of those who surrendered to me in good faith. But I'm forbidden to either ransom or free them. That means only two things: Either Henry wants me to cede my prisoners to him—or he wants me to kill them."

29 September 1402: Warkworth Castle, Northumberland

Harry strode back and forth in the parlor of the new keep, magnificent, eight-lobed edifice, atop a hillock. Replacement for an older structure in the bailey, it was his father's pride and joy.

Drumming into the thick floorboards, his boots competed with the faint sound of water coursing inside the light-well after an afternoon rain. A four-storey shaft that paid tribute to the engineering vision of both its architect and its owner, the light-well brought fresh air and sunshine into the keep and, through a cellar tank and pipes, collected and discharged water for rinsing privy shafts, washing, and cooking—like brewing the blackberry-herb infusion Harry quaffed as he paced and his sire frowned.

A straight-backed old campaigner with muscles bulging on his calves and gnarling his arms, mossy green eyes, a neatly trimmed beard and bushy jet-black eyebrows, the earl both loved and admired Harry and often clashed with him, especially over issues of kings and governance—like the one dividing them this day.

"Confound it! Must you go back and forth and stomp like that?" the earl protested. "It's hard enough to think as it is."

"I'm not stomping." Harry's steps were as light and graceful as ever, if annoyingly energetic. But he paused, finished his drink, and refilled his cup, this time from the wine carafe at his father's elbow.

On his arrival Harry had learned four things: One, that Henry had called a Parliament, to begin the next day; two, that the king had followed his initial order with a decree that all the prisoners be presented to him in London; three, that his father intended to comply; and four, that he urged his son to do likewise. Harry had immediately refused.

"What's to think about?" he asked his father. "Henry wants our prisoners. You yield yours. I don't yield mine. You do as you see fit. I do as I see fit. End of deliberations."

Seated at a carved table opposite the fireplace, Earl Henry crossed his arms. "It's not that simple. I don't want to give up mine any more than you want to give up yours. I doubt there's a choice, though. We can't afford a squabble with the king. He owes us too much money, for one thing. We also can't give him cause for replacing us as wardens of the March, installing some conniving scapegrace like Dunbar or one of those lickspittles at court. I'm not going to endanger my lands and people or have to kiss the cock of some new warden who'll dither like Mowbray did after Otterburn, when you were still a hostage with Montgomery and things went to wrack and ruin around here."

Harry threw himself onto the leather cushions of the window bench. "Given our day at Homildon, Henry wouldn't dare replace us."

"Wouldn't he? I'm not so sure. And there are plenty at court who'd just as soon forget our role at Homildon. I hear that Dunbar has already told all and sundry, including Henry, that the triumph is really his since he 'stayed Hotspur's hand' and kept you from charging 'straight up the hillside.' He claims he convinced you to use archers instead."

"What? Damned lies! You were there. You know what happened."

"Yea, but others weren't there, especially that lot at court. Some want to believe the worst of you. They'll agree with everything Dunbar says and spread it further. So we durst not undercut our position by angering Henry."

"Never mind all the times Henry has angered me!"

"I know the man's a great disappointment as king," the earl conceded. "But king he is, no worse than some others we've had and probably better than a few. And as far as the hostages go, Henry's only doing what he did two years ago. Remember? Some of our lords captured a couple of Scots lairds and their men raiding Redesdale, and Henry forbade anyone to free or ransom prisoners, under pain of forfeiture of possessions."

"Aye," Harry replied. "And we all know that a goodly number of hostages suddenly became invisible: Not ransomed, not 'freed' as such, not turned over to Henry, just vanished from their captors' households—only to turn up, hale and hearty, in Scotland. That tells you what men in these parts think of such orders."

"You yourself forwarded Henry's writ that time," the earl reminded him.

"As was my duty. But I didn't add one of my own, supporting it. Nor did I investigate how hostages mysteriously 'disappeared' and—oh wondrous miracle—ended up back home."

"You may have chosen to look the other way. I don't believe in such 'miracles'."

"Nor do I. That's why I intend to be direct. That's why I'm telling you I won't give up any man who surrendered to me in good faith and whom I've promised to safeguard. I'll say as much to Henry, too."

"That will accomplish wonders, riding off to court to rant at Henry and he at you."

"I won't lose my temper," Harry declared, striving to control it now. "I'll just discuss matters. And if I must, I'll read to him from the rules of war."

"Oh, even better! A knight lecturing a king on the law."

"Someone should!" Harry retrieved a book from the table. "These are the very regulations that Henry himself reissued before I raided Scotland in 1400, when I retaliated for Scots' raids on

Northumberland." He flipped through the *Statutes and Ordinances To Be Kept in Time of War*. "Listen. Here's Number VII: '*Be it at battle or at any other deed of arms, anywhere that prisoners be taken, he that first may have his*' – a prisoner's—'*faith shall have him for his prisoner ... and none other shall or may take him, nor have him for prisoner....*' That means that if I take a man's faith or pledge in surrender, he becomes my hostage, and no one else may try to take him from me."

"I know what it means."

"Number IX is pertinent, too: '*Let no man debate for arms, prisoners, nor lodging, nor for any other thing, so that no riot, conflict, or debate be in the host.*' In other words, there shall be no disputes over prisoners taken by those in the army."

The earl reached for the book. "Let me sec that." He thumbed through it. "Isn't there something that says a man should bring his prisoners to the king? Ah-ha!" His finger tapped a page triumphantly. "Number XXI: '*If any man take any prisoner, anon (right as he is taken in the host), he should bring his prisoner to his captain or master, and ... shall bring him within 8 days to the king, constable, or marshal as soon as he goodly may... .*' That clearly says men must surrender prisoners to the king—within an octave!"

"*If* the king is with the army!"

"It doesn't say that."

"But that is how I and every other man who fights for England has understood it. And our perception constitutes a type of precedence. Besides..." Harry read over his father's shoulder. "It also says a man shall bring his prisoners to the king, the marshal, *or the constable*. You're the constable of England. I brought my prisoners to you at Wooler—as did the others."

His father stifled a curse.

"You, England's constable, gave all of us the keeping of our own hostages," Harry added. "So I've already met that provision. Anyway, beyond what the rules of war say, my authority as warden of the East March explicitly includes the power to settle disputes over prisoners."

"Yea," the earl agreed. "But whatever our powers as wardens, the king holds ultimate authority."

"Yet even he must abide by the law," Harry emphasized. "He can't take what's not his. He can't steal. He can't have my hostages."

"At least give him Douglas."

"Douglas! Douglas is the one, above all, whom I can't cede. Turn him over to Henry, which is tantamount to turning him over to Dunbar, his bitter enemy? After I swore to him on the battlefield that I wouldn't?"

"You had no way of knowing, *then*, what Henry would demand, *now*."

"Knowing what Henry *does* want changes naught. My word is my bond. My word has always been my bond. My word shall ever remain my bond!"

His father sighed.

"Be reasonable, Harry. I realize you value your principles, but sometimes a man must bend or even forget them temporarily. What you and Douglas agreed to won't work. You simply cannot keep him."

"You make it sound like he's a mongrel pup I tried to hide in the cellar. He's a man, for God's sake! And I won't go back on my pledge to him. That's all there is to it." Harry's dark-blue eyes studied his father for a few seconds; then he hastened from the room.

Realizing he would be back, the earl took no offense. Sipping his wine, he stared above the table at the tapestries, scenes from the journeys of Ulysses, a topic much in vogue among artists and bards. In one panel, the sirens leaned temptingly from their boulder; in another, the Greek ship felt its way around perilous rocks while sea monsters raised toothy maws from a roiling surf. *Trying to steer between Scylla and Charybdis is a damned sight easier than trying to negotiate a course between Harry and Henry. Damn their obstinacy—both of them!*

But there was still hope. Douglas was too incapacitated to travel. That could buy time.

Across the way, the aroma of spitted beef and fresh-baked shortbread arose. The earl heard the cooks chattering and the laughter of a pageboy shooing a yapping hound. From the Great Hall, down a short corridor from the parlor, came the thud of trestles being swung into place. Already his mouth watered as he anticipated the feast being prepared in his kitchen—or one of them. He had two, opening into each other and adjacent to buttery-bottlery and pantry, which connected to the Great Hall.

Putting cooking facilities on the same floor as the hall and including both a major kitchen for large dinners and a smaller one for lesser occasions was another unusual feature that he delighted in. It simplified the cooks' jobs and spared servants from lugging heavy trays from a cellar, cookery, or outdoor roast-house. Simultaneously, the kitchen hearths helped heat the keep's middle floor, including the spare bedchamber, to which Harry had apparently retreated.

Kicking off his boots, Harry pushed the curtains aside on the bed—the same one that had been his as a boy, in the old keep. Now, though, unlike his younger self, he needed the entire mattress to stretch out. But he wasn't tired and after several minutes he got up and went into the adjacent garderobe, located side-to-end with one serving the parlor. *Another of Father's architectural ideas.* Admittedly, too, a clever one. He urinated into the stone toilet, then paused at the sink stand, washed his face along with his hands, and splashed the nape of his neck with water, cooling and calming. Toweling dry, he returned to his chamber to linger at the window, watching the Coquet as it snaked around the town. Up that river, to the west, was love, for there Ciarry dwelt. She was probably finishing late-afternoon chores, perhaps, like him, stealing a moment to look toward the sky, crystal clear and beginning to blush with sunset. Perhaps she was thinking of him...

Why was he here, instead of there? Why was he quarreling with his father once again—and not even over deeply rooted differences but because of Henry's arrogance?

The starlings prancing outside his sill had no answers.

With a yearning look westward, he went to rejoin the earl and find a way to agree about disagreeing.

* * *

Sunday, 1 October 1402: Tower House, Northumberland

"Pride is wrapped up in this, too, you know." Ciarry looked up from her sewing.

Across the room, Harry smiled. "Henry's, you mean."

"And yours, too, a little. 'Twas *your* victory, and you resent Henry for coveting your spoils and claiming your credit. Any man would take offense, consider it an affront to his ability and pride."

Leaning against the doorframe, he stiffened. "But I've always despised proud, vain men. Besides, pride is a sin."

Rising, she planted a soothing kiss on his cheek. "Some pride *is* sinful, yea. Some is good, though. Pride in fulfilling your duty to England, pride in honing your skills, pride in upholding justice—those are honorable. That kind of pride we need. And, except for some stubborn pique, that's what's driving you here. Which makes *me* proud!"

"So you agree with me about Douglas?" He

brushed a strand of hair from her forehead.

"Absolutely."

"And you'll help me keep my 'stubborn pique' from taking over?"

"Always."

Bestowing another kiss, she returned to her stitchery, the binding of a book: her own translation from Latin to English of Luke's Gospel, for Sister Etheldreda's new school at Holystone. "Anyway," she snipped a thread, "the issues extend beyond Douglas."

Nodding, Harry knelt by the fireplace. "Other lives are at stake, perhaps for years to come. Men trust each other because of our laws of war, including those governing ransoms. We can't let those laws, that trust, be abrogated. We'd have naught but barbarism and more war."

"Yea. Although..." Her eyes sparkled impishly. "...Others might argue that hostage-taking only *encourages* warfare, to collect money and booty."

Harry pondered briefly. "Sometimes, perhaps. But 'twould be worse were it not for our rules and the bonds we make in being and taking hostages, and holding March Days to adjudicate cross-border complaints, and all the rest." He shoved a log into place. "After Otterburn, Montgomery didn't come a-reiving until now. Archibald 'the Grim' Douglas wasn't *too* terrible, either. To be sure, he raided, and I retaliated. But even Archibald never attempted a full invasion, and I suspect he restrained himself because Montgomery counseled against it, partly due to his friendship with me."

"Too bad Archibald's son didn't heed such counsel."

"True. I doubt Douglas will want more war now, though. He talks as if he'd like a permanent truce. Had he not yielded to me, had I let him die where I found him, that chance wouldn't have come. That's one more reason I can't let Henry or Dunbar claim him and perhaps harm him: It would jeopardize peace. We've suffered too much to allow that to happen. So have the Scots."

She joined him, watching the flames. "Peace would do so much, even beyond the lives spared. We wouldn't be as desperate about crops, for one thing. 'Tis hard enough farming without constant worry that if the weather doesn't turn against us, the Scots will, overrunning fields and purloining cattle."

Harry nodded. "Moreover, with the men home, not in my armies, farming would be easier. Women and old men and bairns would be spared the heaviest burden." He shook his head, marveling. "I don't know how you women, in particular, have managed."

"We're strong. But your love makes us stronger."

"Us too." He hugged her lightly.

Over her shoulder, she glanced at the half-bound Gospel book. "With peace, we could also further knowledge. Children could spend more time in class."

"Older scholars as well, without having to go to Oxford or Cambridge," he observed. "My father has long wanted to establish a college at Warkworth, to educate priests and men learned in the liberal arts."

"Women also?"

"Why not? If the project ends up falling to me, I'll ensure that."

Ciarry's thoughts tripped happily ahead. "Did I tell you? Our Holystone school has five girls already, of a dozen pupils total."

"Then I have even more reason for pride: Pride in you!"

With a lingering kiss, he drew her down beside him on the rug.

* * *

Tuesday, 3 October 1402: Berwick Castle

"Hell!" Montgomery shoved the pastry tray down the table so hard it nearly ended in Douglas' lap. "There's one course only."

"Correct," Harry agreed. "I ride to London and tell the king that I can never surrender Beau or anyone else."

"Dead wrong!" Douglas countered. "The only answer is that I absolve you of your promise. That goes for my knights, too. Then they and I ride to London with you, Harry, give ourselves up and," he swallowed, "take whatever comes."

"No!" Montgomery bestowed a smug smile on Harry. "And no again!" He favored Douglas with the same. "You're both being bullishly stupid. The best idea is that *I* ride to London with Harry and turn myself over to King Henry on your behalf, Beau, and that of all our men. And hc can keep me 'til the royal cows come home."

Harry shook his head. "You've already paid a ransom. You're not a hostage."

"Exactly why it should be me who goes, and me only. I'm a free man. I can go where I please."

"Aye, but..."

"So if I want to ride to London," Montgomery added, "no one can stop me, not even you, Harry. Even if you don't want my company, you can't prevent me from riding the same roads at the same time."

"True. Still, I can't have you chance it. Lord knows what Henry might do."

"I don't like the idea either," Douglas commented. "Damn it, I'll fight my own battles, John. I'm not afeared of Henry or Dunbar, or anyone at the English court."

Montgomery eyed him sharply. "You're not in any shape to ride to London, much less fight anyone once you get there."

"He's right, Beau," Harry put in. "You could bleed to death on the road if your wounds reopened."

"And he knows whereof he speaks," Montgomery

recalled, "having done the same damn-fool thing himself, after your cousin speared him at Newcastle and he stormed across the countryside and nearly bled to death at Otterburn at my feet, with nary a new cut in him. You *are* too weak."

Frustrated, Douglas conceded. "All right. Yet I don't like having you bear all the burden."

"I won't," Montgomery replied. "Harry will bear his share, since we've no way of knowing how Henry will react. Anyway, King Robert charged me with doing all I could to make things easier for the Scotsmen captured. He assigned me as his liaison twixt the two kingdoms. This is a good way to do it. I can probably get Robert to cough up more money, too. Then Henry will love me, for sure."

"Even so..." Harry said skeptically.

"Got another plan?"

"Frankly, no."

"Or you, Beau?"

Douglas shook his head. "I suppose as your overlord I could refuse permission, but..."

"But you're in no position to do anything, since you're a prisoner of Harry. That makes him overlord of us both. And he's acknowledged I can go anywhere I want. So you see, Beau, you can't stop me, either... Thus, 'tis settled."

Montgomery retrieved a jug from an ambry. "Now, for more immediate pursuits, like partaking of my wondrous whisky."

Harry laughed. "Aye. But not too much. One shock to my wits tonight from you is enough!"

Chapter V

Wednesday, 4 October 1402: Berwick Castle

Alone at his desk, Harry kissed a note, laying it aside as Hardyng entered the chamber.

The squire grinned. "Ciarry must've written."

"No, the children."

"Yea? What'd they say?"

Harry passed along a small sheet with his daughter's loopy writing and son's energetic cross-out:

> *Dere Father:*
> *Plese aske good Kinge Henryy to*
> *let Uncl Edmund cum home. He used*
> *to visit alot. We myss him veary*
> *muchhe.*
> *Yur loving childron,*
> *~~Young Henry~~ and Elissa*
> *Fitzhenry*

"Poor bairns." Hardyng gave it back. "Glyn Dwr captured Mortimer in that skirmish in Wales around the same time he nabbed Lord Grey, right?"

"Aye. They were caught in separate attempts to lead their troops against Glyn Dwr's men. Neither of them was ever much good at fighting, you know."

"And King Henry agreed to ransom Grey, who kidnapped Welsh children and turned them into 'servants'—slaves—on English estates and has caused endless other trouble," Hardyng observed. "But he won't allow Mortimer to be ransomed by his own kith and kin, using Mortimer family money?"

"No. I got a letter from Edmund, too. Owain Glyn Dwr sent it to Bishop Trevor, who forwarded it to me. Luckily, any threat to himself notwithstanding, Trevor continues to be a go-between in this insane warfare."

Hardyng nodded. "It's good, too, that you and Glyn Dwr can still communicate, after Henry refused to accept your treaty ending the war. If he had done so, the fighting would be over, Glyn Dwr would again be a peaceful English liegeman, Mortimer would be free, and this mess wouldn't continue to plague us—and so many others—either!"

Harry sighed. "Aye. 'Tis staggering, the extent and repercussions of bad royal decisions, especially those made out of spite. Anyway, here's Mortimer's letter to me."

Hardyng's eyes moved down the page:

> *Harry,*
>
> *Firstly, I congratulate you on what I hear—even in my forlorn place in Wales—is a great victory that you won over the Scots. I turn to you because I have no other recourse. I know you and I were never boon companions. In growing up, I shared my sister Elizabeth's disdain for your Borders speech and preference for military service and horses and the wilds of Northumberland over pursuing the royal court positions that we craved. I'm sorry for that now. Anyway, King Henry ignores my requests to allow me and my family to pay my ransom. I beg you to use your influence with him, for it must be high, after your success at Homildon. It seems he thinks I conspired with*

"As he himself admits, Edmund scarcely regarded you as worthy afore," Hardyng observed tartly. "Yet, in trouble, he appeals to you. He sounds desperate, though."

"Desperation will humble any man."

Irby knocked at the open door. "Pardon, but I've got more missives, delivered to the gatehouse." At Harry's nod, he approached. "Two for you, Sir. And another for you, John." Dispensing them, he left. One of Harry's dispatches bore the royal seal; the other that of the Earl of Worcester. Harry opened the latter:

That much was by a scribe, but Thomas had penned a post-script in his own hand:

> *Also, Harry, I'm aware you've never been close to Edmund and his family, acquired through an ill-suited marriage, arranged by your sire and Elizabeth's pater when you were small and I was still scarce but a youth myself and hardly able to intervene. As you know, after she repudiated you, she formed a loving bond with Lord Camoys, who continues as one of Henry's ranking courtiers. But even Elizabeth and Camoys couldn't persuade Henry to help Edmund. Now Elizabeth suggests to me that you trade Douglas for Edmund. I told her I doubt you'd agree, but she persists. In whatever way you can, please help Edmund—not as a sort-of kinsman but as an honorable soldier taken in battle—and for my sake, as I try to promote peace in Wales.*

> *Your devoted Uncle Thomas*

"Hell!" Harry exclaimed. "I'm besieged on all fronts: by Edmund, by my uncle, and, through my uncle, by Elizabeth, who thinks I can just swap Douglas for Mortimer. As if King Henry would agree! What's more, even if Henry somehow *did* agree, *I* cannot. God help us... I understand why Elizabeth thinks as she does, but I can't spring Mortimer from Glyn Dwr's dungeon by thrusting Douglas into one of Henry's. I can't do justice to Edmund by doing an injustice to Beau."

Frustrated, he took up the letter from the palace:

Harry groaned. "Henry writes as well, demanding Douglas and the rest of my prisoners. Damnation!" He tossed the king's letter aside, threw back his chair, and started pacing, only to stop abruptly when he noticed the unusually glum expression on Hardyng's face.

"Ill tidings? Your family?"

"No, it's from my friend Brother Gildas, the scribe at St. Werburgh's Abbey in Chester. Gildas says the whole realm is getting very disgruntled with Henry. He's hearing from other monks, across the realm, that Henry's minions are running amok, demanding services and taking goods, without paying."

"Sounds familiar. Look how much he owes us." Harry shook his head somberly. "Furthermore, aside from his financial non-feasance, I've gotten complaints he tried to rig shire elections again and pack this latest Parliament with his cronies."

"Even that might not be the worst," Hardyng said. "It seems this king who's no saint has been creating martyrs."

"Huh?"

"Remember how Henry outlawed rumors that King Richard still lives? And banned criticism of himself?"

Harry nodded.

"And his warning that he'd already thrown men into the Tower of London for it?"

"Aye. Well?"

"Gildas sent this with his letter." Hardyng displayed a document. "It deals with a judicial session Henry convened to convict some friars of high treason. Gildas says the text is circulating to monasteries, each making a copy and sending it to the next, until all the religious houses in England are informed, for obvious reasons."

"That's from a trial?"

"Yea."

"Do we know what prompted it?"

Hardyng nodded. "A lay brother in Aylesbury and another monk from Leicestershire fell out with their monasteries. They hied themselves off to the king, alleging that their brethren engaged in treason." Hardyng glanced back at the document. "Various friars and others were carted off to London, where Henry interrogated some himself. One admitted that he preferred Richard as king. So Henry asked what should become of him—Henry—if Richard ruled again. The monk said that Henry should just be Duke of Lancaster." Hardyng shrugged. "That made Henry mad enough to execute him, along with a priest who'd likewise offended him somehow."

"*Jesu!*"

"Next, another whole group was prosecuted," Hardyng continued. "Whereupon somebody, anonymously, made a transcript." He held up the parchment. "Probably it was a royal clerk, doing what he usually does in judicial trials. Doubtless, though, Henry never figured it would leak out through his palace walls."

"Do I detect the hand of Candorinus again?" Harry wondered, referring to the pseudonymous monk and scribe who surreptitiously told him of troubling developments in Henry's court, just as the priest-lawyer Adam Usk had once done.

"Likely. Candorinus has been our loyal colleague ever since the Crown exiled your friend Adam for asking questions or giving advice Henry didn't want to hear. Anyway, you'd better read it."

Returning to his desk, Harry began:

> *Eight more monastic brothers*
> *and their master of theology were*
> *led, tied up, to London. (Meanwhile*
> *another monk accused many other*
> *brothers of other monasteries, but*
> *they fled. Verily, the king then called*
> *upon the archbishops and other lords*
> *and ordered that these monastic*
> *brethren be brought in.) Now,*
> *certain ones among these eight,*
> *young and old alike, were*
> *insufficiently learned. So, in truth,*
> *they responded incautiously. Then*
> *the master of theology admitted that*
> *he, in keeping with his own whims,*
> *had himself expounded the prophecy*
> *that is said to be of the canon of*
> *Bridlington.*

Harry looked up. "What's the prophecy of the canon at Bridlington?"

"I'm not sure. But that reference seems odd because the Bridlington canon, John Thwing, is posthumously revered by many, including Henry's in-laws. One would think Henry would like the comments of a monk who spouts what the Bridlington canon said."

Puzzled, Harry resumed reading:

And the king said to the master: "These brothers are fools and idiots, nor do they even know or comprehend how to read. You, however, ought to be wise. Now, you say that King Richard lives?"

The theology master responded: "I do not say that he lives. But I say that <u>if</u> he lives, he is the true king of England."

The king contradicted him, saying, "Richard resigned."

And the master said: "He resigned, but was urged and forced to do so while in prison, and such an abdication is thus null by law."

To this the king said: "He abdicated of good volition himself."

But the master said: "He would not have resigned if he had been free, and an abdication made in prison is not made freely."

"Furthermore," the king continued, "he was deposed."

And the master, to a certain extent being argumentative, said: "When he was king, he was captured by armed men, incarcerated, and deprived of the rule. And you usurped the crown."

To this the king replied, "I usurped not the crown but was properly elected."

The master explained. "An election is null if the lawful incumbent is still alive. But, if Richard is dead, then he is dead by your hand. And if he is dead by your hand, then you have lost the title and all right that you could have to rule."

To that the king swore: "By this head of mine, you shall lose your head!"

The master added: "You never loved the church, but you took a lot away from her before you were king and now you further destroy her."

"Liar!" said the king. "Begone!" And all these monks were taken out to the Tower.

Then the king took counsel, and one of his knights, who had never loved the church, said: "Never shall we extinguish this clamoring about Richard being alive until these friars are extinguished!

Now the minister-general of the friars got an audience with the king and said that he had prohibited all of his brothers from saying or doing anything prejudicial or offensive to the king, and he sought mercy on their behalf.

Yet the king said: "You chose not to punish them, therefore it is appropriate that they be punished by me."

Next they were brought to Westminster, shackled together, and were arraigned before the judge, along with a sibling of King Richard, a knight (born of a sexual mistress and thus one of his kin), as well as the prior of Laund, a master of theology, who had received letters alleging King Richard to be alive.

Harry gulped. The reference to wiping out English speech reminded him of his embarrassing gaffe in 1400, when, at the urging of his young ward, Prince Hal, he had issued a bigoted statement claiming that the Scots wanted to destroy the English language. Months later, John Montgomery had shoved it back into his face, almost literally...

He read the rest of the account of the trial, learning that a jury had convicted the monks, leaving the judge to pronounce sentence:

*"You are ordered to be drawn
from the Tower of London up to
Tyburn, and there hanged for a day,
and then beheaded, and your heads
placed upon the bridge." And so this
was done, in view of many thousand
folk. At Tyburn the theology master
preached a devout sermon on the
theme of "into your hands, O Lord,"
and swore by the salvation of his
soul that he never said anything
against King Henry. Likewise, he
devoutly forgave all those who were
the cause of his death. Moreover, the
other friars said also: "It was never
our intent, despite our enemies'
claims, to kill the king but rather to
make him Duke of Lancaster, as is
his due." On the morrow, at the hour
of vespers, the minister of the Friars
Minor came by, suggesting that it
might be possible to retrieve their
corpses. And with him helping in the
search, they discovered the bodies
tossed in sewers and against walls,
with great holes instead of heads.
Thereby they bore them home to
their monastery with considerable
sorrow. Afterward, the jurors came
weeping to the Franciscans, begging
forgiveness, saying that if they had
not declared these friars to be
doomed, they themselves were to
have been killed.*

Harry turned to Hardyng. "Henry perverts justice.
'Tis clear he had naught on the Franciscan friars,
beyond comments he disliked, including the statement
that *if* Richard is dead—which, as we know, is true—

then Henry must have murdered him, which is also true. Plenty of folk have said as much, though not to Henry directly.”

“The monks are also accused of sending money to Glyn Dwr.”

“Probably to rebuild their destroyed monasteries. *I've* distributed considerable money in Wales. Even Henry has sent funds to repair monasteries he sacked there.” Harry paused. “By my count, Henry has already executed more than a dozen men. Wasn’t there also a scribe from Canterbury, condemned earlier for saying something Henry found objectionable?”

“Yea.”

“Has he launched a berserker attack on the church?”

“Not merely the church,” Hardyng said. “Those executed include Sir Roger Clarendon.”

“Who was purportedly King Richard’s bastard brother but never made a move against Henry, not even when Henry seized the throne. Clarendon was a devout layman Franciscan, though, just as I am a layman-member of the Premonstratensians.”

“Guess that was enough.”

“Aye.” Abruptly, Harry arose. “Best pack our gear.”

“Where’re we going?”

“London, to see the king!”

* * *

In traveling to London, Harry left his captives behind but brought Montgomery and a group of squires and knights under Knayton, lest Henry harbor notions of throwing him into a dungeon like the ill-fated friars. They arrived on 19 October, bunked at Aldersgate in the inn bequeathed to Harry by his grandfather, alerted the chancellor, and conferred with Earl Henry, whose London manse overflowed with his own Homildon prisoners. Henry summoned both Percies, "with all the hostages," to appear the next morning.

* * *

Friday, 20 October 1402: Westminster, London

King, Lords, and Commons packed the old White Hall, a Norman structure still impressive, if annoyingly smaller than adjacent Westminster. Henry had chosen it for that reason: Filling it suggested a far vaster throng than it actually held, the better to awe ambassadors and foreign 'guests' (like hostages).

Until called, the Percy party waited outside the throne room. To demonstrate their high rank and the grandeur of Scotland, the hostages were magnificently garbed. Earl Henry likewise sported the finery of a leading peer. Harry, too, wore what pleased himself. Although simple and unadorned, his tunic was of deep teal suede and his leggings of soft grey leather, tucked into black knee boots. He carried no sword but wore his knife, with an engraved sheath matching his belt. Hardyng, Kynge, and Montgomery came indoors with him, while his escort waited in the yard.

"Your Majesty," a herald bawled, "the Earl of Northumberland and Scottish and French lords from Homildon... And Sir Harry Percy, warden of the East March against Scotland."

As they entered the throne room, Hardyng and Kynge slipped into the crowd. The others knelt, got up at Henry's gesture, and started to proceed—Earl Henry first, followed by Murdoch Stewart and the other captives. Harry and Montgomery brought up the rear. Before they had taken four steps, Stafford's palm arose.

117

"Halt!" The bishop bustled down the aisle. Pushing Earl Henry aside, he placed his hands on Murdoch Stewart's shoulders and thrust the young Scotsman down. "The prisoners will kneel thrice more in the presence of the king of England: Again here; then midway down the hall; then before the throne."

Half-genuflecting in confusion, Murdoch looked toward Earl Henry. The earl nodded, and Stewart dropped completely to his knees. The others did likewise.

Satisfied, Stafford moved ahead and turned to survey the scene, not yet motioning the Scots to rise.

One foot uneasily rocking back and forth on the floor, Harry watched.

At his side, Montgomery tensed.

Ahead, Henry's confidants clustered around the throne, Lords Lovell, Beauchamp, Aumale, Blount, and more. All, too, were sumptuously dressed, feet in vivid shoes whose spear-shaped toes curved back toward the wearer, as if to point out that this was an important man.

Smile as gilded as his robes, John Beaufort lounged on Henry's left, exuding both confidence and perfume, the latter to disguise the fact that, despite his love of luxury, he failed to bathe enough. Cleaner, if likewise lavishly gowned, Dunbar stood opposite, in silver shoes whose prows didn't bend back like his fellow courtiers' but extended to outrageous lengths, like lances lashed to his feet. Leaning over, Dunbar spoke to Henry, who motioned to Stafford.

The bishop hurried up to the dais, bent to the king, and faced the audience. "That other prisoner, Lord Montgomery, shall likewise kneel!"

Harry's voice boomed. "My Lord Chancellor, he's no pris—"

Montgomery jabbed Harry's side. "'Tis all right, Lad." He, too, sank to his knees.

Henry and Dunbar smirked.

Stafford motioned them forward. Halfway down

the aisle, Murdoch fell to his knees again. So did the others, Montgomery included. After another long pause, Stafford bade them up. They moved ahead to repeat the homage below the dais. Looming above, Henry made them wait another portentous minute before allowing them to get to their feet.

"Welcome, gentlemen!" the king declared. "We are delighted to see you and assure you that you'll be treated with fitting courtesy."

Earl Henry stepped up to make introductions, but the king intervened, pointing to Murdoch Stewart. "You are?" His voice was loud, his tone condescending, and his query unnecessary, for he already knew Stewart and several of the others.

Scottish royalty, as well as the ranking prisoner, Stewart, correctly perceived an insult. Declining to reply, he nudged a lesser captive, Sir Adam Forster. Somewhat hesitantly, Forster announced Stewart, with all his titles, and introduced the others, except Montgomery, who had reclaimed his place alongside Harry.

King Henry's amber eyes singled him out. "Lord Montgomery, is it?

"Aye!" Montgomery stepped forward proudly. "Sir John, lord of Eaglesham."

Dunbar murmured to Henry, who addressed Montgomery gleefully. "And likewise my prisoner!"

"No, Your Highness," Montgomery corrected. "I be no prisoner of you or any man. I come of my own choosing, in the service of my liege, King Robert, who charged me with doing all I could for these, my fellow lords, and to represent Scotland's interests to you."

Stafford broke in. "Sire, this is a most unorthodox embassy."

The king frowned at Montgomery. "You've not represented the Scottish king in our court afore."

"'No, Your Majesty. But he saw a chance to use me, and I urged him to do so. Even so," Montgomery glanced sidelong at Harry, "I left your North freely, in the company of Sir Harry Percy, your warden of the East March, whom—though we spar betimes—I am honored to call my friend."

Dunbar whispered again and the king went on. "Sir Harry captured you at Homildon."

"Aye. But he paroled me."

"In direct disobedience to orders!"

"No..." Harry began, but Montgomery's foot pressed hard against his.

"'Twas not, Your Highness, with all respect," Montgomery explained. "He paroled me long ere you issued orders to the contrary. And afore he ever broached it, I paid him a sum, for transmittal to holy kirk, in recompense for damage we caused, and to meet other needs on your East March. What's more, I bring a comparable sum, courtesy of King Robert, to do with as you will, though he and I hope 'twill be used to ease the burden of these, my fellow Scots and friends." He nodded toward Robert Stewart and the rest. From a sack on his shoulder, he pulled two bulging moneybags, tossing them at the king's feet. They landed with the heft of coins too densely packed to give off more than a muted clink. It came as music to regal ears, however.

Henry beamed. "Tell King Robert of our esteemed delight at his tribute."

At Beaufort's nudge, Henry's expression turned dour. "Sir Harry!"

"Aye, Sire?"

"Where are your prisoners?"

"Residing peaceably in my castles in the North, as is customary in such matters."

Dunbar and Beaufort muttered, and an undercurrent stirred the hall.

Henry regarded Harry in stony rebuke. "You will later attend upon Us *privily* to account for your conduct. Go."

Face flushing, Harry departed, to titters of laughter.

Henry's thumb flicked toward Stafford and then the Scots prisoners. The bishop led them away.

Gesturing grandly to his audience, Henry dismissed it and turned to Dunbar and Beaufort, his half-brother. "Now I would dine with my friends."

* * *

They met in a small audience chamber, off St. Stephen's cloister, in the warren that was Westminster. Whitewashed and airy, the room resembled a monastic chapter house, with a tiled floor, pillars vaulting to the ceiling, and intricate stone tracery. Lancet windows admitted shards of sunshine; against one an oak outside displayed red foliage as magnificent as an emperor's cloak.

At the side of the room, a narrow door stood ajar.

The king reposed on a gilded chair, atop a platform reached by shallow stairs. Chancellor Stafford had wanted to have Harry arrive before Henry, who could then sweep in with imperious aloofness. But Henry had insisted on being there first, omnipresent and omnipotent, high on his throne, as if he never entered a room like an ordinary man.

Three guards stood in boredom, while in a niche, two clerks furiously recorded the day's earlier business. The chancellor leaned over them, periodically darting a cautious eye at the king. Henry had drunk moderately at luncheon, but in the angry funk into which he'd descended he gave the impression of someone well into his cups, simultaneously subdued and aggressive.

Warily, Stafford straightened.

Outlined by cloister light, Harry paused at the door, casting a bold shadow across the threshold.

"Your Majesty," Stafford declared, unnecessarily. "Sir Harry..."

At their table, the monks gathered pens and parchment, departing. The elder hurried toward his dorter. The younger went only as far as the low stone wall dividing cloister walkway from the grass courtyard. There he perched, his back against a pillar.

Entering the chamber, Harry knelt.

Behind him, a guard moved to shut the door, but Stafford objected. "Leave it. We'll have more light if it's open." He looked back at the king.

Henry stared at his visitor, making no move to let him rise. Finally, after a begrudging nod from the king, Stafford motioned to Harry and edged away. As Harry got up, so did Henry, to stand below the royal dais. "Where are my hostages?" he barked.

Harry came forward. "My Liege, if you mean the prisoners I took at Homildon Hill, then they are in safekeeping, as I said afore."

"When do you propose to bring them to me?"

"I propose to move none from Northumberland, Sire. I can't sunder their trust, or the laws of war, or the code of the Borders, or longstanding English custom."

"They're my prisoners! I ordered you to bring them to me, and you refuse."

"Sire, I hold them *for* you, *for* England, but *in* the North. I cannot and will not do otherwise."

"But you freed some and took ransoms for others. You deliberately disobeyed me."

"No, Sire."

Slowly, Harry outlined the individual cases of Montgomery and the rest. "To reiterate," he concluded, "most were paroled temporarily, following usual practice, but have reported back and are in my custody. Some turned over castles to me as surety for eventual monetary ransom. I have received no money yet."

"Douglas?"

"Recuperates at Berwick. He was grievously wounded and blinded in one eye."

"I order you to make him fit and then bring him

to me."

"My Liege, I cannot." Fleetingly, Harry considered mentioning his additional reason for not relinquishing Douglas, the fear of harm from Dunbar. But Henry would only take offense on Dunbar's behalf, and they already had enough to disagree about.

"God's blood! I need his ransom, Harry! I need *all* their ransoms! I need money!"

"Hell, so do I!"

"You? You rule no kingdom. You keep no palace. You have no royal children to place in marriage to benefit the realm!"

"No. I simply fight your wars and preserve your peace." Harry started to pace, remembered protocol, and halted mid-stride near the slightly open anteroom door. A whiff of strong perfume reached him. *Beaufort!* An instant later, he noticed the narrow silver toe, protruding from beneath the door, so long that its wearer had forgotten to allow extra room for concealment. *Dunbar, too, was eavesdropping.* Unobtrusively, he shut and latched the door, almost laughing as Dunbar wrenched the tip of his shoe away.

"M-my me-men r-risk their li-loves da-daily." To Harry's frustration, the stutter that had bedeviled his childhood returned. He paused, tried to calm himself, to banish it. After another couple of sentences, he succeeded. "Wh-what support do any of us get? No-none! Wh-where is the money I need for my duties on the March and in Wales? Where are my men's wages? Or *mine*? I haven't paid myself a salary since almost the day you took the throne; even afore that, I drew little because Richard owed me considerable sums. You were going to improve things. Instead, they've become worse!"

Henry glared. "As I told the Lords and the Commons, when *they* hectored me: *Aurum non habeo et aurum habebis non.*"

I have no gold and neither shall you, Harry mentally translated.

He knew that Henry had recently enacted new taxes, with Parliament's reluctant acquiescence. In return, Parliament had sought an explanation of Henry's constant shortfalls and renewed the investigation of his finances, asserting a Parliamentary right to question his ministers. Again, Henry had refused. Lords and Commons had then asked what had happened to his predecessor's treasury. Henry had caustically replied that they should interrogate the Earl of Northumberland and Archbishop Arundel, implying theft during the pair's negotiations with Richard in Wales in 1399. The insinuation had infuriated not only earl and archbishop but many in the Lords and Commons and relations between liege and legislature remained acrimonious.

Henry muttered something, then reiterated loudly: "I tell you, I *have* no gold!"

"Sterling would suffice."

"Damn you! I've no sterling, either!" Flustered, Henry tried to regain control of the discussion, which Harry had somehow diverted from the surrender of prisoners to the payment of arrears. "This matter of Douglas has naught to do with money, anyway."

"No? You just told me you wanted the ransoms because you need money."

"That's irrelevant. The real issue is your insubordination. And you seem remarkably worried over these Scots, especially Douglas. Odd, such concern for a hostage."

"No odder than yours for Lord Grey. I hear that Parliament has approved a king's ransom for him, £6,666."

"That's different! Lord Grey is an Englishman, not an enemy. And he was taken into my service, defending England."

"Well then, if you wish to talk about Englishmen seized in your service, let's speak of Mortimer. Where is your concern for *him*?"

"He colluded with Glyn Dwr. He let himself be taken."

"No more than Grey. Both were captured on duty. Ought a man expose himself to risk, for you, for your realm, and have you not aid him in his plight? You admit you should extend aid when 'tis Grey. But when 'tis Mortimer, 'it's `different,' you say."

"I'll not let a single pence go to pay Glyn Dwr. He'll use it to fight against me."

"'Tis not *your* pence Mortimer would spend but his own, and money from friends."

"Exactly! So how many Welsh-loving turncoats will want to make a 'donation' on his behalf? What a clever way to funnel money to Glyn Dwr."

"Perhaps. But then why ransom Grey? *That* money will go to Glyn Dwr, too."

Henry couldn't think of a response, which only upset him further. "Enough! I'll not talk of Mortimer, and neither shall you. I want to know about Douglas. When are you going to present him to me, along with the rest of those damned Scots?"

Slowly, Harry shook his head. "Sire, I cannot relinquish them."

Henry's scowl deepened. "You shelter Douglas like you did Glyn Dwr. I ordered you to take Glyn Dwr and execute him forthwith. You refused to do that, too!"

"That was an order to commit murder. An order to do something wrong need not, and should not, be obeyed."

"What kind of liege-man are you? None! In reality, you are a traitor! You want the succoring of my enemies and those of the realm!"

"I am no traitor but a *loyal* man, and as a *loyal* man I speak!"

"You dare contradict me?"

"When you dishonor me!"

"Whoreson!" Henry spat in a shower of saliva.

Averting his face, Harry wiped his chin on his shoulder.

The royal hand balled, and as Harry's gaze lifted, Henry swung with the full force of his weight. His knuckles hit with stunning accuracy.

Tears stinging, temple throbbing, Harry bit back his fury.

Gloating, Henry filled the silence. "In faith, treachery like yours shall be dearly bought in England, at cost of *this*..." His fist menaced again. "... *By me*, giving buffets—and worse!"

For several seconds, Harry stood implacable and mute. Then his words came, coldly controlled. "And in faith, *this*"—he touched his bruised cheek—"shall be the dearest-bought 'buffet' that ever was given *by you* in England."

"You threaten me?"

"No. *You* threaten *me*!"

Groping at the gold girdle on his waist, the king pulled a dagger. His eyes shone with the same berserk frenzy Harry had seen in battle, in men he had slain seconds before they could slay *him*.

The king lunged.

Harry's hand shot out, fingers encircling Henry's wrist with unyielding strength.

Henry writhed in agony. The dagger clanged to the floor.

"You would fight me?" Harry asked.

Teeth grinding, Henry nodded.

Harry released him with a shove toward the throne. "Then not here but on the field!"

Before Henry could look up, Harry was gone.

Mouths open, the guards unlimbered themselves for pursuit.

"No!" Stafford emerged from the corner. "Let him go. He drew no weapon." The bishop rushed forward to assist his distressed king.

* * *

Harry rode in a state of suspended belief.

For the second time in three years, he'd been impelled to flee London after challenging royal policies. For the second time in three years, a king had accused him of treason. For the second time in three years, he was racing north, life endangered. This time 'twas worse than before, too. This time, a king had not only called him a traitor but tried to murder him. In 1399, Richard had ordered him to be gone. So he had gone, into internal exile. This time, he himself had, literally, turned his back on Henry, leaving the palace without royal permission. In essence, he was absent without leave.

Yet, it would have been foolhardy to stay and risk being imprisoned or beheaded, or forced to fight a running battle through the streets of London to escape.

Still, he felt an aching sadness and sense of failure. Nothing had come out right: He had not dissuaded Henry from demanding Douglas, nor had he convinced him to respect the traditional code of ransoms. He had not avoided the volatile argument with the king that his father had predicted. He had not wrung one farthing of pay from the Crown. Nor had he persuaded Henry to allow Mortimer to free himself from Glyn Dwr.

In short, he'd botched everything.

Jaw set in grimly, he rode 40 miles with his horsemen, all the way to Royston Priory, stopping there for a belated supper and accommodations. Doubtless, they were being tracked. Well, he decided, crawling onto a cot later, even if a battalion came in pursuit, he should be safe till dawn. At worst, he could claim sanctuary in the church until he could send for his own reinforcements and make Henry either back down or agree to settle their differences legally, whether by judicial trial in a court of law or on the tourney ground in trial by combat, a fatal duel.

Exhausted, he fell asleep.

The next morning, royal messengers reached him as he finished breakfast. To his surprise, their leader was John Norbury, once Henry's treasurer and quasi-secretary, now filling the less onerous job of managing royal estates.

Cordial enough, Norbury pulled out a vellum. "My Lord: I bring you an urgent message from the king."

"Aye?" Harry's curiosity piqued. Henry's assignment of an eminent royal courier so fast might bode well, unless it only meant he was still eminently and royally enraged. "You bring a letter?"

"Yea." Norbury produced it.

Taking it, Harry saw that it was shorter than usual for a message from Henry and appeared to have been hastily scribbled:

> *Sir Harry: We bid you to return forthwith. Our members of the court await you as much as We do. We regret it if you took offense. And We are sorry for having smitten you and repent Ourself thereof.*

The king had signed it with an almost illegible scrawl.

"May I keep this?" Harry asked, after reading it twice.

"Of course."

Thanking Norbury, Harry briefly deliberated. Was Henry being genuinely contrite? Or was this merely an act of cunning? It seemed he didn't regret his actions as much as the fact that Harry had taken offense at them. Then, too, he was supposedly sorry for 'having smitten' Harry, but not, perhaps, for calling him a traitor or trying to slay him. *In fact,* he reasoned silently, *Henry might regret having hit me instead of trying to stab me first, while my guard was down. If he had used his dagger initially, instead of his fist, he could have killed me...*

He regarded Norbury. "I'm grateful for your efforts to reach me quickly and flattered that you came yourself. Please, join us for something to eat, with your escort, too. Probably you rode hard for hours."

Norbury brightened, eyeing a bun. "With pleasure, My Lord. I *am* hungry and spent." Taking a place on the bench, he gestured to his three squires to fill in the end of the table.

"Now, if you'll excuse us," Harry said, "I would confer with my aides before I respond to His Majesty." Scooping up his mug of morning infusion, he led his companions outside.

"Well, gentlemen? Henry wants me to return to London. What think you?" He sipped his drink as his aides passed the note around.

"Don't go back, Lad," Montgomery advised. "He's up to no good; I'd swear it by all the saints of Scotland."

Knayton's forehead furrowed. "Perhaps he means well... But what if he doesn't?"

Hardyng, too, expressed skepticism. "He worded his note carefully, as if he wanted to convey an impression but not directly say it. I'd be cautious."

Kynge concurred. "Something about his 'apology' seems contrived. And what's it mean that all his courtiers await? Will he further humiliate you before them, or have your head? Then again," he shrugged, "perhaps I'm too suspicious."

"We're all on edge," Harry replied. "Nonetheless, I think prudence is the order of the day. We'll continue north."

They rejoined Norbury.

"Tell my regal sire that, in all humility, I accept his apology and render my own for my temper," Harry announced. "Nonetheless, I must resume my duties on the Borders. I cannot return to court."

Norbury hastily swallowed a piece of roll. "You choose not to return, though Our Gracious Liege himself bids you in all worthiness and majesty? When his nobles wait, eager to offer—as our noble king said—the wisdom of their learned and valued counsel?" A note of genuine disappointment rang through this cloying palace cant. No emissary wants to return with his mission unfulfilled.

Harry reconsidered. But the contemptuous laughter when Henry had chastised him and his discovery of Beaufort and Dunbar, listening behind the door, were fresh in his mind. He smiled apologetically. "No, I shan't return. 'Tis said a man's image can be seen in his friends. If so, I've seen a measure, an image, of the king's 'worthiness and majesty' in those around him; seen too, the value of their counsel. I'll let them keep their wisdom to themselves."

Norbury choked. "Would you have me tell him *that*?"

"Aye. Tell him that."

Chapter VI

November 1402: Berwick Castle,
Northumberland

"Any thoughts?" Harry surveyed his council—senior knights and captains—along with Montgomery and Ciarry, convened at a massive table in the hall. Douglas was there, too, nearly as hale and hearty as before the battle at Homildon Hill, although he continued to walk a bit slowly and was still blind in one eye.

For the benefit of those who hadn't already been aware of the details, Harry had begun the discussion by explaining his visit to London, Henry's message afterward, and his growing sense that something had to be done. Now, he sought their counsel.

"There's little choice," Knayton said. "England, and Wales, too, have suffered enou.' The realm must act, which means someone should take responsibility for initiating action of some type."

Gerard Salvayn stroked his mustache thoughtfully. "Henry abuses everyone from peer and prelate to Parliament and lowly commoner and churl."

"Aye," Sir William Clifford agreed. "And his hand falls particularly heavily on those who tend the defenses of the realm. As your under-constable at Berwick Castle, I can personally attest to the needs here. They're dire. And after the damage your armies caused, My Lord," he nodded toward Douglas, "and ours," he included his colleagues, "harvests in eastern Northumberland were lost. We'll run short afore spring."

"I know." Harry sighed. "I'll have to purchase

staples again, with fresh permission from Chancellor Stafford or Henry in London. Hell! It seems like I just came from London. Also, I'll have to try anew to cash my tallies, since you two," he indicated Irby and Hardyng, "once again got nowhere."

"All the more reason someone must tell Henry that enough is enough," said Knayton. "His Privy Council won't, or can't do that, since he rarely convenes it and closets himself with men like Beaufort and Dunbar instead."

"Heaven save us from *them*!" Salvayn pleaded.

"Far be it from an ornery Scot to tell Englishmen how to run their land," Montgomery put in. "But Henry struck me as corrupt, greedy and both vicious and weak, so he can't stand up to temptation or against the conniving bastards he surrounds himself with. His actions threaten not only you but me and my realm, too, with his belligerence and demands that Scotland subjugate itself to him. You have every right to demand better."

Hardyng nodded vigorously. "We do. And like Tom Knayton said, someone has to rally the realm: lords, knights, commons, clergy, everyone. Then, together, we can convince Henry to make amends—or else."

"Or else what?" Harry asked bluntly.

"He risks being ousted like Richard!"

"I don't *want* to oust him," Harry said. "And we can't bring Richard back—if we even wanted to, considering how badly he ruled. There's no one else in the regal line capable, either, save Hal, perhaps. But Hal is too young. Nor would the Mortimers be fitting."

"Hell, *the Mortimers?*" Clifford scowled. "After this news from Edmund?" He didn't elaborate, but they all understood: Forbidden by Henry to meet Glyn Dwr's ransom demands, Mortimer had accepted Glyn Dwr as his overlord and wed Owain's daughter, trading fealty to an English king for allegiance with a Welsh outlaw.

"If you don't want to oust Henry, what *do* you want, Harry?" Salvayn wondered.

"Good governance!" Harry's palm slammed the table. "I want Henry to observe the rule of law, to stop the injustice he himself encourages, to end the corruption. Likewise, I don't want him ever again to accuse me, or anyone, of treason for speaking out."

He paused. "Listen to me. I'm saying almost the same things I said about Richard."

"Because they again need to be said," Ciarry observed.

"Maybe even more so," added Roger Salvayn, Gerard's son.

A chorus of assent followed.

"When I got back to England a few months ago, I was shocked at the disharmony," Roger added. "King Richard was bad enough. Good men who dared question him too oft ended up dead. But Henry seems all the worse. And good men still end up dead. At least Richard never got bogged down in a war in Wales." A muscular man with curly dark brown hair, ginger-colored eyes, and average height, Roger had been one of Harry's squires years earlier, when they served in Bordeaux, an English-held region of France. On his lord's return to England, Roger had stayed in Europe as a freelance man-at-arms, serving various lords for hire and competing in jousting matches, to earn his employers and himself a tidy sum. Finally, tiring of it and seeking more meaningful work, he had sailed home and rejoined Harry.

"It seems that the first question is how you, Harry, or anyone, would go about getting Henry to make reforms," Ciarry proposed. "He's already called you a traitor. You can't just ride off to London and tell him that he's a tyrant and all of England wants him to change. You'll need a rationale, strong arguments, grounded in evidence and citing precedent and law." She looked at him as she spoke and then glanced around the table before casting her eyes at her hands, feeling a little shy as the only woman present.

"Well said, My Lady," Douglas proclaimed, thinking, not for the first time, that if it weren't for Harry, he'd carry her off himself—if she would have him. With that fiery spirit and red hair, 'twas clear she was really a Scotswoman anyhow.

"Garnering support still won't be easy, with everyone fearful of saying anything, and Henry's habit of taking the heads of those who do. You're right, however..." Harry thought aloud. "I suppose the best way to lay out my position is through letters and parleys with like-minded men." He favored Ciarry with a teasing grin. "*And* women!"

"Earls and bishops?" Clifford inquired.

"Aye, and others: Barons and dames, knights, mayors and town councils, abbots and prioresses alike. I'll have to spend a lot of time in the saddle, as well, even more than usual. Over winter, too." He groaned. "But I'll need to demonstrate that I don't fear Henry and am willing to talk directly, if discreetly, of such matters. Then I trust others will find their voices, too."

"Plus their courage," Douglas interjected.

"But the letter should come first, before meetings," Ciarry advised.

"A further thought, Harry," Kynge added: "Once you've declared your aims, especially in writing, you'll have to be ready to defend them."

Harry nodded. "And you're reminding me what that entails."

Kynge fingered the chaplain's cross he wore on a chain around his neck. "Yea. It will mean that you, and I, and all of us, are willing to resort to arms, if necessary, to get Henry to comply, like the barons did with King John, nearly 200 years ago, in making him accept the Magna Carta."

"Or as Simon Montfort and the lords did in compelling Henry III to change his repressive ways," Harry said, recalling history. Earl of Leicester,

Montfort had died in 1265 in the Midlands but continued to be revered, especially in the North, where a relic of him reposed in hallowed splendor at Alnwick Abbey.

Douglas' brow wrinkled. "Montfort? Wasn't he slain fighting that earlier Henry?"

"Aye," Harry confirmed. "Yet even if everything Montfort espoused seemed to die with him, we reap its benefits today: A Parliament of all the estates, Commons joined with lords secular and spiritual; the right of Parliament to deliberate and act upon the most serious issues in the land; the principle that a king cannot rule as an absolute power unto himself but is the representative of the people, bound by law no less than they are. At least," he added, "we *should* be enjoying the rights Montfort and others secured for us—if our Henry IV, like the aforementioned Henry III, didn't want to play the despot."

"But like Montfort, you could perish," Clifford cautioned.

"Aye," Harry admitted grimly. "Many of you could, too, if you throw in your lot with me."

"God help us," Kynge intoned.

They lapsed into silence.

"Enough foreboding!" Speaking in a lighter tone to ease the tension, Harry stood up. "We all have things to do. I, for one, must put words to parchment. Fortunately, thanks to you, much of what I must say is already composed. It only needs to be written down."

Hardyng reached for his quills.

Harry shook his head. "No, John. I'll take a stab at it myself. Then you and everyone else can tear it apart to your hearts' content."

"Excellent." Douglas pushed back his chair. "Not destroying your letter, I mean, but being free on such a fine afternoon." He smiled at Ciarry. "Now I can take this lady out riding by myself! No ... with Lord Montgomery."

Harry's eyes twinkled. "I don't know, two

rapscallion Scots and one little lass. Maybe I'd better assign a chaperone."

"Definitely!" Ciarry laughed. "We'll bring Thor."

* * *

John Hardyng lowered his goblet and picked up Harry's letter. On reconvening, Harry's council had proposed a few alterations to the draft. It lacked a certain polish, perhaps. Yet even Hardyng had to admit that it sounded good, despite—or maybe because of—the brash idealism oozing from each line.

"No less than the republic, res publica, *the good of the entire public of England, our* common weal, *is at stake in the matters of which I write,"* the opening paragraph stated.

Referring to "manifest wrongs" and "execrable policies," Harry went on to cite everything from the situation on the Borders and the Homildon ransoms to Wales and Glyn Dwr; London, sessions of Parliament (or the lack) and rigged judicial courts; a callously opulent palace; and, inevitably, the Exchequer. *"Taxes and tallages, seized under duress, leave us destitute,"* Harry declared. *"By law and custom, they can be imposed only with consent of the three estates of the community of the realm, meeting in Parliament, and then exacted only for the most serious reasons, in defense of the land. Yet they are not used as meant but are devoured, excessively and uselessly—and wasted besides!"*

Smiling, Hardyng pulled a candle closer and continued reading:

> *We must speak out, for our*
> *sakes; for our collective well-being*
> *and, most importantly, that of King*
> *Henry, who merits our good counsel.*

As loyal subjects, we cannot remain silent. I bid you to join me in reminding him of all that he vowed three years ago and in convincing him to end the abuses associated with his reign. Doubtless, he is unaware of many of the wrongs occurring in his name. Doubtless, too, if he truly loves righteousness, he will gladly implement reforms—true reforms—not more empty promises. Thus, we should demand that he:

i. Pay those whom he owes money, whether it be me for England's armies or merchants, farmers and fishermen for supplies the Crown has commandeered without recompense.

ii. Revoke all orders forbidding those who capture men in battle to ransom or free them.

iii. Allow me or some other lieutenant of North Wales to make just and lasting peace with the Welsh insurgents.

iv. Rescind all writs forbidding comments about his rule or the fate of Richard of Bordeaux, once known as King Richard.

v. Provide honest answers to questions pertinent to the death of this same Richard.

vi. Immediately call a freely elected Parliament.

vii. Cooperate with Parliament in its financial reviews, including those initiated by prior Parliaments.

viii. Let me stand trial before my peers during this same Parliament

Hardyng slowly sipped wine. The fat would be in the fire, once this went out.

After finalizing the text, Harry had departed for London with Knayton, Roger Salvayn, and Irby, leaving Kynge and Hardyng to help Ciarry write out multiple copies for him to sign on his return. He was anxious to get on the road, he had confided, because along with visiting the Exchequer and chancellor he hoped to see Henry.

His aides had blanched.

"Must you?" Ciarry had asked.

"Aye, to give him one more chance to discuss

reforms, ere I send that letter to all and sundry.”

“Approaching him could be dangerous,” Roger Salvayn had warned.

“So could shunning him.”

And with that, Harry had left.

* * *

Thursday, 7 December 1402: London

Harry began at the palace, where Henry refused to see him: twice in response to written requests and ultimately via Bishop Stafford when he appeared in person.

“Why won’t he meet with me?” he asked Stafford. “True, we quarreled and I declined to break my journey to return to court. At the time, I feared our tempers might still wax hot and we’d be at each other’s throats. He’d already tried to slit mine, remember. Now I *am* here, though. Yet he refuses to face me. Why?”

Stafford grimaced. “I don’t know. A king needn’t explain. I’m sorry.”

“As am I...” Harry changed the subject. “I also need new writs, for more emergency food for the North.”

Stafford smiled. “There I can gladly accommodate you. Be so good as to come back at the third hour tomorrow. Meanwhile, I bid you adieu.”

“Aye, till then.”

Proceeding across Westminster, Harry exited an alley to see Dunbar ahead, wrapped in furs and in his own affairs, oblivious. A cloud of *eau-de-rose* followed him around a corner. *Ugh!* Harry’s nose wrinkled. *Hanging around Westminster, he’s gotten as fond of fragrance as Beaufort.*

He entered the Exchequer, to discover that Henry,

having changed treasurers yet again, was on the fourth in three years: Bishop Guy Mone of St. David's in Wales, who had taken office shortly after Harry's flight from court in October.

"So perhaps, Lord Harry, your most-pertinent questions about funds had something to do with my appointment," Mone suggested. He had a youthful face, slight build, and none of the extravagance of his predecessors.

Harry immediately liked him. "If so, I pray my inquiries had a salutary effect on your coffers!"

Mone shook his tonsured head. "Alas." Sighing, he apparently decided he had nothing to lose by forthrightness, though his voice dropped confidentially. "There's hardly a pence. What little is left is for the king alone. His bride arrives anon. He long courted her with letters, you know, and hoped to wed her long afore this. Now, she is coming at last, and he insists he must greet her with abundant gifts, emerald brooches and the like, and bedeck himself, too." The bishop cringed, remembering the solid gold collar Henry had just ordered for himself from a master craftsman, as if his existing hoard of jewelry weren't enough to impress Joanna of Brittany or her entourage.

"He empties the treasury for baubles, while my soldiers get short shrift."

"There's no money for your command, certes... Although," Mone added hopefully, "I hear you've done a magnificent job holding things together of your own resources."

"Which are sore depleted!"

"Still," the treasurer stated, "I have nothing for you. Though you," he added, surveying the slats Harry laid on his desk, "seem to have numerous tallies for me." Grabbing a quill, he totaled them: £4,115. The sum included £200 issued to partly reimburse Harry's expenses in retaking Conway Castle in 1401. Each tally had been issued the previous spring. Collectively, they were about to become yet another "loan" from Harry to the Crown.

Mone laid down his pen. "I'm afraid I cannot redeem them, except by issuing new tallies. I'd be happy to give you *those,* for you to bring back at some future date or take to the customs houses, whatever you prefer."

Harry raised his hands in eloquent aggravation. "What would either accomplish? You could provide fresh tallies *ad infinitum.* As long as you have no money to exchange for them, they won't do me any good. Nor do the customs houses have anything."

"Nonetheless..." Mone watched as Harry signed the back of each tally, as he had done so often before. "...I shall write a receipt, stating that you made this loan. Perhaps someday you can show the receipt and get paid."

"'Someday,' when hell freezes over." But Harry took the receipt and, nodding brusquely, turned to depart.

"Do you ride on today?" Mone asked, trying to send him off on a more pleasant note.

"No. Saturday."

"Well, whene'er you go, safe journey. And Merry Christmas!"

"Aye!" Harry smiled sadly. "Merry Christmas!"

* * *

Friday, 8 December 1402: Westminster Palace

Having evicted his servants from the royal bath chamber, the king of England settled into his tub and engaged in the antic that had fascinated him as a boy— and given his nursemaids fits: Purposely farting underwater, he watched as round bubbles rose to the surface in glistening perfection, only to break at the surface with a stinking immediacy.

After amusing himself, he reached for the soap to suds his toes. He'd scarcely begun when someone pounded on the door.

"God's benighted blood! What is it? I could have your head!"

"With all apologies, Your Majesty..." A guard spoke in muffled awkwardness from behind the door. "It's His Highness, the Prince of Wales."

Henry swore to himself and yelled toward the door. "What's *he* want?"

"Says he would see you, Sire."

"*Christ*! All right. Wait."

From the other side of the door, Hal heard faint sloshing steps, a key in the lock, and more sloshing, followed by a splash.

"Enter!"

He did, to find his father reclining in the tub, one leg resting on the rim.

The boy bent his knee automatically. Then he shot toward a shuttered window, unlatching it.

As the blast of December air hit him, Henry sank underwater. "What the hell are you doing?"

"Opening a window."

"I can see that. Why?"

"Because there's a rare stench in here."

Embarrassed, the king slipped further into the tub. "Perhaps there is. The piss pot wants for emptying."

The prince stepped from the window. "I'll fetch a serva—"

"No! I don't want anyone in here when I'm bathing."

Hal stared at his father and back at the window, though he didn't shut it. The rank air began to clear. Crossing the room, the prince gingerly picked up the handle of the covered chamber pot, opened the door, thrust the pot at the startled guard, and slammed the door again.

"Father ... that is, my liege and father..."

"What? Can't you see I'm busy? What the devil do you want?"

Hal's cheeks flushed. "Only... only to visit. You..." He swallowed. "Father, you never send for me as you say you will. Am I not old enough to be of counsel and advice to you, too? When my great-grandsire was my age, he was already king."

"Is that what you want, too, to be king? *Now?*" Henry angrily heaved the soap across the room. "You see why I lock myself in. I can't rely on anyone, mayhap not even you. There're too many untrustworthy scoundrels out there."

Hal jumped back as if he'd been whipped. "Untrustworthy, me? Never, Father!" A couple of tears splashed across his cheek.

Henry continued to glare, and Hal started to leave.

"Wait, boy!" With a weary sigh, the king relaxed. "I'm sorry, Hal. I didn't mean it. I've had too much on my mind of late."

Hal turned from the door.

"Now, fetch my soap."

Hal retrieved it, handed it to his father, and their eyes met. They smiled at each other, and the prince settled his increasingly tall form on the floor beside the tub. With a wet, sloppy hand, the king rubbed his son's thatch of short hair, brown like his eyes. "So Hal, tell me. How fares your court?"

On Hal's 15th birthday that September, Henry had given him more authority over his own court, separate from the king's, though still well within royal purview. Smaller and far more casual in atmosphere than Henry's palace, it resembled the household and regional court he and Hotspur, his military instructor and guardian, kept at Chester Castle, on the English side of the Welsh border.

"All goes well." Hal brightened, shifting his feet

beneath him. "Quite well, Sir. I modelled it on what Sir Harry and I have done at Chester. I've got good kitchens, a library"—his eyes lit at its mention—"a fine hall, rooms for guests, a little chapel, and an ample stable. However," he added unhappily, "my money chests are almost barren."

"I know. I borrowed from them for gifts for your new stepmother."

Hal's anger flared, though he said nothing. He wasn't pleased with his father's marriage but had little recourse. At least it had left Henry too preoccupied for further attempts at arranging Hal's own nuptials.

"And I've met with the chancellor, nearly every day, as you wish," Hal went on.

"That's good. But from now on, you'd best meet with him less often."

A perplexed look filled Hal's long, narrow face.

With another sigh Henry explained. "I'm going to replace him, though he doesn't know it yet."

Hal was surprised. "Why? He seems to work hard, and to be honest and pleasant enough. He said that before he came to me, he conferred with Archbishop Arundel. And afore that, he said, he met with Lord Harry, about urgent staples for the marches."

"*Hmmph,*" Henry groused. "So Harry Percy is buying more supplies to ship north, is he? I hope to God he's paying the conveyance taxes. Stafford arranged it again for Harry and then ran off to Arundel? *Harrummph!* More proof that Stafford's rather too accommodating to those who would cross me."

"What?"

"As I said, I've enemies all around me, even those you think respectable and true."

"But not Archbishop Arundel, nor Bishop Stafford, and not Lord Harry, who wins all those battles for you!" Hal sounded aggrieved.

Henry studied his bathwater. In his opinion, Hal was far too attached to Harry, even though they spent less time together than they had when Hal was younger. Some three years earlier, though, he himself had appointed Harry as Hal's mentor and guardian, not wanting either of them at court after he had seized the throne. Not that either had aspired to the life of a courtier, anyway.

The king looked at the prince again. "Never mind Arundel, Stafford, or Harry right now. See if you can scare up another pot of hot water. My tub cools."

Hal dutifully picked up a large metal pitcher next to the fireplace and poured it into the tub, taking care not to scald his father's feet.

"Ahhh." The royal body basked happily.

"Lord Harry has been trying to see you," Hal ventured.

"I know."

"You haven't given him an interview."

"No, damn you, and I won't either!"

"But why?"

"There's no need for me to explain. I just won't."

Again, Hal looked hurt and confused. "You don't want to fight him, do you?"

"No."

"But you hit him and pulled a knife on him and lunged at him."

"'Twas naught. A trifling argument."

"Then you don't want to personally kill him?"

Henry hesitated. "*Umm ... uhhh ... uhh.* No."

"Or have him beheaded for treason?"

Again, Henry paused long enough to raise pangs of anxiety in Hal.

"*...Damn you... No! ... No!*"

That sounded sufficiently emphatic. Hal smiled. "That's good. Because I'm going to see him tonight. I miss him. I've not talked to him since he left Chester last summer, before his great battle." Pride and wistfulness filled Hal's eyes. "Homildon... Would that I'd been there, instea—" Barely in time, he caught himself. Instead of accompanying Harry to

Northumberland he'd been slogging through Wales with his father, meeting humiliation at the hands of Glyn Dwr.

"What's that? You're seeing him this eve?"

"Yea. Is it all right? Are you still at odds with him? Do you forbid me?" Hal spoke with a directness worthy of Harry himself.

"Yes! I mean, no! I mean..." Flustered, Henry started over. "I mean, yes, it's all right to see him. No, I'm not at odds with him anymore. And no, I don't forbid it."

"Good!" the prince enthused. "He's coming to dine with me in my hall. I've invited him to be the guest of honor, at my high table. And he's going to tell us all about Homildon Hill."

With a muted curse and royal churning of waves, Henry submerged himself again.

* * *

Mid-December 1402: Berwick Castle

Douglas continued to suffer from physical limitations and political limbo. As the days shortened, he resolved to do something about both.

Although it sometimes exhausted and pained him, he had begun joining Harry nearly every morning for exercise. They ran miles along the river, rode horseback, shot longbows, and fenced with broadswords in the courtyard, or, as the weather became bad, in the great hall. Douglas could not practice as strenuously as Harry, but with each session, he caught up more and ached less. Even if somewhat diminished, his skill was enviable. Nor did blindness in one eye matter; his superb instincts, speed and dexterity more than compensated. Before being wounded, he'd been a champion in his own

146

right, and it was clear that, fully recovered, he'd be formidable once more.

But they knew that they, at least, would never meet in combat again. It wasn't merely that they had become friends. Friends on opposite sides of the border often ended up on opposite sides in battle, like Harry and Montgomery at Homildon. No, something more profound had happened. For the first time in his life, Archambeau Douglas was prepared to play a lesser role on the marches. To do otherwise would only condemn the land he loved to hostile uncertainty and endless conflict. He had no stomach for that, not if it meant fighting Harry. Besides, he was partly handicapped and getting on in years, becoming interested in things beyond battle.

Above all, he could accept reality when it stared him in the face.

Reality was, in fact, stretching its long legs and pondering its next move on the chessboard the night Douglas put thoughts to words.

"We should consider the days ahead," the Scotsman began.

Harry assumed he meant Yuletide. "You should be well enou' to travel to Edinburgh afore Christmas. I can provide a carriage, so you don't tire from riding. Actually, I've been considering your situation. There's little reason to hold you longer. I can't free you outright, according to Henry. Nor am I supposed to ransom you. Nor, I reckon, do you wish to stay as my guest forever, as much as I enjoy your company."

"No," Douglas nodded. "I've matters to tend to in Scotland."

"E'en so." Harry's eyes met Douglas'. "Thus, I propose to grant you indefinite parole, with one requisite: That you report back to me if I ever bid you to do so. Moreover, you couldn't take up arms against me. Your oath at Homildon would stand."

"I'd never violate it. But I can foresee other ties binding us, beyond it."

"Aye, assuming we stayed friends—all but brothers, really—as I think we shall," Harry agreed. "Likewise, as long as we both wanted peace betwixt England and Scotland, we'd be obliged to uphold treaties."

"Also, men usually don't raise arms against their overlords."

"When someday—soon, we hope—you no longer are my hostage, I won't *be* your overlord."

Douglas grinned. "What if I wanted you to be?"

"What?"

"Exactly that. Suppose I wanted you to go on being my overlord? Hell, that's what I propose."

Harry was startled. *"You mean it?"*

"Don't act so surprised," Douglas protested amiably. "And let me speak, for it's not easy to say to a ... damned Sassenach!" After a draught of wine, he continued. "Truth is, I see no reason for further jousting between Douglas and Percy on the Borders. You beat me soundly. Overall, you're stronger militarily." He shrugged. "I can live with that. I can live with *you*. I already have, for three months. I've seen how you act *off* the field. You're fair and upright in governance, and you've got a good head on your shoulders."

"Which so far I've been able to keep, though sometimes I'm not sure how."

"Nor I!" Douglas laughed. "Given all that, I may as well be your vassal as well as your lifelong friend and *de facto* brother. You'll be my lord; I'll be your liegeman. If," he paused, "if I can do so without having to renounce allegiance to Scotland. That would be too much!" He paled at the very idea.

"I understand."

"Nor can I offer the same to any other Englishman—not your father, or cousin Neville, or King Henry. This is between you and me."

"Aye."

"Likewise, my vassalage would only apply to lands

on our common border, not to what I own in the Highlands or elsewhere in Scotland. In regard to the Borders, though, you'd be my overlord. That is, if you accept me."

"*If* I accept you?" Harry laughed, standing. "How could I not? I'm honored, humbled and grateful!"

They embraced.

"Nor," Harry added, as they sank back into their chairs and he poured fresh wine, "do I see problems in your allegiance to Scotland. Of course, you would continue to oversee your lands there. It's just that I'd be your overlord. Furthermore, Scottish law would continue to prevail on your Scottish properties, just as English law does on this side."

Douglas nodded.

"Actually," Harry continued, "'twill be like olden days, when many an Englishman held a fief in France and did homage there for it, while remaining in allegiance to the English throne." He paused, thinking. "I suppose King Robert might protest, though."

Douglas shook his head. "If it means peace, I don't think he will. A lot of that land once belonged to England anyway. And we could do much good: no more raids and conflict, at least in this area. Everyone could go back and forth more easily. Not that it's terribly difficult now, but there's still danger, and this would ease things for us all."

Harry nodded. "Including John Montgomery, who, in visiting me, took the most remote paths and garbed himself like a farmer, to travel incognito."

"Exactly," Douglas said. "So I think we agree. And henceforth, my sword is yours, my friendship and counsel, too." He raised his goblet for a toast.

"May I never need avail myself of your sword," Harry said, as their goblets touched. "As for your counsel and friendship: *Damnation!* You know I rely on those already!"

* * *

Upon returning from London, Harry had dispatched his letters, leaving no corner of England untouched. The answers came back readily, most expressing backing and praising his initiative and dedication. Even those who termed themselves unready "at this time" to jump on his reform wagon applauded. Only a few failed to reply at all, and the positive reaction from the rest heartened him.

On Boxing Day, a messenger from Archbishop Scrope of York invited him, "and aides," to visit over Epiphany, to talk of his concerns. He quickly accepted.

Hardyng was in Cumberland, but Kynge could accompany him, Harry decided. He'd bring Ciarry as well. Their hours together were too few; an excursion to York couldn't be missed. Besides, she was also an aide. Laughing to himself, he wondered if the ever-proper archbishop would allow them to share the same bedroom.

* * *

Thursday, January 4, 1403: Bishopthorpe, Yorkshire

Not only Scrope but Bishop Skirlaw awaited them at the episcopal manor near York.

Harry was delighted, knowing that two less upstanding churchmen might have refused to come under the same roof, given prior events: In 1398, the canons of York Minster had elected Skirlaw as archbishop, only to have Richard II foist another choice—Scrope—on them instead. To his credit, Skirlaw had bowed out gracefully, aware that Scrope

150

was hardly to blame. Retreating to his own pleasant see on the River Wear, Skirlaw had warmly welcomed his new episcopal neighbor and they had gone on to collaborate closely.

Harry looked forward to their discussions, especially since Ciarry would be there, too.

Upon greeting the bishops, he re-introduced Kynge, whom they'd met previously, before turning to her. "And this is my friend, scribe, and advisor, Lady Ciarry Fitzwyatt."

Arms locked behind him, Skirlaw bowed, more like a gentleman than a man-of-the-cloth.

Scrope beamed, waved off Ciarry's attempt to kiss his ecclesial ring, and took her hand in his, touching his lips to it. "My dear Sister Ciaran Caritas, what a joy to see you again! Although I surmise you're no longer a religieuxe, to the church's great loss."

"And my undeserved gain," Harry said happily.

Kynge smiled, too. "Ciarry has also been a blessing to us scribes. Her Latin bests mine—and I thought mine was good—and her writing skills top both mine and Hardyng's. She can probably beat bishops in theology debates as well."

Embarrassed, Ciarry demurred. "I wouldn't even think of trying!"

When Scrope asked about her other pursuits since the failed attempt to set up her own abbey, she mentioned her involvement with the Holystone nuns and their school, and Harry's pride surged. A moment later, he caught Scrope's sidelong, amused glance, and realized the archbishop knew they were in love. He hadn't expected to be discovered so quickly.

After they'd exchanged a few more comments, a servant arrived to show them to their quarters—a large bedchamber for Harry, flanked by adjoining rooms. Kynge chose one, and Ciarry's saddlebags went into the other.

They washed and changed. Ciarry forsook the leggings worn on the journey (and covered by a monastic habit when she arrived at York) and donned a skirt of finely woven violet wool. A matching tunic topped it and a silver choker, intertwined like chainmail, like her beloved's armor—circled her neck. A gift from Harry, it was her only adornment, except for a gold ring, etched on one side with his coat of arms and the other with entwined hearts, everything nestled in swirling Celtic motifs. Atop the ring, a silver rim inscribed with *Esperance* encircled a ruby, willed to him by his grandmother. So dark it was almost purple, the gem mimicked Ciarry's eyes, and he had used it for that reason, along with its symbolism of blood and commitment. He had placed the ring on her finger on Christmas Day, and she had worn it ever since.

They rejoined their hosts.

Given the North's economic uncertainties, Scrope had selected a menu both unpretentious and elegant, and, except for the Bordeaux wine, wholly regional: creamy dried-vegetable soup, beef with gravy, trout with leeks, herbed carrots and cabbage, barley-flour dumplings, assorted cheeses, and pastries of apple and preserved cherries. Talk centered on agriculture and church matters until the various courses had been cleared away. Then, over a new round of wine, Scrope took up more serious business.

"You know, Harry, that what you're doing is quite dangerous."

Harry shrugged. "No more than *not* doing something."

"Ah, but not doing something would perpetuate a situation that threatens the whole land. Whereas what you're doing threatens you personally."

"I live with danger every day; I have for nearly 25 years, since my first battle."

"That's risk of death from war or injury in pursuing duty. This is danger of a different sort—risk of being accused of treachery and treason, risk of torture and a cruel, painful death."

Ciarry shuddered, but Harry nodded, mouth set in a firm line.

"Sooner or later, Henry will hear of your letters," Scrope noted. A man of moderate height and lean build, he had a finely cut face, almost like a hawk in its quick expressiveness. Minimally tonsured, his short iron-grey hair included a wavy forelock, which he absently pushed back as he spoke. "He may know already, and he's unlikely to take kindly to your criticisms, all the more so since they're so utterly accurate and necessary. And he's already brutally executed men—not even soldiers, like you, but simple monks and scribes—who dared question or criticize him." The archbishop tapped an anxious finger on the table.

"I doubt Henry could get a conviction of high treason, not in an honest trial by my peers," Harry responded.

"What makes you think you'd get one?" Scrope asked. "If he seized you, he'd doubtless do everything in his power to twist a trial and get a tainted verdict. You'd be condemned to death."

Harry nodded. "As he might have done, had he arrested me that day we argued, instead of pulling his dagger on me."

"So you know the risk. But if provoked, don't think that he'd let you off with merely being beheaded. No, he'd have you hanged, drawn and quartered—in the most vile interpretation of that." Scrope regarded Harry soberly. "He'd have his executioners strip you naked, hang you till you're almost dead, cut you down, slice your genitals off and probably try to stuff them down your throat, slit you open and pull your entrails out, and then finally cut off your head—ensuring your death if you had somehow failed to die before that..." He frowned. "A man in fine fettle like you might last long enough to still be alive when they finally raise the axe to your neck."

Ciarry half-stifled a cry. Harry slipped his arm

around her. Composing herself, she took a sip of wine.

"I know." Harry's gaze met the archbishop's. "I understood, when I wrote that letter, what could befall me if worst came to worst."

"I'm sorry to have been so frank," Scrope added. "I had to make sure, though, you realize what could happen."

"Aye. But that's all the more reason why Henry must be checked. What kind of realm is this, and what kind of ruler is he, if a man can't call for better governance without fear of mutilation and execution?" Harry's eyes flashed with anger. "That's exactly what Henry counts on—that he's so cowed folk that no one dares say or do anything."

"Conversely," Skirlaw suggested, "even if Henry *did* succeed in arresting you and decided to kill you, you might *possibly* be spared condemnation, in part because of who you are, or rather, who your father and cousin Ralph are: Two of the most powerful nobles in the realm. I doubt Henry would hold a fraudulent trial of the constable's son and the marshal's cousin. Personal feelings aside, they'd consider it an affront to family honor."

"Aye, Father and I sometimes clash, but I don't think he'd want me executed. Ralph might not care, however." Harry smiled sadly. "He and I get along, generally, but he worries too much about his own skin. He'd probably never lift a hand to save mine, or complain if Henry spiked it to a wall."

"Perhaps not," Skirlaw conceded. "But your family's strength notwithstanding, your own reputation and the outrage of your armies and much of the country should give Henry pause."

"All in all, then, it could be difficult for Henry to rely on even a tainted trial to eliminate Harry," Ciarry observed.

"Right. Henry would understand as much, too, were he thinking lucidly," Scrope put in. "That's the rub, though. He might not think lucidly. Crazed with anger, as he so oft seems to be, he's capable of anything." He turned back to Harry. "Even if Henry didn't risk a trial or execution, you might perish, like Richard: starved or frozen or slain God-knows-how in some dungeon."

"True again," Harry admitted, "*if* he managed to seize me and *if* he wanted me dead. Perhaps he doesn't. After all, he could've locked me in that chamber where we met in London and had his guards slay me. He didn't. He just lost his temper and momentarily wanted to kill me himself. When I was there last month, he didn't try to arrest me. He refused to meet. But he didn't try to harm me. And he didn't interfere when I spent a most pleasant evening with his son Hal, and Hal's household and friends."

"Henry may still wish you dead," Ciarry warned.

"Aye, at times. Yet in his wilier moments—and Henry is naught if not coldly calculating—he knows that however he dislikes me, he needs me."

"'Struth!" Kynge entered the conversation. "With war in Wales, friction with the Scots, and the possibility of all-out war with France at some point, he can't afford to kill off commanders, especially not one who's served with little or no pay."

"That might be one reason he's resentful," Skirlaw cautioned. "Harry has the kind of backing, from an army, and the public, that Henry will never have."

A pensive look crossed Harry's face. "Adam Usk once said almost the same thing."

"Adam's an astute man," Scrope replied. "By the way, his erstwhile ecclesial lord, Archbishop Arundel, supports you also. I've had a letter from Arundel saying so."

"I got one, too," Harry announced. "Adam wrote from Rome as well, telling me he'd learned of my argument with Henry and pledging his prayers. He even enclosed a few papal coins, to help, 'come what may.'"

"All of which," Skirlaw concluded, "lends

credence to our belief: That, peril to you aside—and it's very real—you are well placed to lead this effort. Everyone comprehends that, even Adam in Rome. Lord knows I can't think of another man to do it."

"What about you two, and Archbishop Arundel?" Ciarry wondered.

Scrope shook his head. "We might be respected, but this needs a laic, not a cleric, someone the nation holds in high estimation, someone of gallantry in war and integrity in peace, someone Henry will respect, out of fear, if nothing else: Someone like Harry."

Harry flexed his legs restlessly. "I don't know... What if I'm falling prey to the sin of pride, taking it upon myself to redeem king and country when perhaps they don't wish to be redeemed? Acting the savior out of hubris?"

"Never!" Skirlaw exclaimed. "As you made clear in your letter, the realm begs for reform. If you were guilty of the sin of pride and hubris, as your bishop, I would tell you. If anything, in hearing you say that, I fear you might be guilty of another lapse: Scrupulosity, finding fault with yourself when there be none." His eyes narrowed. "Besides, as pricked by conscience as you are, had you *not* opted to do something, then I think you might have been guilty of a sin of omission."

"Which is almost exactly what Arundel wrote," Scrope revealed. "Except that he said that if the church failed to back you, *we* would be guilty of a sin of omission. You've taken the lead on this for the good of us all, Harry. I'm grateful."

Harry smiled wryly. "'Tis an honor I'd lief not have. I've luster enou' to my name. I only want Henry to do what's right, do what I think he's capable of, to do good."

"Amen! That's why I invited you here." Scrope went on to explain that he and Skirlaw had sent Harry's letter to all the priests under their jurisdiction, endorsing it and requesting that they share it with anyone in their congregations likely to be supportive.

"Doubtless," Skirlaw laughed, "your letter will be read at many a Mass, in lieu of a sermon. And it will be far less boring than most of those. Yet that increases the chance Henry will get wind of it."

Harry shrugged. "He's bound to, regardless. That's why I explicitly declared that I'm not being disloyal, that I act out of my obligation, under fealty, to be of counsel to him and stand up when the common weal demands it." He sighed. "Henry won't want to listen. Still, perhaps if enough of us say it, he'll *have* to listen—and give this country the governance it deserves."

"Hear, hear!" Scrope raised a goblet. "A toast, in hope for such a day!"

"Aye." Harry lifted his cup. "*Esperance!*"

* * *

"What do you think?" Propped on an elbow in bed that night, he looked down at Ciarry.

Burning low, the flames of hearth and candle cast a subtle glow, mirroring her copper hair as it fell around her shoulders.

She smiled up at him. "What do I think? That you're fortunate to have such wise, good men supporting you. And that I'm very fortunate to have you and be loved by you."

"And I, you!" He kissed her.

"Beyond that, I'm frightened."

"So am I." He pulled her close. "But not as frightened as I'd be if I neglected to act at all."

Chapter VII

Early spring 1403: England

King Henry retreated on the hostage question in late winter.

By then, his adamancy was difficult to justify, even to his most ardent supporters. Two of them, Ralph Neville and George Dunbar, were in almost the same position as Hotspur and, to Henry's surprise, getting just as stubborn. Having taken men at Homildon and itching for gold, Dunbar remonstrated mightily (if privily) for permission to enjoy the fruits of his triumph by ransoming his captives.

Neville hadn't been at Homildon. But his knights had fought there, and they likewise expected their reward. Ralph, though, wasn't about to empty his coffers to compensate them for prisoners he'd confiscated to pass along to Henry. His liegemen complained to him, and he grumped to the king, bitterly.

Tired of the carping, Henry finally bowed to one of Neville's suggestions and named a commission to determine who should collect ransoms: captors, or Crown. Normally, the High Court of Chivalry, the senior military tribunal, would have adjudicated the case. But it recused itself, for its national judges included Earl Henry and Neville, while Harry was senior judge on its northern circuit. Thus, the new panel took over. Although it could still rule in Henry's favor, military men of all ranks viewed its creation as a significant royal concession. A measure of dissatisfaction ebbed, at least when it came to hostages.

Otherwise, the land churned with unhappiness. Henry blamed it on Harry. The king had yet to see Harry's letter, for no one had dared produce a copy and admit to having received it. Nonetheless, Henry had learned enough to know that Harry not only urged the convening of a new Parliament to launch sweeping reforms, but was riding from one end of England to the other, meeting with anyone sympathetic. And apparently, multitudes were.

"It's time," he moodily told Dunbar, "to divert him. I want him out of my realm and my affairs."

Dunbar's face lit up. "Temporarily? Or permanently?"

"Perhaps both!"

They began considering the possibilities.

* * *

25 March 1403: Warkworth Castle, Northumberland

"Though I'd lief not admit it, your obstinacy apparently won out." Earl Henry regarded his son with grudging respect. "The king has been sore humiliated over this hostage matter. But he seems to bear no ill will, even after your damn-fool letter criticizing him." The earl shook his head.

"Humiliated? Him?" Harry flung his long body into a chair sideways, one boot on the armrest, the other dangling over the floor. "What about him humiliating me? Last May, over Glyn Dwr. Then in October, over Glyn Dwr and everything else."

Earl Henry looked down his elegant nose. "Lot of good it did, defending Glyn Dwr. He whom you so kindly protected showed his appreciation last month by burning Denbigh, where you yourself oft stayed and—"

"And protected," Harry interjected. "It's so damn aggravating! Denbigh has long been part of the traditional territory of the Mortimers, liegemen of the English king. I expect that Glyn Dwr, now that Edmund is his son-in-law, wanted to keep it for Edmund, but that meant ending the castle and town's affiliation with England. So he attacked and claimed it. As we're at war, he also probably regarded Denbigh as fair game, even without its connection to Edmund.

"Hell! If Henry had accepted the pact that Glyn Dwr and I negotiated, Owain and Edmund both would again be subjects of the English king, and Wales would be peaceful." Harry frowned. "Henry— or Hal—will have no easy days there now, since Henry sees no need for me, or my uncle, in Wales anymore."

A week earlier, the king had named the prince as lieutenant of all Wales, prior appointments of Harry and Thomas Percy as lieutenants of North and South Wales notwithstanding. Those had been made at the behest of the Great Council; now, Henry had pulled rank to take matters into his own hands.

"You know why he did that?" Earl Henry asked.

"Oh, aye! He's miffed at me and pissing all over himself and Wales as a result. All he knows how to do in Wales is get his tail kicked, burn churches, and hang folk and enslave their children."

The earl glowered. "Oh, stop it! The simple truth is that even you can't be two places at once, as you admitted last summer when Dunbar was up here boasting and disparaging you and you were stuck in that Welsh hellhole."

Uncorking himself, Harry dropped both legs over the side of the chair. "It's different now. The Borders are quiet after the battle at Homildon. Douglas has taken me as his lord, too."

"Douglas submitting to you and his vassals submitting aren't the same. That's the *real* reason Henry replaced you in North Wales. He and I have work for you here, beyond your charge as warden of the East March." The earl went to a chest and retrieved a scroll. "Take a look at this."

Harry began reading the Latin:

> *Greetings: Know you that we have considered the no small measures, labors and advantageous service to us and all our realm of England by our dear cousin, Henry, Earl of Northumberland, especially and at length against the Scots, our enemies, who for the final destruction of our people presumed to invade our said realm but ultimately and in great numbers were slaughtered laudably by this same Earl. Indeed as he desired, our same cousin gathered his worthy men-at-arms in strength and allowed no one in equal strength to commence anything.*

"Rather clumsy; congratulatory to you, too, with nary a word about *me*."

"Don't get all het up. Keep going."

Skeptical, Harry resumed translating:

> *By special grace and Counsel, for Ourself and Ours, with certain knowledge and unanimous vote and total assent of our heirs, and to the extent that it is Ours to give, to this our same cousin We grant this, as follows:*

> *The whole and intact domain of the Earl of Douglas as well as the*

Harry whistled. "He's given us all Douglas' lands! I thought I'd have to scrap with him over them, like I did over Douglas' person."

"He's ceded *me* all Douglas' lands, and more," the earl corrected, "probably because I'm senior peer in these parts and because he's irked at you for not surrendering Douglas in the first place. So you may have Douglas' fealty, but *I* have Douglasdale, *etcetera*, as far as Henry is concerned."

Annoyed, Harry handed the document back. "Do you mean to spar with me—and Douglas—o'er which Percy should be his overlord and hold all that territory?"

"No, Son. You won him on the field. He's given

you his trust and fealty, he's *your* friend. His domains go with him, in my opinion. Besides, I've enough to deal with, without trying to fight you, Douglas, *and* any Scots who oppose expansion of our rights across the border." He smiled. "Furthermore, Henry gave everything to me *and my heirs*. Eventually, you'll become lord by title, after being *de facto* lord immediately. First, though, you'll have to pacify the area. Many of Douglas' people won't object to our authority. But some will. King Robert may challenge you, too, if he's any men left." Pride filled the earl's eyes. "You're the commander, Harry. The finest in England and well beyond. 'Twill be your task, your campaign, your lands. Agreed?"

"Truly."

"Excellent. There's just one other matter," the earl added. "As high constable, I got a separate writ from Henry, announcing it."

"What is it?"

The earl paused and swallowed. "Henry's granted George Dunbar control over *his* old Scottish lands, if he can reconquer them. Dunbar is going along with you, as a captain."

Harry's feet hit the floor. "For the fryggen love of the Lord! He's a vaunting ass. He dislikes me. And, imitating Beaufort, he's taken to using perfume by the bucket. If his bragging doesn't alert the Scots from miles away, his scent will. He'd do better to drench himself in muck from a privy. At least he'd smell like something remotely human!"

Earl Henry laughed. "You'll have to tolerate him. What's more, you'll have to let Dunbar have that castle and appurtenances his own nephew ceded to the Douglases when George decamped to England."

"Is there no end to this? Having Dunbar along is bad enough. Having him as a captain is worse. But having to step into the feud between Dunbar and his kith and kin is worst yet, especially if his kith and kin are Douglas' friends."

"Merely let Dunbar claim those particular properties. If you agree, Douglas will have to agree, too. Then it will be up to Dunbar to coax the local folk into accepting him, and to hold his own if King Robert tries to wrest everything back."

Harry looked dubious.

"Dunbar will cause no trouble," Earl Henry predicted. "He needs your help. He's *persona non grata* in Scotland. He'll have to be on his best behavior with you."

"Oh all right," Harry sighed. "Hell!"

* * *

Late April 1403: Teviotdale, Scotland

Harry knew the Scots would expect him to come from the northeast, from Jedburgh. Though within Scotland, the town had long belonged to England and was the obvious starting point for invading Teviotdale and its surroundings. So he approached from the south.

"That way," he told his captains before they left Berwick, "by the time we reach Hawick..."

"...a plum in its own right," Knayton interrupted.

"Aye ... by the time we reach Hawick, we'll have Teviotdale and virtually all the Eskdale and Liddesdale borderlands. Then we can take possession of Hawick, go on to Jedburgh, and, from there, arrange our governance of everything."

Dunbar protested. "You're going about this arse-backwards!"

Harry only smiled. "Let's see."

A day later, they entered Scotland near Kershope and proceeded unhindered to Langholm, where castle and town promptly surrendered. So did several other castles or towers as they moved northward. At all, Harry allowed the local garrison to remain as long as its members pledged fidelity to Douglas and him. After all, he told his men, not so far back, Teviotdale had been part of England, before Archibald Douglas and William Stewart had beaten it into submission.

The local folk remembered. At each hamlet and farm, they wandered out to watch the English pass, with a few catcalls but little enmity, and, often, shy smiles.

"This land was long under our protection. It shall be again, safeguarded by my writ against any who would reive, rob and burn," Harry declared at every stop. "I come in peace, not only in my name but in that of your own lord, Archambeau Douglas. Once, he was my foe. Now he's my friend, as I trust you will be, too."

They listened and nodded, some waving as he rode on.

Soon, they were only a few miles from Hawick. There, above the narrow road, perched a castle, known variously as Cocklaws or Ormiston or Cocklaws-*in*-Ormiston. Daunting by any name, it boasted a heavy Scottish 'barmkin' curtain wall linked at the corners by towers. Inspecting it from a distance with his scouts, Harry saw that on three fronts the wall stretched normally. But on the fourth—north—facade, it angled outward, continuing to an immense stone that backed up onto an inner parapet. Breaking off on one side of the rock, the wall picked up on the other side; despite that interruption, it remained forbidding. So did the keep, tall and thick-walled, a bastion in its own right.

Walls and keep swarmed with guards, in a close and hostile watch, under the command, as Harry knew, of one John Grymslaw, a senior man-at-arms. Harry had once met him at a March Day and recalled him as tall and strapping, with fox-red hair and pale blue eyes that didn't miss much, the epitome of the intrepid Scot, little known outside his own valley but adept at bedeviling Englishmen.

Squinting, Harry saw that Grymslaw had removed Douglas' pennant from the keep and flew only the Scottish royal flag and the Grymslaw family colors, defiant against the wind.

The English stroll through Teviotdale had ended.

* * *

May 1403: Cocklaws Castle, Ormiston, Scotland

Grymslaw realized that Hotspur was on the march and that the rest of Teviotdale—and Scotland—didn't seem to care. But Grymslaw cared, dispatching urgent messages to King Robert and watching. Well before the English neared, he ordered his archers to the battlements.

They opened fire the moment Hotspur's vanguard came close.

Veering off into the woods beyond the castle, the English spread out amidst shrubs and scrub. Refusing to be lured into a trap, Grymslaw stayed within his walls.

Night fell without incident.

Before dawn, though, Grymslaw emerged to find Hotspur's troops already arrayed below his barmkin and atop adjacent hillocks, onto which they had somehow dragged trebuchets and mangonels. *"St. Andrew's balls!"* Avoiding an ambush in the forest, he had been blindsided by a maneuver Hotspur had used (as Grymslaw belatedly reminded himself) at Conway in battling the Welsh, at Homildon in Northumberland, and God-knew-where else. Now the scribes could add Cocklaws to the list.

Darting back inside, Grymslaw took stock. He estimated that Hotspur had 1,300 men, plus a couple of hundred reserves to the rear. Grymslaw had 425, his usual garrison reinforced by men from Hawick. Scant help, given the odds...

He hunkered down.

The English, meanwhile, busied themselves felling trees to build moveable towers and short, squat "turtles," which allowed soldiers to advance under the cover of a wooden roof and sides. Upon completion, each rolled into action. From the turtles, sappers probed the ground, while archers in the wheeled towers sniped at anyone daring castle parapets.

The Scots retaliated with intermittent fire, shooting furiously, then ceasing abruptly, only to resume minutes or hours later, hoping to riddle the English with as much anxiety as shot. In the lulls, hecklers yelled obscenities from the walls. Not that it helped much. Viewing bumps in his wards on the third morning, Grymlsaw discovered that, like so many energetic moles, Hotspur's sappers had already tunneled under the barmkin and were pushing toward his keep. He immediately ordered his men to dig counter-shafts, which they filled with rubble, forcing the English to clear the obstructions or start digging fresh tunnels elsewhere.

Under the steady drubbing of trebuchets, the siege set in.

* * *

After several days, dents dimpled Cocklaw's exterior. Chunks of parapet sheered off the top, leaving the crenellation ragged, like the broken teeth of a crone. Streaks dribbled down the stone, left by futile attempts to hurl bucketsful of pitch toward the attackers. And the castle walls began to crack.

So did the Scots.

Heads rarely appeared on the parapet anymore, and uneasiness cloaked the yards. Even the heckling diminished, the occasional curses now aimed as much at Edinburgh as the English.

Across the lines, Harry bided his time.

Before much longer, he knew, the sappers' undermining would reach the height (or depth) of perfection. Likewise, the bombardment would damage the barmkin enough to allow a direct assault and entry, especially if he used his movable towers adroitly.

Toward that end, at dusk on the fourth day, he cased the walls, pausing to study the boulder that bisected the north facade. Throughout the next day, axes and hammers rang out. That evening, a new, shorter tower rolled into view, lurching to a halt toward the northeast.

An hour later, succumbing to constant pounding, a section of barmkin above the portcullis split apart, bringing down several feet of parapet. Grymslaw saw to temporary repairs and returned to his quarters to confront more chaos. On the floor, a Scottish royal courier lay dying, pierced by an English arrow as he had scrambled through the gate. His message had entered with him, though. Grymslaw's spirits plummeted as he read it: With no troops to spare, King Robert ordered Grymslaw to either defeat Hotspur and his invaders or inflict as much damage as possible before surrendering. After a round of preparations, Grymslaw fell into bed, craving sleep ere he brought the English to battle at dawn.

* * *

With the same audacity that had prompted the Scots to nickname him Hotspur years earlier, Harry didn't wait for Grymslaw to move first. Nor did he delay until morning. Instead, as a dry but starless night settled in, his archers and musicians filled the air with the mixed racket of Northumbrian bagpipes, drums, horns and the whizzing of arrows, all complemented by thuds from the bombarding siege machines and the grinding and groaning of the wooden towers as they moved into place against the walls.

Inside the castle, snores gave way to shouts as men became aware of their predicament and dashed outside, Grymslaw among them.

Beyond the lines on the English side, the last sappers climbed from their holes, nodding to their commander, at the fore of the English host.

Harry's upraised sword dropped. *"Loose incendiaries!"*

Wrapped in cloth dipped in pitch and set alight, shafts arced over the walls like shooting stars. The crisp air filled with smoke. Fire jumped from the thatch of sheds to wooden eaves, porches, and stairs. Bleary-eyed Scots scurried to douse the blazes, at the expense of not manning the walls.

Underground, long fuses the sappers had lit burned down to the other end and reached sacks of powder, a mixture of charcoal, sulfur, and saltpeter. Fiery explosions ripped from the ground. Several tunnels caved in, dragging chunks of barmkin down or sundering the walls. A stone half-tower on the front tilted precariously, and the Scots within raced to escape.

Around the back, where the massive rock linked the two sections of north wall, the short English siege tower crawled into place. An upper door opened, and Harry bounded onto the rock sword in hand, shield upraised. Both Salvayns and Hardyng followed, with Umfraville, Lord Talbot, and a pack of Northumbrians. In seconds, Harry had leapt between the crenellation and was running along the parapet, toppling two Scots before he reached a stairway. Five more Scots ascended, but the first crumpled when Harry stabbed his chest, the second fell over the first, and the other three hastily descended, holding fighting stances below. Harry nudged Roger Salvayn, who blasted a call on his horn. Then, with Hardyng and Gerard Salvayn at his elbow, he jumped the last few stairs and closed with the three Scots.

At Roger's horn call, other Englishmen poured through the breached front wall, stepping warily around demolished tunnels. Led by Dunbar, they seized an intact section of wall and yard. Through the damaged portcullis, a 'turtle' entered, housing a battering ram. On Dunbar's order, it began pummeling the southwest tower.

As Dunbar burst through the front and Harry through the back, most Scots retreated to the keep. But Scottish archers remained in the two back towers, shooting fiercely. Others fired from the keep itself. Under their protection, Grymslaw rushed forward with his best men-at-arms. Another small group came from the northwest tower, and the combined force hammered Harry party from two sides.

Harry had scarcely pulled his blade from a dying man when he confronted four or five more swords. Hardyng and Salvayn edged closer, and Roger Salvayn reappeared, too. Overhead, arrows winged and smoke hung in thick plumes, making it harder to tell friend from foe or find footing on the uneven, collapsing ground.

Somewhere in the distance, Harry heard MacKerny rallying his archers and knew that Clifford and Knayton, from the taller siege towers, must be forcing their way into the castle turrets. For that reason, or because they feared hitting Grymslaw's band, the Scottish bowmen decreased their fire.

Harry felt momentary relief before a gigantic axeman reared over him. Ducking, he felt a piece of silk rip from his tabard. His sword thrust upward, and the axe fell. Blood dripping, the Scotsman followed it to the earth. Others remained, however. Methodically, Harry's long forehand and backhand began clearing the space around him—not once or twice but three or four times— before the Scots started to fall back. Jumping over the dead and wounded, he pressed harder, crossing swords with Grymslaw but losing him as the castellan slipped, crawled under someone's legs, and came up in a knot of fellow Scots. Another swordsman replaced him, and Harry's duel went on.

Sporadic arrow volleys resumed. Over the shoulder of his latest, crumbling opponent, Harry saw that it came not from the Scots but from his own side. His men had claimed the corner turrets, shooting when they had clear lines of fire. It helped. So did the arrival of Dunbar, fresh from seizing a front tower and eager to settle old scores with Grymslaw. Harry caught only a glimpse of him, though, before Dunbar, too, vanished.

Instead, Talbot and Umfraville materialized. "Harry, we've got the rest of the castle!" the latter yelled.

"Good! Secure everything."

They hurried off.

Simultaneously, Harry realized that Grymslaw's force was drilling toward the keep. He lunged in pursuit. Reaching the keep staircase, the Scots clambered up, backward, and tumbled inside. Harry was right behind. The massive door slammed against his sword. Throwing his weight against the wood, he glanced up to see metal spikes descending. Shoulders jerking back, he cleared the doorframe, a split-second before the portcullis crashed down. *"Hell!"*

Little matter, though... Once Grymslaw and his men understood the predicament, they would no doubt yield. Meanwhile, the English held the rest of the castle. For now, 'twas prize enough, Harry thought.

By moonlight, Harry stripped to his under-briefs and bedded down in his tent. His squires were still busy, helping with the wounded, or cleaning equipment. His role for the night was over, though.

He fell asleep instantly.

A terse whisper awoke him an hour later.

"Harry. It's one of the wounded prisoners. You said to inform you if anyone of prominence turned up."

"Aye?" Harry blinked into Hardyng's lantern.

"It's young Montgomery. At least, he says he's a Montgomery, and since he knows he might die, I don't imagine he's lying." The squire set the lamp on Harry's armor chest.

"Montgomery? But John has no sons."

"This is a nephew, I think. Want to see him?"

"Aye." Harry threw off his covers. "You said he's badly hurt?"

"Yea. Cut through his leg. He lost buckets of blood. But Kynge thinks he might live. He could ever be lame, though."

"Where is he?"

"In Kynge's hospital tent, on the ground, like some of the other injured, since there were so few cots." The squire sounded apologetic. "I even hauled mine out from here, but by the time we found Montgomery, another man was in it."

Harry lit a candle from the lantern and smoothed his sheets. "Bring him here. He can use mine. 'Tis the least I can do for one of John's kin. We can unroll extra blankets over there for me."

Hardyng ran off to return at one end of a stretcher, with Roger Salvayn at the other. On it lay a nearly naked young man, hardly older than 16. He was more blond and shorter and thinner than the lord of Eaglesham. But in the line of his jaw, color of his eyes, and the smile he tried to give Harry, he bore a distinct resemblance to John Montgomery. He was also very pale, and a red bandage covered his right thigh.

Oh God, Harry thought. Had *he* wounded the lad? Not that it made much difference, or that, in battle, he'd had any choice. Still...

He helped his squires transfer the youth to his cot, drew the blanket over him, and sat on the armor chest alongside. "I know you fought bravely. All your men did. My compliments. And to whom have I the honour of paying them?"

The boy regarded him with inquisitive but weary eyes. "David ... Elliott ... Montgomery." He paused, catching his breath. In the background, Hardyng bustled about before leaving with Salvayn.

"Mostly I'm David Elliott, after my mother's family," the young voice croaked. "My Fath... father..." Harry found his whisky flask and gave the boy a long drink.

With another trembling smile, David thanked him, color returning. "My father was ... Sir Alistair Montgomery, half-brother to Lord John. He went crusading—or something—after my birth. He died ... somewhere far off ... last August."

"And Elliott was your mother's maiden name?"

"Aye. Her kin got me a place with Lord Grymslaw. He has ties to the Elliotts."

"You wear a Montgomery signet ring, though."

David sighed. "My father named me his heir. Per... perhaps he regretted abandoning me earlier. Afore he died, he directed that it come back to Scotland, to me. By then, Mother was already dead."

Harry lifted the boy's hand and turned the ring slightly, as if admiring it but actually to determine if it belonged there. It didn't move easily, though, or show signs of recent resizing. Relieved, he knew the ring hadn't been newly gained by theft. David had worn it for months, doubtless since his father's death.

He gave the boy's hand a friendly squeeze as he laid it down. "And John Montgomery? Know him?"

"No. I've wondered about him, though..."

Harry grinned. "Then you shall stop wondering. He's a great friend of mine. He'll be proud to make your acquaintance."

The boy smiled. "I should like that..." His eyelids shut.

Harry extinguished the candle.

Hardyng had made a bed for Harry on the floor, and he sank into it. Come morning, one more duty awaited: He'd have to write to John Montgomery to tell him he had captured his long-lost nephew...

Two hours later, Harry awoke again. No one was in his tent except young Montgomery, who slumbered peacefully. Yet ... Harry cocked a bleary eye in the darkness. Something had disturbed him.

Perfume cloyed the air, and the noise came again—furtive boots outside, along the tent wall near the cot. The steps ranged back and forth; floral scent mingled with sweat.

The side of the tent lifted several inches. Too slowly, Harry regained his night vision. What looked like an ivory-handled dagger shone dully—and plunged between the ribs of the sleeping David Elliott Montgomery.

Harry lunged in vain.

Young Montgomery gave a soft, gurgled gasp. His eyes popped open and shut again, as blood poured from his chest.

Pulse racing, Harry was torn between pursuit and trying to help the boy. Then he knelt beside the cot, right hand wadding the blanket, trying to stanch the flow, though he realized it was hopeless. In his left hand, he held the boy's limp wrist. "David. David..."

There was no response. The pulse beat feebly for a few seconds before dribbling off to nothing.

Harry scrambled to his feet. *"Murder!"*

From outside came the noise of men running and Roger Salvayn's cry: "O'er there! *After* him"

Grabbing his knife, Harry tore from the tent to see his squires chasing someone. They continued for a quarter mile to the forest, Harry on their heels. Shouting a warning as he caught up, he forbade them to go any farther. "You don't know who's in those woods, or how many. And we've naught but knives."

Hardyng turned, as angry and frightened as Harry had ever seen him. "But somebody tried to stab David Montgomery," Hardyng protested. "*No!* Someone tried to stab you, Harry. 'Tis obvious, because no one but we knew Montgomery slept in your cot. I was too far away to do anything. But I saw him—a man in a hooded cloak, raising a dagger."

"Aye. He killed David. However, 'twas me he was after, I'm certain. Never mind that for now, though."

Hardyng peered into the trees. "But he's in there. We should get him!"

"No, John. Again: We're not properly armed." Even as he spoke, Harry wanted to ignore his own order. Yet he couldn't. One young man already lay dead. He couldn't risk losing Hardyng or Salvayn, too.

"But..." Roger pleaded. "Don't you want to find out who it is? And punish him?"

"Oh, aye, punish him," Harry answered. "But I don't need to find out who 'tis. That I already know."

The rest of the night passed peacefully.

At dawn, in armor except for his helmet, Harry rousted Dunbar from sleep.

The strong scent of *eau-de-rose* infused man and tent.

"You tried to kill me!" Backing Dunbar up against a tent pole, Harry fingered his knife. "I ought to cut your heart open, as you came to cut mine. However, unlike you, I won't slay an unarmed man, even a murderer." He released the Scotsman.

Dunbar smiled sourly. "Surely, as you're alive and well, Harry, you're wrong. You had a nightmare."

"No! And a Scots lad lies dead in my cot because of you."

"Your evidence?"

Gawayn Dunbar, the earl's son and squire, entered the tent, followed by a mixture of Dunbar and Percy men, mutually astonished.

"'Twas your perfume on the killer." Harry noticed the sheathed knife, hilt of ivory, lying by George Dunbar's shoes. Picking it up, he drew the blade. "Your dagger, too. There's still blood on it."

"Of course, you ignoramus! Just hours ago, we fought a battle. My knife and sword are both well-stained, as yours should be."

"My squires or I clean mine immediately after battle. Like you do, I think, unless, like last night, you bloody it again deceitfully." Harry threw the dagger down.

Dunbar waved his arm in disparagement. "Afore you insult me further, enlighten me as to why you make such a ridiculous charge."

Harry explained, and Hardyng and Salvayn backed him up.

"A deplorable act! An outrage!" Dunbar commiserated. "Under the circumstances, I excuse your rashness and won't call you out in a duel for slandering me."

"Liar! 'Twas you who did it." Harry asserted.

"Could you identify this mysterious killer?" Dunbar sniffed.

"He wore your perfume."

"Well? Anyone could sneak in and pilfer my toiletries, or my knife, when I sleep."

Harry couldn't dispute that, so he backed off. "Then you'd best be a damned sight more careful where you leave your dagger and perfume." He strode away, convinced that Dunbar had tried to kill him— and that he'd never be able to prove it.

Chapter VIII

May 1403: Cocklaws Castle, Ormiston, Scotland

As soon as Harry could clear his mind enough to piece together surrender terms, he drafted them. Then he convened his captains. He had donned clean clothes under his armor, and over it wore a fresh thigh-length tabard, its lions and fish bright blue and silver in their gold and scarlet quadrants, vivid against the dark-blue cloth. He had also shaved, but shadows rimmed his eyes. Nor had he breakfasted.

They formed a circle on the grass. Along with the others, he'd summoned Dunbar, who acted for all the world as if nothing had happened. Of course, it hadn't, except that some skulking killer had knifed the wrong man.

Aloud, he read his terms: If Grymslaw yielded the castle, he and his men would be spared further risk or penalty. On 1 August, feast day of St. Peter-in Chains, King Robert could either meet Harry to officially surrender Ormiston (and, by extension, all of Teviotdale) or wage pitched battle for it. Meanwhile, a truce would prevail, extending to Hawick, which came under Cocklaws' protection. Grymslaw would become his hostage, treated with utmost courtesy, in surety for the agreement. The rest of the garrison would be paroled, or, if they wished, allowed to stay at the castle during the ceasefire, though they could neither re-victual it nor replenish its ranks.

There were no other conditions.

"You realize that King Robert would still be free to gather an army elsewhere," Knayton observed.

"Aye. But I'll be free to do likewise and intend to, raising troops from across England, so we're ready if the Scots refuse peace.”

“A truce will give them valuable time,” Clifford pointed out.

“And us,” Harry replied. “We need a respite. Our men must see to their farms and fishing, so we’re not short on food next winter.”

“True enough,” Clifford concurred, drawing nods from the others, except one.

“This is crazy!” Dunbar fumed. “You’re giving away everything we’ve gained. The Scots understand one thing. Brute force! Edward Longshanks knew that, but you’re stupid clodpates. We should give Grymslaw no quarter and take Hawick the same way.”

“Is that how you’ll reclaim your Scottish domains?” Harry asked.

“Yea. It’ll be the only way they’ll remember I’m their real lord. And let me further remind you that every day you delay a resolution here, you keep me from regaining my lands elsewhere.”

“You’re free to retake them yourself.”

“Pah! You know that until England holds Teviotdale and the rest of Douglas’ territory, and convinces King Robert of English supremacy, I don’t stand a chance.”

Harry shrugged. “’Tis your choice. Anyway, I intend to proceed with my terms. Everyone else is with me, I trust.” He looked around the circle.

“Aye,” Talbot began, and the others chimed in, as Dunbar slunk off.

Under a flag of truce, Harry’s proposal soon went to Grymslaw, who responded, also under a flag of truce, that he was considering “these most generous terms” but wanted to confer with his men. Meanwhile, he suggested, perhaps an informal peace could prevail?

Harry agreed.

Then the English finished burying the dead, including Montgomery’s murdered nephew.

Despite the cease-fire, Harry also assigned squads to guard the walls, patrol the grounds, repair weapons, and see to everything else incumbent upon a watchful army, lest King Robert appear, after all. He said nothing further to Dunbar but knew the earl had taken up his assigned post, helping MacKerny supervise the archers who manned the castle towers, arrows notched and bows taut against any sign of peril.

He wasn't sure what had prompted the assassination attempt. Until the moment it occurred, he had accepted his father's assessment that, regardless of personal antipathy, Dunbar needed Percy backing too much to cause trouble. Besides, maybe his suspicions were wrong. As surprised and exhausted as he had been, maybe he'd been mistaken. Maybe, as Dunbar had suggested, someone else had tried to kill him—or David Elliott. Also, in the aftermath, Dunbar was his usual obnoxious self, albeit a bit pricklier. But, if innocent, even a man as callous as Dunbar would be embarrassed about letting someone pilfer his dagger and perfume and use them to get away with murder. And such embarrassment might account for his extra blustering.

Too busy to ponder it further, Harry took up other matters. Like his lieutenants, he continued to wear his chainmail hauberk (topped by his coat-of-arms tunic) and his cowl or hood, plus his protective metal arm and leg coverings, though he eschewed the cuirass—a metal chest-plate—and set his helmet, gauntlets, and shield aside.

Accompanied by Hardyng, he began walking the walls, noting vulnerable points. Once Cocklaws officially became his, as he assumed it would, he would need to improve its defenses. On the north façade, he paused below the massive boulder. As he had found, it was the castle's Achilles' heel. It would have to be protected, perhaps with a moat deep enough to thwart even a hardy siege machine.

Yet what if men got across the moat?

He flashed Hardyng an apologetic grin. "I'm going up that rock."

"Why?"

"To see if it can be done, see if troops could get onto it without a siege tower."

"The top is rather flat," Hardyng said. "But the sides are steep and nearly as smooth as glass."

"Aye. It's probably unassailable, as the Scots reckoned. Still, I want to find out."

"Then I guess I'll also find out." Hardyng spoke without enthusiasm. He, too, was in armor. Unlike Harry, however, he had kept his helmet on, visor open, and his shield hung over his back.

"Leave some gear here," Harry advised, beginning to crawl upward. "'Twill be easier."

"No," Hardyng replied. "If we continue along the walls and come down somewhere else, I'll have to return and fetch them. Besides, 'tis a good test. Anyone doing this in battle would be in helmet and have his shield."

"You're right." Harry pushed on

Amazingly, although his boots slid, the stone's smoothness was no serious impediment, not to a determined man. Tiny lines and clefts cracked the surface at odd intervals, and, using them for traction, he groped his way along. With a last strain of muscles, he pulled himself onto the summit. Resting on his knees, he watched Hardyng, still well below. Doggedly inching onward, sweating under the weight of the shield, Hardyng almost tumbled twice. Finally, he, too, emerged over the crest.

"Not something I'd want to do in a hurry!" The younger man wiped his face and unslung the shield. "You were even smarter than I thought to use that siege tower last night."

"Why exert ourselves for naught?"

They got to their feet, and Harry walked onto the

middle of the rock, debating whether he could build a wall right *onto* the boulder. No reason not to try, he concluded, taking another step forward. "We'll increase the height of the barmkin, move it outward…" He turned his head and pointed, "…to about th——

"Arghhh!"

Without warning, Hardyng tackled him, throwing him onto the rock and dragging the shield over them both.

"Stay down!" The squire yelled. "And, for God's sake, pull your chainmail cowl up!"

Complying, Harry didn't need to ask why. He heard the arrows streak overhead and hit the inner wall beyond, sickening scrapes of metal on rock. He counted 10 shafts in quick succession. Even in his contorted position, he could see the ninth, partly embedded in moss dappling the parapet. The slender wood throbbed, feathers quivering in the breeze.

The shots seemed to come from the nearest tower, at the corner where the north stretch of barmkin met the eastern range. A comparable tower stood at the northwest corner. Raucous shouting rang out from both.

Heart thudding, body sore, Harry wondered if any bones were shattered. As he curled there, he flexed his muscles and decided not, unkinking his leg. Hardyng roughly pushed him down. "Don't move until we're sure they've stopped."

The squire shouted at the towers. "Don't shoot! It's Sir Harry and John Hardyng! Friend, not foe!"

The clamor increased, with MacKerny's voice, furious and profane, loudest of all.

Harry and Hardyng lay frozen. "That's Dunbar's men—his archers—in that northeast tower," Harry whispered. "MacKerny and his squad are in the other one."

"I know. And the shots were from Dunbar's tower. I saw them, out of the corner of my eye, barely in time."

"Thank God you did, John. You saved my life."

"Mine too, I wager."

"Think we can make it to the wall?"

Hardyng peeped under the bottom of the shield. "Probably. The shooting seems to be over."

Like a wounded crab, they lumbered under the shield to the parapet. Balling themselves up again, they nestled against it, with the shield in front of both.

But no other threats came, and in another minute he heard MacKerny again. "It's all right, Harry. You're safe. We've got 'em."

Aching and angry, they stood up, dropped onto the parapet, and loped along the walkway to the northeast tower. Harry pulled the door open. They ascended the twining stairs a pair at a time. One floor up, they found Dunbar seated with two of his archers. MacKerny and several Northumbrian bowmen ringed the room, weapons poised.

Harry yanked Dunbar from his chair, shaking him violently."What the devil were you doing? Trying to kill me—again?"

"It... itttt... wwwasss a mmmisstake." Dunbar's teeth rattled in his head. "You... you....sssaiiiddd... Y-Y-You--s-sssaiiddd-d..."

With another brutal shake, Harry let him go, and he collapsed in his seat, while his archers stared at the floor. "You... told us to challenge any attackers ... anyone trying to breach the walls," Dunbar said hoarsely. "My men saw two ... figures ... climbing that rock. So they fired."

"You were to challenge *unidentified* men. *Unidentified!*" Harry pointed to the coat-of-arms on his chest. "Do you not know my colors? How the hell could you miss them?"

Glowering, Dunbar said nothing.

Harry looked at Dunbar's archers. Uncertainly, one spoke up.

"We... we didn't see well, Sir," he apologized unevenly. "The sun was in our eyes."

"Oh aye! And in Scotland it shines from the north of a morn!" Harry retorted.

"We only did what we were ordered," the other man added.

"That I doubt not!"

"It happened quickly," the archer went on, stubbornly.

"Sure as hell did!"

Harry studied the pair. "You're from London, aren't you?" Their accents had given them away the moment they started speaking.

"Yea," the first answered dully.

"So what're you doing here? Hoping for booty?" Harry's questions shot out, as pointed as their arrows.

Fidgeting, the archers looked at Dunbar, who ignored them.

"Well?" Harry asked again.

"We're from the palace guard. King Henry ordered us to help Lord Dunbar," the first man said.

"And?"

"That's all, to help Lord Dunbar; follow his commands."

"And so you did." Harry nodded. "Even when he said to shoot me."

"They targeted you, Harry, for sure," MacKerny asserted. "I'd just entered the yard, with my lads here, to relieve the men in our tower. I saw it happen. We ran up here and caught 'em fixin' to shoot again." He almost spat at Dunbar. "Cursed swine!"

"It was an honest mistake." Dunbar insisted. "A mistake!"

Harry regarded him coldly. "Aye. Trying to kill me usually is."

"It won't happen again," Dunbar said.

"Damned right!" Harry thundered.

"What do you want us to do with them?"

MacKerny gestured to the royal archers.

"Confiscate their bows, arrows, and knives. Take charge of them. Assign them menial chores, like cleaning up after the horses. They're either murderers or very stupid, with poor eyesight. Either way, 'tis too dangerous to let them handle arms."

"And him?" MacKerny jerked his white-haired head toward Dunbar.

"He says 'twas an accident..." Harry shrugged. "I strongly doubt that but let him go. Any more 'mishaps,' though, and he might well hang."

Dunbar fled down the stairs.

Closing his eyes, Harry sank into a chair. "This has already been a very long day..."

* * *

Two hours later, Grymslaw left the keep bearing a truce flag and approached Harry in the yard. "I accept your surrender terms," he announced.

Harry extended a hand. "Then you have my thanks and my esteem. You and your men demonstrated courage and ability."

"We've had ample practice, fighting you English in the past." Grymslaw returned the handshake. "I only ask leave to inform King Robert."

"Granted."

"And ... permission to send word to Hawick to a special lass, my fiancée," he blushed, "as I shall be leaving to take up residency with you."

"Again granted." Harry smiled. "Give my regards to the lady. Tell her she's free to visit you in Northumberland any time. Meanwhile, your garrison must bring out their weapons. Each man can keep his sword or bow and knife, but I want everything else piled in the courtyard, for wagons to collect."

Grymslaw nodded.

"Afterward," Harry went on, "you and I should inspect the premises to ensure everyone's complied."

"As you wish. But 'twill be as you request. I give you my pledge."

* * *

To expedite the inspection, Harry sent Irby, MacKerny, and Umfraville ahead, reviewing every room of the keep and exploring the remaining tunnels. He was peering down a tunnel himself, contemplating descent, when MacKerny emerged from it, excited and aggrieved.

"Damn it, Harry, we found arms down there! These idiots are violating your terms." The other searchers joined him, nodding, as he went on. "They've tried to hide swords and hammers and such."

Grymslaw stepped forward. "Nay! I forbade it, and my men obey me. We relinquished our weapons as directed." He stared down the hole. "I don't know what you found down there, but it can't be ours. And I challenge any man who says otherwise to meet me in single combat!"

"I accept, on behalf of England," Irby promised hotly. "I saw it myself."

"Whoaaa, lads!" Harry placed a hand on each man's shoulder. "Never be so eager for more fighting." He looked at MacKerny. "Gather everything you found."

MacKerny and Irby disappeared into the shaft and came back trundling a wheelbarrow with eclectic contents: a couple of hatchets; a short sword; three saws; a mace, and two specialized hammers—a tool equipped with both an iron mallet-head and a pick-like prong, useful in mining and warfare alike, and under all that was a slingshot.

185

Picking up the slingshot, Harry chuckled. He'd oft seen it in the hands of his mining foreman, who used it for potting rabbits. The rest, too, looked familiar, and when he examined them, he found the well-worn crest of his great-grandfather etched into the sword blade and that of the bishops of Carlisle on the war hammers. He reddened.

"These are *our* things. And, I'm ashamed to say, in our haste last night it looks like we—our sappers— left them behind." He turned to Grymslaw. "I apologize, Sir, for any suggestions otherwise."

"Accepted!" Grymslaw said, a narrow glitter in his eyes. "But does that mean that I don't get a chance to leave this fine fellow in the dust?" He elbowed Irby.

"No," Harry responded. "Your challenge can stand, to be answered by this young man or another, if he declines. Only now your joust can celebrate a new peace, instead of furthering a new quarrel. And you must use blunted weapons. We don't need any more killing here."

"Aye! And you?" Grymslaw poked Irby again.

"Done!" Irby vowed. "I wager every pence in my purse as winnings if I'm defeated. I won't be, though."

So it was settled, mostly—for in typical Borders fashion the duel soon expanded into inter-army games: archery, spear-throwing, football, tug-of-war, horse and foot races, swordsmanship. The events would begin in late afternoon and continue the next day. Scots and English camps quickly bubbled with anticipation. Harry viewed the whole thing as a godsend. Let them expend any remaining hostility this way, instead of itching for renewed battle...

With a few hours to spare, he wrote to King Henry to announce his victory and truce, dispatching the letter by courier. Finally, he, too, started to relax, helping Irby prepare for his joust. Then, in a spirit of impartiality, he offered Grymslaw use of English arms or armor if, post-bellum, the Scotsman was short. Having yielded most of his equipment as well as his weapons, Grymslaw accepted gauntlets and a stout lance, and the preparations continued.

Only Dunbar opposed the tournament, although he dared say little beyond his tent. "We should be watching this place burn!" He kicked the ground under his bunk. "And if I hear that accursed song one more time, I'm like to shit all over my shoes."

"Best stopper your ears then," his son recommended, tilting his head to listen. "Because here it comes again."

A lilting strain rolled from the far line of tents, picking up momentum row by row:

> 'Tis Harry in full wight,
>   with sword and honor bright,
> There's not a knight in Christendom.
>   to match him in a fight,
>   or equal him in might!
> Nay, or equal him in might!
> Against the Scots, from hill and glen,
>   at Homildon and Cocklaws then,
>   He triumphed over brawny men,
>   and won the day, as well we ken!
>   On castle wall, and tower tall,
>   he does not shirk; he does not stall.
>   He's always there: wherever ... when!
>   'Tis Harry, Hotspur, Harry again!

Hardyng had written it over mugs of ale with Roger Salvayn, who had provided the melody. In the tradition of victory songs, it had caught on, carried from tent to tent and group to group by voice, bagpipe, lute, and whistle, with the tempo enlivened by bodhrans or improvised beating of hands on shields.

"'Tis *Harry, Hotspur, Harry again!*'" Dunbar mimicked sarcastically. "He's actually considered a hero by these English lummoxes."

"And no few Scots," Gawayn added, further irritating his father.

"Harry's a colossal fool," Dunbar snapped. "He won. But instead of extracting spoils and wielding real might, he extends terms so mild it beggars belief. Then he chooses to sport with them like they're long-lost brethren!"

"I don't know," Gawayn sighed, stretching his stocky body. "I rather fancy a bit of sport myself..."

"Bah!" Dunbar tasted his wine, only to toss it outside the tent. "Harry coddles the Scots, and King Henry is going to hear of it. Henry had better get his arse up here, too, to ensure this 'surrender' in August actually occurs. And if the Scots want to fight, Henry should lead the English army that confronts them. It would also be a fine time to drag Harry atop these walls he refused to raze and behead him for treason!"

"Treason?"

"Yea. Manifestly. This dawdling with the Scots here is just one of his traitorous acts!" Dunbar reached inside his shirt, pulling out a document. "Whilst Harry inspected the Scots' weaponry, I got into his tent. In his locked coffer, I found a copy of that letter he dispatched around England. It's treasonous, absolutely. And King Henry shall hear every word of it."

Gawayn said nothing.

"I only wish I'd had more time," Dunbar went on. "Since last night, though, his squires have kept close watch, and I'd barely made it inside his tent when someone approached. But," he grinned, "it looks to me like Harry has also got a stack of other letters, from men offering support. I'm going to read those, too, and learn who those men are. Henry will be most interested!"

"You broke into Harry's locked coffer?" Gawayn's fleshy face puckered. "Isn't that burglary or stealing or something? Couldn't you get court-martialed and even executed?"

"I didn't break into anything. I used this." Dunbar lifted a chain from his neck, displaying a key. "Very ingenious, this. I bought it in Paris years past. Works on almost any lock there is."

He dropped it back around his neck. "I'm getting the goods on Harry at last. He'll soon be gone, one way or another. Then I'll be English warden of the March and rule the North."

Again, Gawayn looked unconvinced. "You sure King Henry would agree? He appointed Harry as warden four years ago. Then there's this ceding of Douglas land to the Percies."

"Hah!" Dunbar chortled. "Henry wants to get rid of Harry even more than I do. Who do you think suggested that Harry might get shot in error by his own troops, if he weren't killed by the Scots? That was Henry's idea. I'm just peeved it didn't work. I should've attempted it earlier. But once the fighting started, I was too busy enjoying myself slaying Grymslaw's men to bother about Harry."

"*Someone* bothered about him, though, *after* the fighting."

"Yea, I don't forget my interests for long." Dunbar flashed a smug smile. "As far as that goes, since we're not far from Edinburgh, we might call on King Robert. Of course, he considers me a traitor, so you'll have to ease the way. But I think he could find it worthwhile to see me and let bygones be bygones..."

"Why would he do that? You insulted and denounced him."

"*Why?*" Dunbar glowed with superiority. "Because I'm prepared to tell him about the English strength in the North, and their plans to overcome him 1 August, and that I'm urging Henry to come up here."

His son boggled. "You'd go to two kings? To King Henry, informing him of Harry, and advising Henry to come north to fight the Scots? And to King Robert, informing on the English—including King Henry—so Robert can defeat them? What if someone finds out?" Gawayn could see their family fortune and reputation destroyed on both sides of the border.

"Who'll find out?" Dunbar laughed. "Besides, I rather enjoy the idea of playing one king off against another. Especially if Harry Percy gets caught in the middle!"

Chapter IX

June 1403: Cumberland, England

Furloughing much of his army, Harry spread the rest from Lanercost Priory to Carlisle Castle, his father's post as warden of the West March. He based himself at Warwick Tower, a fortalice with little resemblance to the great Midlands castle with like name, but sturdy enough. Claiming the uppermost chamber for himself, he used the other three as a headquarters and began preparing for 1 August. The final hours at Cocklaws had gone well, the games bringing victories to both sides, though the Scots' successes included Grymslaw's triumph in the joust. Obtaining his wager from the much-chagrined Irby, Grymslaw had thrown his saddlebags onto his horse, taken leave of his men, and joined the English as surety for the peace agreement.

If he thus became a welcome addition to Harry's force, it also suffered an unexpected loss: Gawayn Dunbar disappeared. Citing a lame horse, he dropped behind one morning in Scotland, promising to soon catch up. But he didn't. His father hardly worried. "He'd go off like this, when we dwellt in Scotland," the earl said. "Certes, he hankered after a favorite Scots brothel again and renewal of acquaintances."

And even without a whorehouse, he found an excuse to escape you, Harry thought. *Would we could all be so fortunate!*

So Dunbar Senior remained in camp and Junior remained at large ... for a time.

After a week, Gawayn abruptly returned, offering awkward greetings but no apology. Welcoming the prodigal with an embrace, George Dunbar followed it with a lascivious query: "Been inserting yourself into an old haunt and enjoying Rood hospitality?"

"Aye," Gawayn winked, "in a palace of unexpected satisfactions."

"I'll hear more, privily!" Dunbar led his son away and could later be spotted grinning and humming around camp.

But his elation faded with the sunset. At the latrine after supper, he urinated and cleared his throat, leaning over to spit down the hole. As he bent low, the chain around his neck slipped from his shirt, snagging on his belt buckle. Automatically, he jerked his head to free it.

The chain broke.

In an agonized split second, he watched it fall into the foul depths of the privy. With it went his prized key, the one he used for picking other men's locks...

The same evening, Harry made the rounds of sentries, ensuring all was in order for the night. Then he joined his lieutenants at the campfire, drinking ale and joshing, listening as Hardyng and Salvayn wandered melodiously through the Borders, with bawdy songs of brawling and beer and mournful ballads of lost battles and lost kingdoms, lost dreams and lost love.

Well after dark, Harry climbed the circular stairs to his tower room. Pausing on the landing, he saw scratches on the door latch, gleaming in the lantern light. An examination showed the iron keyhole curled inward, as if bludgeoned. Warily, he tried his key. It fit clumsily and could not be moved, though it had always turned easily before.

"What the devil?"

Deft use of his knife restored the keyhole's shape, and on his next attempt, the key worked. Knife poised, he opened the door. No one waited behind it. A search of the room revealed no one hiding within, either, so he relocked the door, threw the upper bar into place, and stood, frowning.

Someone had tried to break in and perhaps succeeded. Yet nothing seemed amiss; his cot, like Hardyng's, was undisturbed, and so was his portable desk. Then he remembered his smaller, locked coffer, used to store copies of his letter rallying England and his correspondents' replies to it. Kneeling, he pulled the box from beneath his cot.

Wrenched from the wood, the box's lock hung by a metal shard. *"Damnation!"*

He lifted the lid. Inside, the contents were rifled, several documents torn, and all were out of order. Leafing through them, he nonetheless noticed that there seemed to be as many clean, unsent copies of his letter as before. Nor did any replies appear to be missing. Hardyng would know precisely, though, since he kept a separate tally.

Harry scrambled up and peered below Hardyng's cot. From under a pile of soiled clothing, he retrieved another locked box, containing miscellaneous parchments, including Hardyng's list of respondents to his letter. This was still securely locked, suggesting that the burglar had regarded the mess of unwashed laundry as merely that—a young man's dirty clothing—and not pawed beneath it.

Crossing the room, Harry pulled his large trunk from the wall. Its lock, too, was severed, but it held only his apparel, shaving gear, soap, and towels. Once arranged neatly, everything now lay in a knotty jumble. Again, though, nothing seemed missing. Nor had anyone tried to get into his armor chest, set against the other wall.

Odd. If the culprit had wanted valuables, why hadn't he tried to open the armor chest? Unless the burglar had been searching for documents, like his correspondence—not to steal, but to read. Who would want to do that, though? Dunbar? Perhaps. But could a man already under suspicion be so brazen? Instead, was there another, unknown adversary in his ranks? It seemed unlikely. An enemy Scot? Maybe. The guards were observant, but with so many men coming and going, a resourceful spy might well sneak into camp.

"Hell!" Hastening outside, Harry alerted his aides and doubled the number of sentries.

The following morning, his senior officers convened at an outdoor table, where he awaited them with bread, cheese, and a kettle of Kynge's breakfast herbal infusion. "Where's Dunbar?" Harry wondered, noting one vacant place. The others glanced at each other in ignorance. His gaze fell on Hardyng. "Didn't you inform him?"

"Yea, yesterday, after Gawayn got back. He thanked me and said he'd be here."

"Then he must've overslept, though 'tis hard to see how, with the noise the drovers made bringing those cattle in to replenish our larder." Harry set down his steaming mug. "Someone rouse him. He should be here. I want to discuss Liddesdale."

Hardyng hurried off, to return in a few minutes, excited.

"He's not there, Harry!"

"What?"

"He's cleared out. His tent remains," Hardyng pointed toward a distant line. "So does some of his gear. But his saddlebags and armor are missing. The same with Gawayn. Their horses are gone, too."

Harry got up, followed by the rest. As soon as he neared Dunbar's tent, he knew Hardyng was correct. Dunbar's bivouac was abandoned. He kicked a leather strap left behind in the dirt. "Where the hell has he gone? And why?" Even as he asked, though, he knew; knew, too, that it had been Dunbar who had broken into his chests. Now Dunbar had the names of everyone who had endorsed the call for reforms. Doubtless, too, Dunbar had a copy of his letter. And with those in his possession, there was one place, above all, where he would go: To Henry, bearing accusations of cowardice and treason. Having leveled the same charges the previous autumn and tried to kill him, Henry would be all too willing to accept Dunbar's "evidence."

Harry's throat tightened. Everything over several months suddenly fell into place. Henry's creation of the commission to resolve the hostage issue was only a guise, to lull everyone into thinking he wanted to be conciliatory. Likewise, his grant of the Douglas lands was less a move to put the royal stamp on geographic realities than another ruse, to entice Harry into campaigning in Scotland, where Dunbar could ensure that he died.

He strode off to awaken the men who had been on duty near Dunbar's lines. Groggily, the less tongue-tied of them revealed that Dunbar and Gawayn had left before dawn, citing, "orders from you, Sir, to ride to Lanercost and Hexham on urgent matters."

"I gave no such orders."

"But Lord Dun——"

"'Never mind," Harry interrupted. "You couldn't know. 'Tis not your fault."

Leaving the sentries, he studied the ground, picking up Dunbar's track. It led from the camp onto the main road to Lanercost. There, the hoofprints disappeared, obliterated by the arrival of the drovers and their herd. Reluctantly, Harry gave up.

As he had suspected, though, Dunbar's obliterated route had continued to the first crossroads. But from there it had not proceeded onward to Lanercost and Hexham. Nor had it turned right, southward, toward London and King Henry. Instead, it had turned left—north, in the direction of Edinburgh and the Scottish court.

* * *

King Robert III continued to strongly dislike the expatriate earl of March. They had fallen out after Dunbar had arranged to marry his daughter to Robert's son, Scotland's crown prince, only to see the king subsequently make a more lucrative match with the Douglas clan. Irate, Dunbar had denounced both Robert and Scotland, any and all Douglases, and fled to England, where he also held properties, and where he could get in thick with Henry IV.

Now, however, Dunbar sought an audience with Robert...

Setting personal feelings aside and honoring a promise to Gawayne, who had interceded on George's behalf a week earlier, Robert agreed to listen to whatever George had to say. As he did, he recognized the value of the information Dunbar spilled: Details of Harry's plans; the lords and towns promising levies; troop counts, the number and proficiency of siege engines; the amount of weapons and equipment stockpiled, and more.

"In addition, Sire," Dunbar lied, "King Henry calls you a womanly poltroon who durst not lift a hand to defend Teviotdale or any Scots domain. He longs for 1 August, so he can march to Ormiston and lay claim to them all."

Robert's faded eyes smoldered. "Henry? That usurping bastard? By God, come August, he'll see that day, but not for my surrender or loss of any of our lands. Nay, it shall be the day of *his* doom. I'll destroy him ere he sets one foot inside Cocklaws or anywhere in this realm!" A stooped, oft-sick man with a flowing grey beard, Robert spoke so heatedly that his posture, like his words, hardened in defiant majesty. "He shall have warning forthwith! I'll write to him in my own hand; throw his slanders back at him. 'Womanly poltroon'? Hah!"

Dunbar stared. He had wanted to embolden Robert, but not so thoroughly that Robert contacted Henry, who would thus learn of the falsehoods and might respond by protesting that Robert erred. The earl forced a thin smile. "Truly, my liege, 'twould be beneath your dignity to write to Henry about such drivel. Best not to demean yourself."

"Hmmm." Robert stroked his whiskers. "Aye. And 'twould perhaps be better to keep him guessing, too. Let him wonder about my purpose."

Robert studied his visitor. "Am I correct in assuming that this intelligence you brought, welcome though it is, isn't the sole reason for your trip here?"

"You are correct, sire," Dunbar fell to his knees. "I should like a pardon."

Robert's grizzled jaw dropped.

Unperturbed, Dunbar went on, while the king stood over him.

Once Dunbar had finished, for at least a minute, Robert said nothing. Then the king half smiled. "I remember well that only nine months ago you were seen happily slaying Scotsmen on that blasted hill, Homildon, in Northumberland."

Dunbar swore silently.

"Nonetheless," Robert continued. "Scotland is prepared to offer a pardon—of sorts—for your most serious offenses, as well as for diverse, lesser infractions." He announced his terms, going over each point, and then fixed Dunbar with a fierce look. "These good graces shall, of course, depend on your continued good behavior toward me and my realm. Should you, for example, attempt to deceive me and act in any way in concert with my foe, he who calls himself the fourth Henry of England, all will be ended. As will your life!"

"Of course. Your Majesty has my word."

"Aye, for whatever *that* is worth!"

But Robert motioned to Dunbar to rise, and the two stiffly hugged.

To Dunbar's satisfaction, the king then called in a scribe, who recorded the pardon in writing, though, annoyingly, in it Robert also insisted on royal retention of confiscated Dunbar properties until at least 1405, to guarantee good behavior.

His copy locked in his saddlebag, Dunbar left Edinburgh within the hour, as covertly as he had entered. Crossing the border, he raced south to the English court.

* * *

Late June 1403: Warwick Tower, Cumberland, England

A fortnight after Dunbar disappeared, Harry received a letter from Thomas Percy.

Harry:

You'll soon hear that King Henry is marching to assist you in the surrender of Cocklaws-Ormiston and environs. Do not believe it. He marches forth to seize and execute you. Someone gave him a copy of your letter. Also, Dunbar has returned to court, alleging that you protect the Scots and plot against the English Crown. I, and many others, know it to be lies. But Henry refuses to listen to reason. You cannot stop him from coming north under pretence of helping against the Scots. But you can look to your safety and

A day later, Harry got a note from his friend at the palace:

* * *

Hoping to resolve the situation with the king, Harry left much of his army in place in Cumberland and rode back to Northumberland with his core company. Once again convening them, and other key advisors, he went over Dunbar's attempts to kill him at Cocklaws and the earl's mysterious flight; the warnings from Thomas Percy and Candorinus, and his possible options and actions in response.

"I could leave for Chester and bide there," he told the group, gathered again around the table in the hall. "In Chester and vicinity, I could build support politically and marshal whatever force I need to defend myself. At the same time, though, I dread leaving all we've accomplished here." He got up, pacing in frustration. "We're so close ... *so* close to claiming part of lower Scotland and bringing peace to both sides of the border. So close." Raising a powerful hand, he clenched it, then opened it again, as if letting a phantom escape through his fingers. "Yet it seems 'twill be ruined because of this ... *madness!*"

Slowing his pacing, he turned to his friends again. "But what think you?"

"You mentioned a couple of options: staying here, or fleeing to Cheshire," Kynge commented. "There's a third, as your uncle suggested: Sail for Europe. Turn freelance."

Several of the others concurred.

Why not? Harry wondered silently. He could bring Ciarry along, serve in Flanders or Germany or even Byzantium, like his erstwhile French jousting contemporary Boucicaut. "Sell my sword and shield to the highest bidder, you mean," he said aloud. "Pile up some gold, acquire a castle or manse, and live comfortably enou'."

"Yea," Kynge affirmed. "For your own well-being, consider it."

For several moments, Harry stood there, saying nothing. Then, reclaiming his chair, he sighed. "'Tis considered. And rejected. I can't abandon this land and all it stands for, all I believe in. I've never knowingly shirked my duty, on the field or off. I won't start now."

"E'en so," Douglas put in. "If you don't go abroad, at least quit the North. 'Tis too dangerous if Henry marches here to slay you."

"He'd have to take me first. To take me, he'd have to fight me, and that would mean battle, for I think many of you would fight alongside me."

Every one of them nodded: Douglas and Montgomery, Knayton, Hardyng, Irby, and Kynge; Ciarry, too, along with Bishop Skirlaw and even Robert Stewart of Durisdeer and other Scots captured at Homildon.

"But to fight Henry would mean a great loss of life," Ciarry observed, dark eyes sadly luminous. "Hundreds, perhaps thousands, of innocent men on both sides could perish."

"Aye..."

"And a war on the Borders between Englishmen would only allow the Scots to triumph, not just at Ormiston in August but perhaps for years," Knayton said. "Probably, they'd wait to see who won, you or Henry, and then attack the victor and finish him off—like William the Conqueror did in 1066 with King Harold, after Harold beat Hardraada. Instead of us winning much of lower Scotland, the Scots could seize northern England."

"Aye, I realize that, too..."

"You'd best heed your uncle. You've pulled in recruits by the legion these last few weeks. Depart hence, *with* them—an army," Skirlaw recommended. "That, I suppose, will ruin our chances of holding on to Teviotdale in August, but ... so be it."

Harry frowned. "The army stays here. It has to, to meet the Scots. As you say, to take it with me would end our chances at Cocklaws for certain. I won't do that. I'll not sacrifice all England's gains just because Henry has decided to kill me. Hell. he doubtless decided to do that months ago. Besides, many men in our army came from elsewhere in England to fight the Scots, not go galloping off to Cheshire to save my neck from Henry."

"Most of them would follow you anyway, gladly," Knayton predicted.

"Even so, their place is in the North, defending it and upholding our success in Teviotdale. I won't take them from that."

"Then with or without your army, go hence, Lad!" Montgomery urged. "Do not delay. Over the years, I've grown right fond of your hide, contrary as it be. You mean as much to me as a brother or a son—and mayhap more, even, seeing as you and I started out as enemies and all. Don't deprive me of your company in my old age by letting Henry hang you from your own battlements."

Ciarry winced. "Lord John is right, Harry. If Henry wants to kill you, and I think he does, don't make it easier for him by letting him find you here."

Across the table, Rob Stewart leaned forward. "Yet, as far as that goes, Harry, why *not* confront Henry here, where you know the land like the back of your hand? You could use the terrain, trap him in the Cheviots and compel him to back down, or give battle there and kill him."

Murmurs of approval followed.

"No," Harry demurred. "You're right. I could hole up in the mountains and let Henry come after me. But he might refuse to take the bait. Sooner or later, I'd have to come out, like you had to come down from Homildon. Besides, I could get trapped between hostile armies—the Scots on one front and Henry on the other. No," he concluded regretfully, "'tis probably better for me to make myself scarce, until we can end this peaceably, by resolving things through action by

Parliament. Still, one thing troubles me. If I leave—flee—won't some say I'm a coward? That I ran?"

"Anyone who says that in *my* diocese and does not promptly repent will face chastisement," Skirlaw declared. "Everyone knows that you, of all men, do not lack courage. Besides, would it be flight? Or a tactical retreat, instead? As a commander, you know that at times retreat is inevitable, the only way to ensure ultimate victory. That's what you'd be doing, pulling back out of harm's way now to save lives, including your own, to ensure a greater victory—we hope, a peaceful victory—later."

"Most of us can accompany you, too," Douglas added. "I, for one. Since I can't be part of whatever happens at Ormiston, on *either* side," he chuckled lightly, "I'm free to put myself at your service wherever you need me. And if worse comes to worst, with battle, 'twill allow me to kill Englishmen. *Bad* Englishmen," he amended, "for your opponents in this are mine, and Scotland's too, verily."

Montgomery nodded. "I, too, shall ride with you, right proudly," he pledged, and Rob Stewart and the other Scots volunteered as well. So did Skirlaw and all the rest, though Harry ordered a few to remain behind, to help lead the northern army.

Knayton counted mentally. "By my reckoning, e'en without taking a single man from those we've mustered for August, we've at least seven-score horse. God willing, that should be enou' to get you to Chester safely."

"Aye. 'Tis far too small for an army, but makes a fine escort." Harry looked into each face again. "That is your consensus?"

"Aye," Gerry Salvayn began, and they went around the table, assenting.

"Then we'd best leave within the week," Harry decided.

"Why not immediately?" Hardyng asked.

"Because I must talk to my father. I can't hope to

succeed without his backing."

"He, above all, would never deny it," Skirlaw predicted.

Harry smiled ruefully. "You don't know my father!"

* * *

Late June 1403: Warkworth Castle, Northumberland, England

The Earl of Northumberland flexed his thick brows. "I understand why you're upset, Harry. But I'm not certain that you face a real threat, or need any of my troops. Besides, you said yourself that we must keep the border army in place to await the Scots' decision."

"Aye! Those aren't the men I mean. I'm asking you to call up your levies from southern Yorkshire, Essex, and your other lands—all those who haven't already started northward to assist us at Cocklaws. I want them to meet me in Cheshire."

"I don't like sending men on a wild goose chase."

"This *is* no wild goose chase. And 'tis not merely me who worries. Your own brother and at least one man at Henry's court think likewise." Harry pointed at the messages sent by his uncle and Candorinus. "Read."

Leaning over his parlor table, Earl Henry studied the parchments, then threw them down, perilously close to the fire. "Even so, I suspect you're overreacting. And I wish to hell my overwrought brother and this Assininus or whatever he calls himself..."

"Candorinus," Harry interrupted, retrieving the notes.

"Whatever. I wish they had exercised restraint.

204

Thomas resigned all his offices, too, curse him—and so soon after Henry appointed him as tutor to Prince Hal. That was an act that demonstrated that, however mad he is at you, the king still thought well of this family." The earl scowled. "Nor did your letter-writing help. You knew that Henry has tortured and hanged men for less. Still, you persisted. Your damned-fool pride convinced you that only you could rally England and begin righting all the wrongs in it!"

"Someone had to," Harry replied. "Henry could've done so much good, had he limited himself to his proper role as high steward, correcting Richard's rotten governance. Instead, he let his avarice get the better of him and schemed to claim the throne himself. And since he's had it, he's only gotten worse."

He tapped an ornate book of Scripture lying in an ambry near his father. "Remember what it says in the Gospel: 'What does it profit a man who gains the whole world but suffers the loss of his soul?' That's what Henry has done. He's gained the whole blasted world, or nearly so. He's got the crown, power, jewels, land, gold. But he's lost his own soul—his principles, his decency and kindliness, his sense of virtue, all that was noble and honorable about him. He's ruined himself as a man. I can't let him ruin this country, too!"

Earl Henry snorted. "So, like some new St. George, *you* are going to save England. Single-handedly!"

"Not alone. That's why I wrote those letters, why I continue to write letters, why I rode hither and yon for months. I acted only with the consultation of learned and wise men, including Archbishop Scrope, Bishop Skirlaw, Bishop Trevor in Wales, and even Archbishop Arundel of Canterbury."

"Who are all behaving like a passel of high-minded fools," the earl retorted.

"And I only acted because Henry forced me to, "Harry continued. "I questioned his policies, and he tried to stab me. Then he assigned that dastard of a bastard Dunbar to commit burglary and murder for him."

The earl sighed. "You can't be certain 'twas Dunbar who broke into your locked boxes. Nor even that he was the one who tried to slay you in your tent. Or that the shooting by his archers was anything but an accident."

"No, I can't irrefutably prove anything. But the evidence points to him."

Earl Henry slowly nodded. "That I grant you. But it doesn't help if you go making it out to be worse than it might be. I think you should give both Henry and Dunbar the benefit of the doubt until there's indisputable proof."

"By then, how much more damage will Henry inflict? And by then, I might be dead. You'd have your proof, though: My corpse, knifed in the back. Or swinging from a gibbet!"

"Enough!" The earl covered his ears and slumped in his chair. But his face had paled, and it was a shaking hand that he lifted to wave his son away. "I want to think. Go run around the walls or something, like you did as a boy when you were angry."

Harry left.

Seated on the slope near the postern tower, hands on his knees, chin atop interlaced fingers, he gazed at the river, pondering. *Father's mistaken. He wants to believe the best, perhaps because he's frightened and the worst is too awful to contemplate. He wants to enjoy his old age, not worry that my actions could destroy everything, including me. He's happy here at Warkworth, putting his hoary head together with his master builder, planning his architecture. He still likes court life, too, especially being on the Privy Council, whether Henry bothers to consult him or not... Damnation!*

Footsteps scrunched the grass.

With an apologetic smile, Earl Henry settled

206

himself on the lawn, looping an arm over Harry's shoulder. "All right, son. I was rather intemperate; I'm sorry. I do think you, Thomas, and this silly monk at court exaggerate the danger. But I'm prepared to send you as much aid as you need, *if* there comes a time when you truly need it."

"What's that mean?"

"That if you get to Cheshire and find the situation with Henry has deteriorated, notify me. I'll call out the levies and dispatch them to you."

"There might not be enough time."

"I think there will be, because I don't think you'll need them at all. Henry is desperate to play the conqueror. I've written twice to tell him his presence isn't required at Ormiston. 'Struth, he'll only complicate everything! But he pays no heed. He doesn't want to miss a chance to wallow in glory, like a pig in the shallows on a hot afternoon." His eyes lit in amusement. "Sooo... He'll come north. I'll greet him worthily. He won't find you here, of course. Nevertheless, he'll be so distracted by the chance to claim Teviotdale and lord it over the Scots that he won't care. His dislike of you may be large, but far larger is his conceit. For once, it may actually serve us."

Harry pondered. "Perhaps... I still fear, though, that if I *do* need your help, there will be too little time to get it."

His father sighed. "On that we must differ. I just hope I'm right and you're not."

Harry laughed at the irony. "'Tis not oft I pray I'm wrong, but so do I!"

"Nevertheless, carry this." Earl Henry held out a ring, incised with his coat-of-arms and name and title. "Use it if you truly must, with formal declarations or writs, for instance. Famed or not, you're only a knight. Men reluctant to listen to Sir Harry may heed the man who's Earl of Northumberland and Constable of England."

"Should I use it if I communicate with Henry, too?"

The earl groaned. "If it's absolutely imperative. But only after your uncle has vetted what you write. He's more diplomatic than you."

"Aye," Harry acknowledged, stowing the ring. "I'm grateful for it—and for whatever men you send, if I need them."

"But I assure you, you won't!"

* * *

June 1403: Tower House, Northumberland

At Dogmael's bark, Ciarry peered from the barn. "Dearest!" She ran forward.

Leaning from his horse, Harry kissed her and dismounted to wrap her in his arms—only to stiffen.

"You've cut your hair!" He brushed his hand over her boyish locks, as short as on the day they had met nearly three years earlier.

"The better to go with you and pass as your squire." She looked up at him. "Enochie helped me get chainmail and a sword, like a proper squire. But if necessary, I can join MacKerny's bowmen."

Harry's face clouded.

"You know I'm a good shot," she added, seeing his reaction. "I can out-shoot a lot of your men."

"Doubtless!" He gave her a kiss.

"And I ride as well as any squire."

"Better than many a knight." He kissed her again.

"Besides, you don't want to leave me."

"Never."

"And Agnes, and Enochie and his father, and Sister Etheldreda have promised to keep the farm while I'm away, which, God willing, will be but a few weeks. So 'tis settled!"

"No, Lass."

"What?"

"No."

"Huh ... but?"

He shut his eyes, holding her, feeling her heart beating against his own. He *didn't* want to leave her; that'd be the hardest thing he'd ever done. And *'twould* be easy to bring her along.

But he couldn't.

"You can't come, Lass, as much as I want you with me."

"But why not? Why deny me, when it means so much to me?"

"Because 'tis too dangerous."

"I don't care!"

"I know, Ciarry, but I can't allow it. It's not only risk to you that I fear, but to *me*." He struggled to explain. "If ... if you come, I'll worry about you. I know—" Anticipating her protest, he touched his finger to her lips. "—I know: You'll say you can look after yourself. And you *would* look after yourself as much as anyone can. Still, I would fret over you.

"I love you, Lass! More than I've ever loved anyone else. Even if I *tried* not to worry about you any more than I do about my other aides, all staunch friends, I would *still* worry—because I love you so deeply, as a man loves a woman, not just as he loves a friend, and because you *are* a woman." He brushed tears from each of her eyes.

"You see, Lass, if it comes to battle with Henry, my every instinct as a man would be to protect you. Yet if I'm doing that, I can't be doing all the other things I must do in war. At least, I couldn't do them as well as I would otherwise. And if I'm not at my peak, doing my very best, fighting at the fore, guiding my men with all the power in my mind and heart, as well as all the strength in my body, then I shall be very much in jeopardy—and my men, too."

He toyed with a wisp of hair on her forehead. "Does that make any sense?"

She nodded, dropping her head against his chest. "I ... I think... so."

"Thus you must stay behind ... where I know you'll be safe." He raised her tear-stained face. "Right?"

"I ... I suppose," she answered.

He caught the hesitation. "And you *will* stay behind when I go?"

"*Ummm ...*"

"That means..." A knowing look crossed his face. "... You won't try anything on your own, such as following us in a day or two, to catch up at some point where 'tis impossible for me to send you back. You won't try anything like that, will you?"

"I ... guess not." Already, the idea had been running through her mind.

"Nonetheless, you'd like to!" he grinned. "So, I'll help you avoid temptation. As your lord—remember, you took me as your lord, when we first came to Tower House—"

She nodded.

"—As your lord, then, I *order* you to remain here. And as my vassal, you must obey. Right?"

"Aye..."

"So you promise?"

"I promise."

"Good!"

They smiled at each other.

"I ... I understand, Harry," she added. "'Twas foolish to think I could join you. I should have known it would only hurt you more. I'm sorry."

He kissed her brow. "Shhh. I only regret we must talk like this, about being separated this way. But I'm also very happy, and honored, that you love me so much you'd want to accompany me into such peril."

He lifted her into his arms. "Let's go inside and, later, into the hills. 'Tis a fine day for a walk..."

After supper that evening, he presented her with

a sheet of parchment, densely inscribed and very official-looking.

"What's this?" She pushed her goblet aside.

"The deed to the remaining Tower House property in my name, in case there's any trouble and the king decides to confiscate my lands and chattel."

"You mean... if you're arrested, or ... killed."

"Aye," he said softly.

"But how could you sell me everything when we've made no transaction?"

"In a few steps. The Premonstratensians bought my share for one shilling, seven pence. They sold it for the same amount to the prior of Brinkburn. He in turn sold it to you—and I acted as the agent in your name. I could do that through the power of attorney, under the provisions we made when you first came here. I didn't think you'd object."

"No, but..." Too much was happening, too much too sad and horrible and frightening...

"I didn't want to tell you and alarm you if 'twere all for naught," Harry explained. "Alas, 'tis not. I could die. And unlike all the other times I've gone off to face danger, this time it comes not just from battle but from the possibility that I—and mine—could lose everything in forfeiture if Henry kills me."

She shuddered. "Oh God..."

"I know." He reached across the table. "But if you hold clear title to Tower House and all its lands, he shouldn't be able to harm you."

Leaning down, through fresh tears, she kissed his hand, encased around hers.

* * *

Sunset of his second day caught them lingering in the garden, where he took her in his arms once more.

"I leave on the morrow, Ciarry. Probably I'll

return. Yet if I don't, we will still be together, still be one. You know that, don't you?"

"Yea, but..." Trembling, she pulled away, eyes focused on him, as if every instant he was in her sight might be the last. Then she whirled and ran toward the yard, wanting only to escape to some place where he might follow, but all that they feared could not.

In a few paces, he caught up, hand on her shoulder.

"Oh, Lass, can you not see?" He turned her around to face him. "War can kill my body, death can claim what you see standing here before you, but nothing can e'er kill my spirit and my love for you, *nothing*, ever."

Choking back tears, she nodded.

Arm around her, he led her back to the garden and held her again, speaking softly, finding reassurance for himself as he tried to comfort her.

"Naught could e'er truly take me from you, Lass, or you from me. Not time, nor distance, nor evil, nor death itself." He kissed her cheek and ran his finger down her neck, smiling through his own sorrow. "I... I've tried to tell you this before, and I say it again. Because—because *'tis* true. Because I know it, as surely as I know my own name, and that there is a God, and that He is good. I am always part of you, Ciarry, always with you. And I will always be part of you, and with you, no matter what befalls."

"I know. I love you, Harry, so very much..."

"Aye." He paused, picking his way through his emotions. "So you must promise me that even if I am slain, and if, despite my precautions, Henry seizes this farm, you'll keep going. As I said afore, I don't think he'd be able to reach you. But, if he somehow succeeds, you must go on, keep striving, with hope afore you."

She lifted her head from his shoulder. "How could I go on, much less with hope? I'd have lost everything dear. I'd have lost you; that alone is more than I could bear. Oh, I know, I've always been told how strong I am. Perhaps it's true. I might ... might be able to endure here, on the farm, without you. But for God's sake, Harry, how could I go on without this land, too? I would be twice cursed, twice dead. I'd rather I were dead."

He took a step back, dark-blue eyes insistent, hands gripping her upper arms. "Never say that, Lass. You *must* go on, even without me and without this land. To give up would be to allow deceit, evil, and injustice to triumph. No! You must go on, for me."

He gestured around the garden, to the flowers and fruit arbor where their dead babes lay, to the stream burbling in its grassy bank, to woodlands and mountains beyond, on to the far horizon, and when he spoke, his voice coursed with quiet fervor.

"And where'er you may be—here, or anywhere—Lass, look out on the glory of this earth, and honor it, for *'tis* a beautiful place. Let naught close your eyes and heart to that. There is so much wonder here, so much joy, so much to treasure in and of itself, so much good in this creation God has given us—aye, and in most persons, too."

He smiled wryly. "I realize I sound like some prattling bard, but I've seen such futility and destruction, so much blood on so many fields, so much horror, that each thing I see of beauty—well, 'tis like a resurrection for me, each thing, in itself so small, and yet so important. Don't turn away from it if I die, Ciarry. Cherish it, for me..."

Solemnly, she squeezed his hand.

"Remember what you told me when we met?" he continued. "That when I'm not with you, I must walk strong and tall, as I've ever done, but even more so? That's how you must walk, Ciarry, strong and tall, as you always have done, and with my love always with you, even if I am gone."

A faint laugh escaped her. "I can't walk tall, Harry. I'm too damn short!"

He chuckled, even as anguish showed in his eyes.

"Oh Ciarry, how brave you really are. You *do* walk tall, with a stature that men with far more height than you can never attain. Remember that and remember God, for 'tis He who brought us together, and has given us strength. And 'tis He who will remain with us: I in you, and you in me, and God in both of us, and with our love, always."

"Yea."

A bittersweet smile crossed his face. "Now, let's wander awhile. The stars are starting to come out, and it looks to be a marvelous night. Let's see how many we can count."

"Yea," she answered. "But only if we make a wish on each one..."

* * *

Shortly after daybreak, hoofbeats on the road heralded the arrival of his escort. Within minutes Knayton and Hardyng were at the door.

"Everyone's here," Knayton said, "your usual complement, plus Douglas and Montgomery and Rob Stewart and the Scots, with a few more levies from their estates. And I've got MacKerny and two dozen of his best archers, all mounted. Whene'er you're ready, we can be off." They tromped back down the Tower House stairs.

Ciarry and Harry looked at each other. He wore his chainmail and thigh-length tabard, but his sword belt still hung on the wall.

She took a few steps toward it. Lifting the scabbard, she drew the shining blade, bringing it to her lips. Slowly, she sheathed it again, knelt, and strapped it around him, quoting Psalm 45: *Gird your sword at your side, and in splendor and majesty ride on ... in the cause of truth, gentleness and*

214

righteousness.

One last time, he lifted her into his arms for a kiss. Then, tearing himself away, he hurried into the yard. Mounted, he wheeled Valdus and paused, waving. "I love you!"

Turning again, he trotted out the gate. His men closed ranks around him, and he was gone.

Chapter X

July 1403: England and Wales

From Northumberland, they rode through Cumberland and into Lancashire, watching warily and bypassing the city of Lancaster. Even among his own, though, King Henry was increasingly unpopular and from Lancashire, too, knights and men-at-arms stole away to join Harry. All they knew was that he had dared question the king and now was in trouble, having abandoned his triumphant army in the north to ride quickly and quietly west.

It was all they needed to link their dissatisfaction to his.

Others, too, joined en route, and by the time he reached Wales, Harry felt cautiously encouraged. Pausing at Denbigh, he wrote anew to everyone who had promised support, urging them to make good on their pledges. Again, he focused on their backing for any proceedings at court and in Parliament, though he raised the possibility of military aid, too, should circumstances warrant it. He had mixed feelings about the likely response. 'Twas one thing to offer assistance from a safe distance when it was primarily a question of political alliances; 'twas another to provide help when he was on the run and risked execution or battle.

So far, though, the king was heading northward from Windsor as scheduled, lending credence to the Earl of Northumberland's prediction: Henry wanted to preside over a Scottish surrender more than he wanted to confront Harry. Relieved, Harry interspersed letter-writing with other tasks at Denbigh—getting horses shod and laundry scrubbed;

enlisting tenants and neighbors, both Welsh and English, in his cause; mustering levies, and verifying that castles still under his command were armed, victualed and on alert, not just against Henry but against Glyn Dwr, who might take advantage of English disunity and strike.

From Denbigh, too, one morning, Harry cantered to St. Asaph's and Bishop Trevor, who promised not only continued civic and ecclesial drum-rolling but at least 1,300 men from his diocese.

"They're arraying now," said Trevor, a middle-aged man of medium height and well-honed build. "They'll meet you in Chester. When do you expect to be there?"

"St. Evergilda's day. From Denbigh, I'm first going to Flint."

Trevor nodded. "By then, we should be in very good shape. Our men are fit and eager. You can keep them as long as you wish."

"I owe you much."

Trevor shook his tawny, close-cropped head. "No, Harry, 'tis we—English and Welsh alike—who owe you much." His light-brown eyes lit up impishly. "I'll be leading my force myself, by the way. My mace waits in readiness."

Harry laughed. "Another bishop ignoring the church ban on clergy taking up arms!"

"Few rules are so set in stone as to be inviolate under all conditions. Anyway, you Borderers should be familiar with the 'church militant'," Trevor quipped. "Edward I had Bishop Anthony Beck, and Robert the Bruce had Bishop Sinclair. Then there were the monks who marched out from their abbeys against intruders over the years."

"Some fought alongside my forebears, too," Harry remarked. "Likewise, my own chaplain has been known to take up a weapon. And Bishop Skirlaw joined me last week, replete with armor."

Trevor grinned again. "Excellent! I look forward

to seeing him. But I must tell you one thing more about the force I'm mustering. It's both English and Welsh, including men who'd been with Glyn Dwr and are considered traitors to England. They've always been good to me, though, and promptly answered my call."

Harry shrugged. "I'll gladly accept every man willing to follow my command and the rules of war and who seeks the common good. Anything else we can sort out later—including who's *really* a traitor."

"Amen! But for the moment..." Trevor steered Harry toward the cloister. "You're in time for Mass and then lunch. And for that you can have your pick of the fishpond."

* * *

Friday, 6 July 1403: Flint Castle, Wales

A shadowy figure in armor glided from the chapel.

"My Lord." A Welsh-French knight, Yvon Jacques Giscardier, hailed Harry.

They had met twice before: In 1401 at Cadair Idris, when Harry had defeated a Welsh insurgent force, partly led by Giscardier; then again a year later, when Giscardier, who had briefly returned to France after the battle, had rejoined Glyn Dwr and helped launch the negotiations with Harry that had produced the treaty King Henry rejected.

"I come from Lord Owain." Giscardier stripped off a gauntlet and extended his hand.

Amazed, Harry shook it. "How did you get so far into my castle as to visit the chapel—near my own quarters, too? So much for my guards!"

Yvon chuckled. "Actually, they were quite diligent." He rubbed a bruised cheek. "I got a sword in my face ere I could explain my mission. But when I insisted I'd come in peace, they sent for John Hardyng. You were otherwise engaged. Hardyng remembered me and let me wait here—and was most apologetic for being too busy to entertain me."

"All my men have been under a heavy burden. So have I."

"Perhaps I can help relieve it." Yvon smiled. "I've come to join your company, with four knights bachelor, half a dozen squires, 150 men-at-arms, and 75 archers, with Lord Owain's blessing, if you want us."

Harry's eyes brightened. "E'en so?"

"Yea. But that's not the only reason I came." Yvon offered a parchment. "Lord Owain ordered me to deliver this to you alone."

Ripping its seal, Harry read:

*Lord Harry: I have seen the
letter you sent around England and
know that your intentions are good,
not only in regard to your realm but
to Wales. I remain willing to make
peace with England, if it be a true
and honest peace. That is what you
proposed. Perhaps a generous God
will yet bless our desires. To that
end, I hereby declare an immediate
cease-fire with you and yours: all in
Wales and the adjacent shires or
counties of England under your
jurisdiction. Holdings controlled by
King Henry get no such protection. I
know you're unfairly beset by Henry,
largely because of your sense of
justice toward Wales and your
refusal to seize me in ill-faith and
slay me. You protected me, at risk of
your own life. To reciprocate as best*

Harry's astonishment grew. "I'm grateful—*very* grateful!"

"As Owain is to you. I as well. You brought me my wife."

"I did?"

"Yea. Remember Gwynaith? You found her, sore distressed in Caernarvonshire, two years past. You doubtless saved her life."

Memories of devastation, of a haggard woman and hungry bairn flooded Harry's mind. "Raiders had struck, slaying her kin and destroying their family farmstead," he recalled. "I sent her and a child to Bishop Trevor, under my protection."

"Yea. Bishop John took her in and then, seeing her intelligence and skills, made her sub-cellarer for the cathedral. As you probably know, the bishop has converted the church enclave there into a shelter for refugees displaced by the fighting. Last winter, to succor them, Owain bade me deliver money and goods to it. Gwynaith and I met and fell in love. We wed in Eastertide and adopted her nephew, Yolo, as ours."

"Congratulations!" Harry slapped him on the back.

"Gwynaith sends her esteem."

"She has mine in return. Long may you prosper."

"And Wales and England, around us," Yvon added.

"Aye." Harry led him down the stairs. "Now, let

me introduce you to my captains."

* * *

Whether English or Welsh, the people of Flint had always been loyal to Harry, and he left with commitments from another 1,200 men to join him in Chester. Crossing back into England on 9 July, he took up residence in Chester Castle with most of his aides, though one, Jan Kingsley, stayed with his mother, Petronilla Clark, a prosperous glover and leather merchant. Several others soon decamped from the castle to follow, turning her spacious home into a squires' lair, with ample drink, food, and her motherly presence.

On 12 July, Thomas Percy arrived with warm greetings and wagons of armor, weapons, gear, and—equally welcome—money, partly raised by selling furnishings from his London house. He brought more troops, too: knights, men-at-arms, archers, and infantry from his Worcester domains, along with a notable contingent who had abandoned the armies of Prince Hal.

Harry whistled. "They left Hal's ranks? Does he know?"

"He must, by now."

"How the—?"

"Some of his men had served with me in South Wales. I contacted a few knights I knew to be sympathetic. Now they're here and I'm here." Thomas watched a squad of archers trot by on their way to practice. "How's your mustering going?"

"Overall, well. I only brought MacKerny and 24 of his best archers, but there are scores of able and willing bowmen in Cheshire—plus those Glyn Dwr sent. I've drawn quite a few men-at-arms and knights, too, the cream of Cheshire, though we could use more.

I guess the others don't see the urgency. Even so, our numbers increase daily." Harry wanted to sound optimistic. "In the past, you may have heard me mention Hugh Browe, my chief deputy in Wales. He's done a remarkable job recruiting, too, assisted by two local men, Lords Vernon Venables and Jan Kingsley. We have about 6,700 men, most arrayed and awaiting summons."

Thomas rubbed his chin. "That's a hell of a lot more than you had a fortnight ago. But we still have much work ahead."

Harry's eyes closed in weary resignation. "I know…"

* * *

He had assigned scouts to track Henry's movements, as he assumed Henry had done in regard to him. The evening of the 13th, one rode in to announce that the day previous, Henry had closed the seaports—an act invariably taken to keep traitors from fleeing the country. Shortly before midnight on the 14th, another arrived on a much-lathered horse, with more news: Alleging rebellion, Henry had openly denounced Harry that afternoon. Ceasing his march north to join the action against the Scots at Cocklaws, the king instead swung abruptly west, straight at them.

"This is what the Crown declared." The courier handed Harry a sheet, and as his uncle, aides, and Douglas crowded around, Harry read aloud:

Nottingham, the 14th day of July:
The King is on his way to Chester
and Wales to meet Harry Percy, who
has risen in rebellion and passed

"Damn him!" Fury filled Harry's face. "I'm no traitor or rebel and lead no revolt!"

"There's more," the courier said. "He's got a full army, upwards of 16,000 men, and is issuing proclamations like that to every town and shire in England. Also—I know, having met one of his riders at a tavern—he has written to prominent men in Cheshire and beyond, spreading lies, saying he doesn't know why you're doing what you do and that he wishes only to be reconciled with you."

"The hell!" Harry exclaimed.

"A royal messenger told you that?" Thomas Percy asked the courier.

"Yea, My Lord. I bought him ale, without telling him who I was. Whilst he was well into his cups, kissing the tits of the slattern in his lap, I peeked into his bag and opened one of his letters. I copied it—'twas what you've just read, Sir Harry. And in another message, the king claimed he had sent emissaries, bidding you to meet him and restore your friendship."

"No emissaries came," Harry said tersely.

"No, and won't either," Thomas Percy interjected.

"He *says* he wants peace, Harry. But he raises armies against you," Douglas noted.

"Aye! The lying fraud!"

Like his companions, Harry had been awakened and wore only his robe. Rushing back to his chamber, he flung the robe aside, dove into his chest, pulled on underwear and stockings, and tossed leggings, shirt and tunic on the floor. Hardyng and Knayton sprang forward to assist, but he motioned them away. "I can do this myself. I need you for more important tasks." He nodded toward the doorway.

"Have Kynge get one of his infusions brewing to wake us all up. Send someone over to Petronilla's to roust out Kingsley, Irby, Roger, and anybody else over there making merry. Also, send someone to the abbey for Trevor and Skirlaw. Fetch your writing kit, too, John. We've urgent messages to draft. I want all those reserves pledged to us called up immediately. We'll likewise notify Glyn Dwr. I'll need his aid, if I can get it. And dispatch someone to my father. He's *got* to send his levies."

The castle sprang to life, torches and lanterns flickering from cellars to stables to ramparts, obliterating the night.

"It's clear what Henry has done," Thomas told Douglas, near dawn, as they relayed more letters to riders in the courtyard. "Henry's march north was a ruse, as Harry suspected. The moment Henry got far enough from Windsor to be as far north as we are here, he turned hard west to hunt Harry down."

Douglas nodded. "Harry's own father didn't believe him. Now I worry that whatever Earl Henry does—if anything—'twill be too late."

"Yea." Thomas agreed dourly. "For that, I will curse my brother till the end of my days."

The next morning, from Chester Castle, Harry addressed the townsfolk, who filled the courtyard, spilling through the gate into streets beyond. In armor except for helmet and gauntlets, he stood on the stairs outside the great hall.

Quill poised, parchments across his lap, Brother Gildas, Hardyng's friend from the abbey, scrunched in a corner of a wall, determined to record every word for his chronicles, heedless of the crowd nearly trampling him.

Harry motioned them to silence and began: "My Friends, I come before you today as I have so oft before.

This time, though, is different, and not only because 'tis Sunday, the Lord's own. Today, I'm here not only as your justice. I'm here because I *seek* justice. For that, I need help, *your* help. Never did I expect to appeal to you this way. But never have I confronted what faces me now."

He looked out over the crowd, full of serious and often incredulous faces.

"Four years ago, I rode into Chester to take up my office. You had every reason to resent me, for I followed Henry Bolingbroke. He had marched against King Richard, whom some of you held high, and most considered your own..."

Shouts of assent arose. Gildas' pen paused momentarily.

"Yet you welcomed me," Harry went on. "You gave me your friendship—a friendship I consider one of the greatest honors of my life. Then, I came at the behest of Henry Bolingbroke. Now I come fleeing him. So how could I have backed him that summer? Doubtless, you can guess; you, too, endured King Richard's reign. Many say Richard held Cheshire in great favor. As you knew, though, his favor offered too little and his terror exacted too much. For all his charm and splendor, Richard was a very bad king..."

Harry outlined Richard's misgovernance and the outcry for change it had spawned, as heads in his audience nodded. "I, too, endorsed those demands for reform," Harry told them. "Like many of you, I wanted to make things better. In doing so, I didn't seek to *end* Richard's rule; I sought to *improve* it. Thus, like many, I welcomed Henry Bolingbroke's return. Henry, too, had been foully cheated by Richard and sought redress. Moreover, by heredity, he was the high steward of England. 'Twas both his obligation and his privilege to lead us. And he swore a solemn oath that he would never seek the throne himself."

Pausing, Gildas pulled out a clean sheet as a sad look crossed Harry's face.

"I believed him," Harry said. "I trusted him. And unwittingly, I became one of those most responsible for the expulsion of Richard from the palace and the admission of Henry to it. I believed it would be good for England, and good to give Henry a role. But he not only claimed his rightful authority as steward, he usurped the throne to rule directly. And he proved to be even worse than what we had afore—worse than Richard! In time, I realized that I had erred grievously. And I determined, and still intend, to correct my error by demanding what we should have had in 1399.

"Now I stand here before you, as afore. But to King Henry, I'm not Harry Percy, justice of Chester, or warden of the Eastern March in Northumberland, or knight of the Garter, or anything good and worthy. To Henry, I'm a traitor—a *traitor!*"

Even months after Henry had first flung the epithet at him, Harry's voice rang with incredulity and hurt. Gildas glanced up, though his fingers continued to fly across the page.

"Our liege has raised an army to destroy me," Harry went on. "My treason? I know not, since I haven't been judged and convicted by my peers, which is the only way a man can be rightly called a traitor. But my so-called 'treason' seems to be that I dared to question Henry. I dared speak out against wrong. As an officer of the law, as a knight sworn to serve this realm, as a God-fearing man, I could do no less.

"What were the king's wrongs? These..." Harry proceeded down the list, including the order to kill Glyn Dwr, which he explained at some length. Having heard the account previously from Hardyng, Gildas added a margin note to himself to fill in the details later. Flexing his fingers, he rested until Harry's inflexion warned him to pick up his pen again.

"Twice King Henry and I quarreled over the treatment of Glyn Dwr," Harry told the crowd. "We also argued about other matters. At our last meeting, he struck me with his fist. He called me a whoreson and a traitor. He tried to stab me. I refused to strike back. Nonetheless, I have continued to challenge him. How? At the point of my sword?"

Harry rested his hand on the hilt.

"No!"

He withdrew his hand.

"With the quill of my pen! With letters, like those I sent to town elders here, urging others to join me. Our aim? Not revolt, but reform; not to depose a ruler but to defend a realm."

"*Hurrah!*" Spontaneous endorsements erupted.

"God save you, Sir!"

"Hey-ho, Hotspur!"

"All for Sir Harry!"

Cheers reverberated off the castle walls, echoing up the lanes. Gildas duly noted everything.

Slowly, Harry resumed. "Aye! You understand why I'm here. Here, too, are you, debating whether to heed my call. Let me be precise about it. It isn't, truly, a summons to arms. I seek your weapons and strength. But even more, I seek your hearts, your convictions, your love for this land. I hope that will be power enou'. I want to resolve my differences peaceably. Unfortunately, it seems King Henry wishes to kill me. I pray I won't have to fight. But I *will* protect myself, and England, and all I hold dear. And I *will* stand up for what I want."

"What is that?"

He looked out over the multitude.

"For men to be free: Free to assemble, as we do today. Free to speak and write without fear of having their tongues yanked out and their heads chopped off. Free to wander the roads, as the Franciscans were wont to do for alms, without being unjustly accused of abetting enemies and hanged. I want men to be free of taxation without representation, imposed illegally, without permission of Parliament; free of inequality and corruption on high; free of futile wars that set Welsh against English. I want men to be free to plow their fields, craft their goods, sell their wares, and fill their fishing nets without brigands in royal livery taking everything as fees or charges. I want them to be free to choose their own representatives to Parliament, without threat of ruffians from the king trying to force a vote for Henry's fawning favorites. In short, I want them—*us*—to be free to partake of the very liberties we English have long considered ours. These are ours to enjoy, as our right and privilege. But it is our duty to defend them. That is what I am trying to do. That is *all* I am trying to do. I pray that you will help me."

In conclusion, he raised his hand in salute. "May God keep you."

Whistles, shouts, clapping, and foot-stomping rolled across the area. Before his address, Harry had 7,500 soldiers. By nightfall, he had more than 10,000.

* * *

A day later, the specter of Richard II threatened to ruin everything. Accompanied by Bishops Skirlaw and Trevor, Harry was en route to Davenham and Vale Royal Abbey when Irby and Douglas chased them down.

"My Lord," Irby began. "Some of the local men you assigned to the mustering are telling everyone that King Richard is alive, riding to join you. They're saying folk can meet him at Chester Castle, or Sandiway, when you rally the countryside there."

"Huh?"

"It's that idiot Jan Kingsley and the like. They say that Richard isn't dead, that he's due here anon."

"What?"

Harry regarded the bishops. "I've got to return to Chester. I'm sorry..."

"Be off," Trevor replied. "We can find our own way

to Davenham. You go exorcise the shade of Richard."

With Douglas and Irby, Harry rode back to town, venting frustration. "I can't believe, after what I said yesterday, criticizing Richard, anyone could expect him, dead *or* alive."

"Maybe because you didn't specifically say he's dead, they thought he must be alive," Irby suggested.

"And since you said Henry is worse than Richard, perhaps they decided that Richard could rule anew, on his return," Douglas added.

"If so," Harry asserted, "'twill be the greatest Second Coming this side of Christ's!"

Upon reaching the castle, he raced up the steps, followed by Douglas, past throngs of men waiting to enter. Others milled within. Brushing past them as well, he found Kingsley and two of Lord Venable's squires, at a table, enrolling enlistees to his force.

"Good morning, gentlemen," Harry forced himself to be civil. "On the road to Davenham, I heard that you've landed the most laudable recruit of all: The ghost of King Richard!"

"Not his ghost." Kingsley lurched to his feet. "Richard himself!"

Venable's men arose, too. "'Tis true, My Lord," the senior squire said. "I've a letter from him. It came to my brother, parson of a parish over t' Pulford." He pulled a document from his tunic.

Harry read:

My people: Know that I live and will soon be amongst you to reclaim my rightful rule. Prepare yourselves well and with joy for that most glorious day.

Richard, King of England

On good parchment, the writing resembled Richard's. Yet...

Hanging loose at the edge of the page, the wax stamp caught Harry's attention. He fingered it carefully before walking outdoors, alone, to examine it by daylight. It *looked* like Richard's, though it had a few oddly incised wavy lines.

"Hell!"

Once, within these same walls, he had fingered the seal capable of making such an imprint. That day, in 1399, he had prevented a mob from hanging two of Richard's henchmen. On searching the pair's belongings, he had found a fake royal signet. A ring whose top was inscribed with the king's official seal, the signet was used to stamp certain types of royal writs and letters. Since 1399, Harry had sometimes wondered if such fake 'King Richard' seals would ever be used. Obviously, now one *was* being used. By well-meaning fools, trying to serve Richard?

Or...

What if King Henry was behind this? What if his corrupt cronies were using the fake signet to sow confusion and feed disillusionment—which could certainly occur, if the public thought Harry represented a returning King Richard, but the expected Richard never materialized.

Re-entering the hall, Harry threw the letter down.

"This is a forgery, stamped by a counterfeit seal. I know because four summers ago, right here, I confiscated a signet ring with such a seal."

Venables' men and Kingsley looked dumbfounded. "But ... My Lord, it seems so genuine," the senior squire sputtered.

"It is not."

"There are reports as well, Sir Harry," the junior Venables squire added. "I heard them from burghers, who heard them from fishermen, who got them from Scottish boatmen. King Richard dwells as King Robert's guest in Scotland."

Harry's fist slammed the table so hard the recruiters' inkpot spilled. "I tell you, Richard is dead! I saw his body myself. And Henry killed him and maybe behind these bogus tales." He knew his voice boomed through the hall, but he didn't care. Let potential recruits know that he tolerated no forgeries or deceit and took a dim view of fantasies.

"But…" Kingsley began. "I hear he's been seen in court in Edinburgh."

Harry pointed to Douglas. "This is the Earl of Douglas. He guarded Edinburgh and lived at the Scottish court. He can tell you the truth."

"Lord Harry is right," Douglas agreed. "Richard does not live in Edinburgh. Doubtless, he does not live *at all*. However, there *is* a man whom King Robert shelters, a mystic of sorts, who greatly resembles Richard. Many deem him a bastard of your Black Prince. Because of that—because if he *is* Richard's brother, his life would be endangered in England—and because when he is not out of his mind, he's given to wondrous preaching, King Robert keeps him near. Still, he is not King Richard."

"Understand?" Harry asked.

"Yes, Sir." Kingsley crumpled. "I'm sorry."

The others likewise apologized.

"Good. Make sure that every man in this hall understands as well. I'll not have anyone in my army under false pretences. And you, Beau, stay here to help convince them if they need it."

Douglas nodded. "Where're you going?"

"To announce the same outside, hoping to God we've stopped this nonsense before it goes any farther!"

* * *

Bishop Trevor accosted him after noonday Mass

on Wednesday. "You didn't take communion, Harry. I've never known you to refuse the Eucharist before."

Harry sighed. "I didn't feel in the right mind to receive the Lord. To be honest, I'm angry."

"About what?"

"Oh, everything and naught."

"Only naught, from you? Hardly." The bishop shucked his vestments off over his head and slipped his arm around his friend. "Care to talk about it?"

"If I say no, you'll worm it out of me anyway."

They found a secluded parapet above the River Dee.

Harry's fingers traced a moody pattern on the wall. "There've been all these wild stories about Richard."

"I know. Even I was 'informed' that he would arrive any day with your father."

"Which would constitute not one major miracle but two!" Harry joked bitterly. "I've done my best to squelch such foolishness. I thought I'd succeeded, mostly."

"You have."

"Aye, but now..." Disbelief clouded Harry's eyes. "I've been fielding reports about new allegations: That I'm raising an army so I can replace Henry with the eldest Mortimer lad. I want to do this, 'tis said, so Elizabeth's kin can be kings and I can rule through them."

"Total falsehood."

"Aye, but the hell of it is that if Henry *were* dethroned—by Parliament, not me—then, as the most immediate heir to Richard, the Mortimer boy could wear the crown. But that's not why I've done what I've done. I would have challenged Henry's misdeeds no matter who's in line for the throne."

"I understand; so does everyone who knows you."

"Will that suffice? Doubtless, Henry is making the most of this. He'll spread the lies far and wide." Harry shook his head. "The ultimate jest is that my estranged wife, Elizabeth, and I haven't had anything to do with each other for years. Yet I'm supposedly plotting with her and her kin!" He grimaced. "There's more, too: allegations I want to fight Henry to become king *myself,* rule directly. Hell, if we do battle, 'twill be at his instigation, not mine. And if I fight, I'll fight not for a crown but for the good of a kingdom."

"I know." Trevor rubbed his chin." What have you done about all this?"

"Spent the morn on more letters, emphasizing that the only reason I'm collecting a force is for my protection and that of the realm and to ensure the better governance thereof. And urging my allies to help set things straight."

The bishop nodded. "It's difficult to counteract calumny. Yet you've made a good start, I'd say. You can't do much more, except continue to set a good example, and pray."

"Believe me, I *am* praying."

"And so shall I—harder. And send some letters of my own as well."

* * *

Friday, 20 July 1403: Shrewsbury, England

The scouts revealed that Henry had paused at Burton-on-Trent, interrupting his frantic pursuit to await several privy councilors—and their gold.

Harry's own ranks now had about 14,000 men, though he still awaited additional levies from a few allies. Moreover, while individuals and small groups from Glyn Dwr's army had joined him, he had heard nothing further from Owain directly. But the new Welsh recruits reported that the Welshman was raiding South Wales, diluting and diverting English royalist strength there. In any case, 'twas time to leave

Chester.

Accordingly, Harry chose to march 30 miles to Shrewsbury, an English border town midway between south and north Wales, attractive for both strategic and personal reasons. Built on a rounded hill and encircled by the River Severn so tightly it was nearly an island, Shrewsbury boasted stone walls, a thriving merchantry, well-endowed churches, and the Benedictine Abbey of Sts. Peter and Paul. It contained a strong castle, too, looming over everything else. And the castle sheltered Prince Hal, assigned by his father to counter "rebels" in the area. Maybe if Harry could get past the Beauforts, Hal's latest guardians, he could meet with the boy...

They left Chester under skies with nary a cloud. As they wound through the countryside, however, they noticed a streak of silver overhead. At times nearly invisible, distinct at others, it seemed to keep pace with them. "The *stella comata* returns," the soldiers said. The celestial phenomenon had mysteriously appeared once or twice before, in recent years. Viewing it as a troubling portent, some crossed themselves anxiously. Others smiled in awe, taking it as a sign of God's favor, like the fiery pillar that guided the Chosen People in Moses' day.

Overall, though, it was not the heavens above but the earth below that preoccupied them, bedeviling their path with mud, stones, and wheel-wrenching ruts. At length, infantry trudging, wagons straining, horses wearying, they neared Shrewsbury.

Stopping short of the town, Harry chose a campsite two miles northwest, in pastures dotted by trees, within a graceful bend of the river. Happy to be off the road, the men tended their livestock, pitched tents, kindled cooking fires, cooled their feet in the water, and lolled in the late-afternoon warmth.

Their commander settled on a stump with his writing kit. An hour later, with a small escort and flag of truce, he rode off toward Shrewsbury, bearing two freshly inked notes.

On the outskirts, guards in Prince Hal's livery barred the way across the Welsh Bridge. In the distance, Hal's banner flew atop the castle.

Harry pulled out his messages. "Take those to His Highness, the Prince."

"Yea, My Lord," a sergeant answered pleasantly. Like many in Hal's following, he admired Harry and was baffled by news that the valiant Hotspur had turned traitor.

Harry's first note formally requested entry to Shrewsbury, with the unstated implication that if access were denied, he would bring a siege. His second message was personal:

> *My Prince and Beloved Friend, Hal:*
>
> *As you will know if you ponder it and consult your heart, I am no traitor and no rebel, despite what your father asserts. All I seek is good government. I wish nothing more than to bring my differences with your father to Parliament. There we can resolve them and address other serious issues affecting this land. I think of you as a son—so shall I ever—and will do all in my power to protect you, come what may. If you will meet with me, I'll discuss what has transpired, in person.*
>
> *Lord Harry*

Before long, the sergeant and a royal herald returned, with a document wrapped around Harry's note, which had been opened. With a sinking feeling, he realized that John Beaufort, not Hal, had written the response: *His esteemed majesty, my liege and kinsman, the Prince of Wales, has no dealings with rebellious traitors and outlaws.*

Harry swallowed a curse. "Are the prince's guardians aware that refusing us admittance could have severe consequences?"

"Yea, Sir. But Lord Beaufort said you can take your demand and shove it..." the herald paused over the undiplomatic phrasing "...up your arse."

"I see." Harry's jaw set grimly. "Was there a message from the prince himself?"

The herald hesitated. "Umm ... not in writing."

"Otherwise?"

The sergeant elbowed the herald aside. "As we were leaving, the prince waylaid us and said this: 'Tell Sir Harry I'm grateful for his message and know he is not to blame. Tell him I'm sorry.' Then Lord Beaufort saw us with the prince and ordered us begone. Right angry he was."

"Thank you." Harry turned Valdus.

"Is there anything further, Sir?" the sergeant called out.

Harry circled his horse, casting a long, hard look back toward the castle.

"No!"

* * *

When his squire interrupted him that evening, Harry was seated on the ground behind his tent in camp, back against a tree, writing. Above, Thor strutted along a branch, alternately scolding squirrels in adjacent trees and plummeting to unbidden landings on Harry's arm, trying to snatch his pen.

"I'm sorry," Hardyng declared. "But there's a local delegation here to see you. And they won't take 'no' for

236

an answer."

"Hell!" Harry hastily rolled up his latest letter.
"Oh well, show them around." 'Twouldn't do to offend
the local gentry, though he thought he'd already won
over most. "Best bring some wine."

"I doubt you'll need it!" Hardyng walked away. He
soon was back, surrounded by a dozen children,
ranging in age from about 4 to 14.

Douglas followed, amused.

"Sir Harry!"

"Are you really Harry Hotspur?"

"Lord Harry!"

"Is that truly him?"

Clamoring with questions and greetings, they
pushed forward.

Smiling, Harry arose and bowed. "Sir Harry
Percy: Justice of Chester, Warden of the East March
against Scotland, keeper of Flint and various other
places, layman-monk of Alnwick Abbey and..."

"... terror of the Scots!" Douglas contributed.

"... Knight of the Garter, *et cetera, et cetera,* at
your service," Harry laughed. "What can I do for you?"

"We wanted to meet you," said the eldest boy.
Fair-haired and slim, about 12 years old, he had a
farmer's pouch over his shoulder but, oddly, also
carried a short, smooth board. Putting it down, he
shyly offered his hand. Harry shook it with all the
respect he accorded a mature man.

"Thus you have met me. And you are?"

"Albert Rossayle."

"And your entourage?"

"My brother James and cousins Hammo and
Simon," he pointed them out. "And my sisters
Ermyntrude and Glenda. And my other cousin
Sylvester, there." He gestured again. "The rest are
friends..."

"I'm Johnny Bicton," a gangly lad spoke up. "This
is my sister Annie."

Others rattled off too many names too quickly for

Harry to catch them all. But he recognized several as belonging to rural families, from high-born to low, with a scattering from Shrewsbury as well.

"I'm flattered you've come to see me when you might be playing or riding your ponies."

"We hear you're a great hero," Albert said.

"He is," Douglas affirmed.

"They say you're the greatest knight in England!" Albert enthused.

"Perhaps," Harry blushed. "That hasn't been tested for some time, at least not in the lists."

"Because no one dare joust with you," Albert said.

"Possibly," Harry shrugged.

"Is that your sword?" Albert noticed the belt hanging from a tree.

"One of them. My favorite."

"Can we see it?"

"Best not to trifle with it. 'Tis a weapon, not a toy."

"Can you put it on, then?" Albert persisted. "Then show it to us?"

"And draw it?" another child asked.

"Ohhh! Yea! Yea!" They thought that was a wonderful idea.

"All right." Harry buckled it on. "But stand back."

They retreated two feet, Albert in front. To his glee, Harry picked him up, carried him another several feet, and set him down.

"Stand back, all of you. No closer." Carefully, he drew his sword, holding it aloft and sweeping it from side to side. Catching the last of the sun's rays, the polished steel glinted golden-red.

Eyes on every movement, they cheered loudly.

"This is a particularly good sword, at least for me, because it can be used in different ways," Harry informed them. "Like this"—he whipped it through the air—"it's a slashing weapon, perfect for cutting down beasts or bad men on all sides, whether I'm on horseback or afoot. Yet like this," he lunged toward the bushes, stabbing, "it's a thrusting weapon, for times when I must stop someone or something head-on.

"And when it's not doing any of those things, 'tis a fine pig-sticker for roasting a ham over the fire—as long as you don't get it too hot!"

They giggled.

"What's that on the hilt—that little circle?" asked Sylvester, a stocky, freckled-face boy.

So Harry told them about his coat-of-arms: What the lions and fish represented, and why *'Esperance'* was inscribed on the blade and what *that* meant. When he finally sheathed it again, they wanted to hear more: about battles in which he'd carried it, and about his horses and armor, and the many foes vanquished over the years.

"Is it true that the Scots have tails, and cloven hooves like devils, and long claws, and that they hate the English language and want to stop us from speaking it?" James Rossayle wondered.

"What do you think?" Harry gestured toward Douglas. "He's a Scot, and a most powerful warrior. Does he have a tail and claws?"

They scrutinized Douglas. He growled like a belligerent dragon, further delighting them, and then addressed them courteously in English, dipping his knee. "'Tis a great honor to make your acquaintance."

"No claws!" Annie Bicton tossed her light-brown locks.

"I don't see a tail, either," Hammo announced.

"He … he looks just like us!" another boy decided, and the rest nodded. "Talks like us, too."

"And he's handsome," Ermyntrude, a girl of 14, added coyly.

"What does all that tell you?" Harry inquired.

He got a dozen answers at once.

"That adults lied to us!"

"That the stories aren't true."

"That the Scots are really like the English."

"That … that … I don't know!"

"That you can't believe everything you hear,

especially about how horrid your enemies are supposed to be," Harry summarized.

"Was he your enemy?"

"So I thought. Not more than 10 months ago, his army and mine were trying to destroy each other. Now he and I are the best of friends."

"But...?"

"Huh...?"

"What happened?" Albert finished for them all.

Assisted by Douglas, Harry told the story.

"That's why, even though I'm a knight who's won many a battle, I say that too often war is no good," Harry concluded. "'Twould be better to settle our quarrels through other means, because those we try to kill might be folk who could be our friends, or *are* our friends, only we don't know it yet..."

Watching unseen from his tree, Thor felt left out. Without warning, he streaked low over their heads, prompting cries of delicious alarm. Landing on Harry's arm, he pranced, showing off his wings and screeching appropriately.

"My hawk—more pet and problem than predator!" Harry stroked Thor fondly.

"His toes look funny," a little girl noted.

"Aye." Harry told them of Thor's unfortunate beginning and rescue from certain doom. That led to a digression into falconry.

As he and Thor finished, he saw that the sun had dipped low. These youngsters needed to be getting home to their beds.

"Alas, my friends," he pointed to the sky, "Night draws nigh. I must send you off, before your parents fret o'er you."

They protested noisily until he promised that, if his army were camped there the next night (as he expected), they could visit again. Even then, they were reluctant to go.

"Wait!" Albert thrust out his board. "I almost forgot. I came to get you to sign this, in your own hand.

That is, if you *will*." He searched in his pouch, pulling out a piece of charcoal. "Sign it with this."

"I'll do better than that." Harry retrieved his quill. "I'll sign it in ink and write something." And he did:

*To my friend Albert Rossayle,
and his companions, with much
regard and affection, in
remembrance of a most enjoyable
evening. Esperance!*

Sir Harry Percy

"What does it say?" Johnny Bicton asked. "I can't read."

"Me neither."

"*I* can, but only up real close," Glenda confessed. "My eyes aren't good."

"E'en then I can't read at all..."

"Nor I..."

They crowded around Albert, some staring in incomprehension.

Harry reached for the board again. "May I?"

Albert nodded eagerly.

Seated against the tree, Harry balanced the board across his knees and pulled out his penknife. He laid his left hand on the board and, with the penknife, traced around it with his right, cutting the shape of his hand onto the wood. Then he went over the incised outline with ink.

"There!" He stood, giving it to Albert. "Now even those who can't read can see something 'in my hand'."

"Zounds!" the boy beamed.

"Now be off," Harry directed. "I'll see you tomorrow evening. Then we can talk less about me and more about all the marvelous things *you've* done!"

They nodded happily, thanked him again and trotted off. Bearing the board like a sacred relic in procession, they paused often to look back and wave.

Waving in return, Harry wondered who looked forward more to their next visit, they or he.

* * *

After conferring with his captains, he strapped his sword belt back in place, fastened his cloak, and walked out, alone, into the night. Wandering the camp perimeter, he greeted the sentinels and ensured everything was in readiness, should danger threaten. Nonetheless, his instincts told him no attack would occur before dawn, if at all.

Everything was peaceful—the fragrance of summer rising from the meadows, sweet with hay and wildflowers; the river burbling, the occasional brush of insect wing against the air, the evening dew kissing his boots and glittering on the grass in thin light. Constellations pricked the darkness like tiny sparks, but that strange star, the *stella comata*, outshone them all, darting over Harry's path. He watched it for several seconds, taken aback by its fierce, eerie beauty.

Then he turned his mind to matters at hand.

In a sense, he dreaded the morn. With the king marching to trap him and Prince Hal in place—however reluctantly—and instructed to hold Shrewsbury, he couldn't ignore the town. He knew he could probably take it, with its castle. Yet the fighting might be brutal. That troubled him, but what also worried him was Hal's safety. There was another consideration, too: Attacking a town harboring the Crown Prince would doubtless be considered a form of treason. To date, he had given Henry no legitimate grounds to accuse him of that. Thus, he told himself for the umpteenth time, on the morrow all would proceed with calm deliberation. They would ring the town, seize buildings outside the main walls, ready their archers, and again request peaceable entry. If it were denied, they would press onward but not use their weapons until fired upon. Only then would they act, returning the attack—in self-defense, not treason or warfare, but the justified response of men who had sought access to a town and been denied on spurious grounds.

'Twas the only way, the only recourse he had.

Reluctant to end his communion with the night, he rambled on. Crossing a meadow lumpy with the white forms of sheep, he bid them a soft "good evening" and proceeded, entering an adjacent field, where the larger, darker shapes of cows materialized. A few low moos announced his arrival. But the animals were too sleepy to pay much heed, and he continued onward, through a gap in a hedgerow. Beyond, he found a little lea, thick with the first hay, some already raked and ricked.

The Severn lay to his left, and he strolled to its bank.

In another night, the moon would be full. Even now, it hung huge over the water, shedding shards of light. Several seemed to fracture in prisms; others darted and danced on the opposite bank; more seemed to drown, only to re-emerge in shiny resurrection and ripple across the surface.

The North Star and Big Dipper looked particularly bright, though perhaps that was because of the direction they always pointed. *Homeward.* He yearned for Ciarry, to be with her, talk to her, hold her once more. If opportunity arose during the siege—or whatever action he took in Shrewsbury—he would write to her...

Smiling through his sadness, he saw another gleam on the river, mysterious and marvelous. The *stella comata* tarried along the Severn, too, as if, like he, it was unwilling to take leave of the night.

He murmured a prayer, skipped a handful of stones over the river, and, finally, turned away.

'Twas late, and he was tiring, far from his tent. He retraced his path into the first meadow, kicking up scythed grass as he walked. Ahead, he made out a hay mound, low but densely piled, soft and inviting. Settling onto it, he pulled his cloak around him and stretched out, head cradled on his arms. He'd nap a little before finding his way back; 'twould be better than stumbling through the dark, exhausted.

Dreaming happily, he stirred when he rolled over on his sword. Groggily, he unbuckled it, laid it as far aside as possible, and fell back into deep slumber. Nothing disturbed him for another hour. Ultimately, though, chill seeping through his cloak, he awoke and realized how far he was from his real bed.

He set off again.

The *stella comata* seemed to accompany him. Smiling softly, he thanked whatever angels had provided it to guide his steps. When he reached his tent, he cast a final look skyward and stole inside, peeled off his clothes, and crawled beneath his blankets. Almost immediately, he was asleep.

Above, the *stella comata* came to a blazing halt. For a few minutes, it burned more brightly than ever. Then, with an explosion of flame, it went out, inexplicably extinguished.

The sentries could only gape at the heavens and wonder...

Chapter XI

21 July 1403: Shrewsbury, England

Greeting the dawn with exuberant chatter, the birds shook out their feathers, flitting off to scavenge from the fields. The sun edged from a mist to burn the dew away, dappling wildflowers along the Severn, where fish leaped in their pools.

And Harry stepped from his tent to prepare for the task that seemed so improbable, battering his way into a town that harbored a boy he loved as his own. Clad in a towel, he wiped his freshly-razored face and wistfully dug his toes into the grass, wanting to linger, relishing the coolness against his skin. Instead, he had to don his armor.

Hardyng had arranged everything on the ground, and after dressing, Harry worked his way through the metal pieces. As he finished, he looked down, puzzled.

"Where's my sword?"

"Right there," his squire replied.

"Not that one." Harry eyed the blade. "That's my alternate. I want the other one, my favorite"—the sword he'd carried at Homildon Hill, where he won the battle and Douglas' friendship; the one Ciarry had kissed before buckling it around him when they parted...

Hardyng reddened. "I can't find it. I've searched everywhere. So did Knayton. 'Twas not in your tent, or by your saddle or the fire. We even went through the baggage wagons, though you hadn't been near them. It's vanished, your whole sword belt, gone."

"Damnation! Keep looking."

Hardyng gulped and nodded.

But Harry's gruffness quickly faded. "No matter. This one will serve." Forged alongside his best sword, his second-best was a near twin, although instead of black, brown leather wrapped its hilt, matching its belt and scabbard.

He sheathed it. "Let's be off. Alert the others. Have them bring some of the tents, including mine, and several wagons. Otherwise, leave the camp intact."

Within an hour, they departed with horns blaring, saddle leather creaking, and thousands of feet pressing upon the earth.

It didn't take long to reach Shrewsbury. Harry halted beyond the town walls, on the road that became the castle foregate street. Aligning his men in a wedge, he pointed its prong toward the castle, with the flanks arcing around the town, northwest to northeast. Once more, he instructed his captains: "We aren't here to make war. We only want access to the town and castle. And we aren't here to seize or harm Prince Hal. However, if he's closeted in place that refuses to admit us, a legitimate force under the justice of Chester, and is thus endangered by his advisors' stupidity, so be it."

Hugh Browe, Harry's top deputy on the Welsh Marches, concurred. Long-legged, brawny, and lightly bearded, he had spent years as a sheriff and officer and joined Harry's staff when they had met a few years earlier. "I've always been fond of Shrewsbury," he said. "If it gets wrecked, 'twill not be because I, or we, wanted it. "

The others echoed him.

"Onward!" Harry's sword pointed ahead.

They continued into the town outskirts. Fanned out along the edges, the archers screened the rest. But they met no opposition. Harry smiled. Hal and John Beaufort were smart enough to try to stop him, but had chosen not to. Nor did any fire come from the town walls, though Harry could see men there.

Somewhat encouraged, he sent Knayton and Irby to the town foregate, with a flag of truce, requesting immediate entry. As expected, this was denied, but not, perhaps, irrevocably. Instead, the town fathers said they were instructed to bar the gates until the prince could reconsider his position.

Momentarily satisfied, Harry replied that town and castle had half an hour, and if the gates were not opened "we will find our own way in!"

When the time had elapsed, his men advanced up the foregate street and adjacent lanes, checking residences, shops, chicken coops, and pens. They burned two corner houses whose occupants refused to cooperate, and a barn and shed whose owner likewise declined to unlock the premises for inspection. Otherwise, they left everything alone.

Again, no threats came their way. Nor, when Harry trotted up a knoll behind a few dwellings, did he see any obvious enemy. He rejoined his men.

Proceeding a short distance, they began bringing up the 'turtles' and siege machines. Even then, Harry gave no signal to open fire. As the equipment edged into place, however, arrows flew from the town walls ahead. Harry exhaled in mixed relief and regret. At least he had not loosed the first shot and started the fight.

The barrage accelerated, and he ordered his siege engines to respond.

After a few minutes, the shooting from the town slackened. Perhaps, Harry thought, Hal's archers were saving their shots for a more opportune moment, possibly when his men broke through the gates and surged into the streets beyond.

They were pounding their way toward that goal when he made another routine survey. Atop a knoll, he raised himself in the stirrups. To the north, as well as to the west and south, he saw nothing. But when his gaze swept to the east, he froze. Faint brown haze dusted the sky.

Rubbing his eyes, he looked again. The dirty shimmer thickened and widened, rising from the vicinity of Haughmond Hill, beyond the town. Only a large force could generate such a sudden cloud. Flags bobbed into view. Deep in their midst, a rectangle of color flapped: The royal flag. Next to it, smaller and barely recognizable, was a pennant: Henry's personal banner, declaring his presence in the host.

Harry felt as if he had crashed into a wall at full gallop. Gesturing furiously to Knayton and Browe, he took another look eastward. Preternaturally sharp, his eyes couldn't deceive him. Henry had arrived; Henry had succeeded in chasing him all the way to Shrewsbury. He had to lift his siege immediately, or they could themselves be surrounded and attacked.

Knayton and Browe tore up the hillock.

Harry's outstretched arm said it all. After one look east, they turned to him in alarm.

Reporting from an overnight scouting mission, Roger Salvayn galloped up from behind. "Harry! Henry was in Lichfield yesterday but marched by evening. He's coming on hard. They reached Haughmond o'ernight." Like his horse, Salvayn was lathered and panting. "But Henry wouldn't let them camp. He ordered them forward, by way of Sundorne, which is all bogs. A lot of them drowned." Revulsion filled his face. "Henry wouldn't let his other men try to save the ones pulled under, he just kept marching. Finally, he stopped to regroup. Now he's headed toward town."

"I know. His strength?"

"About 16,000 or a little o'er. Even with his losses, he's got at least 2,000 more than we have."

"Aye." Harry sped downhill, considering options.

Better not try returning to their camp; although the river behind it could serve as a moat, the ground was too flat to afford much protection. Likewise, trying to make a stand on the town outskirts would be foolhardy; Henry might trap them between his army and Hal's men in the castle. 'Twould be best to return to Chester. Marching that far was probably impossible, though, given Henry's nearness. But they could at least move in that direction.

He waved his other lieutenants close. "We've got to withdraw, prepare to defend ourselves, north of here."

Viewing Henry's dust cloud, they nodded.

Roger's horn sounded the order, as officers fanned out through the ranks. Trusting Harry, though they did not understand why they were retreating, the men broke the siege and fell into a march, back through the deserted lanes with their gear.

Hugh Browe trotted up alongside Harry. "Why not go across country, toward the Wrexham Road? I think we might reach Wrexham itself."

"I doubt we'd get that far. And I don't want to be hit on the run. We'd better dig in yonder." Harry pointed. "That way, if Henry comes, he'll be a couple of miles from the safety of Shrewsbury. We can use that slight ridge east of the coppices."

"By Albright Hussey?"

"Aye."

"A wise choice."

Harry nodded grimly. "Our only choice."

* * *

In less than an hour, they were in place, setting up obstacles: overturned wagons, freshly cut abatis, and rocks rolled into position. In the pea fields that spread before them, the infantry laced entwining tendrils into nets, the better to snare pursuers.

Before long, the pursuers became visible. King Henry had paused in town to plant one of his flags above his son's atop Shrewsbury Castle. But his first ranks were beginning to march onward, tiny figures against the horizon.

Harry made one long, last, slow ride around his perimeter. Plunging into the midst of his troops every several yards, he greeted lieutenants and sergeants, pikemen, archers and infantry. They welcomed him, aware of the approaching peril but making light of it, bantering about the way they'd been beating Shrewsbury into submission and would return to finish the task if he'd give the word. The archers turned it into a rhyme, chanting as they tapped their bows on the ground:

"On My Lord's command, we'll take Shrewsbury in hand!"

Cheered, Harry grinned. Leaning toward Knayton, he said something and then rode Valdus in an easy loop, back and forth along his front lines. His sentinels called everyone to attention, and the bagpipes served louder notice. Harry let the melancholy notes die on the breeze. Dismounting, he climbed a downed tree trunk, as several thousand sets of eyes fixed upon him.

His tone was controlled and firm:

"My comrades and brothers-in-arms: We're near Shrewsbury. We had begun to claim it. Some of you still wish to take our bows and swords and bagpipes and, like Joshua at Jericho, make those walls come tumbling down. Alas, instead it behooves us to desist from that, to turn our weapons instead on those who come against us with the king."

He pointed toward Henry's lines. "Yonder, you see the royal standard; nor is there room to doubt, however we might wish otherwise. Accordingly, I beg you to consider our position, both this ground *on* which we stand and the moral grounds *for* which we stand.

"Doubtless some of you are here for me, undeserving though I am. But I hope that others— indeed, all of you—are here not for me, but for this land. For if we must fight, we fight not for one man, or a group of men, but for the republic, *res publica*, the whole populace and its well-being, *for England."*

Someone took up the cry, and *"for England!"* echoed through the ranks, first softly, then like a flood sweeping a desert.

When it diminished, he resumed:

"Yet, 'tis not merely the good of England that motivates us. We also fight for Wales and Scotland, that there may be peace and friendship with them, like there is between you of England, and you of Wales, and you of Scotland here today, united against a common foe: this illegal royal *arrogance."*

His eyes narrowed. "What do I mean by 'arrogance'? Haughtiness? Aye. Selfishness? That too. But above all, I mean 'arrogance' in its foremost sense—an improper arrogation of power, a seizure of control, by one man, beyond reason or law." Once again, he outlined Henry's misdeeds, going back four years. "Such injustice, such arrogation of power, such oppression, must be opposed!"

Shouts and applause followed, to the accompaniment of horns and bagpipes—Scots war pipes, the smaller Scottish Lowlands pipes and their cousins, the Northumbrian pipes, uniting in one tremendous sound. Brow glistening with sweat while his eyes wetted with restrained tears, Harry went on:

"We face great risk. Yonder Henry's banner flies. Yonder Henry's army lies. They're set upon our destruction. They would kill us all in battle. And should they capture you, at least some of you, they will torture and kill you by execution, with no thought or mercy or trials. Be wary of what may lie ahead for those who call themselves my companions.

"Yet, ultimately, 'tis not you they seek. 'Tis *I* who am wanted and hated. Accordingly, I tell you to look to yourselves. Spare yourselves this ordeal, if you wish." He paused for emphasis. "I hereby free any and all of you of fealty or other vows and obligations to me. Your lives are yours. Take them hence should you choose... Even so, I hope you will stay."

They responded with cheers, foot stomping, and more ear-splitting choruses from the bagpipes.

Acknowledging the acclaim with a salute, Harry continued:

"Of course, if we fight and are victorious, the spoils of war will be ours, but that is not why we fight. And whether victorious or not, this day shall bring us glory, for whoever fights for freedom, for righteousness—that man fights in glory. Moreover, however this day ends, we who remain here can regard ourselves as fortunate, because we have so much to fight for, so much even to die for. We are blessed, for if a man has naught to die for, then he has naught to live for."

Glancing down at Ian Kynge and Bishops Skirlaw and Trevor, he smiled.

"This morn, we had no chance for Mass. Let me tell you, then, of today's Gospel. It comes from St. John and it says: 'Greater love than this hath nay man, than he who layeth down his life for his friends.' No greater love *hath* any man than he who dies for his friends, his brethren, his country. Should you choose to stay, I will honor you as kinsmen all: My companions, my friends, my brothers.

"Whatever befalls, I pledge to you all that is in me—any skill, any wisdom, vigor and strength, any daring I possess. I would die a thousand times ere I fail you or England."

He looked out across the fields, toward Henry's troops, and then regarded his own men with an affection and intensity they'd rarely seen, even from him.

"Reckoning draws nigh. Hold bravely, for this day either will vindicate us if we triumph, if you decide to stand with me, or it will free us from royal arrogance forever, if we are vanquished and slain. Yet, 'tis nobler to fall in battle for *res publica,* the republic, the commonweal, than to perish after battle—sentenced by our enemy, condemned and executed. 'Tis far better, too, to die in war than to live in tyranny.

"My friends and brothers: God be with you!"

His hand slipped to his belt and drew his sword, reversing it to lift the cross-shaped hilt. Kissing it, he said a silent prayer and then flipped it again, to raise the tip high.

"For God! England! And liberty! *Esperance!*"

His cry disappeared under a roar from his men. "For liberty! *Esperance! Esperance! Esperance!*"

As he jumped off the tree trunk, they stepped forward, one after another:

"My Lord, I stand with you this day and forever!"

"Sir, I'm proud to fight alongside you."

"Lord Harry, my lance and arm are yours..."

On and on. They pumped his hand, hugged him, knelt before him, laid their swords and pikes and arrows at his feet, weapons dedicated to his cause.

They came as individuals, in twos and threes, by the dozen and by the score, as one and as a multitude: Knayton, Kynge, and Hardyng, Irby, Roger Salvayn, and Jan Kingsley; and Yvon Jacques Giscardier; and a host of Cheshiremen and Welshmen and others.

They came in units: archers, pikemen, and infantry, bishops and priests, local monks and Franciscans from Wales, men of the cloth who weren't supposed to fight, but whose belts hung with war hammers alongside the pouches containing their breviaries.

They came: Bishop Skirlaw, axe in hand, and Bishop Trevor with his mace; men of Northumberland and Cumberland and Westmorland and across the North; men from Flint, Anglesey, and Caernarvon and castles and villages on both sides of the Welsh borders; men he knew slightly, men he'd seen once or twice, men he'd never seen before and might never see again. They came from Shrewsbury, too, soldiers who'd joined his camp the night before, and merchants and farmers who had followed him from town on his retreat, anxious to know his will and now, knowing it, chose to remain and fight.

And there were the Scots: Douglas, Montgomery, and Rob Stewart and others, men who had the least reason of all to support him and whose backing was all the more prized.

Finally, even his uncle knelt before him, having abandoned a lifetime of devotion to kings to defend the nephew he loved more than any man alive.

Harry shook hands, pulled men up, shared jests, embraced them—until, eyes brimming, he had to back away and direct Salvayn to sound the trumpet ordering them to regroup.

They obeyed, his battle cry sounding from thousands of throats. *"Esperance!"*

Harry could only close his visor, hiding his emotions, his buffeted spirit almost exultant.

"Esperance!" The cry washed over him, comforting him, carrying him forward.

The momentum rolled on, far beyond his heart, far beyond his ranks.

In Shrewsbury, they heard it and marveled. So did those across the river; and to the west, on the road to Wales; and eastward to Haughmond and beyond.

"Esperance! Esperance! Esperance!"

In the royal lines, too, they could not help but hear. And many whispered uneasily, even the king, clutching their weapons and staring out across the fields...

* * *

Henry had marched as near as he thought prudent and then established his personal quarters in an old stone croft, instructing his men to erect his tent alongside, as his staff headquarters. Restlessly, he stalked from one to the other, saying nothing. Finally,

254

he sent for Father Desmond, abbot of the Augustinians at Haughmond.

A frail man with a tufted white tonsure, Desmond came forward eagerly.

"You've come to me because you wish me to seek peace with ... *him.*" Unable to bring himself to use Harry's name, Henry spat out the pronoun. "You would have me parley with that whoreson traitor! I want no peace. I want his corpse dragged afore me!"

"Sire, I bid you to consider," Desmond said quietly. "Certainly, Your Majesty wants to avert bloodshed, sparing your men—and the innocents on the other side, too." *Including Sir Harry,* he prayed in an unvoiced afterthought. "Think of your realm, sire," he said aloud.

The king glared. Then his attitude softened. "Very well. Take Prestbury with you. Ask Sir Harry to declare his"—he grimaced—"grievances and cause, in writing, forthwith. Then we shall see."

Desmond fell to Henry's feet and kissed the royal hand. Rising, he blessed the king.

Henry flinched. If there was one thing he didn't want to be reminded of, it was that he might need favor with God. "Just go, man!" He was tempted to give the old man a kick in the rear end.

Unflappable, Desmond bowed his way out, mounted his mare, and set off for the Abbey of Sts. Peter and Paul. Although they were friendly, he hardly considered his Shrewsbury counterpart, Abbot Thomas Prestbury, unbiased. Having fallen out with King Richard, Prestbury, then a prior, had languished under arrest until Henry Bolingbroke had reached Shropshire in 1399 and freed him. Henry had subsequently cajoled or coerced the monks into installing the ever-grateful Prestbury in place of their incumbent abbot, who leaned toward Richard. Ever since, Prestbury had been Henry's man.

Nonetheless, Shrewsbury Abbey and the Benedictines had as much reason as Haughmond and the Augustinians to avert battle. Aside from monastic abhorrence of war (especially sinful, fratricidal slaughter), both had extensive farms, crops, livestock, and buildings in the area, vulnerable when armies clashed. Besides, they preferred other ministries to the sad duties of burying the dead, comforting prisoners, and caring for wounded post-bellum.

To his relief, Desmond found Prestbury of a like mind. Together, they sought out Harry, who greeted them graciously, expressed interest in Henry's request, and did not at all resemble the horrid outlaw Desmond might have expected from Henry's invective.

"Afore noon, he shall have my letter," Harry assured the abbots. "He may not welcome it, though." He extended his hands, self-deprecatingly. "However, given the gravity of the situation, I think I'd best respond with directness and candor."

"To be sure, My Lord, clarity and honesty are always best," Desmond replied. "But forget not the virtues of temperance and charity."

Harry grinned. "I shall bear your advice well, good father."

Desmond raised his hand to bless him, as he had blessed Henry. Though, like Henry, Harry seemed impatient, he duly bowed his head and closed his eyes.

Prestbury added his own prayer, and they departed.

* * *

After announcing his plans to his captains, Harry retired to his tent. Alone, he pulled off his outer armor, relieved to shed both its burden on a warm day and the weight of his worst fears. *Henry apparently wanted to talk!*

He settled at his portable desk.

He began slowly, trying to heed Desmond's advice, couching his sentences in temperate politeness. Ultimately, with his page mostly blank save muddy cross-outs, he gave up. *Damn it, he was angry!*

Across the way, Henry's troops now stretched back toward Shrewsbury. All these thousands Henry had brought, all these thousands to try to shore up his corrupt throne and—above all—trap one man: Harry Percy.

Moodily, he drummed his fingertips across his desk.

Suddenly he knew. Suddenly it was clear—the truth even he had avoided, had tried not to accept: Barring a miracle, Henry would never change.

Thus, Henry had to go—peaceably, if possible, through a settlement brokered by Parliament. But he could no longer rule. He was a ruthless killer who practiced deceit, broke the law, and had usurped the throne. To his core, he was perjured and false—in essence, a liar and a fraud.

'Twas time to say so.

Moreover, in saying it, as a knight and commander loyal to England, Harry knew he had to declare independence and renounce his fealty to Henry, who had failed him personally, as well as failing the nation. As a knight rendering fealty to the king, highest lord in the land, he had pledged to serve, honor and protect Henry and to obey lawful orders.

In turn, Henry was supposed to respect and protect *him,* the king's vassal. Henry had not done so. Instead, he had called Harry a traitor and sought to destroy him because Harry had questioned royal corruption and refused to carry out illegal orders—like the one to commit political murder by slaying Glyn Dwr under the guise of peaceful talks...

Resolute, Harry began anew: *I, Harry Percy, warden of the East March against Scotland...*

He wrote in Latin, the standard form for such

important documents, and this time, the words flowed easily, allegation after allegation against Henry, some followed by a singular refrain: *"Unde perjuratus es, et falsus."* Or, in English:

"Therefore, you are a liar and a fraud."

In an hour, he was finished. The ink in the last sentence still glistened as he called his comrades back. He handed the sheet to his uncle.

"Oh My God!" Thomas Percy digested the first paragraph, looked up, and resumed, nodding as he read. When he was finished, he gave it to Kynge, who read it with Knayton and Hardyng peering over his shoulders. They passed it along to the others.

"By all the saints of Scotland, Lad!" The last to read, Montgomery laid the draft on the table. "If you hadn't given Henry grounds for calling you a traitor afore, this'll do it, for sure!"

Harry smiled sadly. "As I said earlier, I may die ere this day ends. If so, I wish Henry and everyone else to know I died defying his tyranny."

Thomas Percy fingered the page again. "It *is* terribly forthright. You accuse Henry, among other misdeeds, of ordering the murder of Richard. The last man who did that, the Franciscan prior, was executed. As you know, Adam Usk and I once found evidence in Henry's own royal records indicating that he had ordered Richard to be killed. But to state it so bluntly..." Thomas' voice trailed off in doubt.

Harry shrugged. "'Tis the truth. I, like you, always suspected it. Now I'm sure of it, given Henry's attempts to kill me and the way he's murdered so many others. Remember, too: A murderer loses his right to the throne, or to anything else."

Thomas indicated another line. "Here, you refer to him as Henry, Duke of Lancaster, not as king. You're saying he's not a legitimate king."

"Aye. Until today, even I was willing to give him the benefit of the doubt, hoping to reform his rule. But seeing that horde he's brought against us, 'twas obvious: He means to murder me, and you, and all our men in unjust battle. Nor does he care how many of his own troops he sends to their deaths—or that his actions may kill his own son, too."

He faced his uncle. "Four years ago, I considered him unworthy to be king and opposed his coronation. Afterward, bowing to the convention of the country—and to your advice—I accepted him. Maybe that was wrong. At the time, it seemed the right thing to do. Before long, though, he gave me cause to question him. As a result, here we are; here *I* am, hunted like a rabid cur. Enough is enough!"

He rested his hand on the document. "Perhaps I haven't expressed myself in the most elegant way. So be it. At least Henry will know it came from me."

"Definitely!" Thomas considered further. "Another point: If you say Henry is unfit to rule, why not suggest a successor? Let him realize he's not the only man in England of regal lineage. There's young Mortimer."

"I mentioned the elder Edmund Mortimer's plight. But I'd lief not cite the claims to the throne of his nephew, Edmund the Younger. Remember, in 1399, when the issue came up regarding a replacement for Richard, you and my father never proposed young Mortimer. You said it would not be fitting for you to do so."

Thomas sighed. "Yea, but now that you raise the succession question anew, the basic fact remains: Edmund the Younger *is* Richard's most direct heir, under the traditional line of succession."

"I know," Harry acknowledged. "But Edmund the Younger is just 11 years old. Hal, although he's only four years older, would make a better king."

"That's something for Parliament to debate, *after* it votes to remove Henry and the throne is vacant and candidates to fill it must be considered," Thomas replied. "Indeed, 'twould work to our advantage: Cite the Mortimer prerogative now; then, at Parliament, agree to look at Hal as a worthy alternative. That would prove we're opposed to Henry's misgovernance, not to a Lancastrian per se. But first, you must refer to young Mortimer in your declaration. Here..." Bending down, Thomas scribbled something in the margin.

Harry groaned. "As you wish... Anything else?"

"Yea." Thomas went on. "You accused Henry of treason, an extremely inflammatory charge."

"He accused me, so I accuse him. He's betrayed England. Would you have me delete that part?"

"No," Thomas said. "It's true, to this realm's great misfortune."

The others echoed him.

"Nonetheless, Harry," Kynge proposed, "you *could* be a little less blunt, a little more vague."

"No! 'Tis something I learned negotiating with the Scots—with due apologies, my friends." Harry smiled at Douglas and Montgomery. "'Tis best sometimes to hit hard, with the strongest statement of terms first. Later, you can soften a bit and appear conciliatory for doing so."

Thomas Percy scratched his beard. "Yea, there's merit in your madness, Harry. If you bring your case to Parliament, *then* you can be flexible, for at that point you'll have already won the most important contest, simply by being there and compelling Henry to be there."

"E'en so," Kynge agreed.

Harry regarded the others. "Further comments?"

"Everything there must be said," Browe declared. "But I fear for you, Harry. Calling him 'a liar and a fraud' is certain to set him against you."

"He already is. What else?"

"Kynge and I could edit it a bit, remove a few extraneous words and smooth it out," Hardyng observed. "And maybe Bishops John and Walter can polish the Latin. It shouldn't take long. But," he frowned, "even that much time we may not have..."

"Probably not," Harry affirmed.

"Then leave it as it is," Hardyng decided. "And my compliments, Harry."

"I'm grateful!" He flashed his squire a wry smile. "Anything else?"

"Naught from me," Roger said, "unless you want Hardyng and me to put it to music and serenade Henry."

Harry laughed. "That far I won't go." He looked at the bishops. "What saith the church?"

"Your Latin is fine," Trevor assured him, as Skirlaw nodded.

"Good." Harry saw his uncle deliberating again. "Uncle?"

"One last thought," Thomas Percy responded. "It represents *your* views, as if they were yours alone."

"Henry asked for an explanation of *my* grievances and cause. I'm the one he's labeled a traitor. It falls to me to bring the accusations against him and bear the risk."

Thomas Percy shook his head. "No, Harry, it doesn't fall only to you. The risk belongs to me and to your father, too. I think you should add our names. In fact, I insist."

"My father isn't here."

"I know. But did he not say you could use his name—and his seal?"

"Aye. But I haven't thus far."

"You have his signet, though?"

Harry fingered his belt pouch. "Aye."

"Then use it, Lad! 'Twill never be more justified than now! Use it! Mine too." Thomas dug his seal from his purse. "Delay not. Prepare a copy and dispatch it immediately, ere Henry changes his mind about wanting it and starts lobbing arrows instead."

"All right." Harry seated himself as the others stepped back. Quickly, he added his father's and uncle's names to the beginning and made corresponding changes elsewhere. Propping the amended document on the desk, he drew up another chair and motioned Hardyng into it. "I want two fresh copies, one to send to Henry and one to keep. I'll write one, you do the other."

Hardyng pulled out a blank parchment and began.

Harry inked a fresh pen and followed suit.

Kynge tried to dislodge him. "Let me do that."

"No," Harry objected. "I want the one going to Henry to be in my hand. It may be the last thing I ever send him." And in clear, bold lines, his words began flowing across the page:

> *We, Henry Percy, Earl of Northumberland and Constable of England; Harry Percy, warden of the East March against Scotland; and Thomas Percy, Earl of Worcester, as guardians and protectors of the public weal, intend to personally prove this indictment today against you, Henry, Duke of Lancaster (and your followers and supporters), unjustly calling yourself king of England without valid legal title, but through guile on your part and the force of your supporters.*
>
> *When you returned to England from exile, at Doncaster you swore to us upon the holy Gospels to endorse the existing regality and royal administration, excluding only those matters of your inheritance, and vowed that the Lord Richard, our king, should reign until the end of his life, being governed by the good counsel of the lords spiritual and temporal. Yet, this same one, your and our lord and king, you had*

imprisoned in the Tower of London,
until in fear for his life he resigned.
Under color of this resignation, by
counsel of your followers and,
moreover, the vociferous outcry of a
common mob gathered outside
Westminster and collected by you
and your henchmen, you were
yourself crowned as king, contrary
to your oath.

**Therefore, you are a liar
and a fraud.**

You swore to us, at the same time
and place, that you would permit to
be levied no tenth taxes from the
clergy, nor fifteenths from the
people, nor any other such tallages
on behalf of the reign while you live,
except by a decision of the three
estates of the nation in Parliament,
and then not except for the greatest
need and defense against enemies,
and never otherwise. But contrary to
your oath, in actuality you caused to
be levied many a tenth and fifteenth
and other impositions and tallages,
on the clergy as well as the
communities of England and the
merchants, under fear of your
authority.

**Therefore you are a liar and
a fraud.**

You swore to us that King
Richard should reign with his royal
prerogatives as long as he lived. Yet
in your castle of Pontefract, by

betrayal and without his consent or judgement by the lords of the realm, this same lord, our king and yours, for a total of 15 days and as many nights you caused by royal order to be killed, destroyed through murder by starvation and thirst—horrible to hear of among Christians!

Therefore you are a liar and a fraud.

When Richard, our lord and king—and yours—thus was slain, against your oath you unjustly extorted, usurped and deforced the kingdom of England and the name and honors of the kingdom of France from the young Edmund Mortimer, Earl of March, nearest and direct heir to England and France, following the death of the aforesaid Richard.

Therefore, you are a liar and a fraud.

You swore to maintain the laws and good customs of the realm of England, and afterward you swore to protect and preserve these same at the time of your coronation. Instead, by deceit and against the laws of England you wrote to your followers, in every county, to elect knights for each Parliament who would be pleasing to you. Hence, in your Parliaments we could obtain no justice against your wishes.

Often, following our consciences given to us by God, we protested to you without relief, as God is our witness—along with the venerable fathers Thomas Arundel of Canterbury and Richard Scrope, archbishop of York. Thus, before Our Lord Jesus Christ, it behooves us now to seek remedy by force of arms.

Also, whereas Edmund Mortimer, senior, was captured by Owain Glyn Dwr while campaigning in deadly warfare in your cause, and was held in prison in iron chains, you proclaimed him to have been captured by a ruse. And you never acted to allow negotiations by him with the aforesaid Owain or by us, his relatives and friends, using our financial means for his ransom.

Above all, you never allowed the negotiations I successfully conducted for the good of peace between you and the same Owain. Rather, you considered me a traitor and otherwise deceitfully and secretly conjectured and plotted my death and destruction.

Thus you and your accomplices and followers we defy to the death as traitors and destroyers of the commonweal of the realm, and as invaders and oppressors and assaulters against the true and direct heir to England and France.

Kynge extended a lighted candle. Harry dripped a blob of wax, stamped the document with his seal, and repeated the action with his father's signet. Thomas Percy added his own. When the wax had dried, Harry gave the sheet to Roger. "Deliver this to Henry and no one else. Don't bother waiting for a reply. It could be dangerous. Tom," he tapped Knayton, "you'd best accompany him."

Knayton left with Salvayn.

Standing, Harry stretched. Now there was nothing to do but wait.

* * *

Henry's red face contorted. "I'll kill him! Fucking kill him!"

Dunbar watched apprehensively. The tirade had continued for half an hour. At this rate, Hotspur would slay Henry by making him so angry that he died of apoplexy.

"Peace, sire," Dunbar soothed, as if petting a high-strung hound. "He's not worth your wrath. There are better ways."

Henry's arm flailed in the air. "*'Peace'* you say! Look at this!" He waved Harry's declaration at Dunbar for the umpteenth time before dropping it to the floor. "He calls me a liar and a fraud. Says I rigged elections to Parliament. Murdered Richard. And raised taxes illegally."

Well, didn't you do all those things? Dunbar thought. *I would have, too, were I king.* Picking up the parchment, he smoothed it. In his present mood, Henry was likely to rip it to shreds. But that would destroy the written evidence of Harry's galling treason. Harry even had the impudence to allege that Henry was not a legitimate king—an unbelievable assertion, but a dangerous one, and not just for Harry. If King Henry were to fall, whether killed in battle or deposed by Parliament, George Dunbar could be ruined, too. Even if Henry were only censured by Parliament, royal power partly curtailed, Dunbar would suffer, for any diminution of Henry's status would mean a reduction in his own, palace confidant that he was.

The royal rant continued.

"I hate Harry!" Veins on the king's neck pulsed erratically. "I can't wait to meet him in battle. I'll run a lance through him!"

Dunbar batted a dismissive hand. "I dare say, your majesty, 'twill never happen."

"You think I couldn't kill him?"

"No, sire, merely that he'll never get the chance to meet you."

"Yea, he'll be cut down ere he lifts a sword. The fates will ordain it. Or he'll faint in dead fear at the sight of me in arms..."

This wasn't quite what Dunbar had meant.

"How I shall welcome his death! I detest him! *Detes*—" Henry doubled over, shaking.

Helping him onto a couch, Dunbar removed the stylish royal boots and poured a cup of wine. He pressed it into Henry's hands with a fervent whisper. "Rest yourself, My Liege."

Henry sank back against the pillows, sipping delicately. Eyes closing, he seemed to doze.

Dunbar poured a cup of wine for himself. *Why the hell didn't we succeed in killing Harry at Ormiston? Well, there was still time...* He poked his head outside, where Gawayn stood with the guard. "Is my horse near? My armor ready?"

Gawayn's head bobbed. "Have been for hours."

"Excellent."

"Is it war?" Gawayn asked. "I'll fetch the king's charger and lance."

"He won't need them." Dunbar ignored his son's bewilderment. "Just make sure all four sets of his extra armor are available."

Gawayn pointed to shining metal under a tree.

Dunbar grinned, returning to the king. But he'd hardly seated himself when a royal boot whizzed past his head. A moment later, Henry threw its mate. "Pay me heed!"

Nodding, Dunbar got up. "Yea, sire. In fact, I've been considering our strength. By my count, we have knights, men-at-arms, and infantry to the number of—"

Henry cut him off. "I've been counting, too, and not just troops."

He leaned close to Dunbar, his pale, prematurely wrinkled face looking controlled and cunning again. "It seems to me there is more than one way to trap Harry. Call back those blithering abbots. I wish to parley."

As soon as the two abbots arrived, Henry announced his willingness to discuss concessions—if Harry would meet with him in person. Agreeing to inform Harry, the churchmen departed.

When they reached Harry, he greeted them warmly and seemed inclined to accept Henry's offer. Thanking him for listening, they left as quickly as they had come.

Harry turned to his companions and pondered aloud. "I wish that I could trust him. But I cannot. Yet I'd like to go and settle this, once and for all. And *someone* must go..."

"But not you," Thomas Percy cautioned. "It may be a ruse to get you into his clutches. Let me meet with him."

Harry demurred. "I think not, Uncle. Your name and seal are on my declaration, too. By now, he must dislike you as much as he does me."

"No Lad, you're wrong," Thomas corrected. "*You*, he hates more than anyone on earth. I think that inside, though, he despises himself because he knows he can never be half the man you are. Rather than accept his limitations or correct his faults, he tells himself that *you* are the source of all his problems. The more he broods o'er it, with Dunbar and other perverted toads to goad him, the more his hatred grows."

A telling look filled Harry's eyes. "Adam Usk once told me exactly the same thing."

Thomas nodded. "Our friend Adam was right. So let *me* go to Henry."

Unhappily, Harry assented.

"If he's sincere about wanting to reach terms, I'll broker them as best as I can, if you give me leave to do so," Thomas added.

"Of course," Harry replied. "You know my position: First, his misdeeds, spelled out in the declaration I sent him, must be redressed. Second, there must be a truce between us, beginning now and enduring through the Parliament that resolves these matters."

"Yea. That all?"

"Aye, but if you aren't back in two hours, I'm coming after you—with the army."

With Thomas' departure, Harry's aides temporarily drifted away, too, leaving him alone with his thoughts.

Turning over the hourglass, he reclaimed his desk. What he had to write now was the easiest letter in the world, because it was to Ciarry. And it was the hardest, because it was a farewell, to be delivered if he were slain. Marshalling his will and thoughts, he felt his eyes sting with tears—not at the notion of dying but because of the sheer injustice of it, and the grief that his death would cause. Yet 'twould be worse if he perished without a final message. So he picked up his pen: *My very dearest Ciarry, if you are reading this...*

To his left, Thor perched on his stand. The hawk had spent a pleasant day so far, splashing in a horse trough outside Shrewsbury, observing the siege from a tree, flying close by Harry as they pulled back, and smoothing out his feathers as his master wrote. Now, partly bored and partly responding to the tension around him, he craved attention.

As Harry finished his letter, Thor hopped onto his wrist, pecking at the quill. Harry pushed him away; Thor stepped onto his left arm and tried again. Gently, Harry shook him off once more. Folding the letter, he addressed it, placed it in a leather bag with a cord, and slipped it around his neck, inside his shirt. Thor promptly hopped onto his head and pulled at the cord. Harry diverted him with a separate strand of leather, deposited him on the desk, and challenged him to a tug of war.

To be sure, he didn't have time to play with a bird... On the other hand, after the sad task of writing to Ciarry, tussling with Thor cheered him and helped restore his equilibrium, essential to a man contemplating battle.

He looked up as Hardyng approached. "Any word from my uncle?"

"Not yet. But this came, sent secretly between the lines."

Hardyng offered a scroll bearing the seal of his lithe, red-haired cousin and friend, Thomas Neville, Lord Furnival. Restoring Thor to his perch, Harry read it.

Harry,

*I wanted you to know from me,
and not learn by surprise, that I
joined the royal force. You know how
I strove to not take sides. Indeed, as I
told you recently, I thought it better
that way, the better to serve you and*

rally support for you if you stood trial or brought your case before Parliament. Alas, my good intentions have been foiled by King Henry himself. (And I wonder how many others in his army have been brought to a similar pass.)

You know that my beloved wife, Annkeroth, and I married without Henry's permission—she a wealthy widow and I a prominent lord widowed after an unhappy, arranged early marriage. Like you and Ciarry, Annkeroth and I found one another by happenstance. We fell in love, shared our love and our bed, thus plighted our troth, and were seen by all as man and wife, like so many who join in wedlock without any formal nuptial ceremony. But, as you also know, when Henry learned of our union, he was enraged, since marriages of high-born men and women are supposed to occur only with royal permission. Annkeroth and I both had to seek a pardon, and pay steep fines. I thought the matter had ended there. But yesterday a royal courier arrived with an order signed by Henry: I had to immediately join his army, or he would rescind his pardons and seize our property. Probably knowing how angry his order would make me, he also declared that if I joined you, then I, like you, would be guilty of high treason and he would execute me forthwith if he caught me. He also

"My cousin Thom is with Henry, under duress," Harry told Hardyng, explaining.

"Henry is monstrous," Hardyng exclaimed. "I'd forgotten Thom and Annkeroth had already 'offended' him by marrying. As if love depends on a royal writ!"

"I know..." Harry's voice softened pensively, as a flurry outside announced Thomas Percy's return.

Harry rushed from the tent. On his uncle's face, he saw neither success nor failure, only determination edged by sadness. "What says Henry?"

Thomas sighed. "He gave me no chance to present

your terms. And he kept me waiting a long time. While doing so, I reminded his counselors that the church forbids warfare every Friday till Monday morn, under the Truce of God. I also bade them recall that this is the Eve of St. Mary Magdalene's day, a time of festival and holy observance." He shrugged. "Perhaps it helped. When he finally saw me, he proposed a 'postponement of hostilities' until Monday and suggested that meanwhile he consider our declaration, with an eye toward a settlement, if we met certain stipulations."

"Such as?"

"He still demands that you speak with him. He said you and he could resolve this 'personally'—I'm guessing he meant in single combat—but that he won't agree to anything until he talks with you."

"Then I *will* go to him..." Harry thought aloud as his aides clustered around him. "At least Henry hints he wants a truce, if only till Monday. If he waits that long for battle, he might eschew it entirely. I don't want war. Presumably neither does he. Perhaps if other options fail, he *will* agree to meet me in single combat, trial by battle. Then the two of us can kill each other, or try to, and spare everyone else." His gaze encompassed the group. "That includes all of you."

Montgomery objected. "No! Don't go to him, Harry. He means no good. He'll never give *you* the satisfaction of seeking satisfaction from *him* in a duel."

"He's right," Thomas Percy warned. "Henry is likely to have his guards slay you."

"Aye," Harry nodded. "And afterward, he'd simply say that I drew first and his men had to cut me down. Still, maybe I should risk it..."

"No. *I'll* propose your willingness to meet him in single combat," Thomas suggested.

Harry reluctantly agreed and he and his aides settled down for another long wait...

But within the hour, Thomas Percy returned.

"Henry is waxing hot and crazy," he reported. "He says you must come to him, or he'll talk no more. First," Thomas' eyes rolled in disbelief, "he said this is about money, that you're sore wroth because he hasn't been able to pay you in full, because he himself has naught. Then he started shouting, asking how you, a mere knight, could be so puffed up with pride as to criticize him, a king 'chosen by God and man alike'."

Harry's aides murmured curses.

"Next," Thomas Percy went on, "Henry prattled about Parliament, about all the times you supposedly could've expressed your concerns when he held the House of Commons in session. Finally, he kicked the tent post—nearly brought the whole thing down—and kept repeating: 'What does Harry want?' It's as if he's forgotten your declaration, spelling everything out. Yet he bade me convey his remarks to you, and thus I do."

Harry began pacing. "So maybe I need to convey *more* remarks to him! Tell him…" Harry paused. "No, I'll write it out, though he may not heed it any more than he has everything I've already told him."

Quickly, he composed a message:

> *You ask how I, 'a mere knight,'*
> *can question or criticize a king. First,*
> *through my God-given rights as a*
> *man; and, second, as one of the*
> *knights who once rallied to your side*
> *in the name of the community of the*
> *realm, for the betterment of all.*
> *When you snuck back from exile*
> *abroad, we escorted you in, across*
> *England, countering King Richard,*
> *as we thought you would reform*
> *Richard's rule and ensure good*
> *governance. Instead, you seized*

*power. And you rule worse than he.
You despoil the realm and yet always
say you have nothing. Your treasurer
has nothing. You make no payments
on your debts. You hold no House of
Commons. And those sessions of the
Commons you have called have
represented only your interests
because you rigged shire elections.
You are no heir to the realm,
morally, and are of dubious claim,
legally. In any case, you have
forfeited whatever right to rule you
may have had. Unaware of your
duplicity, I supported you four years
ago. In doing so, I committed harm.
Therefore, just as I damaged the
kingdom, so I am prepared to repair
the damage. I want peace and hope
to see a freely elected Parliament
convened to determine the proper
heir to the throne after Richard II
and to clear my name of treason and
any other slander. I trust that for the
good of this country, you will join me
in that undertaking.*

With a furious jabbing of his quill, he signed it. "Take *that* to him!"

Thomas departed, to return not long afterward. "He read your note and fumed. *'I'll kill him! I want him dead!'*" Thomas mimicked. "But Dunbar calmed him, and he told me to wait outside. Within a quarter hour, he summoned me and gave me this."

Thomas handed Harry a parchment with Henry's stamp. Opening it, Harry found no reply to his note or to his earlier declaration. Instead, there was a safe-conduct pass, with a postscript: *I recommend that you place yourself in my mercy. And you shall have it.* It was signed, *Henry, King of England.*

Harry closed his eyes, praying silently. *Oh God... Tell me what to do.*

He wanted desperately to attempt a resolution, to stand tall before Henry and declare his intent. But he remembered other promises, other offers of forgiveness, other plans for safe conduct for other men: Richard Arundel, trapped through enticements from Richard II and other conspirators, including Henry, and going to his doom. King Richard, acquiescing to Henry, who swore before witnesses that he would be protected, only to murder him later. Glyn Dwr, whom Henry had wanted seized and executed, under the guise of a safe conduct pass and peace talks...

Oh God...

"I'd lief believe Henry," he said, finally. "Yet I can't." As Thomas watched, Harry answered Henry's note by adding a postscript to it: *I trust not your mercy.*

"I'll send it by someone else. You may be endangered, Uncle, if you return, especially with this."

Thomas demurred. "No, let me bear it. For all his bombast, I think we've achieved a give-and-take. That must bode well. Let me continue."

Harry hugged him. "Then once more, may God go with you."

Thomas rode off.

With that, Harry could delay no longer. Assisted by Hardyng, he began putting his outer armor back on. They were buckling the first greave when Thor leaned close. With a sharp little cry, the bird landed on Harry's shoulder, to promptly ensnare his talons in chainmail. Hastily, Harry put on his leather gloves and disentangled Thor. With an embarrassed flutter, the hawk hopped down Harry's arm to his wrist.

"Poor friend, you're lonesome." Harry stroked him; Thor closed his eyes, nestling his head against Harry's hand.

Behind them, Hardyng patiently held a vambrace.

Thor's eyes suddenly flipped open, and he stretched, wings flapping, eager to go out on the chase with his master, as on many an afternoon.

Harry laughed lightly. "Aye, let's go hunting. Perhaps we'll catch a king!"

He turned to Hardyng. "I'm sorry, John. Let me take Thor outside and send him off for a spell. He wants for flying."

He walked well beyond the lines, into a broad meadow. For a few moments, he stroked Thor again, touching his lips to the sleek, feathered head. "May we both survive this day, and hunt together on many to come. But now you must go hence, alone. Would that I could rise beyond my cares as easily as you take the breeze." With a smooth motion, Harry sent him into flight. Thor rose and circled over Harry's head and then accelerated, climbing higher and higher, becoming smaller, until no longer visible.

Somberly, Harry returned to his tent.

As he finished donning his armor, he and Hardyng were joined by Knayton, Browe, Montgomery, Douglas and others, all likewise in armor. Adjusting his sword belt, Harry wondered aloud. "Any luck in locating my other sword?"

"No. Confound it," Hardyng replied. "We've searched everywhere."

"I don't understand it," Knayton added. "You had it last night at supper. I nearly tripped over it, climbing past you to get another hunk of beef."

"Later, you showed it to the children," Douglas reminded Harry.

"Afterward, once we'd checked everything around the camp, you said I might as well retire, that you were going out by the sentries a while," Knayton continued. "You were wearing your sword then."

"Aye, I was."

Hardyng picked up the trail. "When I got up to piss, afore dawn, you were in your blankets. You'd left your clothing alongside your cot. So your sword must've been there, too. Where the hell did it go?"

Harry kicked at the ground absently. Suddenly, he stood stock-still. "Damnation! I know what happened. *I* lost it. *I* lost my sword. I'm sorry, lads." He regarded Hardyng and Knayton in chagrin. "Last night, I walked the fields. There was nearly a full moon and that shooting star—almost o'er my head, 'twas…"

Douglas nudged Browe, whispering over what they, too, had noticed.

"Finally, I grew weary and lay down, out where the farmers had cut hay, near the cow pasture."

Lord Vernon, one of the Cheshire gentry, spoke up. "I know the place. Farmers from around Chester use it when they bring sheep to Shrewsbury on market days."

Harry nodded. "I wrapped my cloak about myself and fell asleep. I vaguely remember rolling onto my sword. It wasn't very comfortable. I took it off and slept again. Eventually, I roused myself and found my way back. But I left my sword belt out there."

He addressed Vernon. "You're familiar with that ill-begotten field? What's its name?"

"Berwick. It's called Berwick."

Harry's tall body seemed to sway, his face white. "Oh my God… Then has my plow reached its final furrow."

They crowded around.

"Huh?"

"What's wrong?"

Clenching his left fist, Harry wrapped the right hand around it and spoke softly, mostly to himself. "So the old man was right. And so was Ciarry."

"What?"

"Tell us."

He swallowed hard. "Years ago, a wise priest spoke of my prowess and said that eventually the sword would fall from my hand and I would die 'hard by Berwick.' I assumed he meant Berwick-upon-

Tweed. Alas, I see I deceived myself," Harry smiled ruefully. "'Twas *this* Berwick, this Berwick that I never knew existed; this Berwick and region that claim my sword—and I fear—shall claim my life." He gazed ahead, expression distant. "Another wise person later told me that 'berwick' is an old word that can mean any used, or enclosed, or once-built site beyond a town. That, too, has proven correct."

They looked almost as stricken as he. No one spoke, not knowing what to say. Harry continued to stand alone, submerged in thought.

Montgomery's brogue cut through the gloom. "Oh, bosh and blather! Just because your sword 'twas lost at this lesser Berwick doesn't mean your life is going to be lost, too!" He pushed Hardyng and Knayton aside and wrapped his arms around Harry. "That old priest: 'Twere a Scotsman, right?"

Harry nodded.

"Then an idiot to be sure!" Montgomery pounded Harry's back. "Buck up, Lad. 'Tis hardly over yet. For one, you've not even begun to fight. Nor have I. And you and me, Lad, together we must be damned-near invincible!"

At that, the others joined Montgomery, wringing Harry's hand, praising his abilities, predicting success should battle come. Harry embraced them all in turn.

Over Douglas's shoulder, he spied his uncle, fresh from his latest embassy.

"Good tidings, Harry. The best!" Thomas dismounted. "Henry's given in. He's agreed to a truce and more."

Wild cheering and more back-pounding ensued. Harry's spirits, crushed a few minutes earlier, soared. He laughed in sheer relief, then motioned everyone to silence. "Peace, friends! Let's hear the rest of my uncle's news."

Thomas smiled broadly. "To begin, he dropped all demands that you present yourself to him."

They whistled and applauded.

"Overall, he agreed to your various points." Thomas Percy ticked them off on his fingers.

"First, he concurs that there should be an indefinite truce between us. Both sides are to stand down in readiness and disperse. Second, he agrees to summon a freely elected Parliament and to place your various disputes before it. Third, if it's determined at this Parliament that he holds the Crown illicitly, he will relinquish it to the lords and bishops, for them to turn over to the proper recipient, whosoever that may prove to be. And finally," Thomas concluded, "even if accepting these terms today, should either your side or his change its mind, you are still bound to keep the truce until mid-morning Monday, and then to send formal, written word to the opposing army six hours in advance of any arraying of force. And so, to the—"

Bishop Trevor interrupted. "Back up, if you will, to that third point."

When Thomas repeated it, the bishop shook his head. "Henry will never agree to relinquish his crown," Trevor said. "So why did he accept such a provision?"

"Because he's so damned stuck on himself, he thinks he'll never face the test," Thomas answered. "He assumes Parliament would never truly question his right to rule and risk repeating all the chaos of 1399. He reckons that, at worst, he might have to make a few apologies and suffer some limits to his authority, the kind of restraints he and everyone else proposed for Richard four years ago."

"But he'd never agree to those, either," Trevor objected.

"Ahhh, but he would and will," Thomas replied. "He would and will because he wants to be king, wants that more than anything on earth—or heaven. He'd sell his soul for that."

"He already has," Harry said.

"Exactly. Thus, he'll agree to efforts to rein in his power. He'll also implement some reforms because he knows that if he doesn't, he could be deposed. He'd rather be king, albeit a somewhat constrained king, than a former king, or a duke of Lancaster, or dead—though he damned well knows we'd never murder him, even if he killed Richard."

Bishop Trevor weighed the answer. "Yea, I agree. And Henry is likewise vain enough to think he can portray any reforms as *his* idea and win plaudits for his benevolence."

"Precisely," Thomas confirmed.

Further cheering began.

"Enou!" Montgomery squelched it, grabbing Harry's arm. "I'm still not convinced, Lad. He *is* a liar and a fraud."

Again, Harry's elation dimmed. Gradually, though, he brightened. "Aye. Yet I think he'll go along, for the reasons my uncle and Bishop John gave. More importantly..." He focused on Thomas Percy. "If he wanted war, Henry would've held you, Uncle, to make me try to rescue you. He didn't."

Thomas nodded. "Henry has no qualms about killing, as we know. Yet even he doesn't want to waste his army. No intelligent ruler does, not when better choices exist. Consequently, I agreed to the terms in your name, Harry. I trust that was your will."

"Aye."

"You did it, Lad!" Thomas pumped Harry's hand. "Henry's heralds began trumpeting the truce as I departed. His men should soon pull back."

Harry looked across the fields. "The rear echelons are moving already." He embraced Thomas, exuberantly lifting him off the ground. "God be praised! A happier end to a sorrier day I could ne'er imagine."

Releasing Thomas, he grabbed Salvayn. "Sound the call for everyone to stand down. You two," he nudged Knayton and Hardyng, "instruct our battalions. They should spread out across the countryside—not *too* far separated, but enough that no single locale suffers from our presence. The core, though, our horsemen and half the archers and infantry, can stay here with us."

They nodded and took off.

Harry addressed Kynge, Trevor and Skirlaw. "We didn't hear Mass earlier. Let's take time now, each chaplain with his own companies. I think there's much to be thankful for."

The three went to prepare, arms across each other's shoulders.

Eagerness palpable, Harry's men began demobilizing.

So did the royal troops, for a time. Then they abruptly halted in their tracks, as if too exhausted or harrowed by their earlier experience in the bogs to retrace their steps any farther.

Late afternoon found Harry's ranks greatly dispersed—and Henry's men, their own retreat yet to resume, frozen in place...

Chapter XII

Afternoon, 21 July 1403: Shrewsbury, England

Dunbar's insistent fingers accompanied his persistent whine. "You need not honor a truce. You can abrogate it, instantly." He snapped his fingers again. "Like that, it's over."

Slumped in a chair in the croft next to his tent, Henry raised dim eyes. "Not afore Monday, it's not. I agreed to that, scarce two hours ago."

"So?" Dunbar raised a contemptuous chin. "A *truce?* Means nothing. All that matters is your survival. You could lose your crown, if not your life, if you let this folly continue to the point of an inquiry before Parliament. Harry knows that, even if you don't!"

He was speaking more aggressively than was usual or wise. But the stakes were high. Nonetheless, catching the sharp tone, he moderated his voice. "Forget your agreement. Attack now, when they're not suspecting it. Hotspur's men have spread over the countryside." He shook his head in smug delight. "To think he *believed* us, after what transpired today."

A palace knight, Sir Robert Malveysen, frowned in the corner. "Doubtless that's *why* he believed us. He knows how serious 'tis and assumed we do, too. Besides, we announced a retreat whilst Thomas Percy was present. Thomas probably thought we meant it and told Harry we did. *Christ!*" Malveysen licked nervous lips. "*I* thought we meant it!" Fear mixed with disgust as he glared at Dunbar.

"Oh, we did. Perhaps... Until I—" Dunbar stopped. *Best not to claim too much credit.* "Until *we* perceived there might be another way. So I gave the command, with Our Majesty's approval, to recall any troops already withdrawn. And I bade those still here to 'step back' only till they met the others returning to us. Then I told *all* to maintain position." He waved toward the lines. "I say we should use them!"

Henry stirred. "Maybe you're right. I'll never be rid of Harry, if not here and now. I hate him! *Detest him!*" The venom of early afternoon returned. "A liar and a fraud, he called me! I want his head on a pike!"

"There's only one way to get it!" Dunbar emphasized.

Henry closed his eyes, reopening them in a face etched in harshness. "So be it. I abhor the shedding of blood; let it be on Harry's head."

He got up, chainmail shimmering with gold threads interwoven in the steel. "To arms!"

Dunbar placed a hand on his wrist. "To arms for every man, My Liege, save you."

"What do you mean? I itch to begin!" Henry rubbed the dagger at his waist.

Dunbar led him outdoors, away from Henry's entourage. "It's too parlous for you to engage directly. Your place is behind the lines, commanding from there. Leave the fight to others."

"And be thought a coward?"

"You won't be." Dunbar smiled slyly. "Your sword and armor will be seen everywhere. Men will wonder how you could personally massacre so many or be so many places at once."

Henry listened, enraptured.

"The scribes will be beside themselves," Dunbar went on. "Generations of kings will envy you. 'Another Edward I, another Conqueror, another Caesar,' they'll say. No, a warrior *greater* than those!"

Henry lapped it up, like a cat whiskers-deep in cream—until he remembered something. "How shall I do all that, if I'm not even *on* the field?"

Dunbar pulled him close and spoke in a low tone. "Blount, Stafford, Massey, and Fitzwalter have accepted the honor of wearing your extra armor. They'll be arrayed by your standard, but not so close that two can be seen simultaneously. They'll lure Harry. We'll put our best fighters around them. He won't have a chance."

Henry gaped, then beamed, pleased, though not beyond a lingering suspicion. "Harry's damned good."

"Yea, and he might overcome one or two. But he won't get past all four. Not with those other men defending them."

"'Struth!" Henry rubbed his hands expectantly. "It's perfect. All the more reason for me to take the field. *I* want to be the one who kills Harry." He noticed Dunbar's agitation. "Oh, worry not. I'll let the others have their way with him first. But I want to run him through myself."

"Perhaps," Dunbar suggested, "we should consider your *complete* role. If your hand is raised in battle, on one part of the field, it cannot coordinate your overall strategy, guiding *all* your men to victory. Surely, no one but you has the genius to do that."

They kept at it and eventually Dunbar got his way, or mostly. Henry insisted on leading the assault. But he agreed that if things got too hot, he would quit the field for a place of greater safety. And as far as Dunbar was concerned, that would be right here, in the croft, far behind the lines.

They went back inside to plan the attack.

* * *

Still in armor, Harry and his companions knelt in his tent. Mass had reached the quiet, post-communion interlude. Calmness prevailed...

285

Yet, as they awaited the final blessing, faint squeaks drifted across the meadows. Tinny and uncertain, the noise slowly penetrated Harry's consciousness: *Horns*. Next, he heard muted cries: *"Avaunt! Advance banner."* The trumpets sounded again, louder.

"My God!" Harry leapt over Douglas and his uncle, kneeling in the row in front of him.

About to deliver the benediction, Skirlaw's upraised hand dropped like a rock.

Rushing outside, Harry almost knocked Salvayn down.

"Harry! Henry has launched an attack!"

"Aye!" Harry saw the approaching horde, heard the thud of feet and the repeated royal command: *"Avaunt! Advance banner! Onward in the name of the king!"*

Pulling his horn from his belt, he blasted his own call to arms.

"Get your heralds," he yelled to Salvayn. "Summon those men we sent off earlier."

But while they could recall some, it was too late for many others, scattered out of range. "Send messengers, too!" Harry added, though he knew it might be futile.

Sword in hand, he scooped up his helmet, jamming it on his head. Irby brought Valdus, and he vaulted into the saddle, issuing orders. Around him, horses whinnied and priests cut short other Masses as their congregants sought to re-arm, remount, and reclaim their posts. Training told, however, and from the frenzy ranks took shape— infantry and pikemen, horsemen and lancers, MacKerny and whatever archers remained. A makeshift left and right coalesced around Harry and his cavalry, the archers creating an outer line.

Raw with anger and anguish, Thomas Percy plunged his horse alongside Harry's. "Your forgiveness, Harry. I let Henry deceive me. I thought he wanted peace..." Thomas ducked under the first enemy arrows.

"'Tis my fault, too," Harry replied. "I never guessed he hated me more than he loved his own life."

He gauged the speed of the oncoming army, raised his arm, and lowered his sword.

"Esperance!" The battle was joined...

Enraged at being betrayed, his men reacted with a ferocity that stopped the royal army mid-field. Though their regiments were depleted, their archers equaled Henry's in numbers and outmatched them in ability. As at Homildon Hill, the first success went to the bowmen. One segment, then another, of the royal army gave way. For more than an hour, arrows fell like fatal hail, cutting jagged holes in unprotected flesh, cracking shields and tearing into chainmail, embedding in armor.

Harry saw men in his outermost lines fall and others, in the middle, go down randomly. But most of the casualties were Henry's. Underfoot, once sweet farmland became oozing red muck.

In the center of his host, Henry's flag waved provocatively. Sometimes listing as another of its bearers went down, it always bounced back to reveal that the king himself remained unharmed. "Die, you bastard," Harry muttered, marking the location. "Let that banner be your burial shroud."

Henry's vanguard began to fold into itself. On its flanks, whole rows fell, leaving others isolated, spread out in wavering strips, like thin fingers beckoning Harry.

Before he responded, he huddled with Knayton, Browe, Douglas and Montgomery, ringed by their squires and shields, ignoring the royalist arrows splashing unevenly at their feet.

"I'm dividing our force," Harry announced.

His companions looked shocked.

Undaunted, he continued. "We'll split two-thirds of our strength into five battalions, with archers, mounted men-at-arms, knights, and long pikes. You each will lead one battalion. I'll take the vanguard, at the center, against Henry's middle.

"You, Beau," his head tilted toward Douglas, "take the immediate left. And you, John," he indicated Montgomery, "take the far left, opposite Henry's far right. Tom, you take our immediate right, next to me, and you, Hugh, our far right. We'll leave my uncle, Vernon, and Venables with the other one-third, mostly light infantry. Our archers can cover us initially. Then they'll reduce fire, and we'll counterattack." He pointed. "I'll go in first, through there. You follow. I think we can push them back for good."

"And what a pleasure 'twill be!" Montgomery proclaimed.

Knayton touched Harry's hand. "I... I should like to fight the rest of this battle—and die, perhaps—as a knight. Will you have me, Harry?"

Harry's jaw fell. For years, he had urged Knayton to accept knighthood, only to be rebuffed, for reasons Harry well understood. Knighthood brought prestige, but also extra responsibilities, including special taxes. Accordingly, many men-at-arms, equals of knights in all but title, never sought it. But now Tom wanted the honor. Harry smiled. "Kneel, friend."

Knayton complied, and Harry went through the brief ritual, tapping Knayton's shoulders with his second-best blade. "I hereby dub you knight. Henceforth be known as Sir Thomas Knayton. Arise, Sir Thomas, and be lauded!"

The new knight stood, and Harry embraced him. Both struggled to overcome tears and were only partly successful. Pulling away, Harry shoved Knayton toward the others, who shook his hand and hugged him. But there was no time for celebration. Already, the royal troops were massing again.

Sword in the air, Harry galloped off. Enemy arrows flew over his head as he leaned forward, shield covering his upper body. Yet he seemed immune, like most of the men behind him. MacKerny's archers stung the air with retaliatory fire, aiming above their cavalry to lacerate Henry's men beyond.

"Esperance!"

As Harry neared his targets, MacKerny's bombardment decreased.

But Henry's side enjoyed no respite, for Harry was upon them, smashing through three or four rows at once. Royal lancers who avoided him met the pounding hooves of his horsemen or the hot steel of infantry and pikes before they could employ their own weapons.

Bagpipes adding to the din, Douglas and Montgomery charged, sowing destruction on the left, with Browe and Knayton keeping pace on the right.

Several royalist levies attempted a stand, with numbers too minimal and efforts too haphazard. Scores died, unable to advance because Hotspur's men were in their fore and unable to retreat because arrows raked the ground at their rear. Hundreds braved the fire to flee, abandoning spears, bows and lances. Some made it to their camp; others, mortally wounded, fell on the fringes. All left holes in the royal lines.

Farther back, the royal standard fluttered. But as intense arrow-fire continued, the outer circle of mounted knights protecting it melted. In the eroding middle, Henry sat his sorrel charger, fingers on his sword, heedless of the escalating disaster, obsessed by what he saw everywhere: A pennant with silver fish on deep red, light-blue lions on yellow-gold: *Harry's flag,* constantly changing position yet always challenging him. Closer and closer it came, first on his left, then his right, disappearing only to resurface nearer than before, moving like a whirlwind.

"God damn him!" Henry could abide it no longer. Brutally spurring ahead, he knocked down his own standard-bearer and forced his screen of horsemen aside. Two of Hotspur's infantrymen had wormed

their way dangerously close. Arrows showered down, but the king ignored them as his sword stabbed the air. He forced the first infantryman to the ground, stabbed viciously, and on the upswing caught the other. As he was about to strike again, a spear buried itself deep in his shield, splinters of wood flying. The impact twisted his arm, and with an agonized cry, he dropped the shield. Dazed and aching, he dismounted to retrieve it. A swarm of arrows sent him rolling beneath his mount. When a spear scraped the horse, the king was nearly trampled. Getting to his feet, he staggered, dodged another spear, and gave up. Falling to the earth, he instinctively coiled himself into a ball. Chest heaving, he expected the angel of death.

Instead, human arms lifted him onto another mount.

Dunbar's glove on the right side of the bridle yanked the horse forward, as Gawayn goaded from the left. They hustled Henry away, not pausing until they were well away from the combat. Safe on the far side of the royal camp, the Dunbars bundled Henry into his croft, ordering his ample reserve to protect him. There, the king collapsed on his bed, eyes on the ceiling. Though his mouth opened and shut, no words came.

Gawayn poured wine, which Henry swigged in one sip, groaning. After replenishing the cup, Gawayn poured one for his father, too; then he hastened back to the battle. But the elder Dunbar remained behind. Like Henry, he'd seen enough of war for one day.

*　*　*

Unaware that Henry had fled, Harry cut his way to a place of relative calm and took stock. Through the haze and metallic shimmer of rapidly moving men, he spotted part of Browe's line, unraveling. Over his shoulder, he shouted to Hardyng. "Tell Douglas to reinforce me, over there. His line looks secure enou' and we've got to help Hugh."

Hardyng took off.

When Douglas reached him, Harry's augmented force sped to Browe's assistance. It took more frantic fighting before this segment of the royal army was also in rout. Several of Henry's mounted knights tried to halt their fleeing infantry at sword point. But the soldiers, stubbornness intensified by fright, grabbed the horses' bridles, dumped the knights, and jumped into the saddles themselves. More royal knights and lancers joined the flight, some racing almost as far as Shrewsbury.

Even as the dash continued, though, auxiliaries under banners of the Duchy of Lancaster and the Beauforts poured onto the field.

Harry pressed on to meet them, Douglas at his side, the core of their cavalry behind them.

"Esperance!"

The Lancastrians paused, bracing for the impact, each enemy shield coming into sharper focus as Harry drew closer. This man he knew, and that one, and the knight over there...

Unexpectedly, the Duchy's ranks parted. Rawer troops, moving gamely if somewhat raggedly, edged to the front, as if to bear the brunt of the assault. In the lead, a herald waved a flag: the Prince of Wales' standard.

Harry gasped. A moment later, he saw Hal himself, in armor, astride Aelfred, the warhorse Harry had helped him train.

Hal glanced back at his men and faced forward again. Head moving, he seemed to be counting, ticking off the moments until he would countercharge, exactly as Harry had taught him.

No, my young Stoutheart, not you, Harry implored silently. *Not you.* He tugged his reins, slowing his pace, and saw Hal brandish a sword.

Gripping his own sword more tightly, Harry raised it high—and abruptly lowered it again. *No, I cannot. God save me, but I cannot...*

He knew that Hal had recognized him and was watching, waiting, in the eternity that passed in seconds. Turning his horse in a tight circle, Harry lifted his sword once more, this time in salute. With a deep nod to Hal, he veered off diagonally, putting distance between himself and the prince.

His baffled companions followed.

Douglas caught up to him. "What the hell's going on? We could take them!"

"'Tis Hal we were about to overrun. I can't raise my sword against a boy. I can't fight Hal..." The dismay in Harry's voice was evident.

They rode off, side by side, Douglas peering at Harry through helmet slits. "They're a threat, and fresh. They could go for your uncle or the Cheshiremen next. They've got to be stopped!"

"They will be, but not that way. Henry's own lines are disintegrating. Let's get *them*. Let's kill Henry. Then there'll be no need to go after Hal or any of these other poor devils..."

"But we could capture Hal, use him as a hostage to make Henry yield and agree to terms, *real* terms!"

Harry shook his head. "No. Hal could die in the attempt... I can't do it... Pull up yonder," he pointed to a tree at the edge of the battlefield, "and I'll tell you what I'm thinking."

Douglas nodded.

A few minutes later, Harry concluded their brief colloquy, sipping from his water jug.

"To reiterate: I want to end this—afore many more die. I'm going after Henry himself and not stopping till I find him." Audacity glinted under the cold determination in his eyes. "Are you with me, Beau?"

"Aye!"

"Then..." Harry's visor shut. *"For the republic, the common weal of England!"*

"A-Douglas, for Scotland!"
Their voices rang out, sharp as the blades in their hands. Hurtling ahead, they battered their way back into the king's lines. Their companions thundered after them, horsemen, fighters, friends: Hardyng; Kynge—left fist around the staff of Harry's banner, right hand wielding an axe; Montgomery and Salvayn, Knayton and Browe, Giscardier, Kingsley, Irby and all the others, a potent *V* boring into the heart of the royal host.

Their opponents scattered, like twigs in a maelstrom.

"Esperance! For England!" Shield covering everything but his sword arm, Harry galloped on, armor mirroring the afternoon sun. Lances whirled through the air; two swiped his shield, to no effect.

Henry's infantry again fragmented, though a hardy knot reorganized, to make a stand.

In a long, arching jump, Valdus soared over their heads, as if clearing a stone wall in a Borders chase. He landed between two of the king's horsemen. Swords and shields clattered to the dirt as one royal steed went down, spilling its rider; the other horse reared, lost balance, and toppled over backward, crushing its knight beneath its weight.

Stroke by stroke, Harry carved an opening, systematically extending it into the royal lines, his lieutenants at his elbows. Two royal knights took him on, but the first, wheezing in the fury, collapsed over his saddle. The second wheeled his horse awkwardly, leaving his back vulnerable for the merest instant—enough time to die.

Wrenching the tip of his sword from a third staggering royalist seconds later, Harry whistled. A dozen paces away, a large escutcheon shone, vanished, and reappeared: Henry's shield. Then he glimpsed the royal standard, waving madly, as if taunting him. He was on the standard-bearer in an instant. Vainly, the man stabbed with his flagstaff. Flat of his sword smashing down, Harry felled the man with little ado or blood. He barreled on, into the knights encircling Henry's shield. Again using the breadth of his sword, he overcame three—wounded, not killed, but rendered harmless. Not far ahead the already-unhorsed monarch limped, crown welded atop his helmet, lurching dizzily.

Hardyng and Irby distracted two royal men-at-arms, and Harry saw his chance. Leaning low from the saddle, he kicked his leg free of the stirrup and lashed out with his sword, simultaneously jamming his booted foot into the king. The royal head lolled; the royal shield slipped. Harry raised his sword. "Die, you bastard!"

He felt the blade puncture the king's armor, like a nail drilling into tin. Usually he only stabbed enough to incapacitate an adversary, not wasting time or energy on more. This time, he put his weight behind the thrust, digging deep. The king swerved on his feet, gave a ghastly cough, and toppled.

Harry dove from the saddle atop him.

A final, horrid moan escaped the king and torrents of blood gushed from his chest. Straddling him, Harry tugged the royal helmet off.

"What the hell!"

It wasn't Henry at all but a courtier, Sir Walter Blount. Henry had assigned an imposter to do his fighting—and dying.

"You fiend, Bolingbroke!" Harry exclaimed.

Having taken too much time with Blount, he stood up, to see that Douglas likewise had dismounted and was about to be jumped from behind by another royal knight. Three other men already menaced Douglas from the front. Meanwhile, Hardyng and the others had disappeared.

Harry drove his knife into the royalist at Douglas's back, while Douglas continued to clash with the trio in his face. All were on foot; one wore the royal armor and carried the royal shield.

How many damned 'kings' would England have this day? Harry wondered. He confronted Douglas' non-kingly opponents, thrusting his body against theirs and using his superior height and strength to force each over backward. The sound of ribs cracking was lost, but the ear-splitting cry of pain and terror was not as one dropped, never to move again. A second staggered to his feet, but Harry stabbed him, too.

Douglas dispatched the third and stood over him, gesturing. "You look."

Jerking the royal visor open, Harry glanced, startled. Swiftly, he removed the helmet, to reveal the tender-yeared Lord Stafford, dying.

"Oh my God." Voice hoarse with despair and wrath, Harry raised Stafford gently. "Sorry, Lad. I'd tried to spare you..."

Comprehension floated into the boy's pale-green eyes. Attempting to speak, he could only retch. Helplessly, he gazed at Harry; then the light in his eyes went out forever.

"'Tis Stafford, the little lordling," Harry informed Douglas. "I didn't try to enlist him in my cause, thinking him too young. Obviously, Henry had no such qualms!"

He spat—and saw new danger. Two more palace knights and still another in Henry's armor were closing in, Browe in fierce pursuit. Nearly somersaulting into their midst, Harry slashed, backhanded, hitting the man in royal armor from behind and then piercing a vulnerable gap in his armor. The figure crumpled, dead. From the corner of his eye, Harry saw Browe vanquish one of the two remaining knights while Douglas defeated the last.

Rejoining Harry, Douglas poked his sword at the corpse in royal armor. "And who's this?"

Stooping, Harry removed yet another crowned helmet. "Again a fraud! Sir John Massey."

So Massey, disgraced after a disastrous tenure in

Wales, where Harry had been compelled to deal with his gross mismanagement, had crawled back into Henry's favor, only to pay a steep price...

"I want the *real* king!" Harry protested. "Where *is* he?"

An answer arrived in moments.

A pair of Lancastrian knights lunged toward him. Then a third and a fourth man entered the fray. The fourth, too, wore royal armor. Deflecting one, then another, then a third, only to face the fourth and the first pair again, Harry felt fatigue sear his muscles. When his sword and shield slipped slightly, an axe swiped his upper leg. His cuisses protected him from being cut, but not from bruising. Thigh throbbing, he gritted his teeth, determined that if he died, he would take the king with him. And this one *had* to be Henry.

Like a guardian angel, though, Douglas was at his side, now wielding a mace, accompanying each swat with a rich repertoire of Scottish expletives. In part through luck, in part through ability and coordination, they began forcing the royalist quartet back.

Suddenly, a gauntleted hand grabbed a royal knight by the throat from behind. A brief streak of metal preceded a thump. Within moments, a second royal knight fell to the same brazen maneuver—and Hardyng climbed over the dead men, holding a bloody dirk.

Behind him, Irby dueled with the third member of the quartet. Trading knife for sword, Hardyng went to the younger man's aid, while Harry and Douglas concentrated on the fourth king.

Whoever wore the royal armor had the same height and heft as Henry. He kept Harry and Douglas at bay until, apparently tiring, he let down his guard. Harry slashed his arm. Stepping backward, the king entangled himself in the limbs of a dead horse, toppling onto the animal.

Harry's sword gashed the mesh aventail encasing the royal neck. The king went limp. Air wheezing through his severed windpipe, he briefly flailed and died.

Squatting, Harry pried the helmet off. "Fitzwalter."

"What?" Douglas slammed his mace against the ground. "*Again*, not Henry?"

"No. Another of his fakes."

"How many suits of armor does he have out here?" Douglas wondered. "Must we fight our way through his whole armory?"

"No!" Harry laughed. "He claims he's insolvent! He can't have *that* much armor!" The lighthearted moment faded. "Hell!"

Hoofbeats sounded behind him, and he whirled. It was only Kingsley, however, leading their destriers. Knayton and the other horsemen followed. However, as Harry took tally, he noticed that four or five of his original knights were missing. So was his banner—and Ian Kynge.

"*Please, Lord...*" He beseeched heaven, remounting. "*Not Kynge...*"

But his band had pummeled two-thirds of the way through the royal ranks, and the remainder of the troops in Henry's command had retreated.

Elsewhere, Harry realized his army seemed to be holding its own, including those under Thomas Percy, pushing hard against the prince's men. "*God save them,*" he prayed again, thinking of both his uncle and Hal. But he couldn't worry about them, couldn't consider anything but getting Henry...

Meanwhile, in his sector, a strange interlude prevailed.

He took advantage of it to survey the terrain. Across the open land ahead stood the royal troops his cavalry had just forced back. Behind them stretched two cultivated fields, crops badly trampled. Next came a brush meadow, which in turn gave way to a scattering of trees. Barely visible beyond were wagons and tents and an old building or two: Henry's wagons and tents, Henry's headquarters, where Henry would have stashed the rest of his armor—if he had any left—or hidden additional surrogate "kings," *or...*

The realization hit. Excited, exhaustion dissipated, he turned to Douglas and the others. "We've done it! We've driven Henry from the field! We've driven the fryggen fraud from the field!"

"Huh?" Douglas asked.

"Just that! Why, Beau, have we not killed the *real* Henry? Why haven't we crossed swords with Dunbar? He hates us, you and me especially. Yet have we seen him? No! Nor has anyone. And why not? Because he and Henry aren't here. *They aren't here!* They've turned tail!" He pointed with his sword. "They're in their camp, the caitiff cowards! I'd wager all of Northumberland on it."

"You may have to, if you're wrong!" Douglas replied.

"'But I'm not! 'Tis another ruse. Henry thought he'd lure me with his false kings to have his men kill or capture me when I took the bait. Yet here I am. And there he hides. And there I'll corner him like the vermin he is."

Douglas stared, then nodded. "*Damn!* You're right. I'm certain."

So were the rest.

Harry motioned to Kingsley. "Alert my uncle and your Cheshire friends. Tell them we've discovered that Henry is hiding in his camp and are on our way to get him. Ask my uncle to turn in that direction, if he can, driving the prince's troops before him."

Kingsley hastened off.

"Some of Henry's men fled the field to that camp," Harry observed. "They may still have spleen in them. Henry doubtless has a strong guard, too, stowed like his baggage. Perhaps that's why we've made headway here: Not all his troops are in action. Even so, if we hit hard, I think we can overcome them and finish this business."

Montgomery sidled his horse over, wrapping an arm around Harry. "I'm right proud of you, Lad. Uncovering Henry's guile took wits worthy of a Scot."

Harry laughed. "Sans doubt *'twas* a Scot, that rat's arse Dunbar, who contrived it. But he and Henry will plot no more."

He raised his sword. *"For the common weal of England!"*

Mace tucked away, Douglas drew his broadsword, touching its tip to Harry's. *"For Scotland and St. Andrew!"*

They charged, the rest following.

Arrows peppered their path, and Harry heard horses and riders behind him falter. But MacKerny's archers, tracking his progress, answered volley for volley, anticipated arrow with arrow.

Swords swinging with a fearsome beauty, he and Douglas swept onward, their horses' hooves, like their friendship, beating in flawless rhythm. They slashed first to one side, then the opposite, then ahead or behind, repeating it all in seemingly effortless, tandem perfection, cutting a wide swath through the royal lines. Breaking clear of the fighting, they found nothing beyond but meadows—and Henry's camp.

Nudging Valdus left to avoid a scattering of corpses, Harry gazed hard right, at the trees. Through the limited, frontal vision of his visor, he picked out a royal banner—not the battle standard, but Henry's smaller, *personal* pennant, tacked to a tent, adjacent to a stone croft.

Heart pounding, he blinked, looking again:

'Twas no denying it.

I've found Henry, he rejoiced silently, *hiding like a spineless sop!* With his sword, he gestured to Douglas. The Scotsman nodded, gleefully shouting something.

Oblivious of the arrows wafting haphazardly overhead, of the large bruise on his thigh, of whether and how closely his companions followed, Harry leaned forward, knees tight against Valdus.

They catapulted onward.

"Esperance! For England!"

His battle cry resounded from the royal camp to the hillock where he had arrayed his men hours earlier. As it faded on the wind, Harry pulled ahead even of Douglas, flying across the ground as if Valdus had wings, as if his own resurgent optimism carried him beyond any other mortal.

"Esperance! Esperance!" The word rolled through his mind, resilient and strong.

With his left hand, he shifted his shield onto his saddle. Shoving his visor open and sweaty cowl back, he gulped a lungful of fresh air. Head tossed to the side, he shook the perspiration from his brow, eyes clearing, vision crystallizing on his goal. A smile played across his lips.

"Esper–"

Barbed, razor-sharp, lethal, the arrow came out of nowhere, striking his unvisored temple, slamming him into blackness, piercing his skull. His hand slackened on the reins as blood spattered his horse. Snapping in the saddle, his body held briefly, shuddered, and tumbled, right hand still clasping his sword...

He was dead before he hit the ground.

"Harry!" Douglas' anguished cry accompanied his friend's fall. But it came too late.

Closing the distance, Douglas dismounted, scarcely noticing when his horse bolted. He stripped off his gloves and leaned over Harry, who had landed on his back. Tears welling, Douglas examined the arrow. Its tip penetrated deep into skin and bone, blood dribbling in a long, narrow stain. He felt inside the chainmail for a pulse at Harry's neck. At first, he thought he detected a wavering beat. But as he held his fingers in place he realized it was only the nerves in his own shaking hand. Otherwise, there was nothing. Choking back a sob, he waited agonized seconds and tried again. Nothing. *"Godspeed, my friend!"* Bending, he kissed the ashen forehead. Then he flung himself into Valdus' saddle, waved to their companions to join him, and rode off, straight toward the royal camp...

* * *

When they realized that Harry had gone down, a few members of his cavalry galloped off to regroup or flee. More paused at his body and were later captured there. But most followed Douglas.

Discovering whom luck and a random arrow had slain, Henry's pickets informed the king, whose heralds trumpeted the news: *"Harry Percy is dead!"* Slowly taking hold, it demoralized Harry's remaining troops. They shared his vision, but if he fought for England, they fought *for* him, and *through* him, for England. To lose him was to lose too much. Heartsick and exhausted, many gave up, less by surrendering than by merely drifting off toward Cheshire or over the Severn to Wales. Badly bludgeoned royal troops often let them go.

Thomas Percy and the Cheshiremen fought on until they were ultimately subdued.

Douglas' band, meanwhile, overran a broad swathe of the royal camp before also being killed or captured: As Harry had predicted, Henry had kept a potent reserve.

Through it all, Henry stayed in his croft, unscathed. Only when it was over did he emerge onto the field, pretending he'd been there all along, claiming the day as his...

* * *

Vespers

The hawk knew a loyalty uncommon among men, and so one last time it banked low over the field, its keen raptor's gaze searching amid the gore and agony and carnage of war for the one it trusted above all others.

Only hours earlier, he had stroked its sleek head and whispered a falconer's affectionate secrets, bending his wrist in a graceful adieu to send it aloft on the soft air of an English summer. Briefly, he had watched it soar and then disappear, like his own flickering hopes, before turning to resume the last grim tasks of gearing himself for battle.

All day the young harrier had tarried just beyond arrow reach, until the fighting had subsided in a near-quiet twilight, as the gold and purple of the sunset glistened in the river, and the anguish of the dying replaced the evensong of sparrows. Slowly, it had winged its way back, seeking its master first among the survivors fleeing the field and then among the fallen left behind.

In its third pass over the ground, on a rise littered with the debris of defeat, the bird found the man, lying awkwardly in the dust's embrace, right arm beside him, a powerful hand still gripping the hilt of his great sword, the other slung across the armored chest, helmet skewed, dark hair wafting in the breeze, dark-blue eyes fixed on the sky, half-smile frozen on the still face, arrested in a lingering echo of youth.

At the side of his head, a shaft protruded from a clot of red-brown blood, congealed in a sticky rivulet down his neck.

Instinctively, unquestioningly, the hawk landed and understood. For mere moments, it rested on the stiffening left arm, raised slightly as if to receive it one last time. Then with a sharp cry the bird lifted itself airborne, crossing once above the unmoving form and coursing its way north, alone, beyond the twining Severn and distant outlines of the Welsh hills and far-off silver of the western sea; north to the untamed crags and green glens and crashing streams; north to the desolate mountains and wild moors of the Borders; north to Northumberland, there to glide on the wind in freedom until all of its days were ended...

Chapter XIII

21 July 1403: Shrewsbury, England

As night descended, Furnival searched for his cousin's body. Montgomery and Hardyng accompanied him, but at first, even they didn't realize how close to the royal camp Harry had ridden. So they began looking too far back, amid the piles of dead left when Harry and Douglas had surged across the field. Following the trail toward Henry's now-empty croft, they came to an area with far fewer corpses, the last stretch of meadow Harry had galloped over.

There, they saw the still form.

Something scurried off. Heart sinking, Furnival feared that rats had already begun to feast. But as he shone his lantern, he realized he was wrong. Although covered with a scrim of dirt, in death, Harry was unblemished, lying as Douglas had left him.

"Oh God, why did it have to be him?" Kneeling, Furnival removed the battered helmet and tucked the cowl around Harry's neck. As he did, he noticed a leather string. A careful tug revealed a small bag, damp with sweat and blood. Extracting a parchment, he met Hardyng's eyes over the lantern glow. "It's a letter, to Ciarry, for delivery in case of his death." Furnival's voice shook. "I... I'd better take it. I can protect it better."

Hardyng nodded. Easing the sword from his lord's grip, the squire removed Harry's gauntlets. Holding a pale, cold hand to his cheek, he wept, shoulders bent beneath his grief.

Choking back his own sobs, Montgomery lifted Harry's head onto his lap. Gently, he closed the unseeing eyes and started to coax the arrow loose.

"No!" Furnival protested. "Leave it! 'Twill show how he died: not in single combat. No man could best him in that. But plenty will probably claim to, and Henry is sure to believe the loudest braggart, unless we can prove otherwise."

"Even so." Montgomery took out a handkerchief and wiped the grit from Harry's head, tears falling onto the lifeless face and trickling down the chin. He daubed those away, too.

"We'd better get back," Furnival advised, and they laid their burden in the wagon. Furnival climbed onto the driver's bench and Hardyng into the back, cradling Harry in his arms. But Montgomery paused to retrieve something on the field.

"His shield." Reverently, he placed it in the wagon.

Furnival was startled. "'Tis odd no one purloined it, or Harry's sword or armor, either. Usually, scavengers pillage everything forthwith."

"Got dark too quickly," Montgomery speculated. "Or perhaps no one durst stoop to thievery—afeared of Henry, who'll want Harry's armor himself; or frightened of you and Harry's other friends; or scared of God."

"Yea." Furnival twitched the reins, and the horses set off for Shrewsbury Castle.

There they carried the corpse into a lower parlor, placing it on a heavy table. Montgomery stood alongside, lifting Harry's head and shoulders onto his arm. "Ah, my brave Lad. I could not have loved you more if you'd been my younger brother or son... Like a father or brother, too, I'll keep vigil with you now." His rough, tear-stained face turned upward. "Home is the rover, Lord. Take him to you..."

Hardyng half knelt and half fell over the opposite side of the table, distraught, angry, and exhausted. Like Montgomery, he was a prisoner, though Furnival had interceded for them (and Douglas), to ensure their safety. Both had lost not only Harry but other close comrades, including Knayton and Kynge, while the fate of too many more, like Irby and Salvayn, remained unknown. And Douglas's survival was dubious, for he had been wounded again, the only reason he had been taken. Nor were Thomas Percy and Hugh Browe likely to live; captured and jailed, they faced certain execution, with other men of prominence.

For several minutes, Furnival, Hardyng and Montgomery were alone with their slain friend. Then the room began filling with spectators—among them Beaufort and Gawayn Dunbar—muttering and pointing at the arrow. Harry's companions ignored them.

Furnival had sent for Benedictines from Shrewsbury Abbey to assist with mortuary details, and they, too, arrived. In getting Henry's authorization to retrieve Harry's corpse, Furnival had also obtained permission to bury it in his family's chapel at Whitchurch, about 17 miles away. He intended to cart it there before the night ended, with Montgomery and Hardyng and whomever else Henry allowed to go with him.

As the monks began their sad duties, he slipped away.

Douglas was too weak to come down, so Furnival went upstairs to a room strewn with pallets of wounded nobles. Finding Douglas awake, biting his knuckles in pain, Furnival explained the interment plans.

"Then take this. Bury it with him, if you will." Douglas' quaking fingers held a strip of bloodied cloth. "'Tis our plaid's *plaid*, the Douglas clan colors. I always wore it over my heart in battle. I had it today. He's like a brother to me." His voice grew fainter. "I want it to … to go with Harry."

Furnival took it, clasped Douglas's hand, and went back to the lower parlor.

Methodically, the monks there removed the arrow, cleansed the wound, stripped Harry's body of armor, clothing, and signet ring; washed and anointed it, and covered it to the upper chest with a linen sheet. After placing burning candles at the head and feet, they retreated into the dusky background. The flickering light illuminated Harry's white shoulders and accentuated his sleek, dark hair and the bluish-black sheen to his shaven chin. Somberly, his friends regrouped.

Onlookers continued to traipse in and out. Eventually, even Henry and Dunbar appeared—the latter barely trying to swallow an exultant smile.

Entering, Henry, too, almost beamed. But then his face sagged and his bones seemed to cave inward. Hesitantly, he stepped closer. "Oh, Merciful Father—his blood is on my hands. I wronged him. *Killed him!*" His horror rattled off the walls.

"What? Shhhh!" Dunbar pushed him from the parlor.

"No! Take me back! I must stay. My deeds slew him ... and so many others... I mu—" Henry's wail echoed down the corridor.

Hardyng, Furnival and Montgomery exchanged incredulous glances.

Not long afterward, though, Henry returned, expression firm and steps strong, rising on his toes and flexing his leg muscles, as if he meant to kick the corpse. Perhaps only the arrival of his son restrained him.

Hal staggered in, drained of color, except for a red-soaked bandage on his face. He had remained on the battlefield until struck in the head with an arrow—like Harry. Unlike Harry, he had survived so far. The shaft had been removed, but the arrow point had penetrated deeply. The prince glared at his father before dropping his eyes to the bier. Shaking, he draped himself over the body, hands clutching the dead man's upper arms. "Lord Harry ... *Jesu...* Lord

Harry." Tears choked his words.

Puzzled, anger building, Henry stared at his son. Sensing the tension, the others in the room backed out the door or edged into the corners. Only the boy's weeping broke the stillness.

Finally, marshalling his strength, Hal raised his face and yelled across the chamber at his father. "You lied to me! And you killed him! I hate you for it!"

"He was killed in battle—against me!" Henry answered. "Against *us*."

"You said there would be no battle. You made a truce with him. You announced it. Then you attacked—when his guard was down!"

"Hal..."

"And don't try to tell me otherwise, that it was *his* fault!" the prince declared hotly. "'Twas *your* horns I heard, commanding us to commence battle. Suddenly, we were marching forward, pushed on by those behind us. Your archers began firing. And Harry's retaliated ... and we were at war. I had to fight to save my men and myself. So did he." Hal looked back at Harry's body. "But you started it. You lied."

Henry sighed. "Hal ... Son, I did what I had to do, to preserve the throne for me—and you. He would've wrested it from us."

"He didn't want to fight. He wanted to go to Parliament."

"Perhaps," Henry conceded. "But if he hadn't seized the Crown from us by battle, he would have urged Parliament to depose us. It might have complied, especially the kind of Parliament *he* wanted: members voted upon freely by men at all levels in shires and towns, without any direction from the Crown. Even if Parliament had not taken the throne from us, the Lords and Commons would likely have curtailed my power, making it impossible for me to rule as I wished. Is that what you wanted?"

"I wanted him alive! I needed him. England needed him. *You* needed him."

Henry cursed.

Furnival, Hardyng and Montgomery watched in mute surprise. *He's saying exactly what Henry needs to hear,* Furnival thought bitterly. *'Tis what I would say, if I didn't have to remain on good terms with Henry long enough to bury Harry.*

Hal returned to the bier. "Lord Harry saved my life today. He was aiming straight for me, with all his horse and might. Then he recognized me and turned back. Those behind him turned, too. Had we closed, he and his horsemen would have slain me." He laid his palm on Harry's chest, eyes cast down. "He loved me. And I loved him." Gaze raised, he stared at his father. "But I hate you!"

Henry shifted on his heels. "Talk not that way, boy. You're injured, tired; you know not what you say."

Hal ignored him.

"Listen to me, Son."

Hal's face filled with contempt. "Call me not your son. I renounce you." He patted the dead man's shoulder. "He was my true father. Perhaps you begat me, *Sire!*" His lip curled. "But *he* was father to my dreams and hopes. He made me see what kind of man I want to be: a man like him, not like you! And someday..." his young shoulders squared, "... I shall rule as he would have wanted me to rule, in justice and righteousness. Not as you rule."

Advancing, Henry struck Hal's face hard, knocking the bandage off and bringing an outpouring of fresh blood.

Again, the prince's eyes filled, and he stumbled, but he said nothing.

Henry motioned to his guards. "Take my son to bed. He's out of his mind."

The guards loomed, but Hal shook them off. Leaning over, he kissed Harry's cold cheek. "Farewell, My Friend, My Lord..."

They hustled him away.

Henry gestured toward the corpse. "And get him

out of here, too."

* * *

A few hours later at Whitchurch, Furnival laid Harry's body to rest in an unused vault. Hanging low over the earth, the moon rose to wax full, but with a strange ruby color, encircled by a deep haze. "'Tis a moon eclipsed in blood," the scribes declared. Around it, the stars were dim. And the *stella comata* came no more.

* * *

Night of 21 July 1403: Coquetdale, Northumberland

Low clouds swirled through the valley as Ciarry awoke with a start.

Where am I? When is this? And what am I called by? Confusion engulfed her. Was she at the croft of her infancy? The convent that reared her? Her own abbey? Or somewhere else entirely? Even her name eluded her: That of her early childhood? The convent? As quasi-abbess? Or...

As clarity struck, a moment later, none of that mattered.

It's Harry. He's been killed. He's dead. I know it...

The conviction left no room for doubt; everything became numbingly real.

Too stricken to cry, though her throat constricted and eyes stung, she tried to tell herself she might be wrong. It didn't help.

Somehow, she sought company but hesitated to awaken Agnes. Yanking on clothes, she hastened to

310

the barn and saddled Grandon, the grey Harry had given her. Mounted, she left the farm and picked up the path to Holystone quickly, though the mists thickened as she reached the old Roman road and skirted the mystical Lady's Well, where legend held that St. Paulinus had baptized some 2,000 Northumbrians, 775 years earlier.

The convent lay beyond.

Tying her horse at the gate, she stumbled through the foggy kirkyard, nearly tripping over a root (or was it a tombstone?), ignoring the wet grass that reached out to tug at her ankles, slipping down the softly rolling little embankment to the old kirk. When she reached it, the door opened easily. Of course... even at risk to their security, the nuns wanted anyone in need to have access to them. They especially never barred entry to their greatest treasure, their sanctum, where the Lord dwelt...

Through blackness lit only by the tabernacle candle, Ciarry crossed the unevenly flagged floor. Halting in the sanctuary, she slumped against a pillar, the base of a Saxon arch. There she gave way to her anguish.

And there, arriving to prepare the church for Matins, the pre-dawn prayer service, Etheldreda found her, damp face pressed to the chill, unfeeling stone. Etheldreda realized only one thing could make her friend race across the countryside by dark. She gathered Ciarry in her arms.

"It's Harry," Ciarry's tears wet the nun's veil. "He's dead."

"I know, dear..." Etheldreda rocked Ciarry, even as her own heart began to break. "I know..."

* * *

At sunrise on Sunday, an itinerant friar wandered into the Shrewsbury castle courtyard. "Henry Bolingbroke," he declared, "when you usurped Richard's throne, 'twas foretold you would bring carnage upon the land. So you have, through manifest sins!" He extended a bony finger. "Repent, afore all is lost... *Repent!*"

Henry was transfixed at both the friar's stridency and his resemblance to the Franciscan who had infiltrated Westminster in 1399, before his coronation, predicting doom. Huddled at the window, the king shivered until his guards arrested the old man.

Henry immediately had him executed.

Then he ordered the exhumation of Hotspur's corpse, had it hauled back to Shrewsbury, embalmed, and exhibited, naked, at the High Cross, in the center of town.

Drawn by the tragedy and gruesome spectacle, folk gathered all Sunday afternoon. Some laughed, trading jokes with Henry's guards. More stood silently, faces glum; still others grieved openly, lamenting and praying, crying. Leaning close to those they trusted, some suggested the wrong man had died.

As hours passed, the throng increased. Men in Henry's livery and more in the prince's colors came, too, several swearing unhappily. Dunbar arrived as well to spit at the dead man's feet. Drawing elbow jabs, he retreated again. Other courtiers also drifted by, but no one expected Henry—until horns blared through the streets. "Make way for the king!"

Everyone fell back.

Henry swept up to the High Cross, beard jutting out, haughtily aloof, eyes impassive amber. At first, he gawked. Then his face flooded with erratic animation, his gaze darting over Harry's body. Pink lines shot across each cheek when he spoke, in a voice both imperious and strangled: "I accuse you on the day of judgment of the human blood unwillingly destroyed by me... *Ego appello te! I accuse you!*"

Without another word, he returned to the castle.

But he was back twice before nightfall, eyes vacant, shouting: *"Ego appello te! Ego appello te!"*

Worried, his advisors determined to remove the king from Shrewsbury as soon as he had dealt with the remaining "traitors."

The following day, Thomas Percy, Hugh Browe, the Cheshire lords Vernon and Venables, and others were beheaded or hanged in Henry's presence and at his order. Thomas met his end with stoic courage, despondent not at his own demise but Harry's, scarcely caring whether he lived or not. At least in death they would be reunited... His last words echoed his nephew: "Better to die here than live in tyranny!"

Yet, despite the executions, the king could not rest easily and hours later was spotted making yet another trip to the High Cross, again berating the dead man. *"Ego appello te!"*

His advisors hurried him from town.

Two days later, from Lichfield, he ordered that Harry's body be decapitated, with the head sent to York, to hang over the gate leading north. The rest he had quartered, dispatching arm and leg sections to display on the walls of Bristol, London, Newcastle-Upon-Tyne, and Chester. Then he returned to the splendor of his palace.

Hal wasn't with him. Wound festering badly, the prince was taken to Kenilworth, where only the skills of an expert surgeon-physician and extended nursing saved his life.

At court, Henry prowled his halls, troubled, some said, because his victory had proven so costly. As the aftermath of the battle revealed, despite Harry's death, it was Henry's side that had suffered the heaviest losses. Nine knights had died with Harry, but Henry had lost at least 28. One clerk reported immediate battlefield burials of about 1,850 men, of all ranks, but added that this excluded those interred elsewhere. A second chronicler recorded 8,000 total dead, from both camps. Elaborating, another explained that Hotspur's forces had 700 fatalities, but the king had 7,000. If so, in killing his supposed enemy, Henry had lost almost half his army.

He burned away his frustration with vengeance.

In Chester, Petronilla Clark was dragged kicking and screaming from her shop, losing it and her home, to become the only woman punished by name for supporting Harry. Countless others, however, also suffered from penalties, fines, confiscations, or death sentences imposed on their husbands, brothers or sons.

Her life ruined, her town bereft (for Chester paid a staggering sum to obtain a royal pardon), Petronilla took comfort in one thing: Her son, Kingsley, had escaped to Wales. Dependent on the charity of friends, she haunted the abbey church, weeping, drawing the attention and pity of St. Werburgh's abbot. Along with paying for new glove-making equipment so that she could resume her livelihood, he gave her a cottage near his walls, in return for token rent: One pair of gloves a year.

* * *

August 1403: Northern England

Archbishop Scrope submerged himself in his episcopal duties and ministry. Too heartsick to believe he could truly assist his morose flock, he was also too dedicated to do anything but try.

Eventually, he knew, he would have to move beyond the purely religious and become active in a more political sense as well. Thousands had perished.

Most had been Henry's men, but callously used, they deserved justice, too. So did the living, suffering under the king's atrocious rule. But first, England needed time.

Scrope labored alone now. His colleague from Durham, Bishop Skirlaw, had escaped the battlefield, sheltered briefly with Bishop Trevor at St. Asaph's, and sailed into exile in France.

Trevor himself remained safe, at least as long as Henry didn't invade Wales. But that could happen at any moment, for instead of ending the fervor for reform, Henry's actions in Shrewsbury had stoked it. Soon after the battle, another Welsh county had defected, Flintshire, where English and Welsh alike had announced allegiance to Glyn Dwr. Harry had easily held them. Henry could not and swore to punish them.

Scrope feared war could march north, too.

Parishioners and priests alike spoke of rejecting Henry, of emulating Harry and his battlefield declaration. But at present, the North needed to recover, to learn to go on without many of its sons, without Harry. Writing to his flock, the archbishop advised restraint: *Let us sleep amidst the ruins of our fallen dreams, and try to forget that once we had ideals, and held them high, and dared to follow such a man...*

Someday, he would take up Harry's fallen banner. But not yet; not yet...

* * *

Henry freed Hardyng after he spent a period in Furnival's keeping. While he had fought like a knight at Shrewsbury, Hardyng was still a squire and thus considered less culpable. Moreover, Furnival had urged Hardyng's release. Sensing he had enraged

Harry's cousin enough, Henry had acquiesced.

Montgomery remained a captive, with Douglas. Though less seriously wounded than at Homildon, Douglas was recovering more slowly than he had the previous autumn, a setback that Montgomery attributed to Harry's death and Douglas' dismay at falling into Henry's and Dunbar's clutches at last.

Dunbar himself spent less time at court, infuriated that he was not named warden of England's East March. Instead, Henry chose Prince John, who was even younger than Hal and in whose name power clearly would be wielded by grown men, though not the Dunbars. Likewise, replacing Earl Henry on the West March, the king appointed Ralph Neville its warden.

Friction also arose between Henry and Dunbar with the belated recognition that they had outsmarted themselves at Shrewsbury. If the battle had killed Hotspur, it had also eliminated Dunbar's chance of reclaiming his Scottish estates and Henry's ability to annex a swath of lower Scotland. Unwilling to proceed after losing their commander, Hotspur's lieutenants had disbanded their northern army. The Scots had reclaimed Cocklaws-Ormiston and environs by default.

* * *

Declining to join Furnival's staff, Hardyng headed north to piece together his life. He had maintained loose ties to his family, but it was Harry who had raised him from age 12. They'd been together 14 years, and it was hard to consider any other existence. Yet he had to consider it, though one thing was clear already: Wherever he ended up, it wouldn't be with the house of Percy, for he could never forgive Earl Henry for abandoning Harry.

Otherwise, all he knew was that he wanted to continue as a man-at-arms and a scribe, and, perhaps, write books someday, like Froissart and Chaucer.

Beyond Cheshire, he met several archers returning to Carlisle and learned that MacKerny had fled to Wales with Giscardier to join Glyn Dwr. He rode with the bowmen for a day, then turned northeast, alone. He continued to have the road to himself and to the beat of his horse's hooves, a poem began intruding on his thoughts. He let it come, partly because it was balm for his sorrow, partly because he wondered about Thor, who had disappeared, and partly because the insistent rhyme gave no surcease. Finally, he stopped to jot it down:

The Fields of Shrewsbury

Gone the hawk, from northern sky,
answering valor's ancient cry,
Close by its master's side to fly,
with he who would for justice die,
On the fields of Shrewsbury...

Gone the hawk, from Cheviot's mist,
from twilight moor, by starlight kissed,
Gone with he who left the burn,
and glade and glen, to ne'er return,
From the fields of Shrewsbury...

Gone the hawk from Tweed and Tyne,
with he who won a lass so fine,
and brought her hope, and gave her love,

*Gone he, whom e'er she's
dreaming of,
            Far from the fields of
Shrewsbury...*

*   Gone hawk and knight, from
Coquetdale,
            to fight that righteousness
prevail,
            Gone our lord, from heathered
moss,
            while we remain, to mourn our
loss
            Away from fields of
Shrewsbury...*

*   Gone the hawk, from northern
sky
            answering valor's ancient cry,
Close by its master's side to fly,
            with he who would for justice
die,
            On the fields of Shrewsbury.*

August 1403: Tower House, Northumberland

In Northumberland, as elsewhere, royal messengers had spread news of the battle, but Hardyng was the first to reach Tower House with details. He found only Agnes at home; Ciarry had ridden to Holystone, where, Agnes revealed, Ciarry spent hours, whenever she wasn't laboring frantically on the farm, pushing herself into wrung-out exhaustion by the close of each day. "Trying to drown woe in weariness," Agnes sighed. The old woman confided something else: "She knew about Harry, almost as soon as he fell, long ere reports reached these parts."

As they gathered around the table later that day, Ciarry confirmed it. "Sounds like a fable, I know, But 'tis true."

"I believe you," Hardyng assured her.

Agnes patted the younger woman's shoulder. "God told you, or let Harry tell you. He went straight to heaven, I'm sure."

Ciarry's eyes filled. "Aye. That's one of the things that comforts me, if anything can, after the disinterment and all."

Hardyng winced. "You heard of that?"

Ciarry buried her head in her hands. "Aye...." It was unbearable to think about, yet sometimes all she *did* was think about it: That tall, flawlessly fit body, stretched out naked in Shrewsbury, then hacked apart. The long legs that strode the earth so energetically and wrapped so affectionately around hers in bed, exhibited in towns. The lean, powerful shoulders and arms that had held her, grotesquely affixed to walls. And his handsome head, with the face that had looked on hers with so much love, spiked above the entrance to York...

"If you want to pay your respects, at York or Newcastle, I'll take you," Hardyng said.

Ciarry twisted the ring Harry had given her, its stone like a drop of blood. "Thank you, John. But no. Perhaps 'tis better I not. And were his whole body there, it still wouldn't be Harry."

"No," Hardyng agreed. "Even at the tomb in Whitchurch, Harry wasn't there. He's with the Lord, waiting for us."

"Aye." Ciarry's tears spilled. As he placed his hand over hers, he began to cry, too. They rose, holding each other. Agnes embraced them both, and the three clung together...

Hardyng departed the next day, leaving Ciarry with a copy of his poem, pledging that since Harry had been a brother to him, she had become his sister and he would always look after her.

She knew he would keep his word.

Two weeks later, Ciarry stood atop her roof, tending pots of herb seedlings. Hoofbeats on the road caught her attention. A familiar horse approached, its rider about Harry's height and with a similar build. Her heart caught in her throat.

Astride Redesraven, guiding another horse on a lead, Furnival rode through the gate.

She leaned over the crenellation. "Thom!"

He waved, dismounting.

Ciarry sped down the stairs. Furnival had visited in Harry's company a few times, and she liked him, seeing similarities to Harry that went beyond Neville family resemblances. Below, she extended a palm and smiled. Yet sadness shadowed her eyes—and his.

He kissed her hand, then pulled her into a hug. "I'm so sorry. I'd give anything if it could be otherwise."

"Aye," she murmured. "It's been difficult. I only hope my glumness doesn't weigh on you, too."

"It can't," Furnival said, as they stepped apart again. "Truth is, I've been furious since that moment on the battlefield when I realized what was happening—that Henry had betrayed Harry, and me, and his own army. I was with the king at Shrewsbury. You probably know that."

She nodded. "I assumed you had no choice. None of those men did."

"Yea. I didn't want to fight. But Henry had threatened to harm my wife if I didn't." He shook his head. "It was ghastly: Brother against brother, kin against kin, like Harry and me. 'Twas the worst slaughter I've ever seen. And it should never have been. That night," his eyes closed, voice strained. "I tried to laud Harry, buried him with a funeral Mass and all the respect and accolade I could give. Henry undid it all, breaking his promise to me, again, desecrating Harry's body. I detest him for it, for everything."

"I understand."

"That's partly why I'm here."

"I'm glad you came. But you're doubtless weary and could use refreshment." She led him into the house and fixed a tray with cups of wine, cheese, and berries from her bushes. He carried it to a table in the dappled warmth of the upper garden.

"I was with Henry until I rode here," Furnival explained. "He thinks I was so attentive because I was impressed with his 'triumph.'" He drawled the term derisively. "Really, 'twas because I wanted to do what I could to prevent further havoc. That's why I took up my current mission." He lowered his drink. "I've been named to oversee the confiscation of Harry's goods and properties in sections of Northumberland and Yorkshire."

"Oh God." She blanched.

"It's not as you think," he asserted. "I'm doing it to prevent someone else from doing it. If there's any reason to doubt Harry held a property as the sole owner, I've refused to take it. I accepted this post so I can protect Harry's people, not steal from them!"

Her eyes narrowed. "Are you supposed to seize Tower House, too?"

"No. I assume you hold clear title."

She nodded. "I bought half the property from Harry when we met. Before he left, he sold the rest to churchmen, who conveyed it to me."

Furnival smiled. "That was clever, but legal. Regardless, though, I couldn't seize this place. I know how much Harry loved it and loved you. What he held dear, I will protect. I swear it."

"I'm grateful." She refilled his goblet.

"I've got Harry's saddlehorse," Furnival added. "They found him with the extra horses and baggage. He's yours, if you wish. I've another to ride."

Redesraven. Something more of Harry's to hold onto. She felt a desperate hunger to possess and safeguard anything of his. Yet she slowly shook her head. "I appreciate your kindness. But Redesraven belonged to a knight; he should stay with one."

"And Valdus? Harry's warhorse? I also claimed him."

"'Tis the same. However, if I may make a request?"

"Of course."

"Give him to Lord Douglas. I understand that Douglas was riding him when taken. Let them stay together."

"A fine idea. Douglas will be honored. Until he can ride again, though," Furnival added, "I'll keep Valdus, lest someone snatch him from Henry's stables. Douglas is a royal hostage. I doubt he'll see freedom soon. But I'll do what I can for him—and Valdus."

"Please."

Furnival unbuckled his belt pouch. "There's one more reason I came, the most important. I've brought you a letter from Harry. We discovered it on his body." He handed her a slim leather envelope, which replaced the original battle-stained bag. "I took it, so the king couldn't."

She looked both eager and inexpressibly sad. "Thank you."

"I'll see to the horses." He returned to the yard.

Gently, Ciarry removed the parchment, to read Harry's last words to her:

Shrewsbury, 21 July 1403

My Very Dearest Ciarry,

*If you are reading this, I am
dead. Or, perhaps I should say that I
have gone to be with God, for I hope
and trust that He will take me to
Himself—if not immediately, for my
many sins and failings, then once He
has let me sojourn awhile in some*

purgatory or other. Please pray that I not linger too long there! In any case, I am, I think, in a state of grace, cherished by God, however flawed I may be. And for that I ask you to rejoice for me.

I hope, too, that He will have allowed me the honor of dying a knight's death in battle, and not the death of a traitor on the gallows or the executioner's block—for, as you know, whilst I strove for reforms I am no traitor.

Obviously, though, the manner of my death will not have been mine to say. Only God could ordain that, or, more precisely, only fate, since I believe that oft in this world He brings us to life and takes us to Himself in death, and in between lets the fates buffet us as they will, though He always remains there to guide us through the fens and share our burdens as we go.

However, all of that may have fallen out, know that in death I am in no pain, no longer threatened, no longer pursued. Let that assurance comfort you.

Remember, too, as I tried to tell you afore we parted, that while my life enfleshed as a man on earth may have ended, my true life—my spirit, my mind, my heart, the very essence of my being, the _real_ Harry, goes on. I _live_, but no longer in the form *where you can see me and hold me to you. May God give us both the fortitude, courage and faith in Him to endure that, until the blessed day we can be totally reunited. Nevertheless, I will never abandon you. I shall always be standing with you close under my right arm, my sword arm, the better to protect you as your faithful knight. You once described me as your lord, your defender, your friend and your love: dominus, defensor, amicus, et amor. Indeed, I was, from the moment we met. And indeed I <u>am</u>, and so shall I be, semper, forever.*

Of course, I am also your debtor because I owe you so much. You made me whole, Ciarry. Ere I met you, ere I felt your love, I was an incomplete man, an imperfect man. Doubtless, I remain imperfect, but whatever honing of self, whatever strides toward perfection I made in these last few years, I made because of you. Supposedly I was born "noble," but 'twas a lie! 'Twas you who ennobled me and gave me whatever genuine nobility I attained (and it has naught to do with having barons as forebears). How could I ever repay you? I couldn't in my short existence on earth. But had I lived a thousand lives, I still never could have repaid you. Misfit rascal that I am, I can only tell you how grateful I am. How very fortunate I was to have found you, to have known you, to have been able to love you and—mirabile dictu, wondrous to relate—to have won your love as well.

Last night, afore I slept, I looked to the heavens, and the North, where you are. When you read this, do likewise. Go hence by night and look for our northern stars and know that I am with you, gazing at them, loving you. Perhaps I am like the stars myself now. On cloudy days, or at brightest noon, you cannot see them; yet still you know they are there. In that same way, I am there, too.

Now the day lengthens and my hourglass surrenders its last grains. I must perforce return to my men. Ere I seal these inadequate lines, let me add one more thought, the word by which I have tried to live my life: Esperance!

May hope be yours, my love, always.

Your Harry

Epilogue

In the end, Hotspur had won.

It was so obvious to Henry now, in the last hours of his own mortal existence, with no time left to make up for all the wrongs he had committed, all the evils he had condoned. Harry had lost the Battle of Shrewsbury but won the battle of life. He'd prevailed in the greatest contest of all—the struggle for mastery of self, for defeat of debased desire, for the triumph of all that was good in a man. Harry had been victorious, and he, Henry, Fourth of that Name since the Conquest, ruler of England and Wales and all the rest, had been vanquished. Miserably. Even the circumstances of their deaths made it clear.

Harry had fallen esteemed by thousands, including all those in his army, who, offered a choice, had stayed with him to the last. There had been so many others, too, bishops and nobles, mayors and abbots, farmers and fisherfolk, merchants and lowly churls... For years, it had been Harry "on whom the hope of all the people was riding," as one scribe had boldly declared. Yea, so it *had* ridden on a man lauded in life and mourned in death.

Few would mourn "His Majesty, Henry," though. And he knew it.

Other things troubled him, as well.

Harry had died on the verge of victory, knowing he had already bested his adversary in their private battle because he had put Henry to flight, made him cringe behind the lines, proved his cowardice. And Harry had died championing all he believed in, vigorous to the end.

But here he, Henry, was, dying feeble and incapacitated by a stroke at age 46, only three years older than Harry had been at Shrewsbury. Not much to brag about, those three years, especially since he'd been plagued by disease for many more. Muscles aching and immobile, face distorted from seizures, body bloated and skin ruptured in suppurating boils, he had become so disfigured that even close aides shrank back in repulsion.

Divine retribution, the populace said, punishment not only for Shrewsbury and all that preceded it but all that followed, including the sacrilegious execution of

Archbishop Scrope.

Mustering his courage and the men of the North in 1405, Scrope had urged reform anew and excommunicated the king for his most egregious sins, among them mistreating Hotspur in life and desecrating his body after death. Scrope's supporters had included the Earl of Northumberland; his opponents included Ralph Neville, who became the archbishop's undoing. At Henry's behest, Neville proposed parleys, only to arrest Scrope when he agreed—the same gambit Harry had rejected at Shrewsbury and refused to use against Glyn Dwr. Henry had then had Scrope beheaded. Earl Henry had fled into exile and was killed three years later, attempting to re-enter England.

Now, Henry was about to follow them to the grave.

He had been stricken at Westminster Abbey while preparing to give alms. It seemed as if even God disdained his charity, offered by blasphemed hands, with tainted money.

The location of his deathbed was notable, too. Fortune was playing tricks, as in 1403. Harry had perished "hard by Berwick," but not Berwick-upon-

Tweed, nor on the Borders at all. Hearing the "Berwick versus Berwick" story at Shrewsbury from Harry's captured lieutenants, Henry had laughed riotously. *Harry had died at the wrong Berwick! Harry couldn't even get that right!*

Yet, here *he* was, King Henry, dying in the wrong Jerusalem...

He had aspired to end his days "in Jerusalem," on Crusade or in pilgrimage as an elderly monarch. Well, he was "in Jerusalem" all right—the Jerusalem Chamber of Westminster Abbey, to which he'd been carried, too weak to be borne to his palace. The room's name came from its tapestries and hearth, decorated with biblical scenes.

So much for the Holy City.

His courtiers hovered. Most seemed unmoved by his agony, and he suspected they were present not because they cared about him but because they cared about themselves. Fearing to miss out on any last largesse he might bestow, they also vied for favor from his successor, Hal.

The 25-year-old prince, however, was indifferent to them and coolly polite to his father. If he sometimes regarded his sire with pity, he also left little doubt of his loathing for much that Henry had done.

Nor was Hal alone.

Even some royal counselors urged Henry to repent, at least for murdering an anointed king (Richard) and consecrated archbishop (Scrope), and stealing the throne.

Henry himself fluctuated between stubbornness and sorrow.

"On the first two points, I wrote to the pope," he protested. "He sent me a bull with absolution and penance, which I fulfilled. As for the third point, the crown and any transgression involving it: Truly 'tis hard to remedy. My children would not want royal power to go out of our line. Besides, you mentioned three sins. What of the rest?"

Indeed, "the rest" weighed heavily in his more remorseful moments.

"Sinful wretch..." he whispered. "What a life I have misspent..."

He saw his victims in constant procession, an endless parade of dead: Richard's advisors, executed during that first near-coup 25 years earlier; Lords Arundel and Gloucester, brutally killed in 1397; Bushey, Wiltshire and Green, beheaded at Bristol;

Richard, starved at Pontefract; all those friars and critics he'd silenced so brutally; Thomas Percy and Hugh Browe and the others executed after Shrewsbury; the men in both armies killed in battle there when he violated his own truce; Scrope, of course; and, above all, Hotspur.

Harry, galloping across the battlefield, pointing an accusatory sword, bearing down on him. *Harry,* who chased him even in his dreams, who would haunt him forever...

He whimpered, but no one leaned down to comfort him.

Closing his eyes, Henry shut out his entourage, if not his eternity.

Westminster's monks drew close, replacing the courtiers and chanting penitential psalms associated with King David and blood crime:

> *Lord, rebuke me no more in your anger.*
> *My flesh is afflicted because of your ire.*
> *My bones ache because of my sin.*
> *Foul and festering are my sores because of my folly.*
> *The very light of my eyes has failed.*

*In your compassion blot out
my transgressions.
Wash away my guilt, for I
know my offense.
My sin is always before me…*

Henry listened as long as he could hear. Finally, lapsing into a coma, he died.

* * *

Thirty Years Later—October 1443: Tower House, Northumberland

"Ask the old woman," they urged the traveler, when they themselves could help no further. "'Twas she who knew him best…"

Aye, so she had, in the days when her hair flamed with the color of sunset, when her skin was as smooth as an unfolding petal, her step faster and her hands less careworn, when she was young…

Over 70 now, she continued to dwell on the land her lord had given her, after he'd found her walking the wild hills of Northumberland and carried her heart away. She had lived most of her life without him. But in that one fragile moment when they met, not only her life but her eternity had changed…

Someone as perceptive as John Hardyng had known it all along and understood immediately whom the farmers meant when they said, "if you would speak of Sir Harry, go to her."

To Hardyng's gratification, many remembered *him*, too, from service under Hotspur's command. Relishing the chance to relive war stories, hoary veterans would begin over noon ale and end at dusk, when both their brimming pitchers and recollections were exhausted. Lingering and listening, Hardyng would scribble pages of notes, as entranced as they.

Others who had not been in border armies brought more prosaic reminiscences but no less inclination to share them, talking of what it had been like to call Sir Harry their lord and neighbor, their friend; of encountering him at markets or Sunday kirk; of numerous examples of his kindness and a few of his wrath; of how this land hadn't seen his like afore him and never would again...

Inevitably, everyone concluded with the same advice: "Go hence to Tower House. She'll gladly tell you more."

Thus, one afternoon, when Coquetdale blazed russet and gold, Hardyng made the journey, pausing on the road above to survey the farmstead. So many memories clung to this place, so many...

And his were the least of them.

Overall, it looked much the same as always, although Ciarry had improved some of the outbuildings and added others, similarly expanding the herds and flocks in her fields.

Her neighbors remained, too.

Enochie had grown into the outstanding man he'd always promised to be, inheriting his father's property and buying the mill across the way. A widower, he maintained his lands with his sons and grandsons and continued to assist Ciarry, a partner as well as a neighbor. He rented many of her fields, and her will provided that upon her death, her holdings would be divided between his family and the nuns at Holystone.

Agnes had been gone for some time, dying in her sleep, well over age 80. Her body lay in the garden, next to the stillborn twins.

For Harry himself, there was no grave.

"Another St. Oswald," the Northumbrians said, for like Oswald some 750 years earlier, Harry had died near Shrewsbury, fighting a corrupt king. Like

Oswald's corpse, his had been interred, only to be exhumed and desecrated by the king who had slain him. Again, as in the case of Oswald, his limbs had been scattered. Unlike Oswald's body, however, Harry's seemed to have disappeared from his family's own castle. After months exposed on town walls, the pieces of his skeleton had been boxed and sent to Alnwick, for Elizabeth to bury on one of her trips north. Not long after the battle, though, she had married Camoys. What she had done with her first husband's remains she never divulged, not even to the children. Hardyng had always suspected that, thoroughly estranged from even Harry's memory, she had simply ordered the servants to toss the bones in the river.

Harry's only memorial was the countryside he loved...

By now, many of his companions were gone, too. Furnival had unexpectedly died a few years after Harry, and Montgomery around the same time. Douglas had languished as Henry's captive for five years. Visiting Ciarry on his release, he had delivered a two-fold pledge: That he would devote all his energies to fighting Henry IV and his ilk; and that if in doing so he raided England, he would never touch Tower House. He had kept his word and died in 1424, battling Lancastrian armies in Normandy. Harry had indeed been the only English lord who could command his allegiance and win his friendship.

Like Douglas, Hardyng had remained active as he greyed. After Harry's death, he had accepted a post with Sir Robert Umfraville, serving with him and Henry V, the erstwhile Prince Hal, in the campaign that included the victory at Agincourt.

As a king, Hal had been nearly everything his father had not, making amends from the first moments of his reign. Although hardly perfect, he had been beloved for his courage, intelligence, and innate (if sometimes badly ignored) sense of decency.

Removing Richard II's body from an obscure grave, he had reburied it in Westminster Abbey, in regal splendor. He had likewise reached out to other, still-living victims, including the latest generation of the house of Percy.

Under Henry IV, the Percies had suffered severely. Furnival had tried to mitigate the losses in 1403 and sometimes succeeded. Overall, though, Henry had ruthlessly confiscated everything, all Harry's lands and possessions, down to the most mundane items, including blankets. A few years later, Earl Henry's own clash with Henry, followed by the earl's death, had provided another chance to loot the family estates.

More interested in old friendships than old animosities, Hal-Henry V had returned many properties to Harry's son and named him Earl of Northumberland, restoring his grandfather's title.

Hardyng had gladly served the dashing Henry V in diplomatic capacities. But Henry V had also died too soon, at age 34, in France, after ruling for nine years.

The latest Lancastrian, Hal's son, now held the throne as Henry VI. An artistic young man, vastly different from both his father and grandfather, he had acquired the crown as a babe and disliked politics, governance and war. Whether his reign would flower into greatness or disintegrate into chaos was unclear, though the crass competition at court suggested the latter.

Now 66, Hardyng had seen many of the power struggles firsthand, as he had witnessed so much of the tumult of his age. His experience had been put to good use, for between adventures in warfare and statecraft he had authored a treatise of English history, which he continued to update as affairs warranted or fancy struck. Of late, he had busied himself with another project, too.

Hence, his mission to Tower House.

He trotted through the gate, leaving his horse to Bartram, Enochie's grandson and spitting image. The back door opened, and Ciarry ran out, as slim as ever, Dogmael's latest descendant tripping happily at her heels.

"John!"

Laughing, he greeted her with a hug and stooped to pet the puppy, pleased to see Ciarry so healthy and content—as content as she could ever be, without Harry.

Hardyng's affection for her had increased over the decades, and he had twice asked her to marry him. Both times she had gently declined, not because she wasn't fond of him or he wouldn't have made a good husband, but because no one could ever take Harry's place in her heart. And without that kind of love, she would never wed.

Undismayed, Hardyng had continued to call, and the two were bonded as much by their own friendship as by prior ties to Harry.

"You're in time for supper." Ciarry ushered him into the house. "'Tis a blessed delight to see you, a welcome surprise."

"You didn't get my letter? Sent a week ago, with a friar bound for Brinkburn and Holystone? 'Twas full of my news and plans."

"Doubtless he'll arrive anon. Meanwhile, you can tell me yourself."

Hardyng grinned. "I've started another book, afore any more of us go the way of all flesh. I've waited too long as it is." He accepted a cider flagon and went on. "'Twill be about great men of our time, biographies, as it were, not hagiographies. And I intend to start with Harry."

She glowed with the rare joy that only thoughts of Harry inspired. "Marvelous!"

"I hope so. But you must help. I want you to write your own account, whatever you can say about him. Then I'll put it with mine: A true rendering, 'twill be, by two who knew him well."

Despite her enthusiasm, sadness stirred. Even after all these years, it hurt. She still missed Harry; craved his smile; yearned, sometimes with an almost physical hunger, to see him again, just to hold him. She longed to find those dark-blue eyes teasing her from across the table; hear the rich, boyish laughter; slip her hand into his as they walked their horses down a lane on a moonlit eve. She wanted only to kneel before him again, vowing to be his and taking him as her lord, feel him pulling her up, into his embrace and his keeping and—as he had oft reminded her—into his debt, forever...

At times, alone, she still wept. Yet there was happiness, too. Often, she felt intensely close to Harry, as she recalled his words: *"I shall always love you ... always be with you."*

'Twas true. Somehow, he *was* with her...

Watching a beautiful smile light her face, Hardyng could guess where her mind and heart had been. He lifted his cup: "To Harry!"

That evening, they talked further, two writers deep in collaboration.

"How soon do you want my opus?" she asked.

"Whenever you're ready. I've seen your chronicles of the local monasteries and your texts for schoolchildren. I know you write fast and well."

"I've never written anything like this, though. You might see as many tear drops as ink blots on the manuscript."

"If 'twill distress you," Hardyng said regretfully, "don't do it. I'll have material enou'."

"No," she assured him. "I *want* to do it."

He brightened again. "Whate'er you write will be wonderful."

"We'll see."

"Hah! I doubt it not!"

They toasted the venture with another cup of wine.

* * *

A month later, he returned to find her smoothing a sheaf of parchments. "I've written anonymously, as a scribe and close friend of Harry," she explained. "'Twill be obvious, though, that it wasn't by you. And folks may guess a woman wrote it."

"Let them. We can pair it with mine, two complementary chronicles, and not combine them into one." Hardyng pulled up a chair and began reading. He soon looked up, excited. "This is very good!"

"Aye?"

"Truly!" He happily immersed himself again.

Ciarry tended the hearth, pensively watching the flames. For several minutes, the only sound was the crackle of the fire and the soft brush of another page turning under Hardyng's hand. Then she broke the silence, crossing the room in abrupt inspiration. "May I?" She reached across Hardyng to retrieve the last sheet from the bottom of the stack. "I had an idea: to add a few words at the end, for any who might come across my work, years from now, and wonder how it came to be..."

"Of course."

Returning to her desk, she penned a brief postscript, a final tribute to Harry:

> *Long ago, when the world was a*
> *little bit newer,*
> *   and the risks of challenging*
> *kings never more daunting,*
> *   I fell in love with the greatest*
> *knight in England.*

*Above all other men, he dared to
seek justice
      and defend righteousness.
      And for these he died, for he held
them
      dearer than life itself.*

*To these verities I can attest,
forthrightly
      for I had his heart, just as he
had mine.
      Let these pages tell his story.*

*And someday, if you have read
them,
      know that you have read truth.*

The End

Afterword

Factoids and Fiction

Because I've always believed that entertainment can be educational and education entertaining, I offer detailed chapter notes on what in To Tread on Kings actually occurred, according to the historical record, and what I created. Overall, however, though cast as fiction, the tale told is largely true. To assist readers wishing to explore further, a bibliography follows, with full names of sources mentioned in these notes. The bibliography applies to all 3 volumes in the Epic of Hotspur series.

Liz Sevchuk Armstrong

October 2025

Chapter I

This chapter is mostly made up, although many of the characters in it were real. Sir John Montgomery captured Hotspur in 1388 when the Scots invaded Northumberland and Hotspur spent more than a year as a captive with Montgomery waiting for England's King Richard II to allow his ransom. Montgomery seems to have treated him quite well, more like a younger brother or son than a prisoner, and I suspect the two became close, lifelong friends. Thomas Knayton, John Hardyng, Bishop Skirlaw, and others were real men. Enochie, Ciarry, Agnes, and Sister Etheldreda are fictitious, although I strongly believe

Hotspur did have a sweetheart much like Ciarry. The women's skills, education, self-reliance, and courage exemplify those of many long-forgotten women in the Middle Ages. The preparations that Hotspur and his advisors, including Ciarry and Etheldreda, discussed reflect what probably did occur at times of threats to the North.

Chapter II

Depiction of the Battle of Homildon Hill (or Humbleton Hill) comes from information in the *Annales* (pages 344-347); the *Dieulacres Chronicle* (pg. 177); the *Giles Chronicle* (pgs. 28-29); *the Buik of the Croniclis of Scotland (pg. 480-482)*; and *Scotichronicon*, (pgs. 44-49), and Holinshcd's *Historie of Scotland* (pgs. 405-406). Royal sources (*Calendar of Documents Relating to Scotland*, No. 620) and English chronicles report the incredibly low English losses of 5 men slain (though others may have died later of wounds, unrecorded). If the reports of the English fatalities are correct, Hotspur's victory must rank as one of the greatest English latter-medieval military victories, as significant as Poitiers, Crecy, and Agincourt. Yet the battle seems little known. Perhaps the animus of King Henry stifled early celebrations and awareness of what happened faded over the centuries.

The English archers seem to have played a crucial role in the Homildon victory and are sometimes credited with winning the battle almost single-handedly. (See the *Annales*.) Their contribution to the Scottish defeat cannot be underestimated, but the English cavalry charge and pursuit (including the chase by the fighting merchants of Newcastle) at the end certainly prevented the surviving Scots from regrouping or escaping and thus were crucial as well.

The *Scotichronicon* credits Dunbar with preventing Hotspur from embarking on a charge before deploying the archers, but the incident is not mentioned in any of the English chronicles cited above (not even in the pro-Henry IV chronicles, which would have had incentive to make Hotspur look bad). Given Dunbar's apparent envy of Hotspur, his habit of otherwise bragging about his accomplishments, and his duplicitous conduct against both Scotland and England, any claims that Dunbar essentially "saved the day" at Homildon are highly dubious. I suspect that the story only surfaced as a bit of Scottish and/or Dunbar propaganda to explain the debacle and later help ease the Dunbars back into Scottish society by asserting that the Scots lost at Homildon largely because a fellow Scot—George Dunbar—directed the battle against them and saved the English from their own foolishness. Nonetheless, I think that the story also contains a nugget of truth and that Dunbar and Hotspur disagreed over the issue of coordinating a cavalry charge with the use of archers and that the two held the respective viewpoints ascribed to them here.

Douglas was severely injured—according to the *Annales,* by five wounds—and blinded in one eye, as described here. A "Lord Montgomery" was captured, along with the other prominent Scots. Since the various chronicles do not provide his first name, suggesting confusion even among medieval writers as to which 'Lord Montgomery' this was, I'm guessing he was Hotspur's captor-turned-friend, John Montgomery.

Chapters III and IV

During his long recuperation under Hotspur's care, Douglas became far less of a captive or hostage than a close friend, and Hotspur seems to have quickly dropped any ideas of ransoming him. Ultimately, nothing but a genuine friendship between the two can explain the depth of Douglas's subsequent conduct and deep commitment to Hotspur, even assuming that they made some mutually beneficial political and military pact regarding control of the Borders. However, the scenes here are fictitious, though based on my idea of the way their friendship may have developed. The lines from Froissart's chronicle at the beginning of the chapter, where Hotspur reads of his own prior exploits, are from the Johnes edition of Froissart (pgs. 367 and 371). Hotspur did order a for trial Sir William Stewart, who was eventually convicted and executed. (For Stewart, see *The Scots Peerage*, Vol. IV, and *The Black Douglases*, among other sources.) In Chapter IV, Montgomery's visit and Hotspur's debate with his father are fictitious. However, events demonstrated that Hotspur and his father diametrically differed on the hostage issue. The writs from King Henry forbidding ransom or freeing of the prisoners are from the *Calendar of Documents Relating to Scotland*, numbers 620 and 622.

Chapter V

According to Hardyng, Edmund Mortimer appealed to Hotspur when all other attempts to persuade Henry to allow him to ransom himself had failed. (See Kingsford's article, 'The First Version of Hardyng's Chronicle,' pg. 472, and the Ellis edition of Hardyng's chronicle, pg. 359.) Mortimer's use of Hotspur as a last-ditch channel suggests that, contrary to the portrayals in Shakespeare and elsewhere, Edmund Mortimer and Hotspur were not particularly close. Certainly, Mortimer never seems to have been one of Hotspur's aides or lieutenants, to have campaigned militarily with him in Wales or elsewhere, or to have lent support either during Hotspur's tours of duty in Wales or at the end, at Shrewsbury. The letters from Hotspur's children and wife are fictitious, but he was probably under tremendous family pressure, as well as his own sense of obligation as a senior English official in Wales to help Edmund.

Wording of Henry's writ about making Douglas fit enough to travel and then relinquishing him in London is invented, but based on what the king is known to have ordered. (See Hardyng, pgs. 360-361) The text of King Henry's dialogue with the doomed friars is taken directly from the *Eulogium* (pgs. 389-394). I have translated and slightly edited the excerpt used here. The scene of the surrender of the Scottish prisoners is based on the accounts in Hardyng, in the Kirby biography of Henry IV (pg. 148) and other sources, though I have added Montgomery's involvement. The broad details of Hotspur's argument with Henry IV, including some of the dialogue, come from several chronicles: Hardyng (pgs. 360-361), the *Eulogium* (pg. 396), *The Brut* (pgs. 548, 593), *The Giles Chronicle* (cited under Chapter II, above), and Davies's *English Chronicle* (pg. 27). According to the *Eulogium*, Henry called Hotspur a traitor and pulled a knife on him. *The Brut* reports that Henry slugged him in the face and called him a "whoreson." The *Giles Chronicle* and *The Brut* also state that Henry sent a courier with a conciliatory message after Hotspur, but that the latter, while likewise conciliatory, excused himself and continued on his way—probably distrusting Henry's intentions and, as The *Giles Chronicle* reported, dismayed after having seen the conduct and caliber of the men gathered around the throne. While referring to the medieval accounts for the essence of what happened, I've filled in gaps in describing the scene.

Chapter VI

I have recreated Hotspur's letter, based on his
allegations from his battlefield declaration and the
paraphrased references to his letters in the *Annales*
(pgs. 361-362) and *Historia Anglicana* (pg. 255).
Other sources as well (Hardyng, the *Giles Chronicle*),
mention his correspondence to enlist support for
political reform. Indeed, some of the language in the
Annales may well have been lifted directly from his
correspondence. Also, one allegation cited by the
scribe, that government funds intended for national
defense and other serious needs "were not being used
for what was obliged but devoured, excessively
uselessly, and wasted besides!" sounds very much
like something Hotspur would have said or penned.
(See pages 361-362 in the *Annales* and pg. 255 in
Historia Anglicana, Vol. II.)

According to Exchequer rolls, on 7 December 1402,
Hotspur submitted tallies for £4,115, 17 shillings,
including a tally for £200 in reimbursement of costs
incurred at Conway Castle in 1401. The money owed
to him became another unwanted "loan" to the
Crown. (Exchequer rolls E401/626; E403/574)
Henry *did* go through a series of treasurers, none of
whom seemed to have been able to curb his profligate
ways. The scenes at York with Skirlaw and Scrope are
fictitious, but according to Hardyng and other
sources, both prelates were Hotspur's supporters and
advisors in his government reform efforts. In fact,
Hardyng, mentions that Hotspur consulted widely
with others, numerous bishops and barons alike (pgs.
351-352, 361), while the *Historia Anglicana*
specifically mentions his letters to shire or county
officials, the local government leaders (pg. 255).

Chapters VII and VIII

Henry backed down on the hostage issue, naming a special commission to resolve the matter (*Calendar of Documents Relating to Scotland*, No. 629). He also granted the Douglas lands to the Earl of Northumberland and his heirs, and the wording used here is from his order. (*Rotuli Scotiae, Vol. II*, pgs. 163-164; translation by this author.) Dunbar likewise got his old lands back—if he could conquer them. (*Calendar of Documents Relating to Scotland*, No. 634) The invasion of Teviotdale and siege at Cocklaws or Ormiston are described in Wyntoun's *Orygynale Cronykil of Scotland* (pgs. 89-90); *Scotichronicon* (pgs. 51-53); *The Buik of the Croniclis of Scotland (*pg. 483-484*)*; and the *Annales* (pg. 360). Grymslaw apparently won his match and collected his winner's purse, but still became Hotspur's hostage as surety for the truce. (And it was apparently Hotspur's sappers who left equipment in their tunnel, thereby raising the alarms of Scottish deceit so vigorously disputed by Grymslaw.) Hardyng, Wyntoun, the *Buik*, and the *Scotichronicon* all called the castle "Cocklaws," but in a letter to King Henry of 26 June 1403, found in the Privy Council documents (POPC Vol. I, pgs. 204-205), the Earl of Northumberland referred to it as "Ormiston." Thus, its precise name is unclear, as is its exact location and appearance. My description reflects details of other contemporary castles. The ballad about Hotspur's exploits is original to this novel.

In his Shrewsbury battlefield declaration, Hotspur accused Henry of having tried to kill him. He may have been referring to the king's violent actions during their October 1402 argument, but I think it is likely that he also referred to one or more separate incidents. The campaign in lower Scotland in 1403 would have provided ample opportunity for murder attempts under the guise of warfare or war-related "friendly-fire."

Chapter IX

Dunbar is known to have fled Hotspur's army after the siege ended at Cocklaws. According to a fragmented and long-overlooked document, apparently originally from the Scottish court but included among English Crown records in the *Calendar of Documents Relating to Scotland* (No. 632), Dunbar was in Edinburgh on 10 June 1403, reaching some rapprochement with the Scottish Crown. Thus, Dunbar must have fled Hotspur's camp, parlayed with the Scots' King Robert III, and then hurriedly crossed the border and raced to King Henry. Chronicle evidence reveals that he came to Henry from the Borders, alleging that Hotspur was refusing to speedily return to Cocklaws and was in revolt (i.e., engaged in treason) and urging Henry to move against him. (*Buik,* pg. 485; *Scotichronicon,* pg. 57; *Annales,* pg. 364, *Giles Chronicle,* pg. 33). Since Hotspur had reached a cease-fire pact with the Scots, there was no need to return immediately to Cocklaws, and Dunbar seems to have been manipulating Henry to get him to destroy Hotspur, so that Dunbar could control the English North. Dunbar's visit to Edinburgh also strongly suggests that he was simultaneously engaging in deceit against both kings.

Dunbar's suspicious behavior probably warned Hotspur that he was in danger, and he may have received word from friends at Henry's court, as well. Certainly, his uncle must have been in contact with him, for at some stage Thomas Percy left royal service and sold off or removed his London possessions in order to join his nephew. (*Annales*, pg. 361) The scenes of Hotspur's discussions with his aides, father, and Ciarry are fictitious. Hardyng (pgs. 361-362) later accused Earl Henry of betraying his son by abandoning him at Shrewsbury and failing even to offer him adequate advice:

> *His uncle dere was with hym*
> *there [in]dedde.*
> *His father came not out of*
> *Northumberland,*
> *but failed hym foule, without*
> *witte or rede.*

Chapter X

Hotspur left Northumberland for Cheshire and the Welsh borders with a small company but soon began picking up support. His speech after he reached Chester has been recreated from brief quotes in the *Eulogium* chronicle (pgs. 396-397) and references in the *Annales* and *Historia Anglicana* and Hardyng about his reform proposals. (See note above regarding his letters promoting reform.) The popular belief that Richard II was still alive is mentioned in the *Annales* (pg. 363), *Historia Anglicana* (pg. 256) and in the *Dieulacres Chronicle* (pg. 177). At times, modern historians have attributed such claims to Hotspur, but there is no proof that he spread such fantasies. In fact, in his battlefield declaration, Hotspur accused Henry of having ordered the murder of Richard. It seems indisputable, however, that some of his Cheshire supporters spread the tales about Richard's existence (see the *Annales*).

References to Hotspur's visits to Denbigh and Flint occur in the *Calendar of Documents Relating to Scotland* (No. 646) and by their very banality suggest

that even a couple of weeks before his death, he was
not planning war against Henry. From Chester, he
moved on to Shrewsbury. I suspect he tried to talk to
Prince Hal, who was in Shrewsbury Castle, but was
rebuffed by Hal's guardians, and I thus created that
scene. His interaction with the children is also
created, based on something that supposedly
occurred. According to local lore in Shrewsbury, on
the night of 20 July, Hotspur used his pen knife to
outline his hand on a board and gave it to local
friends as a keepsake.

Chapters XI and XII

In 1401, Lord Furnival had to obtain a pardon from
Henry IV for having married his second wife, a
widow, without royal permission (*Calendar of Patent
Rolls*, Vol. II, pg. 512), which may account for his
obligations toward Henry at Shrewsbury. His letter to
Hotspur is fictitious, however.

Medieval accounts of the negotiations and battle,
including information on casualties, can be found in
the *Scotichronicon* (pgs. 56-59); Wyntoun's
Orygynale Cronykil of Scotland (pgs. 90-92); the
Buik, (pgs. 485-487); the *Dieulacres Chronicle* (pgs.
178-181); the *Annales* (363-371); the *Giles Chronicle*,
pgs. 32-34, the *Eulogium* (pgs. 396-398); Hardyng's
chronicle (pgs. 351-354 and 361-362), which includes
the text of Hotspur's battlefield declaration; and the
Given-Wilson edition of Adam of Usk's chronicle
(pgs. 169-170).

Hotspur's battlefield speech has been recreated from
snippets found in the *Annales* (pgs. 364-365) and
Historia Anglicana (pg. 256). The text of his note to
Henry, outlining how he dared to question or criticize
a ruler, is drawn in part from quotes the *Eulogium*

attributed to him in a statement to the king. His
answer to Henry's offer of a purported safe-conduct
pass and lenient treatment, "I trust not your mercy,"
is from the same source. The account of his missing
sword, revelation that he'd left it at a place called
Berwick, and his shocked reaction to the news,
recollection of a sage's prediction that he would fall
in battle near Berwick, and sad remark that "then has
my plow reached its final furrow," are taken from
material in the *Annales*. The assumption (mine) that
he himself lost his sword while wandering the fields
the night before the battle is based on a line in the
Eulogium that a comet burned high in the skies over
his head, as if signifying the events to befall. Also, I
doubt his squires would have been careless enough to
lose his favorite sword.

Two Scot's sources, the *Scotichronicon* and the *Buik*,
describe Henry's deceit in agreeing to a truce and
then launching battle; Adam of Usk's chronicle says
much the same thing and the *Annales*, despite its
often pro-king slant, strongly hints at such duplicity
as well. Severely wounded after Hotspur's death,
Douglas was captured. *The Calendar of Documents
Relating to Scotland* (No. 640) records the
incarceration of a Scots lord, Sir John Montgomery,
at the Tower of London, as of September 1403. This
is probably the same John Montgomery who was
Hotspur's Otterburn captor and likely also was the
Lord Montgomery captured by Hotspur at Homildon.
Dunbar remained in England until 1408 (Adam of
Usk chronicle, note 2, pg. 231). Still, according to the
Giles Chronicle, in the end, he had to flee back to
Scotland, which suggests that, eventually, he, too,
suffered a falling-out with Henry.

Chapter XIII

For accounts of the aftermath of the battle and desecration of Hotspur's body, see the sources cited above. The *Scotichronicon* (pg. 59) reports that Henry lost 7,000 men slain and Hotspur 700 men slain; it also has the account of three "fake kings" slain by Douglas. Holinshed later wrote that there were four fake kings. The figures on knights slain come from the *Dieulacres Chronicle*. Both the appearance of the comet above Hotspur's head and the blood-red eclipse of the moon are reported in the *Eulogium* (which also mentions the execution of the unfortunate friar who blundered into Henry's presence).

Although he fought on the royal side, Furnival risked Henry's wrath by claiming Hotspur's body and interring it in a family tomb at Whitchurch (see Jacob's *Fifteenth Century*, pg. 53, and the *Dieulacres Chronicle*). But the king ordered its removal, exhibition, and dismemberment. Henry's public denunciation of the corpse is from the *Dieulacres Chronicle* (pg. 181). Furnival later played a role in the confiscation of Hotspur's belongings in the North (*Calendar of Patent Rolls*, Vol. II, pg. 312).

The poem *"The Fields of Shrewsbury"* is original to this novel.

Epilog

The comments Henry makes in his deathbed scene are from Capgrave's chronicle (pg. 302, also quoted by Marie Bruce in *The Usurper King,* pg. 247), and from Lancastrian *Kings and Lollard Knights* (pgs. 103-104 and 112). Capgrave was a contemporary of Henry V (Prince Hal). Other background on the scene comes from Adam of Usk's chronicle and various biographies of Henry and Henry V (see

Bibliography, below). The quotes from the penitential psalms, numbers 38 and 51, are from *The Complete Parallel Bible*, pages 1186-1187 and 1206-1207.

After Hotspur's death, Hardyng joined Sir Robert Umfraville's staff in the North. He later wrote a chronicle of English history and otherwise went on to a long and varied career with Umfraville and the English Crown. He served both Henry V (Prince Hal) and Henry VI (Hal's son, Henry IV's grandson) and wrote out a copy of his chronicle for the latter's successor, Edward IV. Obviously, any resentment he felt toward the Lancastrians was reserved solely for Henry IV. He seems to have lived to be quite elderly and apparently was still active in 1465, when he would have been age 87. See the "Preface" to his chronicle for more on his later life. Whether he ever proposed writing a series of biographies is a matter of speculation. What is not speculation is the fact that throughout his long life, he continued to revere Hotspur, for even in old age, he wrote about him in moving and admiring terms, conveying an ongoing, deep sense of sadness and loss.

Bibliography

Note: *Since I launched my Hotspur research in graduate school more than 30 years ago, other sources have become available, so this list does not necessarily include all of the most recent material. Furthermore, between 2003 and 2006, the British government merged several record-holding departments, including the Public Record Office (or PRO), into a single institution, the National Archives. Because I conducted nearly all my research before the consolidation, I've retained the PRO slugs or titles and similar identifiers on documents cited here.*

Finally, inclusion of a reference here does not mean that I agree with that writer's perspectives or conclusions.

Chronicles

Dieulacres Chronicle: Edited by M.V. Clarke and V.H. Galbraith; in the Bulletin of John Rylands Library, Vol. XIV (January 1930)

An English Chronicle (Davies' English Chronicle): Edited by J.S. Davies, Camden Society series, 1856

Eulogium Historiarum (Also cited as *Eulogium Historiarum sive Temporis*, and as the *Continuation of the Eulogium*): Edited by F.S. Haydon; Longman, Green, Longman, Roberts and Green, London, 1863

Northern Chronicle 1399-1430: Edited by C.L. Kingsford; contained in the book *English Historical Literature* (see below).

The Kirkstall Chronicle 1355-1400: Edited by M.V. Clarke and N. Denholm-Young; published in the Bulletin of John Rylands Library, Vol. XV (January 1931)

*Froissart: Chronicle*s [abbreviated English version]: selected, translated and edited by G. Brereton; Penguin Classics edition, London, 1968

Froissart: Chronicles of England, France and Spain, Vol. II, by Sir John Froissart, translated from the French by Thomas Johnes, William Smith, publishers, London, 1848

Chronicles of the Monks of St. Albans: *Chronica et Annales 1392-1406 (Annales Ricardi Secundi et Henrici Quarti)*; attributed to John De Trokelowe and Henry Blaneforde and the monks of St. Albans, probably under the overall supervision of Thomas Walsingham; H.T. Riley, editor; Longmans, Green, Reader and Dyer, London, London, 1866. Also: *Historia Anglicana, 1381-1422*: by Thomas Walsingham, edited by Henry Thomas Riley; Longman, Green, Longman, Roberts and Green; London, 1864

Scotichronicon, Vol. 8 (Books XV and XVI): attributed to Walter Bower; D.E.R. Watt, general editor; Aberdeen University Press; University of St. Andrews, 1987 (Earlier text edited by W. Goodall, 1759.)

The Chronicle of John Hardyng: edited by H. Ellis; printed for F.C. and J. Rivington, T. Payne, and others; London, 1812

Chronique de la Traison et Mort de Richard Deux, Roy Dengleterre: Excerpted in Myers' *English Historical Documents* (See below for citation on latter.)

Foedera: 'Acta Regia,' Vol. II (abridgement): Usually cited as *Foedera*, or *Rymer's Foedera*; Compiled in the early 1700s from earlier works; the rare-book copy used here was available for reading by request to Georgetown University Library, Washington, D.C.

Chronicle of Adam of Usk: edited and translated by E.M. Thompson; London, 1904

The Chronicle of Adam of Usk, 1377-1421, edited and translated by Given-Wilson, Clarendon Press, Oxford, 1997

Gile's Chronicle (Incerti Scriptoris Chronicon Angliae deRegnis Trium Regum Lancastrensium, Henrici IV, Henrici V et Henrici VI): edited by J.A. Giles; London, 1848

The Buik of the Chroniclis of Scotland, or a Metrical Version of the History of Hector Boece, Vol. III: by

William Stewart, edited by W.B. Turnbull; Longman, Brown, Green, Longmans, and Roberts, London, 1858 (Rolls Series Volume 6)

Creton: A Metrical History of the Deposition of King Richard the Second: Reprinted, with translation from the French, by J. Webb, in *Archaeologia* XX (1824), London

The Orygynale Cronykil of Scotland, Vol. III, attributed to Andrew Wyntoun, edited by D. Laing, William Paterson, Edinburgh, 1879

The Brut, Or the Chronicles of England (Part II): edited by Friedrich W. Brie from 15th-century texts and published by the Early English Text Society, Vol. 136, London, 1908

Chronicon Henrici Knighton (Chronicle of Henry Knighton), Vol. II: edited by Joseph R. Lumby, printed for Her Majesty's Stationery Office, London, 1895

Chronicle of Alnwick Abbey: (excerpts) in *Archaeologia Aeliana*, Society of Antiquaries, Newcastle-upon-Tyne, Vol. III, T. and J. Hodgson printing, Newcastle, 1844

The Westminster Chronicle, 1381-1394: edited and translated by L.C. Hector and Barbara F. Harvey, Clarendon Press, Oxford, 1982

The Chronicle of England, by J. Capgrave, edited by F.C. Hingeston, Rolls Series, London, 1858

Raphael Holinshed: Chronicles of England, Scotlande and Irelande: Richard the Second, by AMS Press Inc., New York, 1965); Richard II (1398-1400), Henry IV, and Henry V (combined volume), by Greenwood Press, Publishers, Westport, Conn., 1917 and 1978; The Historie of Scotland, by AMS Press, 1976

Government Documents and Records

Royal and Historical Letters During the Reign of Henry IV: edited by F.C. Hingeston; Longman, Green, Longman and Roberts; 1860

The Diplomatic Correspondence of Richard II: edited by E. Perroy, Camden Third Series, London, 1933

Calendar of Signet Letters of Henry IV and Henry V, 1399-1422: edited by J.L. Kirby, Her Majesty's Stationery Office, London, 1978

Rotuli Parliamentorum (Rolls of Parliament) Vol. III: (Henry IV), London, (part of 8-volume set published 1780-1832)

Rotuli Scotiae (Rolls Regarding Scotland): Vol. II, printed by command of George III, London, 1819

List of Sheriffs for England and Wales from the Earliest Times to A.D. 1831: Her Majesty's Stationery Office and Kraus Reprint Corp., New York, 1963

Calendar of Patent Rolls (CPR); Henry IV, Vols. I and II; His Majesty's Stationery Office, London, 1903 and 1905

Calendar of Documents Relating to Scotland, 1357-1435: edited by J. Bain (series published 1881-1888)

Calendar of Close Rolls, Henry IV, Vols. I and II: His Majesty's Stationery Office, London, 1927 and 1929

Calendar of Fine Rolls, Henry IV (Vol. XII) 1399-1405 London, 1931

Calendar of Inquisitions Post-Mortem, Vol. XIV: London, 1962

Record of Caernarvon, formally known as the *Registrum Vulgariter Nuncupatum "the Record of*

Caernarvon" (Commissioners of Public Records, London, 1838

The Black Book of the Admiralty, Vol. I: edited by Sir Travers Twiss; Longman & Co., et al, London, 1871 (includes "Statutes and Ordinances To Be Kept in Time of War," circa 1400)

Letters from the Northern Registers, edited by James Raine, Longman & Co., London, 1873

Anglo-Scottish Relations: 1174-1328 (with later supplement), edited by E.L. G. Stones, Nelson & Sons, London, 1965

Scottish Historical Documents: edited by Gordon Donaldson, Neil Wilson Publishing, Glasgow, 1970

Anglo-Scottish Relations, 1174-1328: Some Selected Documents, edited and translated by E.G. Stones, Nelson Publishing, London, 1965

Proceedings and Ordinances of the Privy Council (POPC) Vols. I and II: edited by H. Nicolas, London, 1834

Exchequer rolls (scrolls), in the Public Record Office/National Archives, London: E403/564; E401/619; E401/626; E404/15/57

Chester Recognizance Rolls: Number 25/10, Public Record Office, London

Cotton Collection (Hotspur's letters): In the 1990s, in the Cotton MSS Collection ("Cleopatra" F III series) in the British Library in London, I studied five letters that Hotspur wrote, in Anglo-Norman French, to the Privy Council in 1401 and 1402. The letters were reprinted, in Anglo-Norman French but in modern typefaces, in De Fonblanque's book (see below) and in the *POPC* compilation (see above).

Books

Fourteenth Century Studies: by M.V. Clarke; Oxford at the Clarendon Press, 1937; 1967

The Fourteenth Century, 1307-1399: by May McKisack; Oxford University Press, 1959; 1991 reprint

The Fifteenth Century, 1399-1485: by E.F. Jacob; Oxford at the Clarendon Press, 1961

Fifteenth-Century England, 1399-1509—Studies in Politics and Society: edited by S.B. Chrimes, C.D. Ross, R.A. Griffiths; Manchester University Press, 1972

Constitutional History of England in the Fifteenth Century (1399-1485) by B. Wilkinson; Barnes & Noble Inc., New York, 1964

English Historical Literature in the Fifteenth Century: by C.L. Kingsford; Burt Franklin publishers, New York, 1913

The Receipt of the Exchequer, 1377-1485: by Anthony Steel, Cambridge at the University Press, 1954

The Royal Household and the King's Affinity: by Chris Given-Wilson, Yale University Press, New Haven and London, 1986

The Complete Peerage, Vol. 4 (former volumes IX-X): by G.E.C. (Cokayne), Alan Sutton publishers, 1982

The Scots Peerage, Sir James Balfour Paul, editor, David Douglas (publishers), Edinburgh, 1907

Dictionary of National Biography, Volumes XIV and XV: Smith, Elder & Co., London, 1909; Oxford University Press, series reprints 1949-50

Richard II: by Anthony Steel; Cambridge at the University Press 1941

Richard II and the English Nobility: by Anthony Tuck; St. Martin's Press, New York, 1974

Richard II: by Nigel Saul, Yale University Press, New Haven (U.S.) and London (U.K.), 1997

The Reign of Richard II: edited by F.R. du Boulay and C.M. Barron, University of London, The Athlone Press, 1971

History of England under Henry IV, Vol. I: 1399-1401; Vol. II: 1405-06: by James Hamilton Wylie (part of a four-volume set; 1884-1898) Longmans, Green and Co., London

Henry IV of England: by J.L. Kirby: Constable, London, 1970

The Usurper King, Henry of Bolingbroke 1366-99, by Marie Louise Bruce, The Rubicon Press, 1986

Lancastrian Kings and Lollard Knights: by K.B. McFarlane; Oxford at the Clarendon Press, 1972

Henry V: by Christopher Allmand, University of California Press, 1992

King Henry V: A Biography: by Harold F. Hutchison, 1967; Dorset Press, New York, 1989

Henry V: The Scourge of God: by Desmond Seward, Viking Penguin Inc., New York, 1988

Henry V, the Practice of Kingship: edited by G.L. Harriss; Oxford University Press, 1985

Henry V: The Astonishing Triumph of England's Greatest Warrior King, by Dan Jones; Apollo-Head of Zeus, Bloomsbury Publishing PLC, London 2024; Viking, New York 2024

Annals of the House of Percy, Vol. 1, by Edward B. De Fonblanque (London, 1887)

A History of the House of Percy: by Gerald Brenan; Freemantle and Co., London, 1902

A Power in the Land: The Percys, by Richard Lomas, Tuckwell Press, East Linton, Scotland 1999

Owen Glyn Dwr: by J.D. Griffith Davies; Eric Partridge Ltd., Scholartis Press, London, 1934

Owen Glendower: by J.E. Lloyd; Oxford at the Clarendon Press, 1931

The Revolt of Owain Glyn Dwr: by R.R. Davies, Oxford University Press, Oxford and New York, 1995

The Black Douglases, by Michael Brown, Tuckwell Press Ltd., East Linton, Scotland, 1998

Medieval Scotland: Crown, Lordship and Community, edited by Alexander Grant and Keith J. Stringer, Edinburgh University Press, 1993, 1998

English Historical Documents: 1327-1485: edited by A.R. Myers; Oxford University Press, New York, 1969

War and Society in Medieval Cheshire: 1277-1403:
by Philip Morgan; Chetham Society, Manchester,
1987

*The Historians of the Church of York and its
Archbishops, Vol. II:* edited by James Raine, London,
1886

History of the Battle of Otterburn Fought in 1388:
by Robert White; John Russell Smith, London, 1857

Memorials of the Most Noble Order of the Garter: by
G.F. Beltz; William Pickering, London, 1841

A History of Northumberland: Vol. V, by J.
Hodgson, Reid, et al, publishing, London, 1899; *Vol.
XI*, by Kenneth H. Vickers, Reid & Co. Ltd., London,
1922

*A History of Northumberland, in Three Parts (Part
I: Containing the General History of the County):*
Society of Antiquaries of Newcastle-upon-Tyne, also
attributed to J. Hodgson; Thomas and James Pigg,
printers, Newcastle, 1858

England, France and Christendom, 1377-99: by
J.J.N. Palmer, University of North Carolina Press,
Chapel Hill, and Routledge & Kegan Paul, London,
1972

The House of Commons, 1386-1421, Vol. I, J.S.
Roskell, Alan Sutton Publishing, Stroud, for the
History of Parliament Trust, 1992

Medieval Anglesey: by A.D. Carr, Anglesey
Antiquarian Society, Llangefrei, 1982

Chronicles of the Revolution: by Chris Given-Wilson,
Manchester University Press, 1993

War in the Middle Ages: by Philippe Contamine, translated by Michael Jones, Basil Blackwood printing, Oxford, England, 1984

Armies and Warfare in the Middle Ages: The English Experience, by Michael Prestwich, Yale University Press, 1996

Chivalry: by Maurice Keen, Yale University Press, New Haven and London, 1984

The Knight and Chivalry: by Richard Barber, (revised edition), The Boydell Press, 1995

The Book of Chivalry of Geoffroi de Charny: by Geoffroi de Charny, circa 1350; text, context and translation by Richard W. Kaeuper and Elspeth Kennedy, University of Pennsylvania Press, 1996

War and Border Societies in the Middle Ages: edited by Anthony Tuck and Anthony Goodman, Routledge Publishers, London, 1992

Violence, Custom and Law: the Anglo-Scottish Border Lands in the Later Middle Ages, by Cynthia Neville, Edinburgh University Press, 1998

The Border Reivers, by Godfrey Watson, Sandhill Press Ltd., Alnwick, Northumberland, England, 1985 (reprint); Robert Hale & Co., 1974

The Steel Bonnets: The Story of the Anglo-Scottish Border Reivers, by George MacDonald Fraser, Collins Harvill Publishers, London, 1989 (first published 1971 by Barrie & Jenkins)

English Society in the Later Middle Ages 1348-1500: by Maurice Keen, Penguin Books, London, 1990

Standards of Living in the Later Middle Ages: Social Change in England c. 1200-1520: by Christopher Dyer, Cambridge University Press, 1989

The Ties that Bound: Peasant Families in Medieval England: by Barbara A. Hanawalt, Oxford University Press, 1986

The Medieval Town: A Reader in English Urban History, 1200-1540: edited by Richard Holt and Gervase Rosser, Longman Group U.K. Ltd., Harlow, England, 1990

London in the Age of Chaucer: by A.R. Myers, University of Oklahoma Press, Norman, Okla., 1972

Medieval Westminster, 1200-1540: by Gervase Rosser, Clarendon Press, Oxford, 1989

The Medieval Cookbook: by Maggie Black, British Museum Press, London, 1992

A Medieval Book of Seasons: by Marie Collins and Virginia Davis, HarperCollins Publishers, 1992

The Intelligent Traveller's Guide to Historic Scotland: by Philip A. Crowl, Congdon & Weed, New York, 1986

Fishing in Wales, by Walter M. Gallichan ("Geoffrey Mortimer"), F.E. Robinson & Co., London, 1903

Atlas of Medieval Europe: by Donald Matthew, Facts on File, New York, Equinox Ltd., Oxford, 1983, 1989

Revised Medieval Latin Word List: R.E. Latham, et al, Oxford University Press, for the British Academy, London, 1989

Oxford English Dictionary: unabridged (I used the Compact Edition, 1971, as well as more recent editions)

Anglo-Norman Dictionary: Modern Humanities Research Association, London, 1992

The Complete Parallel Bible: Oxford University Press, 1993

Journals and Articles

English Historical Review: 1912: "The First Version of Hardyng's Chronicle," by C.L. Kingsford; 1917: "The Office of Warden of the Marches: Its Origin and Early History," by R.R. Reid; 1934: "The Parliamentary Title of Henry IV," by G. Lapsley; 1937: "Richard II's Last Parliament," by H.G. Richardson; 1938: "Richard II's Last Parliament" (response), by G. Lapsley; 1939: "The Deposition of Richard II and the Accession of Henry IV," by B. Wilkinson; 1957: "The Wardens of the Marches of England Towards Scotland, 1377-1489," by R.L. Storey; 1994: "Keeping the Peace on the Northern Marches in the Later Middle Ages," by Cynthia J. Neville

The Welsh History Review: 1964-1965: "Owain Glyn Dwr and the Lordship of Ruthin," by R. Ian Jack; 1974-1975: "Richard II's Return to Wales," by J.W. Sherborne; 1988-1989: "Perjury and the Lancastrian Revolution of 1399," by James Sherborne

Bulletin of the John Rylands Library: 1969-1970: "The Cheshire Rising of 1400," by Peter McNiven: 1979-1980: "The Scottish Policy of the Percies and the Strategy of the Rebellion of 1403," by Peter McNiven; 1930 and 1931: see *Dieulacres* and *Kirkstall* chronicles

Northern History: 1968: "Richard II and the Border Magnates," by J.A. Tuck; 1998: "The Scottish Invasion of 1346," by C.J. Rogers

Archaeologia Aeliana: 1950: "Wardens and Deputy Wardens of the Marches of England Towards Scotland in Northumberland and the English Wardens of Berwick-upon-Tweed," by C. Hunter Blair; and "The Forests of Medieval Northumberland," by W. Percy Hedley; also 1957: "The Percies and Their Estates in Scotland," by J.M.W. Bean

History: October 1959: "Henry IV and the Percies," by J.M.W. Bean

Transactions of the Historic Society of Lancashire and Cheshire: 1980 (Vol. 129): "The Men of Cheshire and the Rebellion of 1403," by P. McNiven

Transactions: Caernarvonshire Historical Society: 1978: "The Taking of Conwy (Conway) Castle 1401" by Keith Williams-Jones

Smithsonian magazine: "The Lords of Alnwick, a Castle Great with Art and History," by Israel Shenker, August 1984

Liz Sevchuk Armstrong first heard the name "Hotspur" at age 12 in a production of Shakespeare's *Henry IV*, which sparked a passion for British medieval history and changed her life forever.

After pursuing journalism in college, she embarked on a long career in news at local to national levels, winning awards for investigative-type reporting on government as well as for general coverage and feature-writing, and, in briefer editorial stints with non-profits, for public relations. As a reporter in Washington, D.C., she covered the White House, Congress, and Supreme Court, for U.S. and international daily news operations and worked for a time as a stringer for the Toronto *Globe and Mail*. During a downhill slide in the news business, she entered graduate school to study history. She returned to her childhood interest in the Hotspur-Henry IV conflict, which became the subject of her master's project. That later spawned the Hotspur series. Volume I, *To Remain Vigilant,* won the 1st place Chaucer Award in the Dark Ages/Medieval/Renaissance category of the Chanticleer International Book Awards contest for historical fiction published in 2024.

Liz now resides in upstate New York with her husband and three macaws.

Liz Sevchuk Armstrong's books also published by BWL Publishing

To Remain Vigilant: Book I of the Epic of Hotspur
To Be Worthy in Honor: Book II of the Epic of Hotspur